trigger warning

This book contains: mask kink / masked sex, primal play, blood, biting, spitting, slapping, choking, dub con, unusual toys, double-penetration, unusual toys, mention of sexual abuse, mention of sexual assault, and more.

four masked wolves

Monsters of Durnbone

emilia rose

Cover by: Covers by Christian

Edited by: Jovana Shirley, Unforeseen Editing, www.unforeseenediting.com

Emilia Rose

emiliarosewriting@gmail.com

1
the reunion

sina

UNKNOWN: **Welcome home, Sina.**

As Maxine pulled me toward a large house in the outskirts of Durnbone, I stared at the text message sent to me from an anonymous number, my chest tight in anticipation. Since I had left Dad's home three days ago, I hadn't told anyone that I was coming back to my hometown.

Only Maxine knew.

"Girl!" Maxine shouted, grabbing my phone from me. "We're about to head into your first party since you finally got the balls to leave your father's estate and come back to town. Put your phone away!"

I took my phone from her and shoved it into my purse, tucking some brown hair behind my ear. "I thought you hated partying?"

"My best friend is back in town. You bet your cute little tush that I'm going to party, no matter how much I hate the smoke and drunk monsters trying to crawl up into every girl's bed. Gods, I see enough of that at the pub."

After looping her arm around mine, she pulled me into the dimly lit house. Smoke and haze lay heavily around grinding bodies. People of all species danced and drank together, actually getting along, unlike what Dad had tried to tell me for the past four years.

When I'd finally turned twenty-two, I'd refused to live under his strict rule anymore. Four years ago, he had forced me to cut off all communication with Maxine and the four wolves I had grown up with. They had been my best friends for so long.

One day, something must've flipped in Dad's stupid, annoying head because on my eighteenth birthday, when I woke up, all my bags were packed for me, my phone was destroyed, and I had been in the back of his car on the road to someplace that took me ages to figure out how to escape from.

"Hello?" Maxine said, waving a hand in my face and handing me a drink. Two scars from a wolf attack years ago peeked out from underneath the top of her shirt. "What's with you tonight?"

How could I tell her I had missed this place so much? That I missed those wolves too? That I feared Dad would find me sooner than I expected?

Deciding that I wouldn't let Dad ruin tonight for me, I smiled at her and grabbed the glass from her hand, taking a sip of what people in Durnbone called Midnight Moon, this region's most popular drink that got *every* monster drunk in one glass.

"You don't think this is a bit too strong for a human?" I asked, scrunching my nose at the bitter taste.

Dad had only let me drink sweet white wine these past few years. This brew was stronger than any other alcohol.

"You'll get used to it," Maxine said.

After forcing myself to take another sip, I relaxed my shoulders and blew out a deep breath, as if it would push away all my troubles. I scanned the room, trying to spot anyone relatively familiar to me. But so much had changed in a few years.

"Do you know—"

I turned my head to see Maxine was no longer beside me, but flirting with a demon whose face was half human, half demon with huge teeth and one piercing red eye. She had mentioned him briefly. Xorgor was his name, I believed. And if I was remembering correctly, Maxine had told me that he came from the royal demon bloodline.

My purse buzzed, and since Maxine was distracted, I pulled out my phone.

Unknown: You're back in Durnbone, and you haven't even said hello.

This message was from another unknown number. I scanned the room to see if anyone was watching me, my chest tightening even more. Whoever this was knew that I was back in Durnbone and possibly at this party. This was the only place I had gone besides the supermarket today.

After quickly glancing over at Maxine to ensure she was occupied, I texted back.

Me: Who is this?

Unknown: Downstairs. Third door on your right.

Me being the dumb bitch that I was, I told Maxine that I had to use the bathroom and hurried to find the stairs to the basement. Demons, wolves, vampires, and other monsters danced around me, some trying to pull me toward them, but I continued moving.

When I finally found the stairs, I carefully walked down them without sloshing my Midnight Moon over the edge of the cup. I glanced down the long, dimly lit hallway and walked toward the third room on my right.

Just as I was about to open the door, someone slapped their hand over my mouth and tugged me into the opposite room. I struggled against them, desperate to get out of their hold because I wouldn't spend my first night in Durnbone getting raped.

That would play right into Dad's narrative of monsters.

I threw my elbow back into the hard abdomen and scurried out of the man's hold. Twisting quickly on my heel, I spotted Jaroth grabbing his side and shaking his head with his black horns at me, annoyance written all over his pretty face.

"What the hell, Jaroth?! What are you doing here?" I asked.

"What are *you* doing in Durnbone?" he asked, smoothing his shirt that clung to his body.

"Not expecting to find my ex-boyfriend," I said through gritted teeth.

He stepped closer to me, his eyes darkening the way all incubi eyes did right after they had too much to drink and wanted someone right then and there. But I wasn't falling for that shit anymore.

I moved away and poked him hard in the chest. "And why are you texting me?"

"Texting you?" he asked, taking another daring step closer and grabbing at my hips. "I haven't texted you in over a year now, Sina. But I haven't been able to stop thinking about the way you taste—"

Before he could finish his sentence, someone grabbed him by the collar and threw him out of the room and across the hallway. My eyes widened as I stared at four tall, muscular, sexy-as-fuck wolves.

Holy fuck.

Calder, Gaian, Darius, and Thayer stood before me. When I had left four years ago, they had still been high school boys, barely come into their own, shorter and skinnier then. Now, they were men with tattoos, piercings, muscles, and …

Get those thoughts out of your head, Sina. What are you even thinking?!

"Get the fuck out of here, Jaroth," Calder, the alpha, growled.

I wasn't sure *how* they knew Jaroth, as I had started dating him after I moved away from Durnbone and behind my father's back for the most part. Maybe they had been keeping tabs of my whereabouts or maybe they'd heard whispers of everything my father had been doing with me.

Jaroth stood up from the floor and brushed off the drywall that had fallen around him from the mere impact of Calder throwing him against the wall. He gave me a long and hard look, his gaze dark, then stormed up the stairs.

The four guys turned back to me, and I had to physically tear my gaze away from their muscles. These guys weren't boys anymore.

They weren't the guys I remembered them as. They were wolves now. I could see it in their piercing golden eyes, those long, extended canines, and the veins pressing against their skin around every curve of muscle.

"Pretty Bird," Darius said, stepping forward with his lips curled into a smirk. "It seems like our messages did get through to you. Welcome home to Durnbone. You've been gone for far too long." He looked at the other guys beside him. "And you owe us an explanation."

2

the proposition

AN EXPLANATION?

Nerves zipped through me, and I found myself stepping back farther into the room. The four wolves followed me, their mere stature so much bigger and more confident than I ever remembered.

What kind of damn explanation did I have for leaving them?

None.

"My dad made me leave," I whispered, holding my hands up, as if to show them I wasn't dangerous. Hell, I didn't even know why I was doing it. A human like me could never be dangerous to four ruthless wolves like them. "He smashed my phone and moved me across the country."

"You didn't say good-bye," Darius said.

Dark skin, a single cuffed earring, and a fade with three-inch dreadlocks, Darius stood a bit stockier than the others. If it wasn't for his gold family ring that he wore around his right thumb, I wouldn't have recognized him.

"I didn't think I was leaving," I said.

"You left on your eighteenth birthday," Thayer said, his voice deeper than it had been since I'd last seen him.

Last time I had seen him, he had been skinnier than the other guys, his skin free of any ink or scars and his dark brown hair cut short. But now, tattoos covered his pale skin from head to toe, his hair was messy on top of his head, and he had a large scar that cut straight through his left eyebrow down to his mid-cheek.

Thayer said the words like they should've meant something to me, as they seemed to mean to them.

"I didn't have any choice on the matter," I said, wanting them to believe me.

"We have been searching for you," Gaian said, green eyes softening at me. He ran a hand through his dirty-blond scruff. He might've been the only one who hadn't changed as drastically, the calmer and more collected one of the bunch.

I lowered my hands and sighed softly to myself, hating that Dad had taken me away from them. If it wasn't for them constantly on my mind for the past four years, I probably wouldn't have come back. I sure as hell still would've been off Dad's estate though.

Annoyed slightly because they couldn't see that this hadn't been my doing, I turned toward Calder and crossed my arms. "Do you have anything to say to me? Anything you want to get off your chest?"

Calder and I had never really gotten along. Sure, we tolerated each other, but Calder was always off, learning how to be an alpha with his father. Growing up, he had barely spent any time with me.

Calder clenched his sharp jaw and growled, "You're staying at my pack house."

My eyes widened. "What?"

"That's what I have to say to you," Calder said, turning on his heel and heading back through the door. "Say good-bye to Maxine. We're bringing you home with us, so no other guys like that fucker"—he hiked his thumb back to the stairs, where Jaroth had disappeared a couple of moments ago—"can hit on you again tonight."

"You know, you don't get to boss me around now that I'm back," I said, handing my drink to Darius and following after him with my arms crossed over my chest. "I'm not one of your wolves that you can order to do things and expect me to do them."

"Oh, really?" Calder said, stopping at the bottom of the stairs and turning toward me.

He towered over my body, his frame so much bigger than the other alphas I had seen around town since I had been back.

I craned my head back and stared up at him, tapping my foot. "That's right."

Before I could react, Calder scooped me up and tossed me right over his shoulder. "Bullshit. You'll do as I say, Pretty Bird. You've been gone for too long."

But something deep down told me that there was more than just that. His tone and touch were nothing but possessive, overflowing with jealousy and rage. I scrambled to try to get out of his hold, but he easily walked up the stairs and back into the hazy party.

"Tell Maxine she's staying with us," Calder ordered Gaian, "then get her shit and bring it back to the pack house."

"This is not fair!" I shouted, banging on his back. "Let me down! At least let me walk!"

"No," he growled, chest rumbling. "You're not leaving us again, Pretty Bird. You're ours."

———

Forty minutes later, I found myself standing in an empty bedroom with my two suitcases spread on the bed. I looked from my suitcases to the guys who stood in the doorway, all with their arms crossed and their gazes focused on me.

"If I'm going to live here until I find a place of my own, then I need—"

"You're not going to find a place of your own."

Ignoring Darius's comment, I continued, "Then I need some personal space."

Calder nodded to my suitcases. "Unpack your shit, then meet us downstairs. We have things to talk about."

After successfully pushing them out of the bedroom—where I would supposedly live in forever now—I unpacked my belongings and put away my clothes. This was definitely not how I'd expected my first night back in Durnbone going.

I'd thought I'd get drunk off Midnight Moon, then sleep with some vampire or something.

Not this.

Once I unpacked everything, I placed my diary underneath my pillow and vowed to find a lock to put on it. If they were this forward with me, I didn't doubt that they would snoop around my stuff at some point. And I would *die* if they found what was in there.

"You ready?" Gaian said from the doorway, watching me intently and smiling softly. "I've calmed Calder down. We don't have to talk about anything tonight. It's just going to be a … reunion of sorts, a time to get reacquainted."

"Reacquainted, huh?" I asked, stepping closer to the doorway.

He paused and stared down at me, those golden eyes still the same. Memories flooded through my mind of the night before my eighteenth birthday, the night before Dad had changed my life forever. The guys and I had played an innocent game of Truth or Dare.

And the last thing I remembered before falling asleep was Gaian kissing me.

"Do you remember the last time we got acquainted?" I asked playfully.

Gaian placed his hand on my back, his touch gentle at first. "I do," he said, guiding me down the stairs, fingers curling around my shoulder. "But this time, it's going to be different, Pretty Bird. This time, we all get you."

3
the diary

"WHY DON'T we play Truth or Dare?" Thayer said, glancing at the guys. "You guys do remember that it was our favorite game to play in high school, don't you? We can play the adult version since we're all grown up."

"The adult version?" I asked, arching a brow and feeling the warmth grow between my legs. Our Truth or Dare games in high school had gotten a bit freaky, though not as much as I had hoped at the time. "What does the adult version of Truth or Dare entail?"

"Anything we didn't do in high school, Pretty Bird."

Which translated to anything rated R because we had done almost everything with each other in high school, like grinding against each other at school dances, making out underneath the bleachers, and even getting close to third base.

Close.

It never happened. Dad had forced me to leave town before it could ever happen. He didn't understand the connection that a human girl like me had with these four beasts. He told me that they would destroy me from the inside out.

He hadn't known that I wanted them to do that to me all along.

"Anything rated R," I clarified, "huh?"

"If that's what you want"—Darius curled his lips into a smirk—"then that's what you'll get."

"Fine," I said, trying desperately to suppress a smile. "Let's play."

Darius must've taken that as the go-ahead to get right into it because as soon as I told the guys I wanted a truth to start off the game, he asked, "What's your deepest, darkest secret?" instead of an innocent warm-up question, like, *What is your favorite color?*

I gnawed on the inside of my cheek. "Before I left, I stole my dad's most prized possession."

What I left out though… was that Dad's most prized possession was me.

"Lame," Gaian shouted. "You have to have something dirtier than that, Pretty Bird."

"Don't forget that we grew up together," Thayer said. "We know you better than to believe something like *that* is your darkest secret."

My lips curled into a smile, as I desperately tried to fabricate a wild lie that they would believe so I wouldn't have to tell them the truth. "Would you believe me if I said I burned my dad's house to ashes?"

Calder didn't smile, but the right corner of his lip curled up ever so slightly. Then, he gave me a cold, hard, "No. Now, spill, Pretty Bird."

Truthfully, I didn't have many secrets.

But I did have one.

Just the thought of speaking it out loud made my cheeks flush. I glanced at each of them, then to my lap, fumbling with my fingers and swallowing hard. Out of all the times we had moved, all the housekeepers that had come and cleaned my room, nobody had ever figured it out either.

"She has something," Calder said, his dark gaze focused on me. Though he was the alpha, he wasn't as loud as the other guys. He had a darkness inside of him, one that lurked just below the surface, but one that I had never seen completely, just glimpses of. He growled, "What is it?"

"Can we not?" I whispered. "Please, I'll answer any other question."

"You agreed to the rules. You have to abide by them," Thayer said.

Fuck.

I ran a hand through my hair and cut off all eye contact with them because the more they stared at me, like predators did with their prey, the hotter my body became. This secret wasn't just anything …

This secret involved these four wolves in front of me.

"Come on," Darius said impatiently. "It can't be *that* bad."

"Okay, okay," I started, taking a deep breath and lowering my voice to a mere whisper. "I have a diary with all my sexual fantasies written within the pages."

My four werewolf best friends watched me intensely from the middle of the pack house's living room. I nervously rubbed my sweaty palms together and stared at the wooden floorboards. This wasn't how I had imagined our reunion.

I hadn't seen these guys for four years, since after high school. Now that I was back in Durnbone, we thought we'd play the infamous Truth or Dare game, which had led to so many stolen kisses four years ago.

Oh, how I should've known they'd want me to reveal my deepest, darkest secrets this time around.

"It's filled with unspeakable acts, fantasies that I haven't told anyone about, not even my incubus ex-boyfriend," I continued, not daring to look up at the guys. Nerves fluttered in my stomach, my cheeks flaming red. "Every time I have a new fantasy, I write it down."

"Where do you hide it?" Calder asked.

"Under my pillow," I whispered.

Calder looked at Thayer, who then stood. "Go get it," Calder said to him.

My eyes widened slightly, and I went to stand, but Gaian caught my wrist and tugged me back onto the living room floor. I sucked in a deep breath, knowing this Truth or Dare game might've been all innocent four years ago, but we were maturer now.

And I could already feel the tension in the air.

They wanted to know what kind of fantasies I had. I just wasn't sure if they were ready to learn that all those dreams were about them, that these past four years had been filled with nothing but thoughts of what I'd let this pack do to me if I ever saw them again.

It was so wrong. So dirty.

A couple of moments later, Thayer emerged from the other room with my diary in his hand. He tossed it into my lap, then took his seat beside me. I gripped it against my chest, eyeing my Midnight Moon brew that they had given me earlier, and wondered if I should down it all now.

"Flip to your favorite one and read it to us," Darius said.

"That wasn't part of the truth," I said.

"I don't care," Calder said. "Read us your favorite."

"You guys are going to be the fucking death of me," I said between gritted teeth, my heart pounding.

I really didn't want to do this, but that drink was really getting to me. I had already finished one entire glass after I put my belongings away.

I sucked in a deep breath and stared at the leather journal in my lap, my fingers wrapped around its thick spine. This wasn't how I had expected my first night back to go. After taking another sip of my drink, I opened to the first page and stared at the stupid Table of Contents that I had made.

What a waste of time.

I knew exactly what page I needed to flip to. I had read it multiple times a week and touched myself to it, unable to stop myself from imagining the darkest of fantasies finally coming to life one day.

"Favorite. Page." Calder's voice was stern this time, his alpha tone slowly appearing.

"Fuck it," I whispered to myself, flipping to page fourteen. "Don't judge me for this. Please."

The guys all watched me carefully, all ears and eyes on me.

"Entry number fourteen: I want masked men to use my holes for their pleasure." I stared down at the leather-bound journal in my hands and swallowed hard. My heart pounded inside my chest as I felt the four intense stares from my best friends around me, the mere tension rising in the room by the second. *"I want to be their little fucktoy—slapped, degraded, and choked until I'm begging for air."*

I rested a hand over my throat, feeling my pulse race underneath it. This might've been my fourteenth journal entry, but that was only because I hadn't had the courage before this one to write down something this intense. I'd had this fantasy four years ago, before my dad dragged me away from this town, but I hadn't written it down until much, much later.

And these masked men that I spoke about were my best friends.

"Spit on," I whispered. *"My throat, pussy, and ass all filled at the same time."* I pressed my thighs together, unable to believe I was saying this out loud. *"I want to struggle against and be overpowered by four wolves much stronger than me."*

Once I finished reading the journal entry, I snapped the diary shut and grabbed my glass of brew. I downed it in one go, needing to at least be a little more buzzed before I glanced up and looked into their wolfish eyes.

They had to know that I was talking about them. That last bit had been a clear giveaway.

"You're being really brave tonight, Pretty Bird," Thayer said with a whistle. "Actually reading an entry aloud after admitting you had a little *fuck me* book stowed away in your room with notes so fucking dirty that your little mouth got nervous to speak them aloud."

Warmth rushed to my core, and I pressed my thighs together, not daring to look up.

"Give me the journal," Calder said.

My eyes widened. "Give you the journal?"

He held out his large, callous palm. "The journal."

"Are you going to keep it?" I asked.

"For what it's worth, Pretty Bird, I plan to read every last page of it."

Because I had already screwed myself over by reading my favorite journal entry and because I might've been a bit too drunk to think straight, I found myself handing over my most precious piece of property. If it fell into the wrong hands, then I would be called Durnbone's newest whore.

Being the good girl that I had aimed to be for years, I didn't want that happening.

"Don't give it to anyone else," I said. "Please."

"Oh, listen to you beg, Pretty Bird," Darius cooed.

I nervously rubbed my hands together and watched Calder place the book beside him before taking another sip of his Midnight Moon. He looked at Gaian, who looked at Darius, who looked at Thayer.

Their eyes glazed over the way they always did while they were talking through the mind link, and then, finally, Thayer turned toward me with a smirk so devilish that I knew something terrible would come out of his mouth.

"You got so tense just now," he said to me, handing me a blanket from the couch behind us. "Your cunt smells like you haven't touched yourself in weeks, Pretty Bird. Why don't you relieve some of that pressure between your legs and show us how loudly you'll scream for us when we make that little fantasy of yours come true one day?"

4

the blanket

sina

THE BLANKET barely covered my thighs, but I wrapped it over my legs and tucked it underneath the backs of my thighs, so there would be no chance the guys could catch a glimpse of anything while I stuck a few fingers into my panties.

Warmth gathered between my legs, and I inhaled sharply. I slipped my hand underneath the blanket and under my dress, inching my legs apart slightly. My pussy ached, the anticipation rising in my core already. This wasn't supposed to be how our reunion turned out tonight.

But there was nothing I could do about it now. I had agreed to an innocent game of Truth or Dare, knowing that our Truth or Dare games were *never* innocent. With them as grown men now, who oozed testosterone, I had known this could happen.

Deep down, I'd expected it.

After pushing my panties to the side, I shoved two fingers between my folds. As soon as my fingers touched the sensitive bud, a moan escaped my lips. I hadn't been able to rub my pussy for days now. Dad had been watching me like a fucking hawk.

Breath hitching, I slowly rubbed my fingers against my clit. All eyes were on me.

"Do you … are you sure about this?" I asked nervously.

Even if they told me to stop, I didn't think I would.

"Keep touching yourself, Pretty Bird," Calder said.

Swallowing hard, I moved my fingers a bit faster. There were four incredibly sexy, muscular wolves wanting me to masturbate in front of them so they could watch. Every single one of them could tear my body to shreds in a moment's notice, but I couldn't seem to care.

I glanced over at the guys, realizing that I wasn't the only one turned on. Each one of them had their hand against their crotch, either trying to hide their boner, like Gaian, or slowly stroking himself. Just the thought of them being hard for me made me almost tip over the edge.

Pressure rose in my core, my heart racing. I couldn't believe I was doing this. Touching myself in front of my four best friends? That was beyond anything I had ever done before, even with my incubus ex. He had never compared to them.

The more I rubbed my pussy, the hornier the guys seemed to get. I continued, and before I knew it, Thayer had slipped his hand into his pants, strands of his dark hair falling onto his forehead. I inhaled sharply at the sight, my cheeks flushing.

"Yes," I whispered. "Please, continue."

Next was Darius to undo his jeans button. I glanced over at him and rubbed my pussy faster. Oh God. If they kept doing this, I was going to come.

A few moments later, even Gaian began stroking himself inside his pants. My nipples ached. I honestly couldn't believe this was happening. Maybe this was all some sort of hallucination from one of those Midnight Moons.

But, hell, I couldn't stop myself.

Then, just as I was about to explode, Calder undid his pants and pulled out his huge, hard cock. Staring into Calder's eyes, I continued to rub my sopping wet cunt.

"Oh God," I whispered, tilting my head back and glancing between my four best friends. I moved my fingers even faster against my clit, the pressure rising inside my core. "Fuck, I'm going to … to come."

Unable to hold back, I jerked my legs up, spread them a couple more inches apart, and came. My thighs trembled. A cry escaped my parted lips. Pleasure washed over my entire body so hard and so fast that I couldn't control myself.

Even after the orgasm passed, I continued rubbing my clit because I knew that with these four guys jerking off to me, I would be able to come another time, to come harder, to come with them.

So, I pulled the blanket a couple of inches up my thigh and rubbed my clit harder.

"Just like that," Thayer said. "Why don't you pull it up a couple of more inches?"

Obeying, I pulled the blanket up a bit more and slipped out my left leg, so the blanket still covered my right leg and my throbbing pussy. I curled my toes and threw my head back, biting back another moan. But, fuck, they just stroked their cocks harder.

"More, Pretty Bird," he said. "Give us more."

My gaze flickered from guy to guy, the sight of their cocks hard because of me almost making me explode again. But I wanted them to come with me, just as I had come a couple of moments ago.

I ripped the blanket off my body and spread my legs for my four best friends.

Grunts and growls echoed throughout the room. Canine teeth emerged from underneath their lips, their eyes glowing golden. I rubbed my pussy harder, needing something inside me so badly.

After I leaned back against the couch, I tugged on my nipple with my free hand and let out another moan. Gaian's gaze dropped to my tits and cleavage, his pupils dilating and his hand moving faster against his dick.

Gaian had always loved tits, had touched and groped mine during our Truth or Dare games in high school. I had imagined him sucking on mine so many times these past four years.

That Midnight Moon must've given me a load of fucking confidence because I couldn't stop myself from undoing a button on my dress, my tits spilling even more out of it. Gaian grunted and looked up at me, canines long and dripping with saliva.

"Oh my gods," I whispered, my pussy pulsing.

"Fuck, I want to blow my load deep in that fucking throat, Pretty Bird," Thayer grunted, gaze focused on my lips, taking in how I parted them to breathe unsteadily. He clenched his sharp jaw and stroked himself faster. "I want you to choke on my fucking cum."

Darius watched my fingers move skillfully around my clit, the way my pussy pulsed over and over on nothingness, waiting to be filled.

While Darius, Thayer, and Gaian were all staring at my body, Calder was looking at me. Gaze focused on my eyes, he grunted and rolled his eyes back into his head, coming into his hand and relaxing back against the wall.

I gripped on to Thayer's shoulder and threw my head back, screaming out in pleasure. Wave after wave rushed through me, my arms and legs going numb for a few moments. It felt so good—so fucking good—so much better than when I would touch myself late at night while everyone at Dad's estate was asleep.

But this was wrong. Oh-so wrong.

5

the panties

calder

SINA'S UNDERWEAR lay on my dresser.

They weren't from the Truth or Dare game or even from when I had snuck into her bedroom last night. They were from the day I had found out that she had left Durnbone for good with her dad. It was one of the few fucking things we had found of hers left in the house.

I grasped the panties and tightened my fist around them, her distinct scent rushing through the room. Over the course of the last four years, the smell had faded more and more every single day. But still, it was the only thing I had from her before she had left.

Inhaling deeply, I relaxed only slightly. Not seeing her for four fucking years had driven me fucking mad. It had been her eighteenth fucking birthday when her asshole of a father tore her away from us. I had waited for that day for years because I knew …

I knew what Sina meant to us. It was more than just friendship. It always had been.

After a couple of moments, I glanced at the five a.m. sky outside my window, placed the underwear down on my dresser, and tugged off my shirt to prepare for our morning run. Most of my pack had gone out at four thirty this morning and were flooding back onto pack grounds, but I hadn't had the damn courage to leave this house.

What if we came back and she was gone?

If we left when everyone was back, then no asshole, like Sina's father, would make it inches onto my land without someone notifying me. Everyone knew that humans weren't allowed here, especially after what that fucker had done to us after he took Sina away.

Opening my door, I spotted Gaian, Thayer, and Darius gathered in the hallway, whispering to each other and nodding toward Sina's closed door. Her soft snoring drifted underneath the wooden door.

"Let's let her sleep," Gaian said, following me down the stairs. "It's early for her."

For a human. Werewolves and monsters were up and ready for the day at this time. Humans, on the other hand, had always been late sleepers—at least, Sina had, ever since we had been children.

"I'm heading out for a run," I said, expecting them to follow, like usual. "Come on."

Darius followed Gaian, and Thayer looked one last time at Sina's door before descending the stairs. I walked through the back door as if Sina being here didn't affect me as much as it did. I didn't want my pack to know how fucking weak this girl made me.

It hadn't even been a fucking day yet, and I could barely hold myself back last night.

I kicked off my pants and shifted into my wolf, not waiting for the others before I sprinted through the woods. They followed after me, none of us speaking through the mind link or hunting for game, like we usually did.

Everyone felt it—the tension from Sina just being here.

Now that she was back in Durnbone, I wanted her father to know that we would *never* let her go. She might've thought she was only our best friend back then, but her father had known she meant more than that to us. That fucker had known and still taken her away.

I had torn up that fucking house from ceiling to floorboards, trying to find any clue about where he could've taken her that day.

Wind rustled through my fur. I growled and pushed myself harder, wanting the five-mile morning run to be over already. I needed to get back home and read that diary. I hadn't had a chance last night.

Once we made it back to the house, we were covered in sweat. I collapsed onto one of the kitchen chairs. Instead of making breakfast together, the guys sat beside me, all skirting around what we really wanted to talk about.

"So …" Darius said.

"You got the diary?" Thayer asked bluntly.

After grabbing it from my bedroom, I tossed it onto the table between the four of us and smirked. The leather-bound book glimmered in the sunlight flooding through the windows, the sweet scent of Sina drifting from the pages.

"Open it," I said.

"You haven't yet?" Darius asked.

"No."

Gaian stared at the diary uneasily and scratched the back of his head. "I don't know if we should. I mean, it's her diary. She already read one of the entries to us last night. I don't think we—"

"Come on, Gaian," Darius said, grabbing the diary from the center. "Did you not smell how horny she got last night while she was reading the entry to us? She wants us to act out those fantasies of hers."

Thayer cracked a wicked smile. "To use her."

Gaian shifted in his seat. "If we—"

"Let loose a bit," Darius said, clutching the diary. "I saw the way you kept staring at her tits last night while she touched herself for us. You guys might've had something more innocent in high school, but it's been four years. I bet she wants to fuck you just as much as you want to fuck her."

Gaian pressed his lips together, then grimaced, not refuting a word Darius had just said.

"Open the diary," I ordered.

Darius laid the diary flat on the kitchen table and opened it to the first page after the Table of Contents. We all, even Gaian, leaned forward to read Entry #1. It was dated a day before her eighteenth birthday.

This is wrong. This is so wrong.

I shouldn't be thinking these dirty things about my best friends, but I can't stop. Every time I see their faces, I can't help but imagine them inside me, pinning and restraining me, using toys on me until I come over and over, fucking me out in public behind The Cane Diner dumpster during the daytime.

One Sunday morning, I'll get the courage to bring them back there and kneel on the gravel in front of Thayer to take his cock down my throat, press my tits together so Gaian can fuck them because I always catch him staring, spread my legs for Darius to play with my clit as he fucks my ass from behind, and even rile Calder up enough for him to claim me.

Gods, I want them all to claim me.

A growl ripped out of my throat, my wolf awakening.

He had already been on edge since we had seen Sina at that party last night, but now, he was wide awake, ready to do whatever the hell we needed to do to keep Pretty Bird here and ours. No fucking way we would lose her again. She didn't know what she meant to us.

And when her father came back to Durnbone to try to take her away for a second time, she'd be full with our pups. We would make sure of it. After reading the first damn entry in her little diary, it was clear as fucking day that she wanted us just as badly.

Her father would have no other choice than to accept it or else I'd kill him.

6
the bedroom

sina

FUCK.

I stared up at the bland white ceiling and grasped my pounding head, my stomach twisting and turning from the Midnight Moon I'd had last night. Slowly, I sat up and glanced around the room, my lips turning into a frown.

This was the first night that I'd slept in a bed since I had run away from Dad's estate. It was much needed, a good time to relax. And, fuck, that dream I'd had last night of the four guys taking my diary was wild, telling me that they'd one day reenact all my fantasies and then me masturbating in front of them.

After swallowing hard, I pressed my legs together and pulled the blankets over to cover my body. Embarrassment washed over me, my cheeks flushing. If that had actually happened, I would die right on the spot.

But that *would* be a great new fantasy to place in my diary.

I slipped my hand underneath my pillow, where I had hidden the journal after I moved into Calder's pack house, and reached for it. But it wasn't there. I tore the pillow off the mattress and threw it to the other side of the room. Nothing.

My heart raced, and I jumped out of bed.

Oh no. No. No. No. No. No.

From my bed, to the dressers, to under the damn rugs, I searched for that diary like my life fucking depended on it. Because it did. But the more I searched, the less and less hope I had of finding the damn thing.

If I really had given them that journal last night, then they knew all my secrets.

Every single last fantasy.

I needed to get it back before they read it in its entirety.

After pulling on a silky lilac robe that I might've stolen from Dad's home, I tied it around my waist and stuck my head out my bedroom door. The guys all had separate rooms, but their doors were wide open.

Creeping down the hall, I glanced in all their rooms and found nobody. My gaze landed upon the last door at the end of the hall-way, which was Calder's. He had to have stolen my diary, because he was the most possessive and crazy one of them all. He must've had it in there somewhere.

I looked around one last time to make sure that nobody was watching, then stepped into the large room. Twice the size of my room with a king-size bed, dressed in a black comforter in the center of the room, Calder's room looked like it fit more than just an alpha.

Spotting a pair of panties lying on the dresser, I clenched my jaw. Who the fuck did those belong to? I should've freaking known that he would turn into one of those typical alpha-holes that Dad had warned me about.

After scrunching my nose, I forced myself to look away from them and searched his room for the journal, cautiously preparing myself for more female items lying around here. Thankfully, I didn't find anything else, but I also didn't find that freaking journal either.

I walked out of the doorway, careful to leave Calder's room exactly how it had been—even with those freaking panties glaring at me—and then headed back down the hallway toward the stairs. Four distinct male voices drifted from the first floor.

"Fuck," I whispered to myself, heart pounding. "I need to get that diary."

I didn't want to face them in the slightest, but I needed to get it as quickly as possible. Another minute that I waited was another minute they could be reading about my deepest and darkest desires.

Hell no.

While I might've been best friends with them at some point, I barely knew them now. And that was far too embarrassing.

Once I descended the steps, I took a deep breath and entered the kitchen, where Gaian was at the stove, cooking some bacon while Darius made waffles. Calder and Thayer sat at the table, chatting loudly with each other. They were all completely shirtless with a thin layer of sweat covering their swollen muscles. At least, they *had been* talking with each other, but when I walked into the room, they snapped their mouths shut and looked over at me, even Gaian.

"Good morning," I said, trying to keep my voice strong. I begged myself to ask where the diary was, but I didn't want to say the words out loud. I didn't want them to know how important that journal was to me.

"Morning," Thayer said.

"Sleep well?" Gaian asked.

"Yes," I said quickly.

At one point in my life—four years ago, to be exact—I had been so comfortable with them, even with the most uncomfortable things, like my period. Hell, they had bought me pads from the shops down in Durnbone when I needed them.

But now … everything had changed. *We* had changed.

I teetered from foot to foot, my cheeks flushing. "So, I, um …"

"Spit it out," Calder said, staring at me intensely.

Narrowing my eyes at him, I cleared my throat. "I need my diary back."

The guys all looked at each other, none of them making a single move to say anything. In fact, they all returned to chatting with each other and stabbing at the waffles and bacon whenever Gaian placed it on the table.

Gaian handed me a plate and urged me toward the only empty seat. "Eat."

Hesitantly, I pulled my robe together even further, noticing the way they all glanced over at me one at a time, eyes lingering on my chest. I loathed the way that my core warmed. I was supposed to be getting the diary back, *not* thinking about getting railed by four beasts the same exact way I'd fantasized.

One taking me from behind, grasping my hips and smacking my ass. One sucking on and playing with my tits. One forcing his cock deep into my throat and fucking me until I begged him to stop. One biting into my neck with his large canines as he pumped into me.

I pressed my thighs together tighter and cursed at myself.

Fuck. Fuck. Fuck. Fuck. Fuck.

"Pretty Bird," Thayer growled, "if you don't stop that, I'm going to eat *you* for breakfast."

Cheeks flushing harder, I cursed at myself for being so fucking embarrassing and desperately tried to calm myself. This was *not* how I'd expected this conversation to go, but I couldn't help it. I had fantasized about them for far too long.

"Do you guys have my diary?" I asked, staring at the granite tabletop.

"Do you mean this?" Calder said, pulling the leather-bound book off his lap and holding it up toward me with a wide smirk and dangerously dark eyes.

"Yes," I said, my heart skipping a beat, "that."

When he went to open it, I stood up and reached across the table to grab it, my robe falling open slightly. He pulled it just out of reach, smirk widening, and glanced down at my tits, just barely covered with silk fabric.

"Oh, come on, Pretty Bird," Calder teased. "You're going to have to try harder than that."

I gritted my teeth. "Calder, this isn't funny. Give it to me."

"No. It's ours now."

"It's mine!"

"She's sexy when she's angry," Darius said, leaning back in his seat.

"I'd put that mouth right back in its place," Thayer said, flicking his tongue over a lip ring near the corner of his mouth.

Hell, what had I gotten myself into?

Calder leaned forward toward me, matching my intense glare, and smirked. "I told you last night, and I'll tell you again. We plan to read every last page of your little book, but if you keep acting out … then we'll have to take matters into our own hands."

"And how'll you do that?" I asked, fingers paling on the table.

After pushing out his chair, he tucked the diary close to his side. "Tonight. Nine p.m."

7
the nice guy

gaian

"THEY STOLE MY DIARY!" Sina whispered to someone over the phone.

I leaned closer to her door and grabbed the handle, wanting to barge right in before the guys came back from planning what we'd do to Sina tonight. But I didn't want to overstep. This was the first time that Sina had gotten any alone time since this morning. Calder had been a bitch about not letting her out of anyone's sight.

"So?" the girl said over the phone. "It's just a diary."

"It is not just any diary, Maxine!"

After glancing over my shoulder and down into the empty living room, I realized I needed to talk to Sina now. Calder, Darius, and Thayer would be back very soon with a plan and some supplies for tonight.

Without knocking, I pushed open the door and walked into the room. Sina paced nervously around, her hair thrown up into a high ponytail and her eyes wide.

When she saw me, she gnawed on the inside of her lip. "I have to go, Maxine. I'll talk to you later."

She shut off the phone and gently placed it on her nightstand, watching me curiously from the other side of the room. "I thought you went out with the other guys," she said, glancing from me to the door. "Are you all back?"

"No," I said, shutting the door behind me and inhaling her sweet scent, which drove my wolf wild. "They're still out. I decided to stay behind because I wanted to … talk to you." Hell, I wanted to do more than just that, but I didn't admit that out loud. Not yet anyway.

"What are you guys planning for tonight?" she asked, fiddling with a button on her shirt.

I couldn't stop myself from dropping my gaze to her tits. The longer I stayed in this room with her, the fucking crazier my wolf howled inside me. He wanted to get out and see her again. It had been too fucking long.

She moved closer to me. "It's something from my diary, isn't it?"

"Maybe," I said, glancing down at her.

She was inches from me now, and I felt like I couldn't breathe or else my wolf would take full control of me—ripping off her shirt, bending her over the bed, and sucking her tits until she came all over my throbbing cock.

I wasn't going to tell her what we were planning. I just wanted to make sure she was okay with it. These were her fantasies after all, but still, we had just only met again. So much could've changed these past four years.

"You came up here to see if I was okay," she said, almost as if she knew. A small smile stretched across her face. "You never change." She nudged me. "If it's something from my diary, I think … I think I'll be okay with it. If I'm not and it gets to be too much for me, I'll say … *vampire.*"

"Vampire," I repeated, feeling my canines extend, the saliva pooling in my mouth, from just looking at her.

She stayed quiet for a long time, then looked down and shuffled her feet. "I'm okay with it, but I am nervous. It's just … some of those things are so personal. I never thought that you or any of the guys would ever read something like that from me. I'm so embarrassed."

"There's no reason to be embarrassed," I said to make her feel better.

I was just so desperate, so desperate for her to stay, so desperate for her to say yes and agree to what we were about to do to her. She was all that I had thought about these past four years.

"But now, you know …" She stepped even closer to me, and my breath hitched. "You know what I like. You know what I've been thinking about. You know that …" She took my hands and placed them on her hips, the way she had done the night before she left. "You know that I haven't stopped thinking about that night, about our last Truth or Dare game. Do you remember it?"

"Do I remember it?" I asked, my voice a whisper. "Of course I remember it."

"Do you remember what you did?"

I took another shaky breath and moved my hands a couple of centimeters up her smaller waist, my gaze drifting down to her full breasts. "Yes," I said with a gulp, letting a small rumble from my wolf escape my mouth.

"Tell me what happened that night. I want to hear it from your point of view."

"It was the night before your eighteenth birthday, and we were playing Truth or Dare. High school had been over for almost two months, but we still played those silly games. That night, you looked over at me and smiled, your pearly-white teeth glinting under the moonlight."

I gripped her waist harder. "I was so taken aback by how beautiful you were. When Thayer dared me to kiss you in the hallway closet, I was so nervous. So fucking nervous. We snuck into the dark, cramped space and stood quietly with each other for a few long moments. I knew Thayer wanted me to do more than just kiss you."

Those guys had known that if any one of us had a chance to really break the ice and do more than just make out with and touch

Sina at that time, it was me. She had trusted me then, like she trusted me now.

"You placed my hands around your waist, like you did just now, and trailed them up the curves of your fucking amazing body to your breasts, making me grope them."

"Why?" she whispered.

"Because," I said, claws lengthening. My wolf emerged, and I groped one of her breasts roughly, unable to fit the whole thing in my hand. "You always knew how much I fucking loved these tits."

My cock hardened inside my pants.

Sina took an unsteady breath.

I had been so embarrassed that night, but things had changed since then. I never admitted out loud that I liked her or that I thought about her late at night while I lay in bed with my hand around my cock, stroking until I came to the thought of watching Sina's tits bouncing as I fucked them.

"You moved closer to me in that small closet and trailed your hands down my abdomen, sinking one of them into my pants. When you felt my hard-on, you moaned into our kiss and moved your body closer to mine."

Another growl exited my throat.

"That was one of the first times I smelled how much your cunt was dripping wet for me."

And she had smelled damn fucking good, like she did now.

Only problem was that I didn't want to ruin our friendship because I liked her so fucking much. Almost too much. If I lost her, I didn't know what I would do.

But the next day, after that last game, I had lost her. We all had.

"All I've thought about for the past four years is what could've happened if Darius hadn't opened that closet door on us," she said, pressing her thighs together. "I would've let you fuck me in there."

My eyes widened slightly, my teeth aching to sink into her neck.

"If that's what you're planning to do tonight, then don't hold back this time, Gaian. I want you to do what you want to do to me before something happens, before my father comes searching for me and tries to take me away from you four wolves again."

"You've been gone for too long," I growled. "You don't ever get to leave now."

I might've been the nice guy, but I hadn't come up here to tell her to leave or even prepare for tonight.

For the past four years, my only goal had been to find her again. She would never leave us again, not even if she begged to go. Not one of us would allow it. We had gone years without our mate, years without our best friend.

Tonight, I had come up here to warn her that we weren't the same guys that she had left. Now, we fully understood what she meant to us, and we would do anything to keep her safe. Even if that meant killing her father.

8
the chase

sina

"RUN," one of my best friend's whispered into my ear, voice gruff under a skeleton mask that hid his entire head—both his face and his hair. He wrapped his leather-gloved hands around my arms and pulled me back to him, letting me feel his hardness throbbing against his dark and baggy jeans. "Run away from us, Pretty Bird. Try not to get caught," he growled low against my neck. "You know what happens when we catch you, don't you?"

I swallowed hard and nodded. I knew exactly what happened. *Entry #15.*

Calder, Thayer, Darius, and Gaian hadn't planned just any diary entry, but one of the most elaborate, detailed fantasies that I had been dreaming about forever. It was one of multiple, where they were masked completely so I couldn't see who was touching me where. The only thing I had to tell them apart was their voices.

The wolf pushed me out into the forest, where the other three men were lurking, waiting for me to run past them so they could snatch me deep into the night and take me like I wanted.

"You have one minute to get as deep into the woods as you can before we come get you. Time starts now, Pretty Bird."

My heart beat against my chest, and I sprinted hard and fast through the woods, following the normal path we had created for easy travels when we were young for a solid thirty seconds before I knew I needed to break away. I didn't want them to catch me so quickly. I wanted this chase to be just that—a long and hard chase.

But I knew it wouldn't be that way. With their werewolf senses, they'd be able to smell my scent anywhere I tried to hide. Whether it was in a tree, in a cave, in the mud, they'd find me.

I counted the seconds in my mind as I jumped over fallen branches and tree stumps and sprinted around Cedar Hill. Ten seconds. I had ten seconds to run before they started to come find me.

Though they knew this forest like the back of their hand, I didn't know where I was going. I had been gone for far too long, and my human legs would only take me so far and so fast. I could've been running around the same space for the past minute for all I knew.

Four ruthless howls erupted through the forest. My heart raced, my core warming at the sound. This was really happening. All my dirty fantasies were finally coming true. My best friends were going to find me and fuck me hard.

Running as fast as I could through the forest, I heard someone's quick footsteps behind me. My heart was racing inside my chest as the wind whipped my hair back. Before I could get another ten feet, he wrapped his arms around my waist, tumbling with me onto the ground.

I turned onto my stomach and tried crawling out of his grip, leaves and branches digging into my forearms.

He pulled me back to him with just one of his hands locked around my right hip and growled deeply in my ear, canines brushing against my neck, "You're not going anywhere, Pretty Bird. We've got you now."

Throwing me over his shoulder, he walked with me back toward the property and let out another howl, signaling that he had found me. I squirmed in his hold and scratched his back through his thick black sweatshirt, trying so desperately to break free from him.

"Try to get away all you want. We'll find you again, and again, and again."

9
the prize

sina

WHEN WE REACHED the pack house, the three men were standing around—arms crossed over their chests, masks covering their faces, everything so utterly unrecognizable. The wolf who had found me gripped my waist and tossed me through the air toward another masked wolf.

He caught me in his arms, his growl lower and deeper inside my ear, sending shivers down my spine. He took me into the house, locked all the doors, and placed me on my knees between the four of them.

"Let's get this off her," one of them said, ripping my shirt right down the center. My bare breasts bounced out of it, and his leather-gloved hand squeezed one roughly as he growled, "Fuck, Pretty Bird. I've been wanting to see these for so long."

I remembered my conversation with Gaian earlier and the way he had grabbed me so ruthlessly. The thought of him finally taking me, finally touching me, made warmth explode all over my body.

Another one crouched beside me and ran his razor-sharp claws lightly down the front of my throat. I had seen the guys ruthlessly rip out the throats of wolves far stronger than me before. He could tear mine out within a damn moment if he wanted to.

"Don't move, Pretty Bird." The sharp talons were running so gently against my neck, over my veins, right in the places where wolves marked their mates. With one finger, he ran his claw down the center of my chest and drew the letters *CP* for Caspin Pack between my breasts.

The *CP* on my skin was red and raised, but it marked me as theirs.

The masked wolf to my right snatched my chin and jerked his huge cock against my lips. "Open up, Pretty Bird. We're going to stuff you full, just like your slutty little mouth asked."

When I opened my mouth, he slammed his cock into it, hit the back of my throat, and stilled. My lips were pressed against his hips, my eyes watering. I tried pulling my head back to breathe, but he smacked the back of my head with his hand and forced me even closer.

I opened my mouth wider and tried so desperately to breathe, my cheeks flushing. After smacking the back of my head once more, he snatched a fistful of my hair and yanked me back. Spitting up saliva, I gasped for air, my chest rising and falling.

"You're not finished," he said, collapsing onto the couch and pulling me between his legs. He forced my head down on his cock again, this time closing his fingers over my nose so I couldn't breathe out of it. "Take it like the filthy slut you wanted to be tonight, Pretty Bird."

Bouncing my head on his cock, I stared up at him with wide eyes and pushed my hands against his thighs, trying to get away. Yet two of the other masked men grabbed my hands and wrapped them around their hard, throbbing cocks. I stroked them back and forth, my breasts pressed together against the couch.

"Spit between your tits," one said, pulling himself out of my mouth.

I let a wad of spit drip from my lips onto my chest and between my tits. The masked man stood up from the couch, grabbed a fistful of my hair, and used it to turn me around. He lay on the floor and tugged me onto his lap. Positioning himself underneath me, he pushed his cock up into my pussy, and I screamed out for him.

"Someone, fuck those tits of hers."

One of the other men stepped forward, stroking his cock in my face. "Hands behind your fucking back," he ordered.

I placed my arms behind my back, interlocking my fingers, and pushed my breasts out for him.

He slapped one hard, making it bounce against the other. Then, he slapped the other one. Over and over and over. Left. Right. Left. Right. Left. Right.

"Fuck, they're so fucking nice," he murmured to himself.

After ordering me to hold my tits together, he pushed his cock between them. It disappeared for a moment, and then his head reappeared between my cleavage.

The man under me thrust up into my pussy, naturally forcing my breasts to bounce around this masked wolf's cock. I felt a finger press against my ass, and I moaned out loud, almost screaming from how good it felt.

"Someone, stick a cock in her mouth to shut her up," one man said.

Another wolf walked up beside me, forced my head in his direction, and thrust himself deep down my throat. I gagged on him, holding my breasts together the harder I choked. Tears welled up in my eyes, and I moaned.

Someone knelt behind me and rubbed his wet cock against my ass. I arched slightly for him and let him push it into my backside, filling all my holes up. Hands were all over my body. The masked wolves were all cursing and swearing, calling me all the names in the book, just as I had asked them too.

I clenched around them and felt my body tremble as wave after wave of pleasure surged through me like fucking electricity. My hands slipped from my tits to the chest of the man below me. I gagged more on someone's cock, my throat squeaking and gurgling.

When he pulled out of me, I dropped my head, trying so desperately to breathe. The masked wolf under me clutched my hips and slammed his cock so deep, stilling almost instantly. He groaned and moved his hips slightly to push his cum as deep as it could go.

My pussy and ass tightened as he pulled himself out of me. I dug my nails into his chest, getting thrust forward every time the other rammed himself into my ass. My tits swung, and the wolf who had put his cock between them was fondling one in his large hand.

"I need to be filled," I breathed. "Please ..." I stared up at him. "I need my pussy to be filled."

The man behind me stilled and slowly pulled out of me, his cum dripping down my asscheek. He slapped it hard and stood up. "Pretty Bird is all yours," he said to the other two who hadn't come yet.

Capturing my nipples between his fingers, one masked man tugged up on them. I stumbled to my feet to lessen the pain, yet he stepped back and pulled me forward and toward him, as if using my nipples to walk me like a fucking animal.

"Come here," he said to me, voice filled with such a hurtful kind of dominance that only turned me on. "Your tits are so big that they just drag you forward. Wherever they go, you go, huh?"

After furrowing my brows, I nodded and continued forward to the couch.

"You want your aching pussy to be filled?" he asked me, picking me up and sitting me on top of him, my back against his chest. He hooked his arms under my legs and pulled them apart, his cock brushing against my pussy. My pussy pulsed wildly as he held my legs farther apart, slipping inside of me. "Huh?"

The last masked wolf knelt between my legs, tore off his mask just enough to uncover his mouth, and started eating my pussy. I squirmed around, the pressure rising in my core. So much ... it felt like it was too much. It might've been wrong, disgusting, gross to some people—to be filled by all these men—but I loved every single second of it.

I wanted them to breed me like this every fucking day.

Squirming in his hold, I tried to relieve the tension in my core. I dug my fingernails into his thigh and screamed out as the other flicked my clit with his tongue at just the right angle. He stood up and rubbed his cock against my wet pussy, then slid it into my cunt too. I felt so full—so fucking full with both of them inside me—yet I wanted all of them in me. I wanted to be used by faceless men I couldn't tell apart. It was fucking weird, but my deepest, darkest fantasy was to be used like this, used for their pleasure, especially by four of the strongest wolves in this part of the forest.

The wolf beneath me grabbed my tits, squeezing as hard as he could. The other wrapped a hand around my throat and rammed himself into me even harder.

I stared up at him. "Is that all you have?" I asked, wanting this to hurt fucking bad.

He slapped me hard across my face, making my right cheek sting. Being the bratty submissive that I was, I slapped him right back across that skeleton mask of his. The other guys went silent, and I clenched down on his cock, knowing that he would hit me back even harder.

After letting out a menacing growl, he backhanded me across my left cheek so hard that my head moved to the side, the pain so much worse and so much warmer than the first slap. I stayed quiet a few moments, trying to reorient myself.

"Looks like Pretty Bird knows her place now," he said down at me.

I turned back to him, my pussy pulsing, and spit up at him. After I did, he ripped the bottom of his mask off just slightly to show his lips, showing me that scar that only Alpha Calder wore on his face.

He spit down at me and pulled his mask back on. "Pathetic fucking whore."

His spit landed on the corner of my mouth, and he rubbed it around my face, ruining my makeup. He covered my mouth and nose with his large, callous hand as they both continued to pound into my pussy. I squeezed my eyes closed and arched my back, coming on both of their cocks.

The man behind me stilled inside of me, his cum leaking down my ass as he pulled himself out of me. Calder thrust a few more times deep into my pussy and growled, coming inside of me too. More cum rushed out, making me a dripping mess.

10
the hidden desire

sina

CALDER PUSHED ME OFF HIM, ripped off his mask first, and threw it onto the ground, his jaw clenched hard and his eyes glowing gold at me. He stared at me for a few long moments, then growled, "You're a fucking brat, Sina."

"What the hell, dude?" Gaian asked, taking off his mask and shoving Calder back toward the other room. "Why the hell are you pissed at her now? You're the fucking one who wanted to do this."

I stared at him with wide eyes, my heart pounding inside my chest. My mind was reeling with so many thoughts that I could barely even process how Calder was reacting right now. Everything that had just happened was … was …

Fucking amazing.

My incubus ex-boyfriend had never even made me feel that good.

Calder glared at me so intensely with those alpha eyes that could make any wolf surrender. I thanked the gods that I wasn't a wolf because I would never surrender to him. I was a human by nature and a brat by nurture.

Dad had taken away enough of my freedom; I wouldn't let Calder rule me around too.

And, plus, being bratty toward him got me off. There was something about being ruthless toward the deadliest guy around that ignited a fire inside of me.

But still, even if Calder was annoyed at me for how I had acted while he fucked me, I didn't care. After all these years, my fantasy had finally come true. I had dreamed about it so many fucking times, touched myself endlessly, thinking about their lips all over my body.

Now that it had happened, I didn't regret it in the slightest.

I wanted more, and I would get more. Any way that I could.

Calder stormed out of the room, Gaian following him to talk tensely.

"Don't get a bruised fucking ego over it, Calder," Darius shouted, following him up the stairs and into the hallway. "Come on. You just fucked the girl that you ..." He disappeared from my view, his voice fading off as a door closed.

The only person left in the room with me was Thayer, who stepped closer to me and watched me like a hawk. His eyes were so dark that they scared the living daylights out of me, so much so that I had to force myself to breathe.

He drew his tongue across his canine teeth, and for some reason, my mind finally processed just how angry Calder had been when he left. Only a few moments ago, when I had still been riding out my high, it hadn't seemed that bad.

But I didn't want to let this go. I wanted this to happen again and again.

"More," I whispered.

Thayer dragged his claws down the column of my neck, so close to my arteries that he was millimeters from tearing them and so deep that he could almost rip out my throat and feed it to me. Suddenly, he snapped his hand around my neck and yanked me closer to him, so my body was flush against his.

"Please, Thayer," I said, my body aching in need. "Don't let this be the last time."

"Don't worry about Calder," he growled into my ear, his voice low, gruff, and deranged. "He'll get over it."

Out of all the guys, Thayer had always been the crazy one, suggesting feral and wild acts, always pushing the limits. Maybe that was what drew me toward him. It had just never been *this* sexual before now, but I knew that Thayer hadn't even let completely loose tonight.

"We're not done using you. I have plans to make you my filthy" —he moved his hand from my neck to my chin and forced his fingers into my mouth—"little"—he shoved his fingers deeper into me, reaching the back of my throat and making me gag—"whore."

I coughed on him, spit dribbling down my chin and eyes watering, but I didn't pull away.

I wanted to be his filthy little whore. I wanted him to do insane, crazy, and fucked up things to me, things that I didn't even want to write in my journal because I'd feel way too guilty about asking anyone to do them.

"You'd like that, wouldn't you?" Thayer asked, the corner of his lips curling into a wicked smirk. "You want me to snap a collar and leash around your throat and walk you around like a dog, brand you all over your body again so you know who you belong to?"

Heat gathered between my legs, and I found myself sucking harder on his fingers. He thrust them deeper down my throat, pushing them in and out of me, as if he were throat-fucking me.

"Yes," I moaned. "Please."

"Fuck," he grunted, pressing his bulge against the front of my hips and grinding it up and down, as if he were inside me too, showing me how deep his cock could get. "I wish I were coming against your fucking cervix again, Pretty Bird. You'd look damn sexy, pregnant with one of our pups."

My breath caught in my throat, my pussy fucking beating.

"I read through that entire journal, and I didn't see a word about your breeding kink in there," he said, dropping his hand to my cunt and playing with my folds. "But by the way your mouth started salivating and how your cunt just tightened, I can tell that's what you want."

"Thayer," I whispered, my cheeks flushing.

I didn't know how the fuck he had found out, what I had done to even give him that mere thought. I had made sure not to write it down anywhere, but I couldn't stop my body from reacting to his words. Heat rushed through my aching body.

Before tonight, I had only touched myself to that breeding fantasy one time. I refused to let myself slip into it multiple times, like I had with some of these other fantasies because I couldn't see myself breeding with any other guys. And I had never thought I would see these four wolves again.

"Admit it," he growled. "You want us to shove our cum deep into your holes until you're filled to the brim with it because the thought of us wanting to fill you with pups, to claim you as our own, turns you the fuck on."

Whimpering softly, I grasped on to his hand so he would stop rubbing my clit. It was only turning me on more, but I couldn't get off, thinking about something like that. I'd promised myself that I would never think that about these guys again.

It made me feel so dirty and shameful.

"Thayer," I said.

But he didn't stop rubbing my clit. He wanted me to get off on the thought, on the mere fantasy of these guys wanting to get me pregnant, though I wasn't sure why. One day, they would find their mates and want families with them.

Not me.

"Please, Thayer, don't," I whispered.

I was sure that Gaian had told him my safe word. Thayer wasn't going to stop until I said that single word to him, and even then … I didn't know if he'd stop. Thayer was crazy.

Still, I didn't say it because I didn't want him to stop. I wanted to come at the thought of each of them so desperate to put their pups inside me that they wanted to fuck me day and night, until I begged them to let me rest.

After a couple of moments, Thayer chuckled menacingly at me. "Wolves are good at breeding, Pretty Bird. We're also good at putting pups inside our mate until her belly is swollen and she's lying in bed, helpless. We all love that, but especially alphas."

The way he said it wasn't just a fact, but a promise.

That was what each of them wanted to do to me. That was what they *all* would do to me.

Especially Alpha Calder.

But that wasn't what caught me off guard. Thayer had said that wolves like them were good at putting pups inside their *mate*. Mate, singular and not plural. Mate, as in me. Sina Baker. Pretty Bird. The innocent human girl who had thought that they were just best friends.

"Calder wants you pregnant," Thayer said, dragging his claw down the center of my chest and over the scarred *CP* that he must've drawn on my body earlier to brand me as part of their pack. "So you don't ever leave us again."

11
the psycho

thayer

SINA WAS SCARED, and I loved every single second of it.

I lay back in my bed, drew my fingers over the sharp edge of a knife, and listened through the thick walls to Pretty Bird pacing back and forth in her bedroom. She hadn't been able to stop for the past few hours, and it was nearing one in the morning.

Heat rushed through my body at the memory of her tonight, the way her body had trembled when I carved the letters *CP* into her chest to brand her. I loved when her heart was pounding, her blood pumping harshly through her veins and arteries, pooling against her cheeks and crawling down her neck, making her entire body flush pink.

She might've had a diary full of fantasies about us, but I had a mind full of fucked up thoughts about what I'd fucking love to do to her and that filthy mouth of hers. She had no idea what I had in store.

Tonight, I hoped she lay in her bed, trembling, thinking about me, about what I would do to her, about how much I would someday push all her limits until she was my desperate, begging little whore.

Moon Goddess, I wanted her on her knees every night. I wanted her to beg me to drag a knife up and down the column of her throat, touching the skin gently enough to give her goosebumps. I wanted her screaming my name and fighting me as I shoved her face down into the pillow and she tried to breathe.

My dick throbbed, and I laid my hand over it, squeezing it as tight as Sina's pussy had earlier. I would fuck her every single fucking night, like we had tonight, if she let me. I wanted her filled with cum dripping out of every one of her holes.

Seeing her as a fucking slut, Goddess, it did something to me. Sina Baker had always been the innocent human girl who hung out with us in high school, the girl we all tried to bang, but never once had the chance.

Dick twitching, I laid the knife on my abdomen and shoved a hand into my pants.

"My room," Calder said through the mind link to Gaian, Darius, and me, pulling me out of my damn fantasy. *"Now."*

He still sounded pissed from earlier, but he didn't have a fucking reason. Calder had just never had someone disrespect him or even oppose his demands. These past four years might've been hard on him, but at least Sina hadn't been here to defy him.

After grunting, I pulled my hand away and walked toward my bedroom door, dick still pressed hard against my sweatpants. I didn't give a fuck though. That was what Calder got for asking us to come into his room this fucking late at night.

I exited my room and glanced over at Sina's bedroom door. It was closed, but I could still hear her pacing around endlessly inside and could only imagine her walking around in a tiny tank top with the letters *CP* still fresh on her chest.

"Now," Calder repeated to only me through the link.

Sighing, I walked to Calder's door and stepped into the room. Like Sina, Gaian paced the room and ran a hand through his dirty-blond hair. Darius lay back on the bed, his eyes closed almost, as if he were sleeping. Calder shut the door behind me.

"What the fuck did you tell Sina?" Calder said to me through gritted teeth.

"I didn't say shit to her," I said, sliding onto the bed next to Darius and leaning against the headboard, hands interlocked behind my head and ankles crossed. "Nothing that wasn't true, of course. I just wanted to make sure she knew she wasn't leaving."

"You told her I wanted to fucking put a baby inside her?"

"Don't you?" I challenged. "It's all you've said you'd do to her once we found her."

"You can't just say shit like that to her," Calder said.

"Who cares? And besides, she's our mate," I said. "We don't have to hold back."

Gaian crossed his arms and clenched his jaw. "If Sina doesn't want us to push it, then we shouldn't push it. She got back into Durnbone literally last night. We shouldn't push her or else she's—"

"Gaian, shut the hell up," I said, rolling my eyes.

I loved the guy, but he was a bit too overwhelming sometimes. He cared too much.

"She fucking loves the thought of it," I said, thinking back to mere hours ago when she had been begging me to stop talking about breeding because her cunt was getting hot and tight, her body so flustered, and I knew she wouldn't stop thinking about it.

She might not have written it in her diary, but that fucking look on her face ... she had been terrified at how her body reacted, how good and warm she must've felt all over, just thinking about us plugging up her holes with our cum.

"You don't know that," Gaian said.

"Bullshit. She was putty in my hands after I told her that's what we wanted." I looked over at Calder and curled my lips into a smirk. "You might be pissed off at her for disrespecting you, but that's what she likes, and alphas like you get off on putting someone in their place."

Calder growled in response.

"Anyway ..." I said, standing up and walking to Calder's dresser, where he kept her diary. I flipped through it and whistled softly. "It's not like I lied to her. We've talked about it since her father took her away. We want her pregnant, and Pretty Bird has quite the collection of kinks that we can try out along the way."

Nobody spoke a fucking word, so I flipped to my favorite page of Sina's diary and tossed it onto the bed next to Darius.

"Seeing as everyone is lost for words tonight, I'll step up and choose the next diary entry that we'll enact for Sina. I think this one will do quite well."

"Pretty Bird has some damn kink with not seeing our faces, huh?" Darius said, lips curling into a smirk as his gaze drifted down the page. "But this one is kinda outlandish, don't you think? Definitely a lot more …"

"Rapey," Gaian said, looking at the page uncomfortably and scratching the back of his head. "I mean, that's what it basically is."

"She has a safe word," I said blankly. When nobody refused, I took the book back and snapped it shut. "I'll get what we need this time, and tomorrow, we'll surprise her. It's not like any one of us is going to be able to hold ourselves back. The closer the full moon gets, the stronger the mate bond will be before taking full effect."

12
the tavern

sina

IT WAS two in the morning, and I couldn't sleep.

I paced around my bedroom, counting the seconds, the minutes, the hours that had passed since Thayer had told me that Calder wanted me to be pregnant. My heart hadn't stopped racing at the thought, and I needed to talk to someone about it.

Someone needed to *convince* me that the thought was crazy, right?

A breeding kink and pregnancy were *not* the same thing.

"Come on, Maxine," I whispered into my phone, looking back at my closed bedroom door to make sure nobody walked in on me. "Answer the goddamn phone. I need reassurance, and these guys are not helping!"

The line rang and rang and rang, and then, *finally*, Maxine answered the phone, the background noise loud on the other side.

"Sina? Are you okay?" she asked. "You never call while I'm working."

"Are you at the tavern?" I asked, brows furrowed.

"Yes, wh—"

"I'm coming down to Durnbone now."

After slamming the End button, I shoved my phone into my pocket and opened the second-story window in my bedroom. If I tried to sneak out through the hallway, one of them was bound to hear me. But if I went through the window … I had a better chance of getting out.

They wouldn't let me out of their sight any other way.

"Thank you, Dad," I said, fitting my body through the window and holding on to the edge tightly to brace myself for the fall. "For teaching me the right way to sneak out without getting caught. That's the only damn thing I learned from living in your house."

Once I took the leap of faith and let my hands slip from the edge, I landed feet-first onto a smaller tree branch. I wrapped my arms around the tree trunk and slithered down it until my feet landed on the ground.

Scanning the woods for any sign of Calder, Darius, Thayer, or Gaian, I found the forest relatively empty. I turned on the directions on my phone and followed them to a dirt road that led back into Durnbone.

The closer I got to town, the more people I saw who were out this late at night. I ignored the desperate faces of incubi wanting to get their fixes of human girls. That was what The Dungeon was for —if they wanted to suck a girl dry of blood, lust, or life.

"Can I—" a deep voice started from behind me, a hand coming around my hip.

I whirled around on my heel, about to slap whoever it was, just to see Jaroth, my ex, creeping around behind me. When he saw that it was me, he let his hand linger for a moment longer than it should've, then pulled it away.

"Fuck, Sina," he said harshly, though his eyes were just as dark and filled with lust as they had always been around me. Too bad for him. That fucker had had to cheat. We probably still would've been together if he could control himself. "Why're you still in town? Your father here?"

"That's none of your business," I said between gritted teeth. "I'm busy."

"You're busy at two in the morning?" he asked, then stepped closer to me and sniffed my shirt collar. "And why the hell do you reek of sex? It's coming off you in waves. I've never smelled you so turned on before."

"That's also none of your business," I said, twirling back around and crossing my arms. "Now, point me in the direction of the tavern."

"You're going to have to be a bit more specific," he said, stepping closer to me again. "There is an incubus bar about three blocks down from here. I'm heading there now and looking for a date to share a room with toni—"

I smacked him. "I'll never be your date after what you did to me, and I have no interest in any incubus bars. I'm looking for Maxine. She works at the pub where all the different creatures hang out. Some demons frequent there, like … I think his name is Xorgor."

"Xorgor," Jaroth repeated, his lips curling in an ugly grimace. "You're looking for the Dead Candle Tavern. It's right across the street, about five buildings down. You should see if you can—"

Instead of listening to another moment of his annoying voice ramble on and on, I hurried across the street and five buildings down, leaving Jaroth where I had met him. I didn't have any interest in him anymore, and I was still salty as fuck about what he had done to me.

The girl he had slept with was one of my best friends back at my father's estate.

Emphasis on *was*.

After taking a deep breath, I grasped the wooden door handle and walked into the raging tavern, filled with creatures and monsters of all types, even those species that lived just outside of the town and in the forest with the wolves. I walked through the groups of people and sped toward the counter, where Maxine worked.

She filled two tall glasses to the top with Midnight Moon drinks and handed them to two female succubi, who then wandered off to a table of vampires. I hurried to the bar and slid onto the only empty seat, staring Maxine down until she spotted me.

Once she finished with a couple more customers, she poured me a glass and slid it across the table. "Oh gods, you look like you haven't slept a wink in the past twenty-four hours. What the hell happened to you after the party?"

"They want me pregnant!" I said, unable to stop myself. "That's absurd, right?"

"What?!" Maxine said. "Who wants you pregnant?"

I glanced around the bar to make sure nobody was listening, then leaned forward. "You know … the four wolves—Calder, Thayer, Darius, and Gaian. But especially Calder. Thayer said that he wants me filled with his pups the most, and I mean, I—"

"Girl," Maxine said, resting her hands on my shoulders, "slow down."

All I wanted was for her to tell me that it was weird, that it wasn't normal in the slightest, that I shouldn't *want* to be bred by them. They were wolves for crying out loud, and I was a mere human.

"Sounds like you're their mate," she said.

"Yeah, but, Maxine, *pregnant*?!" I asked, shaking my head. She wasn't helping. "They've all changed so much—except Gaian really—but I have barely seen them for two days. How could they want to … to …" I swallowed hard, thinking that—scratch that, *knowing*—this was so wrong. "How could they want to breed me?"

The words came out so softly that Maxine didn't hear them—or at least, I hoped that she hadn't. It was so embarrassing to say those words out loud. I had suppressed the thought and fantasy for so long, especially while living at Dad's estate.

If my best friend said it was wrong, then it *had* to be wrong.

Still, whatever she said about it wouldn't change the way I felt when Thayer asked if I wanted to be bred again, when Calder or Darius thrust his cock deep in my pussy and forced me to take every last drop of his cum, when my breasts swelled from a baby growing inside me and Gaian became even more of a freak about them and about me.

"To what?" Maxine asked.

"To …" I started, but I couldn't force myself to say the word again. Instead, I sipped the Midnight Moon until there was nothing left. I slammed the empty glass on the bar and sank down on the barstool, dragging a hand across my face. "I don't know what to do."

"Well, you'd better think quickly," Maxine said.

"Why?"

"Because the four big bad wolves just walked in behind you."

13
the alpha

sina

"YOU'RE LYING," I whispered to Maxine, my entire body tense. "They're not here."

By the mere amused expression on her face, I could tell she wasn't lying. They were probably scanning the pub at this very moment, catching me sitting at the counter with two guys on either side of me who kept looking over at me, before barreling toward us.

"Save me." I leaned across the counter and grabbed her forearms. "Please, hide me."

"Why?" she said, a smile on her face as she poured a drink for the customer beside me. "It's kinda sexy to see them all riled up because of you. You should've known that they'd hunt you down and find you in town."

"They were sleeping when I left!" I whisper-yelled, desperately trying to shrivel up so they wouldn't see me.

All I'd wanted was one night of peace because I had gotten barely any time to myself since I had left Dad's estate.

"Who're you waiting for?" the guy next to me said, eyeing me like Jaroth had earlier.

The guy beside him threw us both a sultry smirk that all incubi had mastered. They might be part demon, but they didn't stand a chance against four possessive wolves.

When he leaned closer to me and grazed his fingers against my knee, I swallowed hard and turned away, *knowing* this wasn't good. Not one bit. If he kept staring at me like that, then the guys would surely—

Darius grabbed the guy by his shirt collar and flung him across the room. To my surprise, everyone carried on like it was nobody's business and like nothing had happened at all. I looked around, anywhere but at the four wolves who seemed like they wanted to kill someone. Even good-boy Gaian looked pissed.

"What the fuck are you doing here, Sina?" Calder said between gritted teeth.

"Getting away from your toxic, over—"

Before I could finish my sentence, Thayer grasped my jaw in his callous hand, and I found myself stopping mid-sentence. There was something psychotic in his strong hold, something that shut me right up.

"We're not being toxic," Calder said, like every toxic guy had ever said. "You haven't fucking seen toxic and overbearing, Sina. Or else you would've been chained to my fucking bed since the moment you arrived in Durnbone."

A heavy sigh escaped my lips, and I wanted to protest more, but I was getting damn tired after everything that had happened today. "I just needed some time away from you guys," I said, slumping my shoulders. "I needed some girl time."

"If you want some girl time, then Maxine can come over," Calder said. "You're not to leave the pack house unless someone goes with you. You don't understand how dangerous it is in Durnbone, especially this late at night and with your father looking for you."

While I wanted to ignore everything that he had said, I couldn't. He was right.

Dad had already dragged me away from Durnbone once because he apparently didn't like these four guys. That had been on my eighteenth birthday, too, when I could officially make decisions for myself. I didn't put it past him to have guys searching Durnbone for me. He would try to take me away again.

But still, I needed some space.

"You're being unreasonable," I said, poking a finger into his chest.

I loved pushing his buttons and making him angry. Alphas hated being disrespected and defied, especially in public. So, if they wouldn't let me out of their sight, that was exactly what I wanted to do until they did.

"You can't leave us," Gaian suddenly said, his voice hard but with some vulnerability in it. He pressed his lips together, the dim light making his green eyes look more menacing than the good-boy image he tried to keep alive.

Something darker lurked within him. Something feral.

After glancing over at Darius, then Thayer, I realized they all had that same worried expression suppressed under their anger. It meant something more to them that I had left without telling them where I was going, that I'd just disappeared without a trace.

"This is why," Calder said, gripping my upper arm and dragging me toward the exit.

"Why what?"

"Why I want your belly swollen with our pups."

I ripped my arm away from him and clenched my teeth. "You want me pregnant because of my father?" I shoved my hands against his chest, pushing him back against a table. "Is it because you don't want him taking me away again or because you think you have something to prove to him?"

Rage flooded through me, making every single inch of my body hot. He didn't want me to be pregnant because he wanted me or because I was his mate or anything like that. Calder wanted me pregnant to piss off my dad.

My hands balled into tight fists, and I flung one at him, suddenly overcome with so much aggression, almost comparable to a wolf. Before it could collide with his chest, Calder caught it in his larger palm and growled.

"You don't know shit about what we went through when he took you away."

"You don't know shit about what I went through when he took me away," I said.

He didn't know how hard it had been for me to be away from them. When I had lived in Durnbone the first time, those four guys had been my escape from the hell that Dad forced me to walk through every moment of my life. I had been looking forward to the day that I turned eighteen because I was finally going to leave his house.

I was finally going to be free.

Instead, Dad forced me into a damn prison at a lake house with some of his *business friends*, who made appearances at my bedroom door late at night. I couldn't say no or risk Dad's scolding and punishment. I'd had no freedom, no free will.

And this guy thought he'd had it fucking bad.

Tears welled up in my eyes. I slammed my hands against his chest again, putting all my hatred for Dad and annoyance for Calder into the push, and shoved him against the table, so hard that he broke it.

"I thought you wanted me pregnant because you liked me," I said, hurt in every word.

While sitting at the bar and talking to Maxine, I had begun to accept this little kink that I had because Calder sorta, kinda had it too. I'd thought that maybe being back in Durnbone with my four best friends would be a good thing. Maybe these guys would take me into their arms and show me the love that Dad never had.

But I was wrong.

Calder just wanted revenge. And the others ... I didn't know their intentions yet.

"I hate you," I said between gritted teeth, then stormed out of the pub.

I continued on the path back toward their pack house while they —even Calder—trailed after me. Crossing my arms, I gritted my teeth and refused to cry.

Deep down inside me, this felt like rejection.

I couldn't explain it, but Gaian's sister had once been rejected by her mate. I had watched her cry into Gaian's arms for days upon days. Who the hell knew if these guys and I had that kind of connection? But this hurt. Bad.

It was always about Dad.

Since the moment I had seen Calder at the party the other night, he had treated me as if I was his object or property. Calder only wanted me to get back at my dad. He didn't really want *me*, and if he did, he sure didn't act like it.

14

the nervous one

darius

"DON'T you think they're being a bit overbearing?" Gaian asked the next morning during our run.

Calder and Thayer had run together earlier this morning, and now, they were watching over Sina while we ran with the rest of the pack.

A thin layer of sweat covered my bare chest. I breathed heavily and pulled my dreads back with an elastic to keep them out of my face, then continued following him through the forest, around the path we always took.

I didn't have the same connection with Sina as the other guys. They had all been obsessed with her in high school, but I hadn't been as forward with my crush on her. Sina and I hung out all the time without them, and she came to me for advice about her relationship with the others. Part of me had always sorta felt left out back then.

But now … things had changed.

"Calder and Thayer aren't afraid to be fucking psychopaths with her," I said uneasily.

But then again, maybe they had a reason to be overly possessive.

I hadn't headed over to Sina's house early the morning of her eighteenth birthday the way that Calder and Thayer did, only to be attacked by goons that her father had hired to *exterminate* us. We had been at war with them ever since—without Sina's knowledge.

"I don't want her to leave ever, but they might push her away," I said truthfully.

I thought back to last night when we had followed her back from the pub and she had cried her eyes out because Calder was being an asshole to her, like usual.

"They will," Gaian said, slowing down as we neared the house.

Sina lay outside on a picnic blanket in a skimpy little baby-blue bikini, trying to soak up as much sunlight as she could. I gazed at her ass falling out of her bottoms and found myself tensing when she looked over at us. Calder and Thayer sat outside on a couple of logs, shit-talking with each other.

After hopping up from the blanket, she hurried over to us, her barely covered tits bouncing. She stopped in front of us and crossed her arms over her chest—a sight that I knew Gaian wouldn't be able to resist.

Chewing on the inside of her lip, she let her gaze fall to my sweat-covered chest, then over to Gaian. "Do either one of you want to do me a favor?" she asked, rocking back on her heels and glancing over at the other two.

"What is it?" Gaian asked.

"Sneak into Calder's room and get me my diary back."

A deep chuckle escaped my throat. "No can do."

"Please, Darius," she said, grasping on to my hand.

My entire body tensed, the feeling of her skin on mine making the hairs stand up on my arms. I stared at her softening eyes for a few moments, my breath caught in the back of my throat. Gaian might've been the nice guy, Thayer the psycho, and Calder the overbearing alpha with her, but all I was with her was a bit more nervous.

Nervous as fuck actually.

Because she hadn't looked at me the same way she did with the other guys in high school. The other three had gotten some experience with her before her father took her away, so they were more comfortable with this feeling of being mated to someone. Me? I had to experience the loss of my mate by myself and in my own weird way.

I feared I would do all this shit wrong or that she wouldn't like me the same way.

But her eyes had been saying otherwise since the moment she had looked at me in that dirty basement party. She might've been gravitating toward the others, too, but her hands were now on me, touching me, begging me.

After Gaian told her no too—because he wanted her just as bad as the others—she grasped on to me tighter, her fingers so much softer and smoother than any wolf I had been with these past few years. She watched Gaian walk into the house to shower and to prepare for later tonight when we'd enact another one of her diary entries.

"You got her?" Thayer called. "We gotta head to Durnbone to pick up some … *things.*"

While Sina rolled her eyes—oh, that woman had no idea what was coming—I nodded. They disappeared into the forest, heading toward Durnbone. Sina blew out a deep breath, released my hand, and sat back down on her picnic blanket.

Her lips were tugged into a frown.

I sat beside her, my legs grazing against her skin, and gently nudged her. "What's up?"

"I …" She dragged a hand across her face. "It's nothing."

"What is it?" I asked again.

"They didn't stop watching me like a hawk while you were gone. At least you and Gaian let me walk around the house alone. Those assholes followed me around, never letting me out of their sight once. It's getting annoying."

"They missed you," I said.

She swallowed hard and looked over at me, her full lips now resting softly. "Did you?"

"Did I?" I asked, heart racing a bit faster, the nerves hitting me full force now.

I hadn't been alone with her since she had gotten back into town, so I could hide my nerves and my feelings, especially during the chase last night when she had wanted us to wear masks and clothes that covered every inch of our bodies. She hadn't known which one of the guys I was, which one wanted to devour every inch of her.

"Hmm?" she asked, her lips curling into a smile. "Did you?"

"Of course I did, Sina," I said. "We're best friends."

Her face fell, the lightness in her eyes gone. "So … are you just doing this because you want to get back at my dad too? Because best friends don't just refuse to give me back my diary and fuck me like you did last night."

"No," I said, scratching the back of my head and realizing that I had fucked up. "I … I'm not doing it just because of your father—or because of him at all. I'm really glad that you're back in town. I've missed you a fuck-ton."

She stared into my eyes, then pulled away her gaze. "You're not just fucking with me?"

"No."

"Good, because I don't want my father to be part of my love life anymore," she whispered.

"Anymore?"

She froze, as if she had said something wrong, then shook her head. "It doesn't matter."

"What do you mean, anymore?" I asked, pushing it.

At first, for a split second, I thought she was just referring to him taking her away from us, but I could tell that there was more to it, more that she was hiding from us, more that she didn't want to tell a single soul.

"It's nothing," she said again, standing up and looking down at me. Her gaze was ice fucking cold, and her jaw was clenched hard, but her eyes wavered for just a moment, telling me something more. "It's nothing I want to think about now. I just want to know if any of you really care about me."

15
the sixteenth entry

sina

I SAT in the living room, angrily staring at the blank wall with my hands balled into tight fists by my sides. There was no point in even staying in my bedroom. The guys had made it crystal clear that I obviously had no privacy at all.

When they had taken me home the other night, I should've left then. I had been told over and over that wolves were easily jealous and controlling creatures, especially alphas. They wanted to have things their way all the damn time.

And I was having none of it.

With them being gone—even if it was just shit-talking by a fire outside—I wanted to leave. Maybe not for good, but I did want to sneak out again. I didn't want to be cooped up in this house without any friends and with them lurking over me twenty-four/seven.

Just as I was about to stand up from the couch, storm up the stairs, and throw on some slutty clothes to wear to the pub, someone slapped their hand over my mouth and lifted me off the couch.

"Get off me!" I screamed into the palm, kicking and shoving whoever it was back.

Three more men dressed in ski masks and dark clothes—almost the same fantasy as last time, but different—flooded into the room, each trying to stop me from struggling. This was almost exactly like ...

Entry #16: Intruder Rape Fantasy.

"Shut her the fuck up," someone to my left growled, tossing a roll of duct tape to the man in front of me.

The guy ripped off a piece of tape and slapped it over my mouth so I couldn't speak, then grabbed my wrists and taped them together behind my back while I struggled to push him away, but he didn't stop. He taped them so tightly that I couldn't wiggle out of it. My breasts bounced inside my tank top when I attempted to escape.

"If you need to stop," he said to me, his lips against my ear and his hand flattening the tape on my mouth, "ball your hand into a fist and release it twice."

I knocked my shoulder into him to push him away. Just as I did, someone new tightly wrapped their hand around my throat and pulled me back toward him so my body was flush against his chest. After sliding his hand up to my chin and shoving it to the side, he pressed the sharp edge of a knife against my artery in my neck.

I inhaled sharply but didn't move, for fear that if I did, the blade would slide into my flesh and kill me. My body went rigid against the masked man behind me, warmth gathering in the pit of my stomach.

All I needed was my safe word for them to stop.

Yet, still, I refused because I couldn't stop thinking about what Thayer had told me earlier about Calder wanting to breed me so badly and how Calder had reacted when I confronted him about it. I wanted to fight them, especially Calder, with all my might. I had so much built-up anger because of him, just from these past few days.

When the man slid the knife down my throat, I pressed my thighs together and leaned back into him, wanting the knife as far away from me as possible. He chuckled darkly into my ear, the sound voice low and feral, like a predator. Then, he cut through the neckline of my tank top, gliding the blade through the shirt and between my cleavage until my breasts completely fell out of the top.

One of the other masked men let out a ferocious growl, and I lifted my gaze to stare at Gaian. Once the knife split my tank top in half, Gaian reached forward and ripped the rest of it off my body, so my upper half was completely exposed to them.

"I can smell your cunt, Pretty Bird," Thayer growled into my ear.

He glided his knife up the center of my chest again and to the CP on the exposed part of my chest, which he had carved with his claws yesterday. The scar hadn't healed completely, but then again, the original mark hadn't been deep, just a mere scrape. With the tip of the knife, he grazed it against the letters without sinking it into me.

After sucking in another sharp breath, my breasts bouncing slightly, I pressed my thighs together harder to ease the pulsing between them. The pressure rose in my core quickly. I loved the feeling of being helpless in their arms.

Psycho Thayer had complete and utter control of my life right now.

If he wanted to end me, all he had to do was sink the knife into my heart, rip me to pieces with his claws, and bury me in the back-yard. While the thought might've scared anyone else away, I loved the rush.

Because I knew Thayer would never do that to me.

Just when I thought I'd make it out of this without a scrape, he sank the tip into the top of the C and smirked against my flesh. "Every time you run away from us, I'll carve these initials into your body. One day, you'll remember who you belong to, Pretty Bird." He continued to carve the letters, as he had promised, then twirled me around so I faced him, his knife pressed tightly against the bottom of my chin.

When he dipped his head and licked the blood off my chest, I nearly lost it already. These guys had barely even touched me yet, had only degraded and branded me, and I was fucking putty in their hands.

Thayer pushed me up the steps and toward Calder's bedroom, then shoved me onto the bed. I squirmed around helplessly, trying to escape, but it was no use. The other three guys walked into the room and locked the door behind them.

"Show us that pussy," Darius said, forcefully spreading my legs apart, ripping off my pants, and smacking my aching pussy. Darius spit on my clit, held my legs apart as far as they would go, then sank his face between my folds to eat me out.

When he rolled us over so he lay back against the bed, I sat on his face. I thrust my shoulders back and forth, wanting so desperately to get out of this stupid tape. I didn't want to give them the satisfaction of taking me so easily. Darius grabbed my hips and held them still, his claws digging into my ass and a deep rumble coming from him against my clit.

Someone else crawled onto the bed, standing at my side with his raging hard cock in his hand. He ripped the tape off me with one scarred hand, and because I could tell it was Calder by the way he held himself, I spit at him.

He wiped the spit off his chest and smeared it across my face, then shoved four fingers into my mouth as deep as they would go down my throat until I gagged. "You want to spit at me?" he growled, pounding his fingers into my throat and forcing me to gag over and over. "I'm going to stuff my cock so deep down your throat until you can't breathe, Pretty Bird. Then, maybe you'll rethink being a disrespectful little whore."

When he positioned himself at my mouth, I pressed my lips together and refused to open them. If I did, I would just be giving him exactly what he wanted. It would be the first step in his revenge against my father.

He smacked me on the cheek, but I didn't flinch. He hit me again, this time more forcefully. Still, I wasn't opening my mouth for anyone or anything, especially not him. So, he pinched my nose closed and smacked me over and over and over, not stopping once.

My cheek was burning. I swallowed hard, vowing that I wouldn't open my mouth, and stared up at him through teary eyes.

I wasn't going to back down, but it was getting damn hard to stay like this without breathing.

One last smack against my cheek, and I opened my mouth to gasp for air. He shoved himself into me and let go of my nose so I could breathe again.

"Eat his fucking dick, you fucking bitch," Thayer growled behind me, grabbing a fistful of my hair and shoving me toward Calder, forcing his cock deeper into my mouth. He bounced my head back and forth on the dick until I babbled to him with my throat. Gargling, spitting, choking.

I might've been struggling as hard as I could, but I wanted them to be rougher.

As he sank his cock even deeper down my throat, he plugged up my nose so I couldn't breathe. I curled my toes and stared up at Calder through his ski mask, refusing to look away or gag or submit to an alpha like him.

Again, my cheeks started to flush. I opened my mouth wider to try to get some air into my body, but Calder just plugged my mouth up even more by stuffing his balls into my mouth and grunting.

"Don't you fucking bite down on my cock," he growled as my throat started to close around him and my mouth tightened, my back teeth unintentionally trying to clench. He grabbed the bottom of my jaw with his free hand and held it apart, sliding another inch down my throat.

I was desperate to breathe, but he wouldn't pull out of me, and the pressure rose inside me.

While Gaian pinched and tugged on my nipples and Darius ate my pussy, Thayer grabbed my hair in one hand and forced me to stare up into Calder's dark eyes, then smacked me hard against the cheek with the other.

"Come, you fucking bitch," he growled. "Choke on his cock and come for us."

When he smacked me again, I screamed out on Calder's cock. My entire body shook uncontrollably, tears streaming down my flushed cheeks. Pleasure rushed through my body as the sensation completely overtook me.

Calder pulled out of me and released me, his dick veiny, wet, and throbbing.

Thayer pulled me off of Darius and shoved me onto the bed beside him, grabbing another piece of duct tape and slapping it over my mouth. "She's not going to be needing that mouth again tonight."

Though I might've been stripped of all my clothes and had my face fucked hard already, I wasn't done struggling. If any of them wanted to be inside more of my holes, they would have to fight for it because I wasn't going to let it happen.

When Darius approached me, I kicked him hard in the chest and sent him stumbling back. But that didn't stop the other three from approaching me. No matter how hard I struggled, I was outnumbered.

"Look at her," Thayer cooed. "Struggling like she actually has a fucking chance."

"This pussy is ours," Calder growled, cupping my pussy and sinking his fingers into me like he owned it.

The more I struggled, the deeper he sank his fingers and the stronger his hold on me became.

He pulled me closer by my pussy, his dark eyes staring deep into mine. "Ours."

I shouted against the duct tape, but my voice was muffled.

Easily, they overpowered me by seizing my limbs and forcing me still with their brute strength. Thayer lay down on the bed, pulling me on top of him so I straddled his waist. He positioned himself at my entrance and slammed me down on his cock.

Darius climbed up onto the bed next, his feet on either side of my knees and his dick at the entrance to my ass. He let a wad of spit drip down into the hole, then followed it in with his dick. I clenched, my entire body tensing.

And when I thought I couldn't hold any more dicks, Calder

stood at the edge of the bed with his cock lined up between Darius's and Thayer's dicks, his poking at the entrance to my pussy. He shoved himself into me slowly until he grunted.

"Four cocks in your pussy at once," Thayer said suddenly, thrusting into me. "You know they won't fit, but you can't stop thinking about having us all at once. Four dicks sliding into your tight cunt, stretching you out, spraying their cum in you at the same time."

Calder pumped into me faster and growled, "Best chance at getting you pregnant."

I tried to hold my orgasm back. I tried to hold it back so fucking badly, but as soon as those last few words came out of Calder's mouth, another orgasm ripped through my body and sent me trembling into fucking oblivion.

"Fuck her tits, Gaian, while we fuck this bitch until she's pregnant," Calder growled from behind me as Darius held on to my bound wrists and lifted me off Thayer.

Calder had held back what he truly wanted of me before this, but now, he wasn't backing down.

Alpha Calder wanted me pregnant.

My tits bounced around wildly, and the feeling of three cocks inside me at once made the pressure rise in my core again. I loved being degraded, slapped, spanked, used, called every name in the book.

Gaian—the only wolf not inside my holes—stepped in front of me, his gaze focused on my bouncing tits and his dick hard in his hand. He released it from his grip, letting it smack against his thigh with a thud, and pressed my tits together slightly.

"Fuck, Pretty Bird, your jugs are incredible," he said, sliding himself between them and grunting. He kneaded my tits with every thrust, my nipples rubbing against his rough palms. "I can't stop thinking about how much bigger they'll get when you're filled with our pups."

Gaian's comment must've tipped Calder over the edge because

he thrust one last time into my pussy and grunted loudly. My pussy exploded around the cocks inside me, pulsing and milking out as much cum as possible.

At one point, I had felt so ashamed of my breeding kink, but I couldn't hold it back tonight. I wanted as much of their cum inside me as possible. I wanted my pussy to drain their balls into me.

When Calder pulled out of me and collapsed into an accent chair in the corner of the room, Darius repositioned himself and pounded into my ass, his cock so big that it was still a hard fit in my hole. My ass tightened around him, squeezing harder. Darius slammed his huge cock deep into me.

After he came, he pulled out of me, his cum leaking from my ass down to my pussy and making it a sloppy, sopping mess. He still held on to my wrists to hold me up for Gaian, who continued to fuck my tits. He held on to my nipples, pinching them hard to hold my breasts together.

Thayer ripped the duct tape off my mouth, finally letting me moan.

I stared at Gaian, chest heaving as I tried to catch my breath. "I know you want to come between my tits, but I need you inside me. Please."

As Gaian grunted, Darius released me down slowly onto Thayer's chest. With my hands still behind my back, I stared behind me at Gaian positioning himself at my entrance with Thayer. Thayer stopped for a single moment, letting Gaian slip into me easily.

Then, they went down on my pussy, pounding into me harder and faster. My tits bounced against Thayer's chest, my nipples rubbing against the battle scars that covered his body. Suddenly, he growled, seizing my neck in one of his large hands—his claws just barely breaking the skin—and pounded up into me one last time. He tore off his ski mask, pulled me down toward him, and sucked my bottom lip into his mouth.

When Thayer finished, Gaian pulled on my hair to tug my entire body against his, then snaked that hand around the front of my throat, his thumb on my chin to guide me into a kiss. With his other hand, he grabbed one of my breasts, then grunted into my mouth and came in my pussy.

Entry #16—check.

16
the next morning

sina

FROM MY THROAT to my pussy to even my ass, my entire body ached the next morning. I turned in the bed, whimpered softly to myself, and snuggled closer to someone strong, the muscular body hard underneath mine. He smelled like fresh pine, mixed with sweetness, a scent that had always been hard to forget.

"Good morning," Gaian whispered, his eyes closed but his fingers gently stroking my shoulder in small, soothing circles. "How'd you sleep?"

"Good," I said, watching the way the sun glimmered against his skin.

Small lines appeared around his mouth as he gave me a soft smile. I laid my head on his chest and glanced around his room. Pictures of his family and his pack decorated the cream-colored walls.

"Why am I here?"

"After last night, you fell asleep in Calder's bed. When I went to bring you back into your room, you said you wanted to lie with me," he said sheepishly, his voice so soft and so vulnerable. He was almost nervous. "I hope that's okay."

Glancing down at him, I cracked a small smile. With the sunlight glaring right into his eyes, he was squinting at me now, his face filled with both worry and tiredness. I didn't know what time we had all gone to bed last night, but, gods, it must've been late.

"How are you feeling?" he asked, gently dropping his hand to my breast and groping it softly, almost as if it was instinctual. It didn't even look like he had meant to do it or even realized that he was touching me there. "These past two nights have been really rough. I want to make sure you're still okay with everything."

"I'm okay," I said, heart swelling at the mere thought of him checking in on me like this.

Obviously, Calder wasn't going to.

"Darius and I were talking last night," Gaian said, glancing over at the digital clock on his side table. "We want to bring you out to breakfast in south Durnbone."

"Like, as in a … date?" I asked, heart racing.

Gaian gave me a sheepish smile. "Like a date? If that's what you want."

But by the look in his eyes, I could tell that was exactly what he had meant. He wanted to bring me out into Durnbone this morning and have a good time with me, but he didn't want to overstep—as if they hadn't overstepped yet by enacting my fantasies.

"Thayer and Calder are staying back, if that makes it any more enticing."

My lips curled into a small smirk. "Calder staying back *definitely* makes it more enticing."

"So, you'll go?"

"Yeah!" I jumped out of bed, nerves zipping through me. I might've had a boyfriend before—thanks, Jaroth—but he never brought me out to breakfast. Ever. "First, I need to shower. I still smell of … cum and hot, sweaty sex."

As I went to hurry toward the door, I stopped in my tracks when I saw a picture of all five of us the night before my eighteenth birthday in a picture frame on his nightstand. I grabbed it, my chest tightening at how happy we had all been together.

Back then, Thayer hadn't been half as insane and Calder hadn't been half as pissed off and rude as they were now. I didn't have anything against Thayer being an actual psycho—honestly, it was kind of a turn-on, the way he had talked to me yesterday—but Calder had been annoying as fuck lately.

Last night had been amazing, but now, finally coming down from that high, I realized that everything that Calder had said and done to me was because he wanted to get back at my dad. He didn't want me pregnant, nor did he like me … for me.

Everything had changed these past four years. Everything.

"What happened to Calder?" I asked, running my thumb over his face in the picture.

He looked so young, his skin so unmarked and unscarred and his expression so innocent. It looked like he had been through hell and back these past few years.

After placing down the picture frame, I looked over my shoulder at Gaian, who hadn't said anything. He clenched his jaw lightly and wouldn't make eye contact with me, instead just staring at the blankets.

"Gaian?"

He sighed softly and looked up at me, shaking his head. "Pack stuff, Sina. Nothing you need to worry about. He probably prefers you stay out of it anyway. He'd kill me if I even mentioned it to you."

"It just feels like …" I swallowed hard and stared out the window, where I spotted Darius, Thayer, and Calder coming back from their morning run. "Like you guys are hiding something important from me that I should know about. You guys tell me how dangerous Durnbone is, but four years ago, it wasn't that dangerous."

The only dangerous thing four years ago had been staying home with Dad for too long.

"What is it? What happened in Durnbone when I left?"

Again, Gaian stayed quiet for a long time. "Sina, let's save this for when we can all talk about it." He swiped a hand across his face, his fingers lingering on a scar that I hadn't noticed yet, just underneath his jaw. Whatever had happened was … horrid. "Please."

Once I finally came to terms that I would have to find out on my own—maybe from Maxine—I sighed heavily. Even Gaian—the good boy who told me *everything*—wouldn't say a single word about it.

"Okay."

"Okay?" Gaian said, taken aback. "You're okay with that?"

"Yes."

Because I planned on finding out on my own now. Living with Dad for four years by myself was proving to be very useful. He might've been a monster, but during my time with him, I had found ways to sneak out and figure out information that people were keeping from me.

"Oh, and by the way, can we stop at my old gynecologist on our way home?" I asked, lingering by the door. "I just want to make sure that my birth control is … working. I refuse to get pregnant just because Calder wants revenge on my father."

That was the lie I told Gaian *and myself.*

Gaian tensed and sat up in the bed, the blankets falling down his torso, revealing his ripped abdomen. I'd missed so much fucking time these past four years with them. I wished I could've been here to watch them grow, especially him.

"Sure," Gaian said, awkwardly scratching the back of his head, biceps flexing. "If that's what you want. We could just use condoms?"

My lips curled into a small smile, and I walked back over to him and leaned over the bed, placing my lips on his. I wasn't sure if it was appropriate—I still didn't know what we were; if we were mates, wouldn't they have told me already?—but Gaian didn't mind.

"If we used condoms, Calder would probably poke holes in them," I said against his lips.

Though, as I said it, I wondered if they had found the diary entry that mentioned *that* yet.

When Gaian opened his eyes after the kiss, his irises were golden pools. His wolf was close—so damn close—and Gaian was doing a hell of a good job at keeping him controlled right now. If it were Thayer, he would've grabbed me by the throat and told me that I'd enjoy *that* scenario—and he wouldn't be wrong.

I was kinda fucked up. Just a little.

"Don't tell me you want my belly full too," I joked with a smile, gently pushing him away and walking to the door once more to head for the shower.

"Of course I do, Sina," Gaian said. "We all do."

17
the date

"THIS PLACE IS SO NICE," Sina said, walking into the Black Crow Café. She wore a yellow sundress that not only clung to the right places, but also had a low-cut neckline that showed off just enough cleavage. "Is it new? I don't remember it."

"It opened, like, three years ago," Darius said. "I used to bring chicks here all the time."

She scrunched her nose. "Ew."

"Ew," Darius teased. "At least I don't have a handsy incubus ex."

When she playfully pushed him, I walked up to the counter and gave the hostess my name and the number of people that would be dining with us this morning.

She handed me a menu to look over during our wait. "It should be five, ten minutes until the next table is open."

I took the menu from her and walked back to Sina and Darius, who looked a lot more comfortable with Sina than he ever had in high school. A strand of her dark hair fell into her face, and her lips pulled up into a huge grin.

"Are you jealous, Pretty Bird?" Darius asked, smirking.

"Yes, I am."

"And why's that?" I asked, pushing her hair off her cheek with my middle and forefinger knuckles and really taking her in.

These past few years, all I could think about was having her again. I'd missed her smile, her laugh, the lightness that she gave us all.

"Because ..." she said, crossing her arms. Her cheeks flushed. Instead of answering and owning up to the fact that she had liked us all this time too, she pulled away and shuffled a couple of feet backward. "I need to use the restroom. I'll be back in a couple of minutes."

"Sina!" Darius called as she scurried to the back. "You're really gonna leave me hanging like that?"

If we were on the bad side of Durnbone, I would've gone into the restroom with her, but the south side of town was relatively safe.

Before she disappeared into the women's room, she threw us a wicked grin over her shoulder. I inhaled her scent, lingering heavily in the air. My wolf was going fucking crazy inside me. Ever since last night, when Sina had come at the thought of being pregnant by one of us, I hadn't been able to think clearly.

"Sina doesn't know about her father, does she?" Darius asked me a couple moments later, leaning closer to me. "I heard you guys talking before we left."

"She doesn't know anything yet, but she doesn't seem like one to sit back. She knows that we're all keeping something from her— something bad. She's going to find out one way or another." I ran my hand through my hair. "I wish this war with her father would end for good."

Darius ran a hand over his dreads. "We should've stayed back with Thayer and Calder."

"They're running through war plans and didn't want Sina to be around for it."

"Yeah, but I've got a bad feeling about today." He tugged on a Moon Goddess necklace around his neck, the way he always did when he was nervous about something going on with this war. "Somethin's not right."

Sina's father's goons *had been* quiet ever since she'd been back in Durnbone. We hadn't been attacked once, and Calder kept saying that his alpha senses were acting up, telling him something wasn't right either.

We just couldn't pinpoint exactly what it was.

"All I'm saying is that I think her father is more dangerous than even *we* think. Yesterday, when you went to shower, Sina mentioned that she didn't want her father to be part of her love life anymore, and she sounded extremely upset about it. Like … he had done something—more than just take her away from us."

My chest tightened, my canines extending. "Do you think he hurt her?"

"She wouldn't say a word more about it. I didn't want to press it."

"Table for Gaian!" the hostess called out. "Gaian!"

Darius and I followed the hostess back to a table near the rear of the restaurant, one that overlooked the town outside the window.

A few moments after we sat, Darius stood back up and nodded toward the restrooms. "I'm going to make sure she's okay."

Once he disappeared into the crowd of people, I sat back in my seat and ran a hand over my face, hoping to the goddess that Calder was taking care of this now. We needed to pinpoint where her father was and kill him for good. If he had touched her …

I tightened my hand around my glass of water so tightly that it shattered in my fist.

If he had hurt her, *I* would kill him myself.

Blood seeped down my forearm from the shattered glass lodged into my palm. I glanced up to see Sina hurrying over with Darius, her eyes wide in fear.

"What's going on?!" she said, gently taking my hand and pulling out a shard of glass. "What'd you do this for?"

After she pulled the last piece of glass from my hand, my palm started healing almost immediately with the help of my wolf senses.

She poured some of her water on a napkin and ran it across my hand. "Why would you do this?"

"I'm pissed," I said, finally taking a deep breath and relaxing. "Sorry."

She widened her eyes at me. "You never get pissed."

"He does," Darius said, leaning closer to her on their side of the table. "You've just never seen it."

As the last of my palm healed, I pulled my hand away and clenched it into a tight fist underneath the table so Sina wouldn't see. I didn't want her to think of me like she thought of Calder; I didn't want her to hate me too.

"Why are you so angry?" she asked. "I can see it written all over your face."

"Did your father hurt you?" I asked, unable to stop myself.

"What?" she whispered.

"Did your father hurt you?"

Her cheeks paled. She ran her tongue across her dry lips and stared down at the wooden table, gently playing with her hands in her lap.

Darius looked over at her, brows furrowed. "We need to know, Pretty Bird."

Sina suddenly clenched her jaw. "My father is gone. I don't want to talk about him."

"But—"

"No buts," Sina said, calling over our waitress to order. "I'm hungry."

18
the doctor

sina

AFTER AN AMAZING MORNING—BESIDES the fact that Gaian had asked about Dad—I sat in the lobby of the doctor's office with Gaian and Darius, waiting for Dr. Stormmark. My knee bounced uncontrollably, my nerves getting the best of me. I didn't have to come to the doctor to get my IUD checked.

I had two more years of it being usable, and I could check to make sure it was still inside me at home. There was a string that I felt around for multiple times a week to make sure it was still in place, especially while I had been dating Jaroth, my ex, after the move away from Durnbone.

While I didn't have an appointment and the waiting room was packed full, the nurse said she'd get me in within a few minutes. I filled out the rest of the paperwork that she had given me and returned it up front, then collapsed back next to the guys.

"I'm nervous," I said, clutching my stomach.

"It's going to be fine, Pretty Bird," Gaian said, gently rubbing circles on my knee.

Darius brushed his hands on his jeans. "I never got to ask … did you enjoy last night?"

I snapped my gaze to him, feeling a smile stretch across my face. "Did I enjoy last night?! What kind of question is that? Did you feel how hard I came—both times?" I let out a small giggle and relaxed slightly in the chair. "Who chose that diary entry?"

"Thayer," Gaian said.

Darius slapped Gaian on the back. "I get to choose the next one. I'm already calling it."

"Sina," Dr. Stormmark said, peeking her head out from behind a door. Usually, the nurses came to get patients, not the doctors themselves, but Dr. Stormmark always loved me. "I haven't seen you in forever. How have you been? I'm ready for you."

After Gaian gently squeezed my knee, I stood and walked over to the doorway, following her into the back. She grinned widely at me and ushered me into room 4, which looked exactly the same as how I remembered it.

Dad had forced me to get an IUD at sixteen when I started getting closer to the guys. Dr. Stormmark had made me feel so at home, so comfortable here. She was one of the few people—besides Maxine and the guys—that I could trust.

"I'm doing well," I said.

Once I undressed and sat on the table, Dr. Stormmark looked between my legs to give me a checkup. Every now and then, she would make small talk, asking me how I had been these past four years.

"You've had sex recently," she said.

It wasn't a question, but a statement.

How could she tell? Was there ... cum still inside me? Even though I hoped it wasn't true, I wouldn't doubt it. Calder's sperm was probably just as stubborn about getting me pregnant as he was.

"Yes," I said.

Suddenly, she pulled her fingers out of my vagina and sat up between my thighs, staring at me with worry in her eyes. "Is everything okay at home?" she asked, eyebrows drawn together. "Is anyone hurting you?"

"Everything is fine. Why?"

"Because ..." She swallowed hard. "There is an *excessive* amount of sperm inside of you, more than the usual amount a woman has after having sex. Not even an incubus has that much cum. And you have a large wound in the center of your chest."

My cheeks flushed. "Yes, I'm fine."

"Would you tell me? You know you can trust me."

Mouth drying, I stared at her for a long time. "You can tell if I'm being ... hurt?"

"Yes. If you were having consensual sex with another human, then it would be much harder to tell if something was wrong. But with claw marks on your hips and around your throat, this seems to have been done by a werewolf."

She continued talking, but I really didn't listen to her after she confirmed she could.

"But if the sex was rough enough, human with human, you could tell if I was being abused?" I asked, wanting direct confirmation. My entire body was tense, my chest tightening by the second and my throat closing up.

"Yes."

A weight that I had been suppressing for so long felt as if it was crushing me. I held back my tears and stared directly at her, knowing that she had lied to me all these years. She had been my doctor when Dad started having *business meetings* and inviting over men to ... sleep in my bedroom.

They were rough. So rough. Sometimes rougher than the guys.

And they left bruises on my inner thighs too. She would've seen them because a couple days after those late nights, Dad would force me to come to the doctor to make sure that I wasn't pregnant and didn't have any ... STDs.

"Is there something going on?" she said, pulling the sheet over my legs to give me privacy. "Sina?"

"Everything is fine."

"Sina?" she said, hands on my knees. "Talk to m—"

"Everything is fine," I snapped.

"You're holding something back. I can tell. You've never been so cold before."

"Lots of things have changed in four years, Dr. Stormmark."

After staring at me for a few long moments, she sighed and nodded. I pulled my legs together and watched her walk around the room. Maybe she hadn't noticed years ago, or maybe she had but refused to care.

Either way, I realized that maybe *nobody* was on my side. Maybe everyone—besides Maxine and the guys—around here in Durnbone who I had trusted four years ago had all been paid off by Dad, had refused to care or help out an innocent girl, had let me be sexualized by old, creepy men.

At the thought of coming here this morning, I'd had so many nerves racing through me. I didn't know if I should've even come here at all, but now that I had found out she could tell I was being abused and hadn't said anything back then …

I was certain that this was what I wanted.

This was the only thing I could control now.

Dr. Stormmark flipped through some pages within a manila folder. "From the forms you filled out in the waiting room, you had a Pap smear a few months ago. You get regular checkups at your doctor where your father lives. And you say that you're not being abused. So, why are you here today?"

I sucked in a deep breath. "It's about my birth control."

"It seems that your IUD is in place, as it should be. Was that what you—"

"No," I interrupted. "I want you to take it out."

19
the disappointment

sina

"NO."

One simple word that crushed me entirely.

From her chair, Dr. Stormmark snapped my file closed and stood to strip her gloves and wash her hands in the sink. "I am not taking out your IUD now, Sina. It's good for the next two years, and that's where it's going to stay until then."

While any normal doctor would most likely listen to their patient's wants and needs, Dr. Stormmark didn't even consider mine. She had stood up and given me a cold, hard no without room for argument.

Sure, I would be able to understand her stance if she really thought I was being abused, but she had never even asked about it years ago, when there had been bruises all over my body and I had been showing up for STD tests every few weeks.

"You've never cared about me, have you?" I asked, pulling my gown closed and following her to the door. I snapped my hand on the wood and refused to let her open it to escape this conversation. "Did my father pay you off too?"

"Let me out, Sina," she said, struggling against me to pull open the door.

But I had fought far too many of my father's *friends* in bed, who were stronger than me, to just be pushed to the side by someone who was merely a hundred and twenty-something pounds. Besides, I wasn't nervous about anything now. I was furious about it all.

"I'm not going to let you out until you answer me!" I shouted, and I wouldn't be surprised if everyone in the doctor's office and the waiting room heard me. "This isn't fair! You can't do this to me!"

"You're being unreasonable and psychotic, Sina," Dr. Stormmark said. "Which is exactly why your father asked me to place an IUD inside of you in the first place. You're going to get yourself pregnant and be stuck in a bad situation."

"That's not why I was in your office every freaking week," I said, poking her in the chest. Tears pooled in my eyes, threatening to spill over and down my cheeks. She made me sound and feel like a crazy person. "And you know it."

"Security!" Dr. Stormmark yelled from inside the room. "I need security in here!"

Alone.

Gods, I felt so alone. Not even my doctor would help me.

Before any security could arrive, I pulled on my clothes, flung open the door, and stormed down the hallway. Other doctors tried to block my way of getting out—they probably wanted to arrest me or some shit for putting my hands on one of their colleagues—but they didn't know half my story. Nobody did.

I pushed everyone away and hurried out the door to the waiting room. As soon as I spotted Gaian and Darius, I burst into tears and ran toward them. They stood almost immediately, Gaian taking my hand to ask what was wrong and Darius quickly pushing people out of our way for a quick getaway.

Thankfully, we escaped before the police or security showed up and hurried down the cobblestone streets of south Durnbone, taking back alleyways to flee the town as quickly as possible. I didn't want to stay here another moment.

What had been a nice morning turned so sour, so quickly.

"What did they do to you?" Gaian asked. His voice was tense, as was his body and stance, his canines lengthened and dripping with saliva.

Gaian might've been nice to me, but he looked like he would rip someone apart for me.

He looked like a possessive mate.

"I can't tell you about it," I said, cursing myself for it.

Gods, I wanted to tell them so badly. But I couldn't.

How would I tell them that Dr. Stormmark wouldn't *remove* my IUD? How would I tell them that the abuse from my father had started earlier than four years ago, when I was still underage—or *ripe*, as he had called it? I didn't want to live through that again. I couldn't.

"This way," Darius said, grabbing my hand and pulling me through a back exit out of Durnbone before anyone could catch us.

I had done nothing wrong, so I didn't know why exactly I felt like I had, but … who knew who I could trust here?

They could all work for Dad. They could turn me over to him.

Once we made it out of the town and were deep into the forest— close to Calder's property, but not on it yet—Darius forced me to stop. His eyes were dark, black almost, and his claws looked long enough to slit someone's throat.

"What happened?" he asked.

I wanted to lie to them. I wanted to tell them nothing had happened.

But I hurt so badly.

Instinctively, I wrapped my arms around myself, the way I always used to after Dad's friends used me and left for the night. I had felt so alone, but acted as if nothing were wrong. These guys had been my only escape.

"She …" I started. "She …"

I couldn't get the words out of my mouth. I couldn't fucking stand my father, yet I didn't want them to know how weak I was. I didn't want them to think of me any different or stop this little thing we had going on.

If I told them, they might … stop with the whole diary thing. And I didn't want that to happen because they were the first people who actually cared about me. Besides Calder—he was a different problem entirely—the guys didn't leave me after sex. They held me, took care of me, did things only a mate would do.

Not only that, but letting them take me, use me … it also helped me in some fucked up way. The guys might have been dominant during our sexcapades, but I could stop it at any point. I had a safe word. I had control.

With Dad's *friends*, I'd had absolutely no control at all. If I said no, they wouldn't stop. They would keep pushing into me, keep dragging me along, grabbing my hair, my breasts, my pussy until I was screaming and burning and thinking about ending it all.

Unable to say anything, I buried my face into Darius's chest and cried as hard as I could. I hadn't been able to let it out in front of anyone for years now. Nobody had held me like they did for so long.

Darius wrapped his arms around me and pulled me closer to him, dragging his fingers through my hair. I tried to tell them I was sorry that I was crying, that I'd ruined our nice morning, that I'd fucking ruined everything. But I could barely talk through my sobs.

I wanted Dad to pay for everything he had done. I wanted to show him that he didn't own me anymore. I controlled my life. I controlled who I let inside me, both emotionally and physically. And I also got to choose who made me pregnant.

With or without Dr. Stormmark's help, I would take my IUD out of me. Only then would I be free.

20

the argument

calder

"I DON'T CARE what you do with him," I said to Thayer, staring at the pathetic man who worked for Sina's father that we had captured on an early morning raid while Sina and the guys were out for breakfast. "Just get me information."

Thayer smirked wickedly at the man, running his fingers along the sharp edge of a blade and cutting his own flesh in the process. He drew his tongue across his wound, licking up his own blood and stalking closer to the man. "No problem."

After deciding to let Thayer do what he did best, I walked up my underground prison steps and exited through the hatch above. Once I locked the door, I lifted my nose to the sky and sniffed the air around me.

It smelled like … Sina.

When I spotted her, she was walking back to my pack house alone.

I gritted my teeth and glared at her, wondering why the fuck she wasn't with Darius or Gaian. If she had snuck away from them while they brought her out to fucking breakfast, I would fucking lose it. She couldn't be walking around the forest without protection.

Not when her father was searching for her.

After looking me right in the eye—almost as if she was fucking challenging me to do something about it—Sina walked past me and into the pack house. I balled my hands into fists and stormed after her, trying to contact Gaian or Darius through the mind link, but they must've been out of range for it to work.

As I reached the house, Sina slammed the door in my face, knowing I was behind her.

Rage burned inside of me. Sina didn't understand how dangerous her father was because if she did, she wouldn't be walking around without protection. He had hundreds of people searching the forest outside of his estate for her.

"Where are you going?" I asked once I flung the door open and stepped into the house.

"To my bedroom that *you* so graciously let me have. Emphasis on *graciously*."

Before she could make it up the stairs, I grabbed her elbow and yanked her back. She stood a foot shorter than me and stared up at me, her eyes filled with annoyance and fury, like they usually were, except they looked bloodshot, as if she'd been crying.

"What happened?" I asked, instinctively knowing something was wrong with my mate.

"Nothing."

"What. Fucking. Happened?"

She turned her back toward me. "Noth-ing."

"Why the fuck are you so aggravating?" I said, growling at her. My gaze dropped to her throat, like it always did, my canines aching to sink into her and claim her. Maybe then I would finally be able to get inside her head and figure out what she was thinking, what she was hiding from me too.

"Me?!" she said, whizzing around on her heel to stare at me. "I'm aggravating?!"

"Yes, Sina, you are."

"You're the one who won't let me out of your sight!"

"For your safety."

"If anyone cared about my fucking safety, they would've helped me years ago!" she shouted, but then she immediately pressed her lips together, as if she had let something slip out of her mouth that she didn't want anyone to know about.

But I didn't understand it.

After tearing her gaze away and staring at the floor, she turned back around and ran up the stairs. I followed after her again, not wanting to let her go that easily because this was the first time I had been alone with her since she had made it here.

"Where were you?" I asked. "You guys went out for breakfast, like, five hours ago. And where the fuck are Gaian and Darius?"

She turned around to face me again and crossed her arms over her chest, pressing her tits together. "You want to know where I was? Huh? Well, I was at the gynecologist to make sure my IUD was still working, so guys like *you* don't get me pregnant."

A growl escaped my lips, my canines lengthening. I grabbed her harshly by the jaw and shoved her against her bedroom door, my body flush against hers. "You sure as fuck wanted us to get you pregnant last night. You came all over my fucking cock, thinking about it."

"I did not," she said, lying through her fucking teeth.

"I can smell your fucking cunt salivating at the thought of it right fucking now." I dipped my free hand between her legs and groped her pussy through her jeans that tightened around her ass. Her body tensed, her pussy clenching in my hand. "Did you leave that little fantasy out of your journal, Sina? Was it too dirty for a *girl like you* to write?"

"No," she said through gritted teeth. "I would never want to have your pup inside me."

Another growl exited my throat. I could barely contain my wolf, my inner fucking demon, any longer. I wanted to throw Sina back onto her bed, pound her tight little hole raw, and make her pregnant as fuck for me.

I unbuttoned her jeans and shoved my hand into them, my

fingers immediately finding her swollen clit. She flared her nostrils at me but pressed her lips together to not say a fucking word, to not let out a moan that I could tell she was desperately holding back.

My dick stiffened inside my pants, and I pressed myself against her stomach. I moved my fingers in quick, rough circles around her clit until her cheeks flushed. Then, I slipped them inside her sopping cunt. "Fucking tell me you don't want my pups again. I want to feel how tight you get when you try to deny it."

She glared up at me, brows furrowed and lips still pressed together.

"You don't want my pups, Sina?" I growled. "Fucking tell me. Don't be scared."

"I don't want your—" She took a deep breath and grabbed my wrist. "I don't want your …"

"It's not that fucking hard to say it without clenching around me, Pretty Bird." I pumped my fingers in and out of her hole, my palm pounding against her clit. By the fucking look in her eyes, I could tell she was close. So close to coming for me. "Unless you want it."

"I-I don't."

"Then, say it."

"I don't want your pups inside me," she managed to get out, her eyes immediately rolling back and a loud moan escaping her lips. Her pussy contracted around my fingers, pulsing harder than it had last night around my dick.

Before she could come down from her high, I pulled my fingers out of her pussy, shoved her jeans to her knees, and twirled her around. Once I bent her over, I slammed my cock into her and grunted, "I don't give a fuck, Sina, because I'm going to give you them anyway."

She exploded around me again, digging her nails into the wooden door. "Oh my God!" she screamed, legs trembling so much that I thought they'd give out.

So, I wrapped one arm around her waist to hold her up myself, then placed her hands on her belly. "You feel that fucking bulge inside of you?" I growled into her ear, picking up her right leg with my free hand and spreading her legs to give myself better access. "I'm so fucking deep, Sina, that I'm in your stomach."

"Calder," she whimpered.

"Tell me you don't want my pups again."

She bit back another scream and glanced over her shoulder at me. Her tits bounced against her bedroom door, but I didn't stop destroying her tight little cunt. It was mine, and I was going to do as I pleased with it.

"I-I ..." she started, pleasure rushing over her face. "I can't."

As soon as the words left her mouth, I stuffed my load as deep as it would go inside her. She screamed out again, her pussy emptying the cum right out of my fucking balls. I slammed myself into her one last time, then slowly pulled out of her.

Before any cum could drip out of her, I pulled up her panties and jeans, forcing her to stew for the rest of the day with a part of me inside her. She turned around and pressed her back against her bedroom door, chest rising and falling quickly.

"I ... I ..." she started, cheeks flushed.

Instead of finishing her sentence, she quickly opened her bedroom door, stepped in, and slammed it closed behind her.

21
the removal

AFTER MY LITTLE run-in with Calder, I locked myself in my bedroom for the entire night. Darius and Gaian must have come back a few hours later because I heard Calder literally screaming at them for leaving me alone. But he didn't know that they had gone back to the gynecologist to *talk* to her.

And by talking … I assumed they had meant something much worse.

When they had left me, I had already made it onto Calder's property and past the pack guards. I had been safe the entire time, but I had known Calder had been searching for a reason to get me alone, to throw me up against my bedroom door.

I paced back and forth around my small room and thought about nothing but all the filthy words he had spoken to me tonight. For the life of me, I couldn't tell him that I didn't want his pups. I wanted to defy him for so long.

But the way he had touched me … the way he'd talked to me …

Gods, I fucking loved it.

So, when the guys slept, I snuck into the hallway bathroom and stared at myself in the mirror. My cheeks were flushed, my chest bright red with the scar that Thayer had left on me the other night. I couldn't hold myself back any longer.

Calder had gotten me so hot and so bothered that I couldn't think straight anymore.

Once I pulled off my pants completely, I sat on the toilet and stared at the wooden floorboards. My heart raced inside my chest at the mere thought of … doing what I was about to do. I didn't want to be Dad's prisoner anymore. I hated the feeling of being trapped.

If Dr. Stormmark wouldn't take out my IUD, then I would do it myself.

After preparing myself for the worst, I thrust my hand between my legs and reached my fingers up inside me. They only got so far in at this angle, and my pussy was so tight, for fear that I would rip the IUD out the wrong way.

I took a deep breath and tried to relax, but I couldn't seem to do anything right now.

So, I ran a warm bath. Once the water filled half the tub, I sank into it and thrust my hand between my legs to play with my pussy. It was the only way I could think of to get myself to relax; otherwise, I would be clenching so tightly that I wouldn't be able to reach the IUD string.

My fingers moved gently against my clit at first, thoughts of which diary entry Darius would choose next drifting through my mind. This might've all started as a damn breeding kink, but I wanted to be bred for real.

Thayer had planted that seed in my head, and Calder had goddamn watered it with his filthy mouth and his cum.

A wave of pleasure rushed through me, and I sank lower in the water, spreading my legs and resting my feet on either side of the tub. Slowly, I slipped two fingers into my pussy and sank them as far as they would go. They moved inside me with ease, my pussy tight, but not as tight around them as it had been when I sat on the toilet.

I dug around for a few moments until I finally found the IUD string.

This was it.

This was fucking it.

All I had to do was tug on this string slightly, pull it out of me, and then I would be free. I would finally get to make my own choices and not have to worry about a paid-off doctor or an abusive father running *and* ruining my life.

Suddenly, someone flung the door—which I swore I'd locked—open. I scrambled in the water, pulling my hand out of my vagina and sitting up in the bath. My eyes widened as Thayer walked into the room with blood all over his hands and splattered on his face.

But it wasn't his.

"What are you doing here?!" I whisper-yelled so I wouldn't wake the others.

Thayer looked at me with the same surprised expression, then shut the door behind him. He pulled his shirt off his body and washed his bloody hands in the sink. "I was about to take a bath to wash the blood off me. As much as I love it, blood ruins my sheets."

I narrowed my eyes.

"What are *you* doing here?" he asked. "It's three in the morning."

"I wanted to … to take a bath," I said, the words not convincing in the slightest.

After turning off the sink with clean hands, he pushed down his pants and stepped into the tub with me. Tattoos and scars covered his taut, naked body. I inhaled sharply, my pussy tightening in the water as I watched him.

He sank down in the water, leaned his head back, and let out a long sigh. While I imagined Gaian would be one to take baths, I could *never* imagine Thayer in one even though he was sitting across from me.

Once I pulled my knees to my chest, I took in every aspect of this man. He was always so tense, so crazy, but now, he was quiet and looked sorta, kinda peaceful. He opened his eyes, leaned over the side of the tub, and pulled a bottle of bubble bath from the cabinet under the sink.

My eyes widened even further. "You take bubble baths?"

Thayer's eyes darkened as he dumped the bottle—the entire fucking bottle—into the tub with us, making the bubbles pile up far past the edge of the bath and spill over onto the floor, a mess that I didn't plan on cleaning up. It'd be a good surprise for Calder tomorrow morning.

"I bought it for you the day before you showed up in Durnbone," he said.

"Wait," I said, sitting up in the bath and focusing my gaze on him. I wanted to really understand this because, all this time, I'd thought that he and Calder didn't really give a fuck. "You bought this for me before I even got to Durnbone? How'd you know I was coming back here? I could've gone anywhere. And … why?"

"Why?" he asked, taking some bubbles in his palm and blowing them at me.

If Gaian had done that, I would've almost thought it was cute. But Thayer—the tattooed psycho of the group, who had just been covered in someone else's blood—made shivers run down my spine. I could only imagine how many people he had tortured with those hands.

"Because you like taking baths."

I stared at him in confusion for a couple of moments, not even remembering the last time I had taken a bath. Dad forbade them at his estate. I didn't know why. He had stupid-as-fuck rules that I needed to follow all day, every day.

But four years ago, I must've taken a bath almost once a day. All I'd asked for on my birthday was bubble bath, bath bombs, and all that glittery self-care shit that I would use to try to forget everything that happened in my bed.

My lips curled in a small smile, an undeniable warmth spreading throughout my body. "I do," I said quietly, watching the bubbles float on top of the water around us. "I forgot I did, but I do. I love them a lot."

Now, if I could only stay in the bath with him …

I balled my right hand into a fist and stood up in the water to get out, dry myself off, and get back to sleep. But he captured me by the waist and pulled me down to him, making the bubbles splash over the edge of the tub again.

"You're not going anywhere," he growled against me. "You went out with Darius and Gaian for breakfast. Calder put *lunch* in your stomach. Now, I get a midnight snack, Sina. It's my turn to have you."

My pussy tightened. I didn't want to leave, but …

He dragged his canines down the column of my neck, sending shivers down my spine again.

I leaned over him, wanting more of his mouth on my neck, and unballed my fist outside of the tub, letting the IUD that I had pulled out of me just as Thayer walked into the room fall to the ground. I'd pick it up later.

22

the bath

sina

MY PUSSY ACHED from me pulling out the IUD moments ago, but I wasn't going to stop Thayer from slipping himself inside me. I *didn't* want to stop him either. After everything that I had been through, I just wanted to do what *I* wanted to do for once.

Thayer grabbed my hips and steadied them on top of his, gently pulling me down and guiding his cock toward my entrance. I curled my fingers into his shoulder muscles and braced myself for any type of pain.

I didn't know how much sex would hurt after I just forcefully removed my IUD, but I couldn't seem to care anymore. Dr. Stormmark hadn't wanted to do it because she wanted to follow my father's orders. So, I'd had to take matters into my own hands and start taking back my life.

"Fuck," Thayer growled against my neck, the head of his dick right at my entrance.

A whimper escaped my throat, and I clenched on to him tighter and squeezed my eyes closed.

Thayer gripped a handful of my hair and pulled my face back, then growled, "Open your eyes."

When I opened my eyes, he ground himself against my entrance. My pussy pulsed as the thought of him slipping inside me and giving me a huge load of his cum making me wet. I might've had a breeding kink, but this was the first time I could *get* pregnant from sex.

This was unprotected.

"I'm going to make you into a little fuckdoll," he growled, making me tighten even more around the tip of him.

His cock twitched against my pussy, and I couldn't help but whimper again.

"I'm going to fucking ruin you. Say good-bye to good-girl Sina, Pretty Bird, because you're mine."

As soon as the last word left his mouth, he slammed his cock into me. I threw my head back and moaned louder this time. My pussy ached for a brief few moments, but then a wave of ecstasy rushed through me.

Water sloshed over the edge of the tub, spilling onto the ground and soaking our clothes. Thayer pounded up inside me, his claws digging into my ass to hold me in place, to spread apart my cheeks and give himself even better and deeper access to my pussy.

I could get pregnant from this.

I could fucking get pregnant.

I could finally give Dad a big *fuck you.*

Something inside me took hold, and I seized Thayer's throat in my smaller hand. He was right that good-girl Sina was gone. I had been wanting to get rid of her for a damn long time, and the only thing holding me back had been a little piece of plastic lodged inside my uterus.

Thayer growled quietly, the sound vibrating against my palm. "That's what I want from you, Pretty Bird. Choke me hard. Bite me. Hit me. Go fucking crazy on my cock. I want to see the part of you that you've been holding back all these years."

Snapping, I sank my nails into his flesh and pulled him closer to me to place my human teeth at the crook of his neck. I used his body to bounce up and down on his cock, not caring how much water splashed onto the tiled bathroom floor.

Pleasure rushed through me, and the thought of claiming one of the four guys was driving me wild. I had only seen wolves claim their mates in the wild, the innate, feral urge to sink their teeth into the other's neck.

That was what was rushing through me right now.

That was all I could think about.

"Fucking do it," Thayer growled. "Bite me, Pretty Bird."

Unable to stop myself, I sank my teeth into his neck and slammed my hips as far down onto his hard cock as they could go. I wanted him deep inside me when he came, so none of his cum would spill out onto my thighs or into this water.

He was mine.

Gods, I wanted him to be mine.

"Oh, you're so fucking cute, Pretty Bird," he said, grabbing my chin and running his thumb across the tips of my human teeth. He chuckled crazily. "Trying to break my skin with these dull teeth."

I wanted to show him I might've been a good girl four years ago, but Dad had made me half as crazy as Thayer was.

Thayer seized my hip with one hand and my hair in the other, pulling it back again so I stared up at the ceiling. He continued to slam his cock deep into my hole and pressed his canines against the vein in my neck.

"Do you feel them against you?" he asked, running his teeth up and down the column of my neck, scraping the tips against my skin so it turned a blotchy red color, making me shiver in delight every time he brushed his canines against my soft spot. "These teeth could kill you, Pretty Bird. Your cute little human teeth will do *nothing* to me."

The pressure built higher and higher in my core. I tightened around him, at the mere thought of being this helpless in his arms. I should've hated this feeling because I had felt it so many times with my father's men, but I knew that Thayer would never hurt me.

I trusted him.

If I wanted him to stop, he would.

"I'm going to come," I whimpered already. "Gods, I'm going to come for you."

I squeezed my eyes closed, the pleasure rushing to my core and driving me higher. My pussy was moments from exploding around his cock, plunging me deep into ecstasy. Thayer moved around, gliding his teeth against my bare neck. All I could think about was him sinking his canines into me.

Just as I was about to tip over the edge, he pulled away from me and stopped pounding into my pussy. I grabbed on to his shoulders, desperately trying to bounce on his cock and keep up the high, but he held me in place with one hand around my waist.

"Hit me," he said, gently smacking the side of my cheek.

I tightened, the heat nearly exploding in my core.

"Come on, Pretty Bird." He slapped me on the cheek again, this time harder. "Hit me."

It had been different when they were all wearing masks, when we were in the middle of a scene and could hurt each other as long as we were all okay with it. Now that it was just Thayer and me … it felt like it had with Calder earlier.

"Hit me," he growled. When I smacked him across the face as gently as I could, Thayer chuckled menacingly at me and slapped me again. "I said to fucking hit me. So, fucking hit me. I don't want this gentle shit. I told you, Pretty Bird, go fucking crazy."

I gathered up all my strength—at least, all the strength I had left after I pulled out that IUD and took Thayer's cock deep inside my hole—and hit him as hard as I could, so hard that my palm burned as it made contact with his cheek.

He howled in pleasure, his canines lengthening even more. "That's what I'm talking about, Pretty Bird. There is that fire."

He thrust into me faster than he had before, over and over. My breasts bounced against his chest, my nipples aching.

Then, he smacked me on the cheek again. "Now, harder. Hit me fucking har—"

Before he could finish his sentence, I slapped him again.

Thayer suddenly stilled deep inside my pussy and growled lower and more ferociously than I had ever heard him. My pussy exploded around his cock. Wave after wave of pleasure shot through my body. I threw my head back and stared up at the white ceiling, thighs quivering as he pumped his cum into my cunt.

As his tense body relaxed underneath mine, I gently rubbed his cheek. Reality slowly set in that I had hit and bitten him. I hoped that I hadn't hurt him, and relaxed on his body, thoughts suddenly running through my mind.

While I might've been protected from getting pregnant with my IUD, we had *nothing* to protect us now. Thayer could've really gotten me pregnant just by coming inside me. I could … I could have his babies. I could have *all their babies.*

23

the next morning

thayer

WHEN I WOKE up the next morning, Sina was lying in my bed, curled up into the crook of my arm. The CP mark that I had left in the center of her chest glimmered in the sunlight that flooded in through the cracked window along with a gust of wind.

Goosebumps rose on her bare skin. Still sleeping, she turned onto her side, moved closer to me, and pulled the blankets further up her body to cover her shoulders. After mumbling something incoherent in her sleep, her breathing evened back out.

I brushed some hair off her forehead and tucked it behind her ear so I could see her perfect fucking face. My dick twitched under the sheets, my wolf growling for control inside me. We had been so close to taking her last night, to *claiming* her before anyone else.

One night, I would be the first to sink my teeth into her.

One night, my wolf would get to have his mate first.

But we had all agreed that we could claim her only after we took care of her father. And he was being a bitch to find, and so were his goons, who he had sent out to every town nearby to find her once she left. They were crawling *everywhere*, which was why nobody had dared to attack us *yet*.

In her sleep, Sina pressed her tits against the side of my chest and again murmured something incoherent against my scarred skin.

Something about her had seemed different last night when I found her in the bathroom.

She looked shocked when I entered, but her pussy was so wet that I slipped right into her. And when she had bitten down on my shoulder, almost hard enough to draw blood—a shiver ran down my skin, a smirk crossing my face—gods, she had fucking nearly ripped my dick off with how tight her pussy got.

After Sina shifted once more, this time onto her back, I noticed that the CP I had engraved on her skin wasn't healing at all. Her body had gotten so tight when I did it that first night that I had been too harsh with her. I had forgotten that a human like her didn't heal like we did.

So, I brushed my fingers against the mark—right where the skin was splitting open again—and let a ring of healing fire echo out from my palm. I didn't do this shit often, but at least my mother had taught me something useful for once. Gods only knew what realm of hell she had sunk to now after she killed Dad.

"Where the fuck is she?!" Calder growled in the hallway.

I rolled my eyes and pulled Sina closer to me. With that fucker, I would only have a couple more moments alone with her. Calder might've been able to keep his cool, but he was twice as fucked up as I was.

Sina's family had broken him, like they had broken us all.

"Sina!" Calder roared.

She curled up into my arms and rested her head on my shoulder, her lips set into a soft smile, even in her sleep. She looked so fucking peaceful right now, unlike when we had taken her from that party the other night.

A moment later, Calder threw open my bedroom door and found Sina lying in bed *with me.* Sina shifted once more, blinking her eyes open until they finally widened. Suddenly, she twisted out of my arms and up to the headboard.

"What are you doing here?" Calder asked.

Sina glanced from her naked body to mine, then reached between her legs and let her eyes grow even wider. "Fuck," she whispered underneath her breath, staring down at the bedsheets. "Holy fuck, I really did it."

"Did what?" Darius asked, peeking his head into the room behind Calder.

Suddenly, Sina snapped her head up to look at all of us, then scrambled out of the bed, pulled the sheets off my body to wrap around her naked one, and pushed past Calder and Darius to run to her room.

I lay back on the bed and let out a long sigh, my dick hard as a fucking rock. Of course, that asshole had had to ruin my fucking morning with her. I just wanted to be able to spend a few hours alone with my mate.

But with Calder, we would never have a few hours.

So, I hopped out of bed and walked to the door to go downstairs.

"You scared her with your ugly mug," I said, smacking him on his shoulder and walking past him and into the hallway. I glanced over my shoulder to see Sina's door shut—and probably locked—then continued downstairs to the kitchen.

"What the hell were you doing with her?" Calder asked, following me.

"Sleeping."

"Don't give me that shit," he growled.

I clenched my jaw, turned around, and shoved him hard. "The same fucking thing you did with her yesterday in the hallway. You fucking told us all that we'd fuck her together until we took care of her father, and then you fucked her and tried to hide it from us. So, I did what I wanted with her, too, because fuck you, Calder."

"I thought you wanted us to wait," Darius said to him.

Gaian stood behind Darius with his arms crossed, staring down at the kitchen table and probably thinking about all the ways he could get Sina alone, too, so he could see her tits because, gods, she had a nice set of them. Gaian wasn't as innocent as she thought.

"My wolf couldn't control himself," Calder said. "I have nothing to apologize for." He lowered his voice. "She's our fucking mate."

I snatched the milk from the fridge and grabbed a bowl from the cupboard. "What the hell are you even doing here anyway? Isn't it your time to go for a run or some shit? We still have a pack, Calder. You can't be obsessing over her every hour of the fucking day."

"I already ran to the prison this morning. Does Sina know that you killed one of her father's men before you fucked her last night?" Calder asked, showing me his canine teeth. "I found our prisoner dead in the cell this morning with your scent all over him."

This asshole thought he would try to fuck with me.

"No," I said, sitting back and smirking at him as I ate. I brushed my fingers across the skin she had bitten last night, leaving indents with her dull teeth. I hadn't let my body heal it yet because I wanted it to be on me fucking forever. "But if she had known, she probably would've come so much harder. Pretty Bird has a dark side."

And I wanted to see just how dark she could get.

<h1 style="text-align:center">24
the confrontation</h1>

darius

IN THE MIDST of a tense breakfast, Calder stopped mid-chew and glanced at the table, his eyes glazing over, the way they did when he was talking through the mind link to one of the warriors in our pack. I watched him carefully and listened as Sina moved around upstairs in her room.

Suddenly, Calder shot up from the table, eyes completely golden, and hurried toward the front door. "Darius," Calder called before looking back at him, "watch Pretty Bird. There are two of her father's men at our borders that we need to take care of."

Thayer stood up from the table, his eyes turning almost black, then stormed out the front door before Calder could. But Gaian lingered behind with me, his movements slower than usual.

"You don't want my help?" I asked, knowing that I'd be more helpful than Gaian.

"Gaian," Calder growled because we all knew that Gaian would be the one to fuck Sina alone next if we left him with her.

They were the closest out of all of us and had always had a connection that Calder was jealous over. But it wasn't Gaian's fault that Calder was cold and callous and didn't know how to speak to his own mate.

"Come with us."

After they disappeared out the front door, I locked *every* lock on all the doors and windows and walked up the stairs to see Sina. While she wouldn't get out, I didn't want to risk it. If her father's men were really here, then *anything* could happen.

Once I grabbed Sina's diary from Calder's room—to pass the time—I peeked my head into Sina's room without invitation. She lay back on her bed, curled up into a ball and clutching an oversize pillow to her chest. When I walked into the room, she glanced up at me and stayed quiet.

"You good?" I asked.

She sat up and beckoned me over to her. I locked her door too—just in case—and then lay next to her.

She glanced at her diary curiously and then at the locked door. "Where are the others?"

"They went out," I said because it wasn't a total lie and flipped open the journal. "It's my turn to choose which diary entry we get to enact next. Do you ... have any preference?"

Sina shook her head and watched over my shoulder as I flipped through the pages aimlessly while listening to the guys shout through the mind link about the men who were on our land and trying to find the pack house.

"I did something bad last night," she whispered suddenly, looping her arm around mine and resting her head against my shoulder, her gaze refusing to meet mine. "And I don't know how I feel about it. It wasn't what I should've done, but I couldn't help myself."

"What?" I asked, flipping through the pages. "You sleep with Thayer?"

"No—I mean, yes, I did ... but it's not that."

I glanced over at her, brows furrowed. "Then, what is it?"

Sina chewed on the inside of her flushed cheek and peeked a glance up at me. "I ..."

When she didn't finish, I pushed some hair from her face. "You what?"

"I want to be bred," she whispered, fingers digging into my forearm and arousal filling the room, awakening my wolf and making me feel fucking crazy. She moved closer to me somehow and pressed her thighs together. "Next time we have sex, I want all of you guys to come inside my pussy. I know you like fucking my ass, but please, Darius … I need it in my cunt."

A growl escaped my lips, one that I couldn't seem to hold back. "Pretty Bird …"

"Please, Darius," she whispered, grabbing my hand and thrusting it between her legs, laying it right upon her hot, sopping cunt. "I want my pussy so full that it's spilling out of me, that your cum runs down my thighs when I stand. I want you guys inside me all the fucking time."

"All the time, huh?"

I asked, flipping to Entry #8, where there was merely one word on the page.

Toys.

If Sina wanted us to use toys on her *and* wanted us to be inside her as much as we could, then I knew just the shop in town to bring her to find something that all five of us would enjoy—Arsenal's Trinket Shop.

Suddenly, the sound of howling and the scent of battle drifted through Sina's open window.

Sina snapped her gaze toward it and furrowed her brows. "What's happening outside? Where did the others go?"

"To deal with someone," I said. "Now, what did you do that was so bad?"

Sina glanced at the window nervously again, then opened her mouth. Just as Sina was about to tell me her secret, a gunshot, followed by a low howl—this time closer—rang out through the air. I could immediately tell that it was Gaian who must've gotten hit by a silver bullet from Sina's father's men.

Sina sat up and hurried over to the window. "Who is here?"

After dashing up next to her, I placed a hand on her waist to draw her back. I didn't want her anywhere near the window because if one of them made it past the guys and saw her, then took her from us, I would never forgive myself.

"Come on, Sina," I said, snapping the diary closed and seizing her arm. "We need to get you somewhere safer. I don't know how much longer the others will be able to hold them off. I need to protect you."

As I tried to pull her away, Sina ripped her arm away from me and rushed back over to the window to pull it open even wider and try to see through the trees. I wrapped my arms around her waist, about to use all my strength to pull her back this time.

I hated manhandling Sina. Calder and Thayer might've not had a problem with it, but I did. She deserved respect, especially after what had happened yesterday at the doctor's office, but I needed to get her out of here.

I couldn't wait any longer.

Just as I ripped her away from the window, I spotted someone in the woods. In the distance, Gaian was limping back to the pack house with one arm wrapped around his bare and bloody abdomen. He stumbled to his knees and spit up blood in the backyard, a low and feral growl escaping his lips.

His body was growing more rigid by the second, his cheeks paler than I had ever seen them. He looked worse than any silver bullet would've made him. He looked like he was about to double over and die.

"Gaian," Sina whispered, eyes growing even wider. "He's been shot."

25
the cleanup

gaian

FIND MEDICAL SUPPLIES NOW, my wolf growled throughout my head.

If we didn't pull this silver bullet out of me within the next few moments, it would severely damage my nervous system. This wasn't a regular bullet, but one that had been laced with poison. From the moment it had left the barrel, I could smell the stench of wolfsbane coating the edges of it.

I hurried toward the pack house, stumbling to my knees every so often and praying to the gods that I could stand back up and make it the rest of the way without problem. But my knees landed on the dirt again, the howls from Thayer and Calder filling my ears.

This was bad.

Really bad.

Before, Sina's father's goons had never used guns, especially not guns with silver bullets that had been laced with wolfsbane. They had been strong as fuck and so fucking annoying before, but now, it was worse.

They must've known that we had Sina. We hadn't really been hiding it anyway.

I stared at the earth and used the last of my strength to push myself to my feet. My entire body ached, pains shooting through every single one of my muscles until they trembled once more. Another gunshot, and no response from either Calder and Thayer.

Someone grabbed my arm from behind, and I shoved them hard off me. I refused to let Sina's father win this time. She was ours, and I would do anything to protect her. So, I used the last of my energy to shift and turn around, a menacing growl exiting my throat.

Sina stumbled back onto her ass, staring at me through wide eyes. "Gaian," she said, my name rolling off her lips as a mere whisper. She scurried back against a tree. "I just want to help you. Please, don't hurt me."

When I heard those last few words escape her lips—they sounded like she had spoken those words with fear so many times —I shifted immediately and collapsed onto my hands and knees. "I'm sorry. I didn't think it was you."

Darius stood a few feet behind her, between her and the battle happening less than five minutes from the pack house. He hiked his thumb back toward where Thayer and Calder lurked in the woods. "I'll go help them finish off the last of them. Heal him, Sina."

"Darius," I growled, wanting to fight alongside my packmates too.

This wasn't just an empty, meaningless war anymore. We had to protect Sina.

Darius shifted into his dark brown wolf and looked back at me. *"What?"* he asked through the mind link.

"Be careful. They're strong, and they have weapons."

Once he left, I stumbled into the pack house. Sina pushed me down onto the couch. I held a large hand over my abdomen to hold the bleeding wound closed, my chest rising and falling quickly. As Sina scrambled through the house to find the medical supplies, I took a deep breath, bit my tongue, and slipped my fingers down into the gash. I felt around my insides to try to find the bullet, but it was lodged too deep.

When Sina came back over to me, she stared at me in horror.

"What are you doing?!" she exclaimed, pushing my hands out of the way and using a utensil to slide into my wound. "You have to be careful! You can't just poke around inside there."

Within a few moments, Sina clamped down on the bullet with the utensil, winced, and slowly pulled the bullet out of me. She dropped it into a small dish, then cleaned the wound with some alcohol and some potion that we had bought from witches who lived down in Durnbone.

"What did they lace this bullet with?" Sina asked, picking the piece of metal up with the utensil once more and examining it. Suddenly, her cheeks paled, and she dropped the bullet and utensil into the dish. "No. No, no, no, no, no."

"It's wolfsbane, Sina," I said.

"No," she whispered, standing to her feet. "It's not. You're lying to me."

"What?"

"My father experiments with this stuff." She shook her head. When she tore her gaze away from mine, a wave of guilt washed over me. "You knew that this was my father's men and didn't want to say anything to me, didn't you?"

"Sina," I whispered, still holding the wound. "I'm sorry. It's complicated."

Sina stormed upstairs to her bedroom and shut the door, leaving me to rot on the living room couch. I shuffled to my feet, bit back a howl, and followed her up the stairs because I didn't want her to be angry with me. We were *always* on good terms.

When I pulled the door open, I caught Sina rummaging through her backpack. She glared up at me, then pulled out a container of glowing pink liquid.

"Is this what you guys have been hiding from me?" Sina asked, screwing off the cap.

"I said that it's complicated, Sina."

After marching right over to me, she put the jar of liquid to my mouth. "Take one small sip."

"What is it?" I asked, eyeing it.

"*It's complicated*," she said, sending my own words right back to me—petty, as always.

But I didn't mind it. We were the ones keeping this secret from her and the ones keeping that she was our mate from her. There had been so many fucking times that I just wanted to come out with it already. I just wanted to tell her, but we needed to keep her father out of our business.

The only way to do that and ensure her safety was to kill him. If she knew that she was our mate and mistakenly told her father, then he might hurt her worse than … he already had. I didn't know what he had done to her these past few years, but I could tell it had fucked with her mind and made her furious.

As soon as the pink liquid hit my tongue, my wolf let out a feral growl. This tasted like vampire blood, mixed with some sort of … of witch's brew or something. I couldn't really tell exactly what it was, but my strength was becoming restored quickly.

"What is this stuff?" I asked again.

Instead of giving me another snippy response, Sina screwed the cap back on, stuffed it into her backpack, and shoved it underneath her bed. "My father used to …" She paused and licked her dry lips. "He used to sneak that green juice that you thought was wolfsbane into my drinks before I went to bed. It …"

When Sina's voice broke, pain shot through my entire body. And not the kind from the bullet wound. This was emotional turmoil that Sina didn't tell anyone about. But I had seen that pain more than once just in the past few days, especially after we went to the doctor.

"What'd he do?" I urged, tucking some hair behind her ear.

"That juice would paralyze me, so I couldn't move for hours," she whispered, glancing down at the ground with tears wavering in her eyes. Suddenly, she grabbed my hand and squeezed tighter than she ever had. "I couldn't fight back. I couldn't fight any of them back."

"What do you mean any of—"

Before I could finish my sentence, Sina's bedroom door was ripped off its hinges and thrust open.

26

the war

sina

CALDER, Thayer, and Darius stood at my bedroom door and saved me from spilling all my secrets to Gaian. I wanted to tell someone so badly, especially after I caught my father using the same type of shit on Gaian, but I … I didn't want to relive those nights again.

Calder stared at me through golden wolfish eyes. Thayer stood beside him, covered and dripping in blood from head to toe.

And Darius glanced between Gaian and me, brows furrowed, and said, "You okay, G?"

"G is fine, thanks to me," I said, crossing my arms over my chest and stepping forward before Gaian could say anything. I narrowed my eyes at Calder and pursed my lips. "Why didn't you tell me you've been fighting my father?"

Calder cut his gaze to Gaian. "You fucking told her?"

I pushed my hands against his chest and shoved him backward. "Don't talk to Gaian that way. He didn't tell me shit. I figured it out myself. If you had just told me, I could've helped you all out."

Calder grabbed my hands, so I couldn't push him again. "He's coming for *you*."

"I know he is," I said between gritted teeth. "But I know what kind of shit he has experimented with. I know what he's going to use in war against you guys—or *anyone* for that matter. I could've freaking helped!"

"We don't need your help," Calder snapped. "You're our—" Before he could finish his sentence, he stopped short and bared his teeth at me. "We're supposed to fucking protect you, Sina. No matter what. He's already taken you away once. He's not going to fucking do it again while I'm alive."

"Well, you're not going to be alive for much longer if you keep shit from me!" I ripped my hands away from him and pointed to Gaian. "That bullet that Gaian was shot with was coated with a poison that affects *all* species and paralyzes them on the spot."

"How do you know that?" Darius said. "You've watched your father use it?"

Suddenly, I smacked my lips closed and stared at him. I didn't know what to say. I wanted to *avoid* this conversation, not make it about me. I couldn't make it about me. I didn't want them to know how weak I had been these past four years.

I wanted to be strong, not only for myself, but for them too. I had adored wolves for far too long, since I'd met these guys, and every day, I aspired to be as strong as them. How would they look at me, a human who had been taken advantage of by her own family? They already thought I was weak because I was human. All species did.

"Did they experiment on you?" Gaian asked, stepping forward.

All I could do was glance down at my feet. Pain shot throughout my entire body, and I felt the hands of all those creepy men all over my body. I wanted the memories to vanish forever, so I didn't have to remember how helpless I had been.

Lying in my bed. Unable to move. Letting man after man come inside me.

I didn't know why Dad had allowed it.

I didn't understand why he hadn't protected me from them.

Ever since I'd been a young age, he had told me that he would do anything to protect me. So, why the hell hadn't he protected me from all those filthy guys? Why had he willingly let them sleep with me every single night, before I could even understand what was going on?

"Yes," I finally whispered. "For years, even before he took me away."

Thayer let out a ferocious growl. "I'm going to fucking incinerate him."

Calder placed a hand on Thayer's chest to hold him still. "What did he do to you?"

My chest tightened. I opened my mouth to say something, but the only thing that came out was a deep cry that I had been trying to hold back for years. I didn't want to reopen this chapter of my life because it hurt too fucking badly.

This wasn't even the beginning of everything. There was so much more.

They all stared at me, as if they were waiting for me to continue, but that was all that I would tell them for now. That was all I *could* tell them for now. The memories were far too atrocious to remember all of them.

"It's okay, Pretty Bird," Gaian whispered, moving closer to me. "You don't have to tell us anything else right now, if you don't want to. We've, uh …" He looked at the others. "We've been at war with your father for the past four years. He had two men waiting for Thayer and Calder at your house on your eighteenth birthday. Those goons nearly killed them."

"He did?" I whispered, feeling even more betrayed by my own blood somehow.

I glanced up at Calder and Thayer, who both refused to make eye contact with me. In fact, Calder glared at Gaian and bared his teeth, as if Gaian wasn't supposed to say what he had. Thayer glared out the window, his dark eyes flashing a fiery orange color.

"We've been killing all the men he sends to us," Darius said.

"Killing them," I whispered, tasting the words on my tongue.

All these years, I'd wanted to kill them myself. Every night, as I lay paralyzed in my bed and they pounded inside me, I would stare up at my bland ceiling and think about how I would kill them. I had dreamed about things far worse than biting or slapping them the way that Thayer had made me do to him last night.

I wanted to feed them that green poison and torture every last one of them the way they had to me.

"Is that what you did with Dr. Stormmark?" I whispered.

Darius and Gaian shared a tense look. They didn't have to say anything for me to know that they had gone back to Durnbone after my doctor's appointment and slit her throat for making me *cry.*

Darius and Gaian had both been so sweet four years ago, and now … now, they were just as deadly as Calder and Thayer.

"The men are taken care of for now," Darius said, looking at the others. "We have guards posted all over Durnbone and the land around the city. Why don't we take an afternoon to relax?" He glanced down at Gaian's abdomen. "I think we all need it."

"Where?" I asked.

"The tavern, but … we have to make a stop first," he said. "To the trinket shop."

27
the toy shop

sina

"YOU GUYS HAVE BEEN HERE BEFORE?" I asked, stepping into Arsenal's Trinket Shop on the outskirts of town.

Glancing around the shop, I scrunched up my nose. For all the weird, unnecessary junk that the shop owner sold here, the shop was bustling with people of all backgrounds—from werewolf to human to demon and even an angel or two.

When I stopped to stare at an unusual device that looked like it could saw me right in half, Darius grabbed my hand and pulled me to the front register, where a scantily clad woman in nothing but a damn apron stood, smiling a bit too sweetly.

The thin apron straps barely covered her breasts. I mumbled under my breath, possessive of my guys and not wanting someone like her to even draw their eyes. I tightened my grip on Darius and dug my claws into Gaian's bicep, jealousy taking over.

"Hi! My name is Mindy. How can I help you today?" the woman asked.

"We're looking for Odrin," Darius said.

A couple of moments later, an older man with bifocals walked out from behind a red curtain, which must've led into the back storage room. "Ah, the boys! It's nice to see you all. That, erm ... trinket that you asked for is available after all."

"Trinket?" I asked, brows furrowing.

The man turned toward me. "And who is this?"

Calder growled, "She's none of your business."

"My name is—"

Thayer growled at me, glaring at me not to say another word. I pressed my lips together and glared back. Jeez, possessive assholes much? It was as if they didn't want this man to even know my name, like he'd use it against me with some sort of magic or something.

"Well, why doesn't Mindy show you around? I'm sure there is something here that suits your fancy, hmm?" Odrin gently ushered Mindy in my direction, her breasts nearly bouncing out of her apron when he did. "Boys, you can follow me."

When the boys disappeared in the back, I glanced around the shop, my gaze landing on the seat behind the counter, where Mindy must've been sitting. A huge ten-inch-long dildo was suction-cupped to the leather chair, covered in a thick layer of juices.

"So, this is a sex shop?" I asked, arching a brow.

Mindy giggled. "No! We sell trinkets and gadgets. Nothing like that."

I eyed the dildo. "Right ..."

There was something about her that I couldn't quite put my finger on. Her eyes were glazed over, a smile plastered on her face, and she willingly listened to her boss with so much enthusiasm that it was fake—it had to be fake. Nobody was that enthusiastic about anything.

"Do you want me to show you around? We have a wide selection of trinkets and gadgets that you can use while hunting monsters, or for everyday activities, or honestly anything that you could want."

After walking around the shop with Mindy—a bunch of older men staring at us like we were some sort of prey—I stopped at the edge of an aisle and smiled at a gadget that might be fun to use with the boys … or maybe they'd hate me for it. I wasn't sure.

"I'll take this," I said.

Mindy clapped her hands together, grabbed the gadget, and hurried toward the register, checking me out at lightning speed. After handing me the bag, she excused herself to scrub the floors with a bucket of soap and the smallest sponge that I had ever seen.

I stared at her, finally understanding why there were so many creepy men here, just staring at her, and turned back toward the red curtain. A couple of moments later, the guys walked out from the back room with a small black bag.

Darius opened the bag for me to look into, and I saw a small black pair of panties.

"You should go put them on now," Darius said.

"But the underwear I have on now is—"

"Not going to suit you for what we have planned," Darius said.

After I sighed, Darius handed me the bag. They all stared at me impatiently. We wouldn't be leaving here anytime soon without me putting on the underwear in the back room. So, I snatched the panties from his hand and marched into the bathroom, hooking my fingers into my current underwear and pulling it off.

I shoved them into the plastic bag, knowing that Thayer would want them—or at least, one of them would. They were all fucked up in the head anyhow. After pulling out the clean, fresh pair, I furrowed my brows at them and eyed them for any sort of … weirdness.

Those boys hadn't come to this store to buy normal lingerie.

But the more I examined it, the more normal it looked.

Deciding that the piece of clothing wasn't going to destroy my pussy somehow, I pulled them on under my dress and blew out a deep breath. They were a bit tight around the inner thigh area, but that was about it …

"You ready?" Gaian asked, peeking his head into the bathroom.

Jumping in surprise, I held a hand to my chest and cut my eyes to him. "What is wrong with you guys today?! First, you take me to a sex shop, and now, you're peeping on me!"

"You're ours," Gaian said, like it was the most normal thing in the world. He clutched his side, where his bullet wound was. "We can do what we want with you."

After snatching my purse and bag, I hurried out of the bathroom and toward the main room, where the guys were chatting among themselves and not staring at Mindy like the rest of the shoppers were.

"Come on," I said. "Let's get out of here. Odrin gives me the creeps."

"Bye!" Mindy said, lifting her head slightly and waving to me. "See you next time."

I gave her a small smile and rushed out of Arsenal's Trinket Shop, heading right in the direction of home. Realizing that the four guys were lagging behind, I looked over my shoulder to see Darius handing Gaian a small, circular rubber-like loop.

My brows furrowed, and I stopped, arching a brow. "What was that?"

"Nothing," Thayer said, grabbing my hand. "Come on. Let's head out to lunch before we go home."

"But ..." I blew out an angry breath.

"But nothing," Calder snapped, always pissed off at the world. "You're coming with us."

28
the toy

sina

I SAT inside the tavern with my four guys and eyed them suspiciously. We had come in and ordered drinks only five minutes ago, but I couldn't figure out what they were up to. What would these stupid panties do to me? Why'd they force me to wear them?

"Hey, stranger," Maxine said, standing to my left with a bunch of Midnight Moons for us. She placed them on the table inside the tavern and beamed at me. "Where have you been? I thought these guys nearly killed you with the way they dragged you out of here the other night."

My lips curled into a smile. "I've been dealing with my dad."

"Well, make sure you stop in more often. I miss you." She smiled at me and took off her name tag that glimmered under the tavern's dim lights. "I'm off for the rest of the night. Have fun, and I'd better see you soon."

Once Maxine left, I eyed Gaian's pocket, where he had hidden that circular loop thing that all the guys had been exchanging on our walk over here. Thankfully, the tavern wasn't as busy as it was at night, so we had the whole corner to ourselves, and they could do whatever the hell they were planning.

"All right, well … we gotta use the restroom."

"All four of you at once?" I asked when they all stood.

They didn't even answer me as they walked through the tavern to the restroom together, like they were part of some sort of cult or something. Pissed off, I angrily tapped my foot on the ground and stared at the men's restroom door. I shifted in my seat, rubbing my thighs together and feeling the wetness between them already. My underwear tightened around my hips, and I discreetly tried to loop my finger around it to make it a bit looser.

But when I tugged, it tightened even more, almost as if it was locked on to me.

Breath catching in my throat, I glanced back up at the restroom and tugged harder on it, but it didn't budge. Suddenly, something huge was pushed between my pussy lips and slid into my sopping pussy with ease. I gripped the table and inhaled sharply, my nipples hardening.

It felt like … like Gaian's cock.

It had been inside of me so many times, so I knew what it felt like.

After glancing around to make sure nobody was watching, I pulled the front of my dress up and stared down at my panties, watching another throbbing dick enter my pussy from the inside of my panties. I tightened around the two cocks even harder and whimpered.

Holy fuck.

What kind of panties were these? How was this even possible? Was that—

Before I could even finish my thought, I felt something push at my backside and enter me. *Fuck, fuck, fuck, fuck, fuck.* A moment later, a fourth dick entered me, stuffing me fuller than I had ever been.

I wiggled in my seat, trying to relieve the pressure inside me, and parted my lips in delight, aching for them to start fucking me. I could only imagine how it would feel to have four cocks thrusting in and out of my pussy, all at different paces and different rhythms and all at once.

As if nothing had happened, the guys walked out of the restroom together. I glared at them and bit my lip, whining softly when they approached.

"What are you doing?" I asked breathlessly. "What kind of panties did you buy for me?"

They all took a seat beside me, scooting into the booth.

"One that lets us fill you with cum all day, every day, even when we're not with you," Gaian said, staring across the table at me with those dark, hooded eyes. "You said that"—he reached under the table, thrust his hips up and his dick harder into me, and grunted—"you wanted to use toys."

I moaned in response, feeling so tight down there. I gripped Calder's bicep and leaned over his shoulder. Calder reached under the table too, where he unzipped his pants and pulled out his cock that had that rubber loop around the base. He grabbed the loop and moved it up his length slowly, his dick sliding out of my pussy.

When he pushed the loop back to the base with so much force and filled me up, I found my body jerking up, my breasts bouncing slightly, almost as if he were really inside of me. I slapped a hand over my mouth to stop myself from moaning out loud.

Darius and Thayer followed, undoing their pants right in the middle of the tavern and stroking the rubber loops up and down their cocks. I pressed my lips together, feeling four cocks thrust in and out of me, my body jerking up and down, breasts bouncing inside my thin dress, nearly coming out each time.

"We've got another one for that mouth of yours," Thayer whispered into my ear, pulling me onto his knee and gently rubbing my clit through the panties with his free hand. "A mask just like ours, except we can fill your throat when you use it until you're choking on each of us and you have spit running down your pretty little chin and neck in front of everyone."

"You-you do?" I asked breathlessly, glancing at each of the other guys, who nodded in agreement.

They thrust themselves in and out of my pussy, driving me higher and higher. Warmth pooled between my thighs. I leaned back against Thayer, letting him touch my body however he wanted.

On the edge of an orgasm, I curled my toes. "I need your cum, please."

Gaian and Calder completely pulled the loops off their cocks and pulled themselves out of me. Darius and Thayer pulled out of my ass and pressed the head of their cocks against my entrance, coming all over my pussy lips. I moaned in response, wave after wave of pressure rushing out of my core, and let Thayer rub their cum against my clit.

Both grunting, they pulled away, leaving a thick layer of cum at my entrance. Gaian and Calder pushed back into me, shoving the others' cum deep inside my pussy. After a few thrusts, Calder and Gaian stopped. My pussy pulsed on them, milking the cum out of the balls.

Calder pulled out, then Gaian. The panties finally loosened around my hips and thighs, and I relaxed against the booth, both pleased and excited to use the mask. At the start of this, I'd never thought I'd be sitting in the middle of a pub, using a trinket that let my guys fill me whenever they pleased. But here I was, aching for more.

29

the secrets

sina

AFTER TAKING THOSE PANTIES OFF—BECAUSE I didn't know if I'd be able to handle another round of public sex—I walked through Durnbone with my guys in the direction of home. I was calling the pack house home now, I guessed.

"Before we head back, do you think that we'd be able to stop in Durnbone?" I asked, spotting a witch's shop that had poisons and potions in the window. "If you're fighting my father, I need to stock up on supplies to help you guys out."

They glanced at each other, and then Calder clenched his jaw and nodded. "Be quick."

Not having to be told twice, I hurried across the street and toward Witch's Brew, which looked to be a magic shop with golden-accented windows. I glanced into the door window, then walked into the black-mystical atmosphere.

Filled with skulls and colorful potions, the room might've been small, but I could feel the magic floating around in the air. It sorta, kinda felt like Dad's experiments all over, like my nightly tea, like revenge.

I brushed away the thoughts and the feelings, then continued into the room. A woman dressed in black with dark purple lipstick crushed some herbs at a counter in the back, then sprinkled them into a cauldron. When I walked over to her, she glanced up at me, then behind me at my four guys.

"Can I help you?"

"I would like some herbs," I said before Calder could butt in. "And vampire blood."

As soon as the last few words left my mouth, the witch's face paled. "Vampire blood?"

"Yes."

"But you don't do magic. You're a human."

"Give her the fucking blood," Thayer growled.

Once the witch placed down the herbs, she disappeared into a back room. I shifted back and forth on my feet, glancing over at the others, who all waited impatiently for her return.

"If you guys want to be strong against the potions that my father creates, then you need to be willing to drink vampire blood. Your wolf powers won't heal you alone."

My gaze landed on Gaian, who looked to be doing better after I gave him the healing potion this morning, but his cheeks were still a bit pale. When we got home, I would have to give him some more medicine.

"Are you sure about this?" the witch said, clutching a vial of vampire black blood.

"Yes."

She took a deep breath and handed the vile to me. "Please be careful. This stuff is very dangerous. If you need help or directions on how to use it, please come back to my shop. One wrong move, and you'll create a potion that'll kill you."

"I'll be safe with it," I said, paying her for the items.

Hell, Dad had already pumped me full of this stuff. Who knew that it could've killed me?

———

Back at the pack house, Gaian looked worse. While the others went upstairs, I mixed together the herbs with the vampire blood and poured it into a glass of juice in the kitchen. Part of me *hated* giving it to Gaian because this felt like what Dad had done to me. Still, he needed to get better.

Once he placed the cup to his lips and took a big sip, I grabbed the cup from him and drizzled some potion over his open wound. Even with his advanced healing abilities as a wolf, the gash had barely healed. His skin sizzled as the potion came in contact with it, some green steam almost boiling off on contact.

Gaian flexed every muscle in his body, his abdomen thick and glistening. I pressed my thighs together and reminded myself that I'd bought this to heal him, not to jump on his cock and ride him all fucking night long.

Not that either of us would mind.

I stretched my hand across his stomach and gently curled my fingers against his abs to hold him steady. "I have to do it again," I whispered, unable to make eye contact with him because I was so much hornier than usual. "There's still some poison inside you."

From the corner of my eye, I caught Gaian clenching his jaw and staring at me. His gaze was so intense that I couldn't resist the impulse to look up at him, which was a huge mistake. My heart raced, and I had an innate urge to jump on him.

He was sex. Pure, animalistic sex.

A feeling that I hadn't experienced prior to last night with Thayer rushed through me. There was something, some compulsion that had made me rip out that IUD, bite Thayer on his neck, and become a starved, feral beast. Though … I didn't know what it was.

After forcing myself to look away, I returned to healing his wound and poured some more potion onto it. A heap of green steam boiled off it, the wound healing only slightly. Gaian winced, muscles tensing even harder.

Heat spread throughout my body, a single bead of sweat dripping down my back.

Gods, he was making it so hot in here.

When I *finally* finished with him, he pulled his shirt over his abdomen and grabbed my hand. Tingles shot up my arms, my heart racing so freaking fast for some reason. Gaian must've felt it intensely, too, because a low growl exited his throat, and then he pulled away.

I took a deep breath and quickly turned away to put the blood and the potions away. Hopefully, we wouldn't need it anytime soon, but I needed to make some vials of healing potion this weekend. I needed to be prepared.

"I would've told you about your father sooner, but … Calder wanted to keep it a secret."

Gritting my teeth, I glared out the kitchen window. Why was Calder such an asshole? All he did was keep secrets from me and act as if I *belonged* to them. It didn't make any sense to me, especially because I wasn't their mate.

Okay, there was a *slim* chance that I was, BUT if I was, I would assume they would've told me by now. Or at least, their wolves would've taken control of them and claimed me as theirs, right?

Almost as if he knew what I was thinking, Gaian let out a low sigh and grasped my chin, forcing me to look into his desperate eyes. "There is more that Calder won't let us tell you." He paused for a long moment, his voice filled with nothing but sadness. "So much more."

30

the suffocation

sina

ALL NIGHT, I twisted and turned in the bed, unable to keep my mind calm. The only thing I could seem to think about was how much of a jackass Calder was to me. I didn't understand his reasoning *for anything,* but these guys followed his orders because he was the alpha.

And I fucking hated it.

After grinding my teeth together for the hundredth time tonight, I threw my blankets off of me and stormed to my bedroom door. The house was quiet tonight, which meant that all the guys were actually in bed or out, but I didn't give a fuck.

I slipped into the hallway quietly and hurried to Calder's door, grasping the door handle firmly in my hand. It seemed like every-thing had been annoying me tonight—from how hot it was in my room to how I couldn't get him off my mind.

Why the hell was he the only thing I could think about? And who the hell did he think he was?

When I stepped into the room, the first thing I caught sight of were those skanky panties that I'd spotted last time. I didn't know who the fuck wore a neon G-string *that* slutty, but I sure as hell wanted to put up a fight about it.

Heat engulfed my body, my cheeks burning. I slammed his bedroom door, probably waking up all the other guys, and rushed to his bed. All I wanted was for him to hurt. He had done nothing but be an asshole to me and parade around those fucking panties, stashing them in a place he *knew* I'd see them.

Didn't he know that I liked him—even if he was an asshole? I'd *always* freaking liked him.

I grabbed the nearest pillow, climbed onto him, and straddled his waist. At first, he shifted underneath me, his strong body feeling *huge.* Then, when he blinked his eyes open and saw my furious face, I pressed my hands hard against the center of the pillow and suffocated that freaking bitch.

I didn't know what had come over me, but I couldn't stop.

He struggled underneath me again, twisting and turning his body and *trying* to push me off him. But I didn't stop. I pressed as hard as I could because I wanted him to freaking pay. I wanted him to hurt. All I had been doing was hurting.

A layer of sweat covered my back, my lungs burning. Why the fuck did he keep things from me? Did he not think I was strong enough to handle them? I hated all these secrets. It felt like Dad's house all over again.

Calder couldn't protect me these past four years from all the monsters who had bent me over the side of my own bed and fucked me until my eyes filled with tears and I was begging—*fucking begging*—them to stop. He couldn't protect me from experiment after experiment that Dad had done on me to make me a perfect specimen, a perfect fucking suitor for any type of species who could want to use my body.

I had done fine, escaping Dad's estate, all by myself. I had gone through torture worse than that poison that Gaian had taken and those men who wanted to find me. I didn't need him to protect me.

Doubling down, I put all my weight onto the pillow to hold it in place. I looped my legs around his and ground my hips against the front of his to stop his body from spazzing. If I had to use fucking force to show him that I was strong and capable of the truth, then I would.

But, hell, it was getting hot in here. He even had the windows cracked open, and it was October.

A low growl rumbled through the pillow. Hot tears welled up in my eyes from everything that I had been holding back lately. I shoved my hands down against the pillow over and over and over, hoping that he'd die.

Not really, but still.

His movements and struggles became stronger. I needed a way to show him that I was serious about all this shit. That I could handle anything he would throw at me. That I didn't want to see any more panties lying around his room.

Just as he ripped the pillow away from me, I spotted a silver knife sitting on his bedside table. I grabbed it, released the pillow, and shoved the sharp edge of the blade right against the artery in his neck.

"Don't freaking move, Calder," I growled, breathing hard. His room suddenly felt hot, burning, scorching, *suffocating*. As my chest rose and fell, I pressed the knife harder against his skin. "Stop acting like you're the big bad alpha and tell me what you've been hiding from me. Tell me whose panties those are. Why do you keep hiding shit from me?!"

"Mate." The word came out low and feral, his voice almost not even his.

Blinded with rage and hurt and agony, I shoved my hands into his chest to push him further against the mattress. Hot tears filled my eyes to the brim. My skin burned under the heat in this room. I wanted him to hurt.

I didn't want them to be his mate's. I wanted them to be mine.

I wanted to be the one leaving panties in his room. I wanted to be the one sleeping with him every night of the week. I wanted to be the one who birthed his pups, one after another after another until this pack house was full of them.

"Tell me!" I screamed at him, control completely fucking gone. *What is happening to me?*

Suddenly, he seized my waist and turned me around, so I was lying on the bed. He growled, his eyes glowing a golden tint and his canines lengthening under the moonlight.

"Heat," he said. "You're going through the first few symptoms of heat."

"I'm a human, jackass!" I shouted, the knife slipping from my hand and clattering onto the ground beside his bed. I shoved my hands into his chest, sweat pouring down my neck, and gripped his flesh. I couldn't go through heat, only werewolves did. "Get off me!"

Gods, maybe I really *was* just going crazy. Maybe I had blown this all out of proportion.

All I knew was that I couldn't breathe, and all my body wanted was him right now. I wanted to fight with him because Calder fucked the best when he was angry. I wanted to feel full. I wanted to milk out his cum with my pussy. I wanted him to breed me right here and right now on his bed.

31
the heat

calder

"CALM THE FUCK DOWN, SINA," I growled.

My wolf clawed at my insides, simmering right underneath my skin. He wanted me to let him out now. He wanted me to lose control. He wanted to have Sina all to himself right now, to put her out of her heat and her misery.

The only explanation that I had for it was that she was going through heat earlier than she should've been, even before we fucking marked her. It was unheard of that a human female mate went through heat after her mate found her. And this seemed worse than the first few symptoms of a she-wolf's heat. It was punishing her for us not marking her.

But I couldn't. Not right now.

"Gods," Sina muttered, hopping off the bed, pacing around the room, and stripping off her clothes. "It's so hot."

"Put your clothes back on, Sina," I said through gritted teeth, my control slipping. "Now."

Instead of listening to me, Sina hurried over to the window and pulled it open, so cold fall air would drift into the room. She placed her hands on the windowsill and leaned her head out of the window a few inches.

As she leaned over, I could see the layers of sweat on her back. She was sweating profusely, her skin all over her body flushing. She wiped sweat off her forehead with the back of her forearm and turned toward me, her nipples hard.

"You said that this was heat," she said, breathing heavily. "How? I'm human, not a wolf."

"Sina," I growled, tearing my gaze away from her and feeling my cock stiffen.

From the corner of my eye, I watched her grind her thighs together, as if she was trying to relieve the pressure and aching between them. All I wanted to do was bend her over the bed and fuck the heat right out of her.

My wolf was begging me. He wanted her as much as I did.

"Calder," she whimpered.

I should've gone over to her and marked her to put her out of her fucking misery, but I turned around and faced my bedroom door. My claws dug into the wood so hard that splinters stabbed at my fingers.

Canines extending, I found myself losing control. Quickly.

With every second that passed, her scent was becoming irresistible, overwhelming. My wolf howled inside me, finally thinking that tonight would be the fucking night that I took her after four long and hard years for the both of us.

"Calder," Sina said, her voice faint and frail. "Calder, please."

After balling my hands into tight fists, I gritted my teeth and glared at the door. Vowing that I wouldn't move toward her. Vowing that I wouldn't even look back. I fucking couldn't. We needed to take care of her father first. If he captured her after I marked her, I would go fucking insane. It had been bad enough last time.

"Calder, please, look at me," she begged.

Unable to stop myself and my wolf, I turned my head to the side and caught sight of Sina by the window. Her thighs pressed together, she had stripped her panties, and a bead of sweat rolled down the center of her chest.

"Please, breed me," she whimpered and rubbed her legs together. "Make it go away."

"Fuck, Sina," I gritted out, a low growl rumbling from my chest.

"Please, Calder. I know you want to put a baby inside me, so do it already. Gods, I can't handle this anymore." She took a step away from the window and toward me. "I want it so badly."

When she was feet from me, she dropped to her knees, her legs spread and her pussy inches from the floor. It was fucking dripping onto my rug, staining it with her sexy-as-fuck juices. She grabbed my hand, and I fucking lost it.

I turned, picked her up into the air, and threw her forcefully onto my bed. She landed with a thud with her legs spread, her eyes wide as hell, and her full tits bouncing slightly. After scurrying up to the headboard, she shoved a hand between her legs and rubbed her cunt as she watched me stalk closer to her.

With my wolf in complete control, I crawled up onto the bed and between her legs, hungry to taste my mate. I lay flat on the mattress, wrapped my arms around her thighs, and buried my face between her legs, eating her. She thrust a hand into my hair and tugged.

"Please," she whispered. "I want you inside me. I want you to fill me with your pups."

Another growl escaped my throat, and I continued to eat her pussy, hoping it would satisfy her. I couldn't fuck her tonight because if I did … I would mark her. And I had already fucked her first without the others.

I shouldn't give a fuck about them. She was my mate too.

But I couldn't handle what had happened after Sina left. I couldn't stand to see my packmates, my fucking brothers, get so torn up on the inside. I forced myself to bury my hurt to be the alpha they fucking needed.

"Breed me!" she cried. "Please!"

After dropping her thighs from my arms, I moved up the bed and toward her, my mouth all over her hot body. She was burning up, her scent drifting off her in fucking waves and her pretty pink lips begging me to take her.

I kissed up the column of her neck to her jaw, then back down to the crook of it, my canines brushing against the sensitive skin that I would mark. That I ached to mark. That I fucking had to mark. Now.

"Calder," Thayer said through the mind link.

Ignoring him, I let my canines lengthen even more and grazed them against her skin, giving it goose bumps.

"Men at the border," Thayer said. *"Where the fuck are you? You're usually the first one here."*

I snapped out of the trance that Sina had put me under with her delicious fucking scent and tore myself away from her incredible body. As I hurried to the door, promising that I wouldn't look back, I listened to her crawling up the bed toward me.

"Where are you going?" she said. "Please, don't leave. Please."

Those were the same fucking words that I had mumbled over and over when I found her home completely empty four years ago. I'd wanted that all to be a fucking lie, some sort of sick joke, so hearing Sina beg me to stay when I couldn't tore me apart on the inside.

She jumped up from the bed and hurried after me. "Calder, ple—"

Knowing that I wouldn't be able to handle it any longer, I walked out the door and slammed it right in her face. One more moment, and I would've lost it. Then, I shifted into my wolf, right in the middle of the pack house, and ran toward the borders.

32

the borders

sina

ALL FOUR OF the guys had left, leaving me alone with some random woman from their pack. I hadn't really interacted with the other packmates since I had been back, but I remembered some of them from before Dad dragged me away.

But not this chick.

I sat on the top of the stairs with barely any clothes on and prayed that this pain would be gone soon. The heat was only getting worse, only growing hotter until it felt like my insides were scorching fucking hot.

Digging my nails into my skin, I scratched at the flesh in hopes that it would stop the pain. I had never felt anything like this before today. I didn't know what the fuck it was because it couldn't be heat … could it?

Only if …

My entire body tensed, and the heat was suddenly slowing. There were only two ways that I could be going through heat right now. If I was fully mated to a werewolf or if … Dad's experiments had worked.

A sudden chill ran over me, and I grabbed a shirt from Gaian's closet. What was that? Just some symptoms of heat? Was it going to come back one day? Was it going to be worse? How could his experiments have worked?

When the door opened, I jumped up in surprise and hurried toward it. "Was it my dad?"

"False alarm," Gaian said, walking into the house.

After placing a hand over my heart, I took a deep breath and closed my eyes for a brief moment. Last time he had come home, he'd had a large bullet wound in his side. Hell, that had only been yesterday. I could only think the worst.

A few moments later, Calder walked into the house after Darius and Thayer, his gaze immediately reaching mine. We stared at each other for a few moments until I got pissed the fuck off because he had left me earlier. I had been begging for him, pleading that he take me, that he explain to me why I was going through heat.

And he had left.

He'd freaking left.

"What?" I snapped.

Instead of answering me, this ho of a man walked up the stairs to his bedroom. Not wanting to deal with it anymore, I followed him and grabbed his wrist to stop him halfway up the stairs. He froze as our skin touched, then yanked himself away from me.

"What is wrong with you?"

"Don't fucking touch me, Sina. I'm not in the mood."

"You sure were in the mood ten minutes ago."

He hardened his glare at me, and then, suddenly, it softened. He stared at me with so much hurt, so much love—I didn't know exactly what it was. All I could seem to do was stare back at him and wonder what his damn problem was.

One moment, he hated me. The next, he was looking at me like this …

"I'm fine," I said, answering the question he was giving me with his eyes. "Don't worry about me. You're the one who left while I was supposedly in *heat*." And then I strolled back down the stairs, ignoring the stares from the other guys, and walked to the kitchen to make myself some breakfast or lunch or whatever the hell meal it was.

I couldn't figure him out. I didn't know if I would ever be able to figure him out either.

The only logical reason for his bipolar personality was that I was their mate.

I wasn't blind and definitely not stupid. When it came to me, they were all possessive and reckless assholes who had gotten way too close the moment I entered Durnbone again. After days of coming up with any reasons as to why they had wanted me back so badly, this was the only one.

If I wasn't their mate, I didn't know why they reacted the way they did. If I wasn't their mate, they would've forgotten about me these past four years and shouldn't care about what had happened to me. To them, I had just left.

"You went through heat?" Darius asked from the living room.

Calder stared at me for a couple more moments, then walked up the rest of the stairs to his bedroom. When he slammed the door, I poured myself some much-needed coffee and swallowed hard.

"I don't know for certain. Maybe I was just having a hot flash."

But deep down, I knew that it really had been heat.

I, a human female, had gone through heat.

I, my father's experiment, had proven to be a success.

After taking a huge gulp of my coffee, I sat at the kitchen island and rethought all my life choices and everything that had happened lately. These guys had searched for me for the past four years, then taken me in because I was their mate. But what I couldn't wrap my head around was that they hadn't marked me yet. Calder had come close last night, and Gaian had mentioned that they were hiding something from me. Still, what was stopping them?

Thayer walked over to me and forcefully grabbed my arm, examining the scratches and cuts that I had given myself only a few short minutes ago. I'd wanted to get out of my skin so badly that I cut my flesh open with my fingernails.

"Who did this to you?" he asked.

"I did."

"Don't play around with me, Sina," he growled. "Your human nails couldn't do this shit."

Not wanting him to question me anymore, I pulled myself away from that man and continued to drink my coffee. "It's none of your business. I was feeling hot, so I did it to myself. If you don't want to believe me, don't."

Thayer glared at me even harder than Calder had, and then he grabbed my arm and pressed his palm against the cuts. I went to pull myself away, but he didn't budge. Instead, he held my arm even tighter and closed his eyes.

My arm burned for a moment, and I whimpered. "Thayer, let go."

When he reopened his eyes, his irises were as red as a demon's. He let my arm go. I glanced down at my forearm and saw that he had healed the cuts, every last one of them. His eyes returned back to normal, and he walked back upstairs.

"Don't lie to me, Pretty Bird. Those cuts were done by a wolf."

And then he disappeared into his bedroom.

33
the ex-boyfriend

sina

AFTER LAST NIGHT, I really needed a drink. So, somehow and someway, I convinced the guys to bring me out to the tavern where Maxine worked. As soon as we walked into the room, I scanned the place for her but instead found a couple of unfamiliar girls behind the bar.

She must be off tonight. Or maybe she was out with Xorgor.

I hurried away from the guys, spotting the bartender handing a man a huge glass of Midnight Moon that was just calling my name. My mouth watered at the sight of him, and if I were anything other than human, saliva might've started dripping off my canines and onto my chin.

Thank goodness I wasn't one of *those* nasty creatures because then I would've been a thousand times more desperate last night with Calder. I scooted onto an empty stool and leaned forward. I hated how I'd begged for him last night.

"Give me a Midnight Moon but stronger," I said to the bartender.

She furrowed her brows. "Are you sure? We have some human—"

"A Midnight Moon," I repeated.

There was no way in hell that I could stand some cheap human drink that barely had any alcohol inside it. I needed something strong as fuck because I was trying really damn hard not to lose my cool. I refused to go through the heat again tonight.

Before Calder could sit next to me, I pulled Darius into the empty seat.

I especially didn't want to be around Calder tonight.

That man had the audacity to glare at me *after he left me during heat*! He was lucky I hadn't found one of his unmated packmates to spend the night with. Hell, Calder freaking deserved something like that to happen after I found those skanky girl's panties in his room.

After sending Darius a death glare, Calder walked over to the farthest seat away from me and sat down, then asked the bartender for a Midnight Moon too. This chick flirted with my guys right in front of me, unbuttoning a button on her shirt before she handed the guys their drinks.

She hadn't even given me one yet, and they each had a glass sitting in front of them.

"While this drink comes *very slowly, apparently,*" I said, "I need to use the restroom."

The guys eyed me as I stood, daring me to walk away from them. But I was about one more eyelash-bat from this chick away from snapping her neck with my own two hands. Heat crawled up my neck at the thought of someone else trying to take them away from me.

"I'm going to the bathroom alone," I ground out. "I don't need you guys holding my freaking hand. I'm not going to run off with anyone. Don't worry."

Before they could give me another look, I hurried to the restroom, slammed the door closed, and splashed some water on my face. Gods, it was warm in here. Warmer than it had been the last time we were here, playing with that toy.

I gripped the porcelain sink and stared at myself in the rusty mirror, noting how all my facial features looked the same and reassuring myself that this heat was a coincidence and not because Dad had succeeded in his experiments.

After I thoroughly convinced myself, I took a deep breath and headed out the door, bumping into the one and only incubus Jaroth. He smirked down at me, his eyes surprisingly clear and not lust-filled, like usual, and grabbed my wrist.

"What are you doing?!" I whisper-yelled at him, then tugged my wrist out of his hold.

"I want to talk."

"We are not getting back together," I said between gritted teeth.

"I know that, Sina," he said, glancing over his shoulder, as if to ensure nobody was listening to our conversation. When he turned back to me, he scratched the back of his head. "I know you told me not to ever talk about this again, but …"

He paused for a long moment, and I swallowed.

"But what? Spit it out."

I had four possessive assholes sitting at the bar, waiting for me. If he didn't say something soon, they would come looking for me and find me with my ex-boyfriend. Then, they *really* wouldn't let me out to Durnbone again.

"It's about your father."

"My father," I whispered, mouth drying. "What about him?"

"Listen, I know that we're not together, but what he did to you isn't right."

"Why do you care?" I asked, stepping to the side so I could walk by him. "You're the incubus who fucking cheated on me. We were never going to work out, and you didn't care while we were together. Don't start now."

"If you had told me, then I could've helped you. I didn't know."

While I wanted to snap at him some more, he was right. I hadn't told him because I didn't know how, just like I hadn't told the entire story to the guys yet. How could I relive something like that over and over? It had taken so long to become numb to it. Hell, it had taken so long to understand that shit like that wasn't normal.

That other women didn't become paralyzed every night and have men rape them.

That other women weren't used as science projects for their fathers.

That other women had rights.

I had been living without any since I had been a damn child. I hadn't known any different until, one day, I found all of Dad's shit, until I found the courage to escape for the night with Jaroth and finally understood that sex didn't have to hurt me.

"I told you not to bring it up," I said, the hurt flooding back.

"You need to talk about what happened to you," he said, glancing around, then moving closer to me. Unlike his usual flirty self, he gently rested his hand on my shoulder. "It doesn't have to be me. I just wanted to warn you that I heard he's gathering soldiers in the north."

My chest tightened. "What? How many? Do you know anything else?"

"I can't be sure, but from what I've heard, his army is large and enhanced."

"Enhanced … as in enhanced humans?" I asked, knowing the answer before I even asked the question.

Of course they were enhanced humans. It wouldn't be any kind of monster that lived in Durnbone. They were humans like me, humans that … were more powerful than anyone thought.

All because of his experiments.

"I'm heading that way this weekend," Jaroth said. "I'll find out—"

Before he could finish his sentence, someone grabbed him by the back of the neck and hurled him across the pub.

Darius stood before me, his canines long and his eyes golden. "What the fuck are you doing with your ex-boyfriend, Pretty Bird?"

34
the damage

sina

"GET IN THE FUCKING HOUSE, Pretty Bird," Darius said, pushing me into the pack house behind my best friends and slamming the door behind us all. With blazing black eyes, he glared at me, pulling me closer, then growled into my ear, "What the fuck was that? Why the fuck were you with your ex?"

My eyes widened slightly, nipples hardening under my shirt. After that night in the woods, when my four masked best friends had run after me and devoured every inch of my body, everything was supposed to go back to normal. We weren't supposed to do it a second time, or a third, or even a fourth, and none of us were supposed to catch feelings for each other.

But I was knee deep in feelings and heat.

And, gods, I wanted them to take me tonight. Hard.

"Let me go. I didn't do anything," I said, yanking myself out of his grip and backing up until I hit Thayer's taut chest.

Thayer snatched the back of my neck, his claws almost piercing my skin. "You didn't do anything?" he asked, pulling me back and against the wall, pinning me there. "You didn't do fucking anything, huh?"

"No," I said.

Though … part of me wanted to lie and say that I had done something. I wanted them to be angry. I wanted them to be jealous, I wanted them to admit their feelings for me, and I wanted Alpha Calder to feel like the biggest piece of shit for leaving me in heat.

I had seen the way he looked at me, but something had held him back. And I couldn't wait any longer for him.

I wanted all of them. As mine. And mine only.

Gaian snatched my chin, nostrils flaring, and forced me to look at him. "What were you doing with him?" he asked, voice soft but filled with underlying jealousy.

"Fine!" I lied. "What the fuck do you want me to say? You want me to tell you that while all four of you were out at the borders this morning, after all four of you left me in heat alone, that I asked him to come over to fuck me in Calder's bed to get rid of it?"

It never happened. I would never want that to happen.

But it pissed them off—I could see it in their darkening eyes.

Standing behind Thayer, Darius, and Gaian, Alpha Calder balled his hands into fists and growled so loudly that everyone in the room went silent. Except for me. I wasn't going to let him try to intimidate me into submission. He fucking wanted me, and I'd make sure that he admitted it tonight, no matter the cost.

"He's a better fuck than you ever were, Calder," I growled back through my human teeth.

Before I could say another word, Calder shoved the other guys aside and wrapped his big, callous hand around my neck, canines extended, dripping with saliva all over my throat, the throat that I'd get him to mark one of these days.

"You'll never fucking compa—"

He snapped my mouth closed, pulled me to his bedroom, kicked open his door, and dragged me into the room. "Get the fuck into the bedroom and shut your fucking mouth," he sneered, throwing me onto the bed and undoing his belt.

Darius, Gaian, and Thayer followed Calder into the room, each peeling off their clothing and touching, grasping, groping, tugging on all parts of my body, their hands all over me and in places I had been aching for them to touch me since my heat.

Calder grabbed my ankle and yanked me to the edge of the bed, almost immediately thrusting himself into my pussy. "We're going to fucking breed you," Calder sneered in my ear, his canines gliding against my soft spot every time he thrust into me. "You're not leaving this bed until you're fucking. Full. With. Our. Fucking. Pups." He thrust into me one last time and grunted, his warm cum filling my insides and spilling out after he slowly pulled himself out.

When he crawled off me, I turned onto my side, placed a hand over my entrance, and whimpered out. He had come so quickly but so ruthlessly inside me, and my pussy already felt so full, so used. Yet, still, I wanted more of them. I wanted them to fuck me to sleep, until tears slid down my cheeks and I begged for them to stop. It felt like they hadn't touched me in so long.

They couldn't stop now.

Darius crawled up behind me on the bed, lifted one leg into the air, and pushed my hand away so he could slide himself right into my aching and cum-filled pussy.

"Beg for it," Gaian growled at me, grabbing a fistful of my hair and forcing me to stare up at Darius as he fucked me. "Beg for him to come inside of you. Beg to bear his pups."

"Please, come inside of me. Please, please, please come." I stared up at him, pleading with my teary eyes, my lips swollen and my hands gliding around his shoulder muscles. "Please, give me your pups. Please, Darius. Make me yours."

After a few more thrusts, Darius grunted and stilled deep inside my pussy, slowly sinking himself even further into my sopping cunt and filling me with his cum. My body relaxed, a weak orgasm rushing through me. I laid my head back, my makeup running down my cheeks, and sucked in a deep breath, my pussy pulsing on Darius's cock.

When Darius pulled out of me, Thayer shoved himself into me

without much of a warning. I yelped out, his huge cock stretching my insides, and grasped on to his muscular shoulders.

"Th-Th-Thay—"

"Oh, Pretty Bird? Have we fucked you so hard already that you can't even speak?" he asked me, his words so fucking degrading.

My pussy tightened around him, and I threw my head back against the pillow.

He reached between my legs and rubbed my clit. "Come on, Pretty Bird. You can do it. Sound it out slowly, if you have to."

"Fuck you," I spit at him, thrusting my hands against his chest.

He caught them in one of his and pinned them above my head on the pillow, smacking me across the cheek. "Guess we haven't fucked you enough if you can still talk back to us," he said, pounding his cock deeper and deeper into me. "We're going to leave you a slobbering mess of a slut."

My pussy tightened around him even harder, his fingers rubbing torturous circles around my clit. I sank my nails into his shoulders and cried out as wave after wave of pleasure rushed through my body. Was it fucked up that I wanted to get them this angry every day? Fuck yes, but I wasn't going to stop being a brat.

It got me what I wanted—to come over and over and over on their cocks.

"Say my name," Thayer said again. When I didn't respond, he slapped me on the cheek. "Say my fucking name, Pretty Bird."

"Thay—"

He rammed his cock so deep into me that my legs shook.

"Ohhh," I moaned.

"Oh? Oh what?" Thayer asked, slapping me right across my cheek again. "Huh? Oh what, Pretty Bird?" He grabbed my waist, his hands so big that he could almost wrap them completely around me. "Say my fucking name."

"Th-Th—" I tried. I tried so fucking hard to get his name past my lips, but the harder he fucked me, the harder it became. I couldn't get his name out of my mouth. "Thay—"

He stilled inside of me, his warm cum filling me up, and grunted into my ear, "That's what I fucking thought, Pretty Bird." He pulled out of me and tossed my legs to Gaian, who grabbed me and pulled me toward the edge of the bed. "Fuck her until all that's coming out of that slutty little mouth of her is slobber, drool, and cum."

Gaian turned me around so my head hung off the mattress and shoved his cock into my mouth, stuffing my throat full.

Calder grabbed my legs, as if he was ready to fuck me again already, and spit on my pussy. "You like being bred, Pretty Bird? You like us stuffing you full with so much of our cum until we know that there's no fucking way you aren't carrying one of our pups when we're finished with you?"

I gargled on Gaian's cock, spit and drool dripping down my cheeks, my nose, and my forehead. They were ruining me for anyone and everyone else. After tonight, I'd be theirs, and they'd be mine. Nobody would touch them, nobody would get to sleep with them, nobody fucking else.

Gaian wrapped his hand around my throat and jerked himself off, his fingers tight around my neck. "What was that?" he asked. "Did you say something?"

I gargled again, and when he started pounding into my face, I became nothing but a slobbering mess. I balled my hands into fists, grasping the bedsheets between them, and tugged up on them.

Calder slammed his cock into me and slapped my tits, over and over and over until both my pussy and breasts were bright red and stinging. The tension rose in my core, and I curled my toes, feeling another orgasm split through my entire body.

Gaian stilled deep down my throat, his cum filling my mouth. I choked on it, spitting up cum when he finally pulled out. It rolled down my cheeks and face, sticking to my eyelashes and gliding into my hair.

Calder rubbed the spit, the drool, and the cum around my face, smudging my red lipstick and mascara. Then, he wrapped a hand around my throat and pulled me up to his level. "Your small-dick asshole ex-boyfriend still fucking better than us, Pretty Bird? You want to call him up after this and ask him to fuck in my bed?"

I parted my lips, wanting to bitch him out so bad but I couldn't.

"No," I whispered, voice raspy. "I don't."

Calder slammed up into me one last time and sucked on my bottom lip. "Good, because you're ours fucking forever. Nobody is taking you or claiming you again. We'll fuck your tight little hole until this world burns."

35
the truth

TWENTY MINUTES LATER, Sina lay back on Calder's bed, thoroughly fucked. "What am I to you guys?" she asked, not making eye contact with any of us. "Why won't you guys tell me the truth? Why do you want to breed me so badly? To make me yours?"

While she hadn't had any other man over in Calder's bed, especially not her ex-boyfriend because I made sure that fucking asshole didn't come close to our property—us demons could sniff out other demons easily—that didn't mean that Sina would be okay with *this* forever.

She had gone through heat. Fucking *heat* as a human. And Calder hadn't done shit.

And I refused to lose her.

Gaian and Darius looked at Calder, waiting for him to tell Sina that she was our mate. But that fucking asshole wasn't going to say two fucking words to her. I knew how he thought. I understood what he thought he was doing—protecting us all.

But I couldn't do this shit anymore. I couldn't keep lying.

"You're our fucking mate, okay?" I said to her, then looked at Calder. "Look, dude, I'm fucking done with keeping this from her."

I stalked closer to Sina and roughly took her chin in my palm, cupping it. "You're ours. Nobody else gets to lay a fucking hand on you, or I'll rip their fucking head off."

Sina pressed her lips together and crossed her arms, as if what I'd admitted to her didn't surprise her. I mean, why the fuck would it? She was smart as hell and had obviously seen how possessive and jealous we all became around her ex-boyfriend—or around *any* guy for that matter.

"If I'm your mate, then why haven't you mated with me yet? Why haven't you bitten me?"

Well, that was Calder's fucking idea.

So, I released her jaw and crossed my arms. "Calder, you wanna take that one?"

Calder bared his canines at me. "No."

"You're an annoying fucking ass," I said to him, gritting my teeth and glaring at him. Later on, I was going to kick his fucking ass for all this shit he had been forcing us to do. "He doesn't want any of us to mark you until after your fa—"

"If you wanted to mark her, you could've," Calder growled. "Yes, I said what I fucking said, but I was protecting you. I'm not going to let us go through what we did again. I can't fucking carry that on my back for four more years."

Sina shook her head, as if she didn't understand where this was going or what we were even talking about. Hell, I didn't blame her. Sometimes, with Calder, I didn't fucking know either. He was even more of a closed fucking book than I was.

But in his sick, fucked up mind, he thought that if we marked her, our connection with her would go through the fucking roof. If her father took her away from us again, we'd all go insane and not think clearly, do anything to get her back—even if it meant sacrificing ourselves.

He didn't want Sina to go through something like that either—to be reunited with her mates and find out that two or three of us had died, trying to protect her. Hell, it had been bad enough four years ago when she left.

"Is it because you want to see other women?" she asked Calder directly, standing.

"No," Calder growled. "Don't even say shit like that."

"So, that's why you have another girl's panties just sitting in your room?"

"That thong you found"—Calder stared at her—"is yours."

Sina shifted from foot to foot, arms crossed and wide eyes rageful. "It's not mine!"

"It was the only fucking thing that was left behind at your old house," I said.

She glanced from me to Darius to Gaian, then finally to Calder, her eyes softening. "Are you being serious? You're not lying to me?" she asked. When none of us came forward, she frowned and collapsed back onto the bed. "They're mine?"

"Yes," Gaian said.

After running a hand across her face, she sighed and pulled a blanket over her body. Suddenly, tears wavered in her eyes. She shook her head and stared down at her legs underneath the blankets.

"I don't remember," she whispered, wrapping her arms around her body. "I'm sorry."

I glanced over at the guys, wondering why she was reacting this way. It was only underwear. She'd probably had a hundred different pairs of them over her lifetime. Why was she suddenly freaking out about them?

None of the others really seemed to understand either.

"Comfort her," I said to Gaian through the mind link.

Because I sure as hell didn't know how to. He always had the easiest time with her.

Gaian walked over to the bed and sat on the edge, next to Sina, as we all watched. It was fucked up that we didn't even know how to speak to our own mate, but we hadn't been around any other women for four fucking years.

"It's fine, Sina," Gaian said, gently rubbing her leg. "You don't have to cry over it."

"I'm not crying over the underwear," she whispered, a hiccup escaping her lips. "I'm crying because I don't remember. If I can't remember a simple pair of underwear that I wore—and they're bright fucking neon-colored, so how *could I* forget?—what if I don't remember other things? What if I ..."

Fear and terror crossed her face, her cheeks paling.

"What the fuck did your dad do to you, Sina?" I asked when she didn't continue.

It was a question that we all wanted to know the answer to, but Sina had shut us down last time we asked her. The more information that we learned, the more and more I wanted to just rip her father to fucking pieces.

She was terrified that she'd forgotten her memories.

"What if they did more than what I think they did?" she asked, more to herself than to us. "What if it was so much worse? How could I just forget? How could I ... how could I forget?"

Sina looked up at each of us, tears heavy in her eyes. She parted her lips, as if she wanted to tell us, as if she was just about to let her terrors slip past her lips, but then she smacked her mouth closed and curled up next to Gaian.

"I'm sorry," she whispered. "I'm so sorry."

36
the potions

sina

SMALL POTION BOTTLES sat around the kitchen table, the thick scent of vampire in the air. I poured some vampire blood into a large bowl, then sprinkled in some herbs, just the way that I had at Dad's estate to keep myself alive.

After last night, I felt so fucking bad. I had been moments away from telling my guys everything, but I got so caught up in the thoughts of what Dad could have done to me. I'd just wanted to be left alone.

Or maybe I was just making excuses now.

Jaroth had told me I should talk to someone about what had happened. He might've been my ex-boyfriend, but he was right. I had to tell my guys about how strong and powerful my father really was. I had to warn them.

Tonight.

I would tell them tonight.

But first, I needed to clear my head.

"How do you know how to make this stuff?" Maxine asked, pulling me out of my own thoughts.

She stirred the bowl every time I sprinkled some more herbs into it. In order for this potion to work, we had to ensure that it was mixed constantly and mixed well. Otherwise, it'd work for only a few moments, and then the body would become paralyzed.

"Trial and error," I said, hoping that she'd drop it.

She might've been my only female friend in Durnbone, but I didn't want her to know the monster that my father really was, mainly because I didn't want to involve her. I wanted her to worry only about herself and not me.

"I would've never thought to mix vampire blood and herbs, and I'm a bartender."

"Yeah, well ..." I scratched the back of my head and added more blood. "You know ..."

She didn't know. She had no fucking idea. She didn't even know what we were making this potion for. I didn't have the heart to tell her that we were making it because my father wanted to kill my four guys and take me to experiment.

"Yeah, I get it," she said, then looked around the room to make sure the guys were still upstairs, doing gods knew what. They had been in Calder's room for the past hour and a half, coming up with some sort of game plan. "I heard that Jaroth was at the tavern the other night."

I rolled my eyes and grabbed a couple of empty potion containers, pulling off their corks. "Yeah, he was."

"And you talked to him?"

"Yeah, I did."

"With the guys there?!"

"All right, it wasn't my *best* idea ever," I said, a small smirk coming onto my face. "But it did give me some information about the guys, like ..." Dad gathering men to come find me at the northern Durnbone border, like Jaroth had said.

What surprised me the most about all this was that Jaroth wanted to help. He wasn't going to sit back and not give a shit. He'd actually told me the information he had about my father instead of keeping it to himself.

But I couldn't tell Maxine. Though that wasn't everything I'd learned from that experience.

So as to not to lie to Maxine, I grinned. "I'm their mate."

"You're their mate?!"

"Yes," I said, peeking up at the second floor and catching Thayer storming out of Calder's room.

His eyes were as dark as the night and tinted with redness that only someone part demon could have.

"I had symptoms of heat too."

I watched as Thayer stormed down the stairs and out the front door without so much as a good-bye. He headed straight for their pack's prison, and I could only think about how he had come home from the prison the other night with blood covering his body right before he fucked me in the bath.

Maybe they had found another one of Dad's men wandering around the property.

"Girl, why didn't you lead with that?" she asked. "We've been making potions for the last half hour, and you didn't say a peep about it to me! What kind of friend are you? I need to know *all* the juicy deets."

My cheeks flushed, and I shook my head. "Nothing's really happened. They refuse to mark me for some fucked up reason. I don't know. I'm trying to think positively, you know? Otherwise, I'll flip."

"I get that," Maxine said.

After we fell into a comfortable silence, Maxine pulled off some more potion corks and let me fill them. "Anyway, I'm hosting a Halloween party next weekend at my place. Xorgor is coming and a few demons. Wanna come? It should be fun!"

"Gods, yes!" I said, my lips curling into a wide grin. "That's the best thing I've heard in, like, days now. I need some desperate girl time and to finally relax. These guys are driving me so damn crazy."

"In a good way," Maxine added.

Sometimes, she knew me better than I knew myself.

"You could say that," I said, cutting my gaze to Calder, who walked out of his room with Gaian and Darius behind him. He walked with such poise, such confidence that it aggravated me. "Or in an annoying-ass way."

"Halloween party?" Gaian asked, hoping off the last step and heading toward the kitchen. He grabbed a potion bottle and pulled off the cork, his biceps flexing. "Making plans without us, Pretty Bird?"

"Oh, I'm sorry." I rolled my eyes playfully. "Can I go to a Halloween party, my dear men who will not leave me alone for a single moment? I know I *always* need your approval for anything and everything. I'm so terribly sorry."

Every single word was dripping with sarcasm.

Calder growled at me and stormed out the front door, heading in the direction where Thayer had disappeared a few moments ago. Darius followed.

Gaian grabbed my ponytail and pulled it back, so I stared directly up at him. He planted a kiss right on my lips, then dipped his head to whisper into my ear. "You don't have to ask us to go. You just have to make sure we're invited."

"You're invited," Maxine said, throwing me a wink. "Sina even told me that she wanted you guys to dress her in the *sluttiest* costume that you could find."

"Maxine!" I shouted, cheeks flushing. "I do not!"

"One that shows off her tits," Maxine continued.

"Oh, I have the perfect costume for you," Gaian murmured to me, his lips curling into a smile against my neck. "You're going to fucking love it, Pretty Bird, and we'll get to check another one of the diary entries off your list," he said, lowering his voice toward the end.

"What do you mean? I don't have any Halloween party fantasies."

Gaian pulled away from me and chuckled deeply, his pale cheeks rounding. "You'll see."

I wasn't sure *what* he was going to have me wear, but I couldn't wait to find out.

37

the dead candle tavern

gaian

LATER THAT NIGHT, Calder, Thayer, and I went out to the Dead Candle Tavern in Durnbone to regroup and chat about Sina and what we were planning on doing. We needed to act quickly because I knew that her father would attack us soon, but none of us could even think clearly around her.

"What pisses me off the most is that she won't tell us shit," Calder said, tightening the glass in his hand and growling. Calder's eyes turned a shade of gold—the color of his wolf and whenever he thought of Sina.

"Because *you* piss her off," Thayer said through gritted teeth. "*You've* been the one lying to her and keeping shit from her. You almost ruined it again. She's not going to tell us anything if she doesn't feel fucking comfortable with us."

"What do you expect me to do?" Calder growled. "Her father took her away from all of us for the past four years. We had to learn to live without her. Without our fucking mate! What the hell don't you understand about that? Yes, I'm fucked up. I get that. But I don't want her to go through any more fucking pain."

His words trailed off, and I realized that, all this time, he had been there for us. He had been holding in so much pain, had been trying to protect Sina since she had gotten here from everything that had happened.

We all knew how much she had been hurting. But while I wanted to understand her pain, Calder wanted to eliminate it. He thought that keeping shit from her was the best way. And while he might've been wrong about that, I could tell right now that he couldn't stand to see Sina this way, so torn up.

When she had cried in my arms last night, he'd looked devastated. Absolutely fucking devastated. And when she'd sobbed about how she couldn't remember some things that had happened in the past … maybe he'd feared that she'd forgotten how much he loved her too.

"Maybe she'll tell Darius," I chimed in for the first time tonight.

"Or maybe she'll fuck him," Thayer said, trying to get under Calder's skin.

"Darius isn't going to do shit with her," Calder growled. "Not alone."

I sipped my drink and let Calder live in whatever damn fantasy that went on in his head. Sometimes—scratch that, most times—I didn't fucking understand him. He thought that Darius, who was one of Sina's mates, wouldn't try to get with her while they were alone.

Calder seemed to be in his own little world sometimes. I totally got it. He did it to deal with the trauma of finding out his mate had left on her eighteenth birthday, then getting attacked by her father's goons a few moments later. He and Thayer were both fucked up that way.

Thayer rolled his eyes and sipped his drink, turning toward me. "Heard she invited us to a Halloween party and that *you* are planning to dress her up that night. What're you going to dress her up as?"

After drawing my finger around the base of my glass, I smirked. "You'll see."

Jaroth, Sina's ex–incubus boyfriend, walked into the tavern and toward the back. Calder sat up straight as we all watched his every move. Sina hadn't dated him while she still lived in Durnbone, which meant that they had met while Sina lived at her father's estate.

"You think he knows what happened to her?" Calder said, upper lip curling in disgust.

"We're going to find the fuck out," Thayer growled, shooting up to his feet and storming over to Jaroth with eyes completely red. While Thayer didn't like many people, he especially hated demons like *him*, who had tried to get with his mate.

Once Calder stood, I hurried after them. Not only to keep them out of trouble—sometimes, I felt like a fucking babysitter with them —but I wanted to hear what Jaroth knew too. I didn't know if Sina would ever tell us.

If we didn't know what her father was capable of doing, then who the hell knew how far he would go? Would he be using humans who were armed with guns loaded with silver bullets and magic? Would he use other species against us? His obsession with Sina wasn't normal.

Before Jaroth could reach his destination—which looked like the back of the bar, where a bunch of other demons hung out—Thayer grabbed him by the back of his jacket. "We need to have a little talk, you fucking ass."

Jaroth stopped completely and looked over his shoulder. His eyes were hazy and looked as if he had just had sex at the Monster Dungeon, just down the road. Incubi were easy to read, especially after they just had their fill.

"Get your hands off me," Jaroth said, shrugging out of Thayer's hold. "What do you want?"

"To talk about Sina," Calder said, stepping forward.

Calder towered over Jaroth, his figure overcoming Jaroth's smaller and scrawnier one. But Jaroth didn't look even a bit intimidated or scared.

"About what? How I want her back?"

Calder growled.

"Of course I fucking do," Jaroth said. "She was the best thing to happen to me."

Before Calder could rip his head off, I stepped between the two of them and clenched my jaw. Hell, I was moments away from ripping off this man's head too. I didn't want him anywhere closer to our Sina.

"We want to know about her father …" I said, trailing off. "And what he did to her."

Jaroth suddenly dropped the act and stiffened. "What do you want to know?"

"Did he … did he … sexually abuse her?" I asked.

We were all thinking it, but nobody wanted to say it out loud, especially Sina. She wanted to keep this all under wraps and not go through the pain of it again. I fucking got that. But I needed to know.

I needed to know how we had failed to protect our mate all these years.

Jaroth clenched his jaw and didn't say anything.

"What else did he do to her?" I asked.

When he didn't respond again, Thayer grabbed him by his collar and thrust him against the wall. "What the fuck did he do to her? I know you fucking know. You're still obsessed with her even though you two broke up. You know some shit."

"You guys knew her before Sina's father took her away," Jaroth said, shoving Thayer back into a table. "You should've figured it out. As long as Sina has lived with her father, she's never had freedom. What the fuck do you think happened to her mother?"

My chest tightened, my throat drying. Sina never talked about her mother. She had died when Sina was barely seven years old. Did that mean that … Sina had been taking her father's abuse for that long? What had he been doing to her at that age?

"She was being abused for far longer than you know," Jaroth continued. "It's not my fucking place to talk about it. I don't even know the extent of it all. You should ask Sina, and if she doesn't want to tell you, that's a fucking *you* problem. It's not mine."

After one last hard shove, Jaroth pushed past us and walked toward the bar in the back, where there were a couple of succubi waiting for him. He slid onto one of the barstools, but didn't even look in their direction.

Jaroth might not have been Sina's mate, but that didn't mean he didn't care about her.

Only problem was that I wouldn't let him get in the way again. He had come so close to Sina multiple times since she'd been back in Durnbone, and I knew he wouldn't think twice about trying to sweep her off her feet and whisking her away from us.

Sina was ours.

38
the confession

sina

"SO, uh, Gaian told me that we're going to a Halloween party," Darius said, lying next to me in his bed and staring up at the ceiling.

All night, after the guys went out without me, we had been chatting about everything under the damn sun, it seemed. And I … really loved it.

Why hadn't we been this close four years ago? All I remembered was feeling so awkward around him and coming to him about problems with Calder. I never listened to any of his advice because I lost every train of thought around all of them. Reason had always gone out the window.

I inched closer to Darius and brushed my fingers against his. "Yeah, Maxine invited me."

When the others were out, Darius usually left me alone and gave me space to myself because Calder and Thayer didn't know the definition of personal space, apparently. But tonight, I didn't want to be alone. I wanted to be with someone.

I could think of nothing but what Jaroth had told me the other night—that Dad was close.

My stomach turned, my fears eating away at my insides. I didn't want it to be true, but I knew it was. Jaroth might've wanted to get back together with me, but he knew that I would never consider dating him again. But that didn't mean that he didn't still care.

Deep down, he was a good person. Or at least, he tried to be.

Shifting around on the bed because it was getting a bit warm in here, I moved closer to Darius, finding myself cooler around him when our skin touched. And before I knew it, I'd laid my entire body on his, straddling his waist with my head on his chest.

Heat wasn't as bad as it had been last night. Just these little touches felt good.

When we fell silent and the thoughts of Dad became too much, I lifted my head off his chest and looked him right in the eyes. "I need to tell you something. I wanted to wait until the others were here, but it's too much sometimes with Calder."

"Calder can be a bitch," Darius joked and sent me a small smile. "What is it?"

"About my father," I said, my voice strained and my entire body going rigid.

"You don't have to tell me," Darius whispered, brushing some hair out of my face.

"I need to," I whispered, clutching on to him tighter. "I need to tell you to protect you all."

Instead of pushing me—like Calder or Thayer would—he didn't say a single word and instead pulled me against his chest and moved his fingers back and forth across my hips. I sank deeper into him, deciding to put all my trust in him.

If I fell back into a nightmare or was going to live through hell again, just to get what had happened out into the world, then he would be there to hold me. He would be there to help me. I wasn't alone anymore. They weren't going to hurt me.

"My father has been experimenting with that poison since I was seven," I whispered, my chest tightening. "He gave the first few doses to my mother and killed her brain. Her body was still intact, but her brain was fried. Then … when he couldn't use her anymore, he shipped her away from me."

Pain shot through my body, tears filling my eyes. I clutched on to him tighter because I couldn't believe that I was saying this out loud. I had never told anyone, not even Jaroth, about my mother. I had been living a lie since I had been a child.

"When she was gone, he started giving it to me. The first few doses hurt me really bad. I couldn't go to school for months. I'm not sure if you remember when my father told you guys that I had the measles whenever you came to visit."

Darius tensed. "You didn't have the measles. It was … that poison?"

A sob escaped my lips. "Yes."

While Darius stayed quiet, he pulled me into his lap and leaned against the headboard, forcing me to look right at him. His black eyes were filled with so many emotions—so many—but I could only recognize the pain that mirrored mine.

"I'm sorry," he said, voice breaking, "that we couldn't protect you."

"I … I'm not finished," I whispered, curling my fingers into his thick chest muscles. "He would give me that poison and paralyze me with it. The first few times, he left it at that and studied my body. Then, he'd …"

Another pain. Another fucking stab in my heart.

"He'd what?"

"He'd invite his friends over," I whispered, body heaving back and forth. "I was seven! Seven years old when they started raping me, and I thought that was what everyone did. I didn't know any different. I thought it was normal! I thought it was fucking normal!"

More sobs escaped my lips. My body trembled violently back and forth. I couldn't stop myself, nor did I want to. I needed to get this out and tell someone so badly. I couldn't bottle it up anymore, not when I had finally realized that all this was wrong.

"They hurt you," he whispered, fingernails lengthening into claws against my flesh. "Who were they?"

"Powerful people," I whispered. "The most powerful people in each species."

"What are their names, Sina?" Darius asked, his canines lengthening. "Tell me."

"There is no point. You'll never be able to kill them all. There was a new man almost every night, and I can't … I can't remember them all. I can barely remember any of them. I fear that … my memories are so blurred that I'm just hallucinating this all."

"You're not," Darius confirmed.

"But what if I am? What if I'm just crazy?"

Darius gently grasped my face in his large hands. "You're not."

I stared down between us and placed my hands over his. Sometimes, it felt like I had gone crazy though. I'd had to endure so much shit from my father. What if it was all … just in my head? When I'd confronted him about it the first time and all the other times, he'd denied doing anything. He'd told me it was all a dream, that it was all made up.

"That's not all," I croaked out. "After he gave me the poison and his friends used me, they would do experiments on me. He wanted to try to create the perfect specimen out of me, the perfect *mate* for other species."

"Mate for other species?" Darius asked. "No other species has mates like wolves do."

"He never brought home a wolf," I said. "Not that I can remember anyway."

What I wanted to tell Darius—that I couldn't seem to say aloud —was that somewhere along the way, Dad's experiments went south. He had used my body too much, but instead of getting rid of me like he had with Mom …

He did something worse.

He had resurrected me as something much more … advanced.

39
the suspicion

darius

SINA HAD DETAILED MORE encounters than I could count.

I knew she needed to talk to someone, so I held in my anger with her father and held her for the entire night until she finally fell asleep in my arms after crying her eyes out. She needed me right now.

Staring out the window into the forest, I wondered why the gods would do something so horrendous to Sina. She had gone through so much fucking torture all by herself because she thought it was normal.

It didn't make sense, and it wasn't fair to her.

At one a.m., I heard the guys walk into the pack house. Calder growled about something having to do with Sina's ex-boyfriend, then barreled up the stairs and down the hallway. I gently rubbed Sina's head and closed my eyes, wondering why we hadn't seen this before.

We had spent so much time with Sina as children and teenagers. How could we have fucking missed that she was being abused at her own house by men thirty or more years older than her? Why hadn't we seen it? We were her fucking mates.

Calder must've been looking for Sina because he came banging on my bedroom door a few moments later. Instead of waiting, Thayer opened the door, and they all walked into the room, their gazes landing on Sina.

"Si—" Calder started.

A growl escaped my lips, and I bared my teeth at him. Sina had been through so fucking much tonight. I wasn't about to let her deal with Calder, the fucking asshole. As if he had never been talked back to before by me, he stared at me with wide eyes.

"Don't," I said through the mind link. "She's been through too much tonight. Don't start."

"We need to talk about what her father did to her," Gaian said.

"I already know," I said. "She told me everything. She doesn't need any more stress tonight."

"She told you?" Calder asked.

While he didn't look angry per se, he looked upset, and I didn't know why. He was the one who had hidden shit from Sina, and he was the one who had pushed her away. But seeing the cold, hard-headed alpha upset made my stomach turn.

"Yes," I said aloud. "She told me."

"We ran into her ex-boyfriend," Thayer said.

Immediately, I tensed and placed Sina down in the center of my bed. Once I knew that she wouldn't wake up, I scooted out of the bed and grabbed a shirt to pull over my head. Instead of waking Sina, I nodded toward the hallway.

We all walked out of my room, and I shut the door softly behind me. "What'd he say?"

"That he wants her back," Thayer growled. "We gotta fucking watch out for him. Something about him doesn't seem right to me. He's too fucking nice to her, and demons in Durnbone are not nice at fucking all. There's nothing good about any of them."

"He's her ex," I said, shrugging. "He probably knows what happened."

"I agree with Thayer," Gaian said, shocking us fucking all. "Something is off about him."

"What is it?"

Gaian paced back and forth in the hallway, crossed his arms, and shook his head. "I don't know. I just have a bad feeling. I've never seen the guy in Durnbone before Sina escaped here. Now, all of a sudden, he's just here all the time."

"He wants Sina back," Calder concluded. "Of course he's going to be here."

"But what if it's more than that?" Gaian asked.

"It's not more than that," I said. As much as I wanted to get rid of him, we couldn't. "Sina told me that he knows her father is gathering men at the border to come find her. He's going to find out as much information this weekend as he can for her."

"Goddamn it," Calder said. "Why does she keep that shit from us?"

"I told you at the tavern," Thayer growled. "It's because you're an ass."

"There is no time to fight," I said. "We gotta get through this weekend, and then we can confront him to see what kind of information he found. If we think he's lying, then we can take care of him."

"*I'll* take care of him," Thayer clarified, eyes glinting red. He turned around and stormed down the staircase, heading in the direction of the prison, where he loved torturing and killing people who had betrayed us. "In the only way I know how!"

40
the rogue fight

calder

SINA DIDN'T TRUST ME.

I balled my hands into fists and paced around my bedroom, breathing in her thick scent drifting underneath my closed door. All the others had gone to bed hours ago, but I couldn't sleep tonight. It seemed that all I could think about was how terrible I had been.

Why hadn't I noticed that Sina was being abused for years—for fucking years? Had I been that bad of a mate, that bad of an alpha, that I couldn't figure out that Sina being sick was just her father's disgusting excuse for being a piece of shit?

My chest tightened, my throat closing. I should've fucking been there. I should've taken the pain away from her, just like I had tried to take all the pain from the guys these past four years. It was the least I could've fucking done. And I had fucking failed at that.

I'd failed my mate.

After tearing off my clothes, I sprinted down the stairs, out the back door, and into the woods, like I had done every night for a year straight after we lost Sina the first time. I ran through the forest, toward enemy territory, and lurked through the thick fog. If I strayed too far from Durnbone, then I'd enter the Vaneroy Forest, where all types of monsters hunted.

A pack of rogues stalked along the edge of Durnbone's forest, howling and searching for prey to feast on for tonight. Instead of watching them carefully, like I had learned to do these past four years, I ran right out into the open, where they could see me, and growled menacingly at them.

Anger and rage and fury pumped through my veins. I wanted them to hurt me. I wanted them to cut my fucking flesh to pieces. I was a shitty alpha and a shitty mate after all these years. I fucking deserved it.

Licking their lips hungrily, five rogues surrounded me. I growled again and bared my teeth, wanting one of these smaller wolves to pounce on me so they all would. They thought they had found an alpha they could feast on tonight.

But I had found five lone wolves that nobody gave a fuck about that I could kill.

Fucking finally, the leader sprinted at me. I let him sink his teeth into my shoulder and rip out a piece of my flesh. Pain shot through my body—that familiar feeling that I had come to love. Another jumped on me, slicing his claws through my side and right over my ribs.

Before I knew it, all five were on top of me, biting and scratching and chewing on an alpha's flesh. They probably thought that I was some weak man that they could overtake, and they'd be right about the first part.

I was weak as fuck.

Collapsing to the ground, I barely held my head up straight. Blood pooled out of my body from various open wounds. When I closed my eyes, I saw Sina smiling at Darius, Gaian, and Thayer and not even sparing me a glance.

While my nightmares used to be about Sina's father tearing her away from me, all I had been dreaming of lately was Sina hating me for the rest of my shitty life. She'd always turn in the other direction, smile, and laugh with the others, leaving me the fuck out.

Someone pierced their claws into my neck, dangerously close to my artery. I growled in response, kicking the guy off me and killing him instantly. The other four came at me harder and faster. My vision blurred with the blood loss, so I had to make this quick.

From either side of me, two jumped toward me. I stepped out of the way, letting them smash into each other, and then I slashed their throats and killed them too. Stars filled my vision, and I knew that if I didn't heal soon, I'd pass the fuck out for real.

After tearing into the fourth's underbelly until his guts spilled out, I turned toward their leader and sank my teeth into his neck, ripping out his pathetic throat. And when I had killed the last rogue, I shifted into my human and collapsed in a puddle of their blood in the middle of the forest, where nobody would ever find me. No sane wolf came down to these parts of the woods that surrounded Durnbone.

I curled my knees to my tightening chest and stared through watery eyes at the moon. The Moon Goddess would be so fucking disappointed in the mate and man that I was. I couldn't protect my mate then, and I feared that I wouldn't be able to protect her now.

No matter what my pack thought, no matter what the guys thought, no matter what Sina thought, I wasn't a strong alpha. I couldn't do half the shit that I promised. I feared that everything would crumble for a second time.

Sina deserved more than me. She knew it. The guys knew it. Everyone fucking knew it.

"I'm no good for her," I whispered, shaking my head and letting a single fucking tear fall.

Nobody knew how many times I had cried these past four years. Every day that passed without seeing Sina, my heart had shattered just a bit more. And now that she was finally back, I couldn't be the man she needed because I had been the alpha the guys needed.

I had been strong and protected them when they were broken. But nobody ever asked how I was. Nobody ever fucking asked if I was okay. Nobody fucking cared about me the way that I cared about them, especially not Sina now.

As I lay helpless in the middle of the forest, my wounds from the rogue fight began healing. And I cursed my enhanced wolf senses. All I wanted was to feel the pain, to simmer in it for a few moments longer.

So, I lengthened one of my nails into a talon and cut through the wound to keep it open. Blood slowly seeped out of it, drooling from the wound and onto the twigs and leaves underneath me.

I closed my eyes, finally feeling my body relax and letting another tear fall down my cheek. "I love her so much," I whispered to myself. "And I can't do anything about it anymore. I can't even make her happy."

41
the breakfast

sina

THE NEXT MORNING, I padded downstairs to grab some breakfast and to finish packaging the last of the potions. I wanted to find a couple places around the forest and around Durnbone today to hide them, in case something went terribly wrong within the next couple of weeks.

"Morning," Gaian said, cracking eggs over a pan on the stove. "Sleep well?"

I glanced around the kitchen at Thayer, who looked pissed like usual, and Darius, who gave me a small smile. Calder wasn't here this morning, which surprised me. Usually, he liked fucking with me from the moment I woke up to the moment I fell asleep.

"Okay," I said, wanting to keep the conversation short.

If I gave him a real answer, it'd be that I'd barely slept all last night. Pains kept shooting through my entire body, as if someone were stabbing me with their claws. Not only that, but the sleep I had gotten was filled with nightmares about Dad.

"You don't look too sure about that, Pretty Bird," Darius said.

Thayer growled. "Leave her the fuck alone."

After grabbing the potion mix and potion bottles from the closet, I opened the last few containers and began pouring in the liquid in silence. For it being almost ten a.m., Calder not bothering me was sorta, kinda weird.

"Has anyone seen Calder?" I asked, shutting the cap on a bottle.

Just as if the asshole knew I was talking about him, he opened the back door and walked into the house, completely naked. Scars and blood decorated his tan, muscular body, and dark bags lay under his eyes.

My eyes widened. While something inside me urged me to hurry over to him to help him clean his wounds, I stayed glued to the spot. It wasn't like he'd do something like that for me even though I was his mate.

But still, I couldn't do nothing, so I said, "What happened to you?"

He didn't look over at me. "Nothing."

"Calder."

Instead of snapping at me like I expected him to, he stopped in his tracks with his back flexed and turned toward me. "What, Sina?" he asked, voice surprisingly quieter and softer than usual but hoarse.

"I ..." I started. But I didn't know what the fuck I wanted to say to him.

Screw that. I knew exactly what I wanted to say to him. I wanted to ask him who the fuck had given him those scars and wounds, whose blood was on his body, and where I could find them. My chest was tight with anger, a wolfish, blinding rage rushing through me.

"Who gave those to you?" I asked through clenched teeth, my voice low.

All the guys—even Calder—snapped their heads in my direction, as if they were surprised about what I had just said, or maybe it was the way that I'd said it. I didn't know, but either way, I wanted answers.

"Why do you want to know?"

"Gods, are you an idiot?!" I asked, eyes wide and teeth aching … teeth aching to rip into someone, to kill them for the wounds they had left on my mate's body. Heat quickly engulfed my body, making it flushed and pounding and red.

Why couldn't he understand that even though he was a fucking jerk sometimes, I still cared about him? If I hadn't, then I would've left here a long time ago. I'd escaped Dad's estate without him finding me, so I could've easily escaped his pack house.

Even though I'd tried before, I didn't really want to leave. I never wanted to leave them.

After running my hands through my hair, I let out a low growl and turned back to the potions. I didn't want to say it out loud because I feared that I'd look like a dumbass. Gaian, Darius, and Thayer knew that Calder treated me like shit sometimes. And my stupid ass still liked him for some damn reason.

None of the guys moved as I continued packing the potions. I pursed my lips and stared down at the liquid, making sure to use every last drop of it. Maybe I would have Gaian take me back down to the witch's little shop in Durnbone, so I could get more ingredients.

"I'm going to hide these around the property today and some in town," I said.

"I'll come with you," Calder said, grabbing some spare clothes from a closet, then walking into the bathroom. "Give me a second."

I arched a brow and began placing the potions inside my backpack. While I didn't want him to come with me, I really didn't have a choice in the matter. He would come with me whether I wanted him to or not.

Sighing, I zipped my bag. Calder walked out of the bathroom with the blood wiped off his body and toward the back door, where I now waited. Once I smiled at Gaian and told him that I'd try his new breakfast egg recipe later, I walked out into the fall air. Calder trailed behind me at first, then jogged up next to me, surprisingly being quieter than any other day. Usually, he was a loudmouthed asshole.

I found a couple of spots around the pack house to hide the potions in, then started toward Durnbone, loathing that Calder still hadn't said a word to me. In fact, he even helped me place the potions.

"All right," I said, stopping in front of him and crossing my arms. "What the fuck is up with you? Why are you being nice and quiet to me today? You're usually an annoying-ass prick who won't leave me alone."

"I can't be nice?"

"No! You're Calder. You're not nice." I stepped forward and craned my head up at the alpha. "So, what's your problem?"

"I don't have a problem, Sina."

"You obviously do."

Calder clenched his jaw, that golden spark blazing in his eyes. His wolf was back and wanted out. But instead of letting him run free and bitch me out, Calder kept him contained. "Forget it. Let's just go to Durnbone to drop these off."

"No, I'm not just going to forget it."

"Goddess, Sina," he said, running a hand through his hair. "I don't know what you want from me. One minute, you're bitching and complaining and hating that I'm an asshole to you. The next minute, you won't stop bitching and complaining that I'm *not* an asshole to you."

My heart raced a bit faster, my breath catching in the back of my throat. "I'm not bitching and complaining," I exclaimed, but I mighta, sorta been bitching and complaining.

Around Calder, I couldn't help it. I wanted him so badly.

"Don't fucking do that," he growled through his canines, glancing down at my legs pressed together. He squeezed his eyes closed and took an unsteady breath. "Don't fucking do that to me, Sina. Just tell me what you fucking want from me."

While he was giving me every *freaking* chance to tell him how I wanted him to act around me, how I didn't want him to be an asshole all the time, how I wanted him to care about me and not just about the idea of his ideal mate, I found myself completely throwing all that out the window.

"I want you to breed me, Calder."

42

the tree

sina

A LOW, throaty growl escaped Calder's throat. Heat rushed to my core, and I ground my thighs together, unable to stop the pressure building between them already. Calder wrapped one hand around the front of my throat and shoved me against a tree.

"Don't fuck around with me, Sina," he growled into my ear, his voice straining and every one of his muscles flexing against my body. "I'm trying fucking hard to be … to fucking be different for you, and then you say shit like that."

I curled my fingers into his chest and whimpered, the heat engulfing my body. "I'm not fucking around with you. My panties are soaked at the thought of you taking me right here and right now, of you emptying your cum into me."

"Sina," he ground out, like if I said another word, he'd completely break. "Don't."

My pussy was pounding, my clit aching. I wanted him so badly that it hurt me. The heat might've been taking full effect, making me want him more than anything, making me not care about the asshole that he'd been to me. But deep down, I knew it wasn't controlling me.

"I'm sorry, Calder," I whispered, grasping his wrist. "I can't help it."

Calder's eyes glimmered a bright gold, his jaw twitching.

"Breed me," I whimpered, rubbing my body against his. "Breed me. Please, breed me."

Before I could react, Calder swiftly shoved his hand down the front of my leggings, sank his fingers into my panties, and touched my sopping cunt. He growled underneath his breath and pressed his hardening cock against my stomach.

Whimpering again, I moved closer to him, aching for every single part of his body to be pressed against mine. He was already touching me, but I wanted him closer. I wanted him inside me, pumping in and out, burying deeper and deeper inside me.

"Please, Calder," I begged.

When Calder reached down to undo the zipper on his jeans, I shimmied out of my pants and went to turn around to press my chest against the tree. But he twirled me back around so I faced him and tightened his hand around my throat.

"You stay like this, Pretty Bird."

After he pulled out his huge dick, he wrapped his hands underneath my thighs and lifted me into the air. I fastened my arms around his shoulders and my legs around his waist, clenching when I felt him position himself at my entrance.

"Breed me, please!" I cried as he thrust his huge cock inside my tight pussy.

With one hand on my ass and the other trailing up my body, he pumped in and out of me. An overwhelming pleasure rushed through me. I tightened around him, feeling every single ridge of his cock move against me.

"Deeper," I whispered. "Please, deeper."

He tucked one hand behind my head and placed his lips against mine. I kissed him hard, letting his tongue slip into my mouth. He roughly sucked on my lower lip, and I realized that I'd never really kissed him like this.

For the past couple decades of our friendship, we had only ever really pecked. The other times during sex, they really didn't count. They hadn't been filled with passion the way that this kiss was—with raw want and need.

I couldn't get enough of it.

"I'm going to kill every bastard who's ever hurt you," he murmured into my mouth.

Pulling him closer, I moved my lips against his and whined, "Deeper, please, Calder."

"Pretty Bird," he growled, kissing me harder as he leaned back against the tree and bounced me up and down on his cock. He grunted, the sound making me clamp down on his cock, and then he stopped pumping into me. "Fuuuuck, Sina."

"Empty your balls into me," I whimpered, my body tense and on the brink of orgasm. "Please, I'm begging you."

He leaned his forehead against mine, slipped his tongue into my mouth again, and slammed up even higher into me, grunting and groaning into our kiss. I clutched on to him, feeling his body tense and relax, and couldn't help myself from crying out into his mouth.

Pleasure rushed through me, my pussy pulsing around his thick cock. My arms slipped from around his shoulders, but he wrapped his arms around my torso and hugged me tight to him so I wouldn't fall over—or maybe he hugged me because he wanted to.

Secretly, I hoped it was for the latter reason.

After a few deep breaths, Calder finally pulled out of me and let his cum-covered dick smack against his thigh. He hugged me for a few moments longer, even when he didn't have to, and then sighed against the crook of my neck.

When he released me, I took a wobbly step toward my leggings on the ground and pulled them on as he redid his pants. His cum filled my pussy, and I knew it'd end up staining my underwear and maybe even my leggings today too.

"So, are you going to tell me why you're acting so nice to me?" I asked, glancing up.

He turned toward me, jaw twitching. "You told Darius what happened to you."

"So, you're being nice out of pity, I suppose," I said, feeling hurt that Darius would just tell the other guys. But I didn't know why I'd expected him not to say a word about it to anyone. They were all overly possessive mates.

"No," he growled. "Because I'm a jealous asshole—that's why. Now, come on."

When he started down the path toward Durnbone, I quickly hurried after him. "Well, of course you are." I rolled my eyes and moved closer to him to steal his body heat as a crisp fall air chilled my skin. "But that still didn't answer my question."

"If you can't figure out that I want *you* to be as comfortable around me as you are with Gaian, Darius, and Thayer, then I don't know what to fucking tell you, Sina." He clenched his jaw and continued down the path.

"If I didn't feel comfortable around you, then I wouldn't have let you come with me today."

"Pfft, you didn't have a choice," he said, but his voice sounded lighter now, and his shoulders weren't as hunched over and tense. He peeked a glance over at me. "I'm not letting you out of my fucking sight, Pretty Bird. Never again."

43
the demon's family

thayer

CALDER AND SINA had left the pack house a while ago, and I couldn't fucking stand sitting in this house, doing nothing. Last night at the tavern, something had been off about Sina's ex-boyfriend, and I needed to figure it the fuck out.

I walked down the main street in central Durnbone and growled to myself, shaking my head in disbelief that I had actually walked all the way here to see the one person I despised more than anyone in this fucking world.

Nobody else in the pack had connections to demons, except me, which meant that I had to go see that dreadful woman who forced me to call her mother down in the demon sector of Durnbone. I hadn't seen her in years now.

After finding my way to a demon club that she attended frequently, I gritted my teeth, cursed myself out, and stepped into the building. Fire burned through the first room, the flames licking the ceiling and the heat hotter than fucking hell. It ensured that only demons stepped into this space; no other species were allowed.

Once I walked through the fucking fire that seared the edges of my clothes, I opened a heavy metal door and stepped into The

Inferno. Demons in their truest forms sauntered around the room, their horns out and lengthened and their eyes a piercing red.

Some incubi danced with women, others with corpses. A group of wrathful demons threw knives at innocent slaves to see who could kill them first. I gritted my teeth and scanned the room for *her*.

When I caught my mother sitting near the back with a glass of blood in her hand, she looked over at me almost as if she sensed—or smelled—my presence.

I made a beeline toward her, grabbed the man flirting with her, and shoved him out of his seat. "We need to talk."

She placed her glass down on the glass coffee table, crossed one leg over the other, and smirked at me. "My son, it's been too long. Four years already?"

"Cut the fucking shit. I'm not here to forgive you. I need answers."

"Answers?" she asked, arching a sharp brow. "About what?"

"The same fucking thing I wanted answers to four years ago," I growled, attracting the attention of some demons. Usually, I could blend right into this crowd, but not when my canines grew three times the length of theirs and I couldn't stop my wolf from coming out. "What do you know about Sina's father?"

Rolling her eyes, she picked up her glass and took another sip. "I know nothing."

"Don't give me that fucking bullshit," I growled through my canines. "Where the fuck is he? I know you fucking know something, and I know you know what he did to her for her entire life, don't you?"

While my mother kept up a harsh expression, I could tell that she knew exactly what I was talking about. She might've been hard for others to read, but she was an open fucking book to me. Mostly because I hated her.

"I know you blame me for her and her father's disappearance, but I can assure you that I know nothing, *son*."

Even her mere voice made me want to kill her.

"Let's get one thing fucking straight," I said, smacking the glass table and shattering it to pieces. "I didn't blame you for Sina's disappearance. I blamed you for not trying to help me find her after she left."

She had the fucking senses to sniff out *any* scent better than a wolf. She had powers far greater than almost any other demon around. She was one of the highest-ranked demons in all of Durnbone. She could've found them.

"But you didn't want me to find her, did you?" I let out a lifeless laugh. "You're working with him."

Instead of denying everything I had said, my mother took a sip of another drink and sat back on the plush white couch. I gritted my teeth and balled my fists, the fire burning from my palms. I wanted to end her life right fucking now.

But if I tried anything *here*, the other demons would kill me.

"Why does Sina interest you so much?" my mother asked.

"Because she's my mate."

She rolled her eyes. "You and your father with all that mating crap."

Knowing that I wouldn't get much out of her, I leaned forward and watched her carefully. "What do you know about Jaroth?"

Suddenly, my mother choked on the fucking drink she sipped. While she quickly recovered from it, I ached to force more down her sick throat so she'd fucking die already. Demons lived for centuries longer than humans, and I didn't want to wait that long to see *my dear fucking mother* go.

"What are you going on about now?"

"Who is he?"

"He's nobody important."

"A rumor has been floating around that he's going to be the next ruler of demons," I said, tilting my head and finally feeling as if I had one-upped her.

I didn't know shit about Sina's ex-boyfriend, but everything I had said up to now seemed to strike a chord with her, and there had been talk around the demon world that a new ruler was coming to power soon once the demon queen stepped down.

"I'm not answering any more of your idiotic questions."

My lips twitched. "I'm right."

"You are the furthest from the truth." She seethed. "And you're no longer welcome here. The Inferno is for demons only, and you're nothing but a wolf who is up to no good. You're banned from this place forever."

"Fucking good. I'm going to find out whatever the fuck he's up to," I growled, smacking the drink out of her hand and storming out of The Inferno.

I might not have found the answers that I had come here for, but I had found out enough.

44

the coven

sina

IN DOWNTOWN DURNBONE, I stepped into Witch's Brew to buy more vampire blood and herbs to make my potions. Calder followed me into the small store and toward the back, where the same witch from the other day eyed us.

"You're back?" she asked, arching a brow and adjusting her black stocking, caught on the corner of her desk. After moving closer to us, she leaned against a table and crossed her arms. "Are you back for more blood and herbs?"

"Yes."

"Don't have much left," she said, walking to the back of the shop and grabbing the last small vial of vampire blood. "Last night, I had a couple of customers come in to buy almost all the vials I had left. Good thing I forgot about this one way in the back."

"Someone …" I asked, mouth drying. "Someone came in to buy them all?"

She handed me the last vial and held out her hand for money in return. I rummaged through my purse to give her whatever I could find because I wanted to get out of Durnbone as soon as humanly possible.

"A tall, slender human man."

"No," I whispered, backing up until I hit Calder's front. "Gods, please, no."

I would bet that tall, slender human man also had brown eyes so friendly that anyone would trust him, a smile that could win over anyone, and glasses that amplified his intelligence and attractiveness to others.

"There was something evil lurking within that man," she said. "Something that none of the customers could see, but I could feel it. A witch can always tell the intentions of others, especially those with murky malice lying within their soul."

After swallowing hard, I gripped the vial in my hand and grabbed Calder's bicep with the other. He thanked the witch as I dragged him to the exit of the shop. She had been nicer to me than she had been the other day but … if Dad had been here, I wanted to go home.

We would head to the Halloween party tonight, dressed in costumes so nobody would recognize us, and then I wanted to be locked away in their pack house for good. I didn't want them to let me out, no matter how hard my heat got or how much … I wanted to help them.

I didn't want Dad to hurt me ever again.

Once we stepped into the chilly fall air, Calder grabbed my hand in his larger one and gave it a good squeeze. "I told you that we're going to protect you, no matter what. When we find your dickhead father, I'll kill—"

"No," I snapped. But then, because we had shared that one small moment earlier, I looked down at my feet and shook my head. "Look, I'm sorry. I know you want to protect me. I know you want to kill anyone who has hurt me, but you can't."

No matter how hard anyone tried, they wouldn't be able to stop him. The only person who could stop him would be me because I knew everything about him and knew exactly what kind of world he wanted to build. I knew his secrets too.

Calder dropped my hand and gritted his teeth. "Fuck, Sina. Just let me fucking protect you for once. Why the hell don't you believe in me, in *us*? You don't know what your father threw at us when he took you away. You don't know the hell we had to go through to fucking survive."

"You don't know the hell that *I* had to survive!"

My words came out harsher than I'd meant them, but I had so much anger built up inside me from these past four years. I thought I was the only person who'd had it rough when, in reality, my guys were hurting just as bad.

Sighing through my nose, I stopped in the middle of the street and stared up into Calder's eyes. He had so much hurt and fear and agony built up in his eyes, pain that I had never once stopped to try to heal.

Sure, Calder was fucked in the head a bit. But weren't we all?

"I'm so—"

Before I could finish my sentence, someone growled lowly from behind us. I looked over my shoulder to see Thayer rushing out of the town center, too, with his brows furrowed in an angry stare and his canine teeth dripping with saliva.

"What are you doing here?" I asked.

Thayer stormed past us, his fiery fingertips blazing against mine as he grabbed my hand and pulled me away from Calder. We walked down Durnbone's main street, back toward the pack house, and Calder jogged up next to us.

"I had a nice visit with my mother," Thayer said between gritted teeth. "Turns out that *someone's* ex-boyfriend is in the running to become the next leader of the demons. And if that's not fucking *suspicious* to you, I don't know what the fuck is."

"Who? Jaroth?" I asked. "What do you mean by suspicious? He's going to see if he can get any information out of my father this weekend."

"We heard," Thayer snapped, glaring at Calder. "We saw him last night."

"Yeah, I know," I said, taking a peek at Calder too. "But what does that have to do with him being suspicious?"

Calder and Thayer shared an intense look, and then Thayer looked away. To my surprise—and Thayer's too, it seemed—Calder growled.

"We don't trust him," Calder said, scanning the woods. "None of us."

"Just because he's my ex?"

"No," Thayer snapped, squeezing my hand tighter. "Because he knew what was happening to you and decided to do nothing about it. They all fucking did, and yet you were held captive by your father for four years."

"He couldn't do anything about it," I reasoned. "He didn't know what had been happening to me until after we stopped dating, until I caught him with another woman. After that … he found out through *other* means."

"Like what?"

"Like he tried to come to my home at four in the morning to win me back after he sleazed around in the incubi bars, fucking all types of women from all different species, and found me unable to move in the center of my bed."

"But—"

"No buts," I said, shaking my head. "He didn't know."

But it seemed like Thayer and Calder still didn't believe me because they shared another silent look, their eyes glazing over, as if they were speaking through their mind link connection.

"Let's go," Thayer said, picking up his pace. "I don't want to be out in the open any longer. We're going home, and then tonight, we're going out to the Halloween party, and that's it. No-fucking-where else until this is all over."

And I wasn't going to complain about that.

45

the costume

gaian

THREE HOURS AFTER SINA, Thayer, and Calder came home from Durnbone, I knocked on Sina's door. Thayer and Calder had gone out to *talk* about how to protect Sina, to make battle plans, or do whatever the fuck they did whenever they left.

"Come in!" Sina called.

I opened the door and stepped into the room, making sure to shut it quietly behind me. Sina lay on the bed, dressed in a little tank top and shorts. While Calder and Thayer might've wanted to talk about protecting her, I wanted her to relax for once. She had been nothing but stressed the fuck out since she had left her father.

Tonight, I wanted her mind at ease.

"We don't leave for the party for another couple of hours," she said, sitting up and leaning against the headboard, her knees bent and feet flat on the bed. "You're in here to dress me up already?"

After tossing a plastic bag on her bed, I smiled. "Maybe I'm a bit early."

"So," Sina said, smiling back and glancing down at the bag, "what am I wearing?"

It was filled with pieces of her costume. Her gaze flickered down to it, eyes widening slightly as she pressed her legs together. Ever since she had gotten back earlier with Calder and Thayer, her cunt had been salivating so much that I could smell it through the door.

And my wolf wouldn't let me have another moment of peace by myself. I had been aching to come into her bedroom and dress her in a slutty little Halloween outfit. Just thinking about her in this had had me hard all last night.

After pulling out piece by piece—because this costume came in many small pieces that didn't cover much—I laid it on the bed and curled a finger at her. "Come here."

She glanced down at the latex material that would cling to every inch of her body and whimpered softly, the sound making my dick twitch. She crawled over to me, sitting on her knees and staring up at me, eyes wide.

I gently grabbed her chin and brushed my thumb across her bottom lip, inhaling the thick scent of her arousal. She might've only been experiencing some heat these past few days, but she was driving me wild.

"Let's get you dressed early," I said, glancing down at her full lips. "Take off your clothes."

Pressing her thighs even closer together, she fingered the hem of her tank top and slowly pulled it over her head, letting her breasts fall out of it. I clenched my jaw, wanting to take them into my hands and squeeze them.

But if I touched her … I would fucking lose it.

"Your shorts too," I said, picking up the tiny black latex costume.

She jumped out of the bed, her breasts bouncing, and shimmied out of her shorts, standing naked in front of me. I held up the costume to the front of her body, imagining how it'd look on her. I didn't even know if her tits would fit inside it.

"Why don't you shimmy into this?"

Sina sucked on the inside of her cheek and took it from me, pulling it through her legs first. Once she got it past her wide hips, she placed her arms through her straps and pulled it over her breasts. The material clung to her body, the little pieces of fabric covering her nipples but showing underboob and enough cleavage to make me hard as fuck.

If this was what her breasts looked like now, I couldn't fucking wait to see what her tits would look like while she was pregnant. Her full breasts would be even bigger and rounder, waiting to be groped and sucked on.

"You look so fucking good, Pretty Bird," I growled.

She stepped closer to me and drew her fingers up the bulge in my pants. "I can tell."

Another low growl rumbled from my throat, and I had to force myself to step away from her or else I would say fuck this Halloween party and take her for the rest of the night.

"Last but not least …" I picked up a mask, which would cover her mouth and nose, from the bed and handed it to her. "Put this on."

"This?" she asked, eyebrows furrowed. "But why? I won't be able to wear lipstick or—"

"Forget about the lipstick," I said. "Wear the mask."

"But—"

"Wear it, Sina. Trust me."

Sina didn't know what we had in store for her. Tonight, she was going to be our good little cumslut.

46
the party

sina

DRESSED in a tiny black latex costume that didn't hide *anything*, I curled my arm around Gaian's and stepped onto the sidewalk that led to Maxine's Halloween party. While Maxine might've been hosting, I hadn't been to her home in over four years, and I was in awe.

Maxine lived alone in a house that her ancestors had passed down through the generations. Sitting on the outskirts of Durnbone, the gray stone house stood three stories tall against the foggy night. It was covered in cobwebs and fake spiders, blood and gore.

"Sina!" Maxine shouted as we approached the doorway, as if she had been waiting for us. She threw her arms around my shoulders and pulled me into the house. When she finally pulled away, she looked me up and down, her gaze lingering on my barely covered body. "Yes! You look so sexy!"

"Maxine!" I said, covering my breasts with my hands, not enjoying her sudden attention. "Can you lower your voice?"

The guys might've dressed me tonight, but I didn't want the attention from any other species or people besides them. I had too much other shit to worry about than wandering eyes.

"No, bitch," she said with a grin, shutting the door behind my four guys. "You're sexy AF."

My cheeks flushed as Calder grabbed my hand.

"Thanks for the invite, Maxine."

I cut my gaze to him, knowing well that nobody had invited him or *any* of them. They'd all just decided to come once they figured out that Maxine had invited me over. They weren't about to let me out of their sight, and after earlier, I didn't want them to either.

"Come on," Maxine said, pulling me through the crowd. "I want you to meet Xorgor."

"Xorgor," I repeated.

I had only seen her boyfriend a couple of times in passing. He seemed to stay out of the crowd and the drama in Durnbone, and I didn't blame him. I didn't want Maxine to be messed up in all the craziness. She'd already had a shit time, growing up, from bullies who joked about the scars from a werewolf attack on her chest.

Thankfully, growing up, Calder, Thayer, Darius, and Gaian had completely slaughtered the pack who had done this to her. Or at least, I thought they had because I had innocently asked the day after my sixteenth birthday to make things right, and the next day, she had found their leader's head on her front steps.

Still, nobody looked at her the same for the rest of her time here. It pissed me off.

"Xorgor!" Maxine called, pushing through the crowd and into the back, where a group of demons hung out.

Thayer walked closer to me, snatching my hand out of Calder's and growling at the demons who looked me up and down. "Don't fucking look them in the eye, Pretty Bird. Don't trust any one of these fuckers."

A couple of moments later, a tall demon sidestepped around other rowdy guys. One half of his face was humanlike—a green eye, pale skin, and shaggy brown hair. The other side of his face was stuck in a demonlike form—a red eye, charred skin, and jagged teeth that couldn't be covered by his lips.

People stepped out of his way and made it a point to avoid him altogether, as if he had some sort of disease. Most demons that I had met could usually switch in and out of their demon forms, but he seemed to be stuck like this.

Thayer eyed him for a long time, then nodded to Xorgor, as if he accepted him unlike everyone else. Demons seemed to stick with their own kind—sex demons with sex demons, wrathful demons with wrathful demons. I guessed, being a half-wolf, half-demon mix made Thayer an outcast too, just like Xorgor seemed to be.

Maxine wrapped her arm around Xorgor's and beamed up at the man who stood at least a solid two feet taller than her. For the first time, Maxine looked truly in love. I grinned back at her, happy as hell that she'd found someone to accept her.

Once she disappeared into the crowd with him, talking to a couple other people who had walked into the party, I scanned the room for any sign of my ex-boyfriend. Like expected, Jaroth hadn't shown up tonight. When I used to date him, he would be at every party, no matter how big or small. If he wasn't here tonight, that meant one thing … he still really cared and wanted to help out.

I didn't want to date him, and I *never* would again after what he did to me, but something stirred inside me at the mere thought of him actually trying to find information about my father's plans and whereabouts. I wanted this to be over already.

But if what the guys believed was true and Jaroth really wasn't to be trusted, then I was glad that he wasn't here tonight either. My guys might've wanted to show him that I was theirs, but I didn't want them to be in danger.

So, throughout the night, I walked around the party and chatted with a couple of people who ogled my body. At some point, Calder, Gaian, and Darius had all dispersed through the crowd to talk to people they knew around Durnbone while I stayed glued to Thayer's hip.

"Can I take this mask off?" I asked Thayer, squeezing his hand to stay close.

More and more people began crowding into the room, the air becoming heavier with everyone's body heat. Hundreds of scents flooded through my nose, and I desperately needed some fresh air. This mask wasn't doing shit right now.

Not to mention, the way some people were staring at me was sorta, kinda making me horny.

Thayer took one longing look at me and smirked, as if he knew something about my costume that I didn't know. "No."

"Why? What does it—"

Before I could even finish my sentence, something slipped all the way into my mouth and down my throat. My eyes widened with tears as I gagged on the object and grabbed on to Thayer. I tried to open my mouth to speak, but I couldn't get out a single word.

Instead of helping me, Thayer grinned even wider, wrapped an arm around my shoulder, and pulled me closer to him to whisper into my ear. "Tonight, you're our cute little cumslut, who's going to take our cum anywhere we want you to."

I let out some muffled words that even I couldn't understand.

"Do you remember that trinket shop and the underwear that let us use you?" Thayer said, strumming his fingers over my shoulder and making the hairs on my arms rise. "Well, we got one for your bratty little mouth too. And we plan on enjoying it tonight, Pretty Bird."

47

the drool

THAYER WRAPPED his arm around my waist and guided me through party as Calder, Darius, and Gaian used that toy to fuck my throat. And I could do nothing and say nothing without globs of spit and drool running down my throat.

Demons that Thayer knew had come up to us and directed questions at me, but I kept my lips sealed and let Thayer do all the talking. It wasn't like I would actually be able to say anything in return. And while I knew that Thayer didn't like any of these guys, I knew he loved watching me be a mess.

"Look at your filthy little mouth," Thayer said, using his finger to wipe some drool running down my chin once a couple of demons left us by the bar alone. He moved his finger lower and lower to trace the cock buried deep inside my throat. "Do you think anyone has noticed yet?"

For a moment, whoever was buried in my throat pulled out to let me breathe. I inhaled sharply, my chest rising and falling in this slutty little outfit. "I … I don't know," I whispered, heart racing and cheeks flushing. "I hope not."

But truthfully, I believed that *everyone* had noticed me being face-fucked.

"Well then," Thayer growled, pulling out a hair elastic from his pocket and fisting my hair in his hands, "let's make sure that everyone does." He pulled my hair behind my shoulders, letting only a few strands slip out. "After tonight, everyone is going to know not to mess with what's ours."

"You're psy—"

Before I could finish my sentence, someone slipped their dick back into my throat. I gagged on it and grabbed Thayer's hand, tears welling up in my eyes again from the sudden movement.

"Open your mouth wider," Thayer ordered, gently pushing the hair out of my face.

I opened wider to breathe, but the only things that came out of my mouth were sloppy, spit-filled squeaking and gagging sounds as my guys used my mouth. Thayer wrapped his arms around me from behind and ground his cock against my barely covered ass underneath my skirt.

"Everyone is staring at you," he murmured into my ear.

Glancing around the party, I realized that everyone really was staring at me. Demons, wolves, vampires, witches, and even some majestic faeries that rarely attended Durnbone parties. I moved back against Thayer to hide myself, but he was having none of it.

"You look like my easy little slut tonight," Thayer growled into my ear.

A small whimper escaped my throat, and I pressed my thighs together. I loved being used and abused by these four guys who I trusted more than anything. I loved their filthy mouths and the way they wanted me to dress up like their whore for tonight.

After whimpering again, I turned around to face him and wrapped my arms around his shoulders. As spit and drool rolled down my chin and my makeup smeared from the tears slipping from my eyes, I furrowed my brows and begged him with my expression to fuck me.

I needed him inside me so badly. I needed something inside me. Anything.

He wrapped his hand around the front of my throat, his thumb rubbing across the dick in my throat and his knee gliding up between my legs. "Is Pretty Bird getting desperate for it? Hmm? Does she need to relieve herself here in front of everyone?"

Layers of drool ran down my throat. "Mmhmm."

He ground his knee against the latex material that covered my pussy. "Get yourself off on me. I want you squirting all over me, making a mess of yourself in the middle of the party, in front of all your old friends."

Gripping on to him tighter, I swallowed around the cock and glanced around the party. While most people had gone back to dancing and having a good time with each other, some were still watching me intently. And I knew that Calder, Gaian, and Darius were all here somewhere, watching me too.

I must've looked so desperate and needy because I couldn't stop myself from dry-humping Thayer's knee. I glided my clit back and forth, over and over, driving myself higher and higher.

The pressure built up, my pussy tightening on nothingness. I gripped Thayer's shoulders and stared up at him through wide eyes, my face absolutely ruined from all the face-fucking that my guys thought would be a good idea tonight.

"Is that all you fucking got, Pretty Bird?" Thayer growled, eyes shimmering demon red. "You got a throat full of cock, and you're still a horny little whore for us tonight." He slipped a hand into the latex material that covered my pussy and cupped my cunt. "You want this? Hmm?"

Whimpering, I nodded.

"Then, you'll fucking beg me to take you right here."

I gripped on to him tighter and begged, but my words came out gargled and full of spit. Someone slipped their cock all the way down my throat, fucking me harder and faster and deeper until their warm cum filled me all the way up.

When they pulled out, my mouth was full with so much cum that it drenched the mask I wore and ran down my throat and between my cleavage, making my tits glisten under Maxine's dim living room light.

"Please," I pleaded with Thayer. "Please, fu—"

Before I could finish, another one of my guys slipped their dick into my throat to fill me up. I gagged and gargled on his cock, bucking my hips back and forth against Thayer's long, thick fingers. Gods, I needed it so badly. So fucking badly.

Heat crawled up my body, slowly igniting it in what felt like flames. It was the same kind of desperate, flaming heat that had made me into a wild mess the other day with Calder. Now … it was coming out with Thayer too. I wanted—needed—to be bred, to be full with cum.

Thayer slipped onto a barstool behind him and pulled me onto his lap, my back against his chest and his cock pressed against the latex material covering my cunt. He pulled up my skirt just enough and ripped off the latex panties underneath it.

"You're a fucking mess," he growled against me. "A sloppy, slutty mess."

"Please," I begged, words still muffled. "Please, fill me!"

"Fuck, Pretty Bird," Gaian growled to my right, hurrying over to me without trying to even hide the bulge in his pants. He pushed through a small crowd, grabbed my arm from Thayer, and tugged me into a hallway that Maxine and I used to play hide-and-seek in when we were younger.

After Gaian thrust me into a coat closet, Thayer walked in and shut the door behind us. I curled my toes at the thought of them both taking me while Darius and Calder took turns, using my tight throat for their pleasure.

"God, I couldn't fucking wait my turn out there," Gaian said, shoving me onto my knees and whipping out his cock.

Thayer sat back against the wall, pulled me onto his lap, and spread my thighs farther apart in order to give himself better access to my pussy. I moaned on the cock in my mouth, cheeks flushing and pleasure rushing to my core.

After undoing his pants underneath me, Thayer rubbed his cock against my glistening pussy. Pushing it between my pussy lips, he teased my clit by rubbing and slapping it with the head of his cock. I whimpered and moved my ass back on his lap to hover over him.

"Ple—"

He shoved himself inside me, his cock filling my tight hole. I curled my toes, letting whoever was inside me fuck my throat until I could barely breathe. My legs trembled slightly, and I squeezed my eyes closed.

Gaian stepped closer to me and shoved his cock between my cum-covered cleavage. His cock disappeared between my breasts for a moment, and then the head appeared at the top, my drool dripping onto it. He groped my breasts through the latex material, rolling my hardening nipples between his fingers and tugging harder with every thrust.

Pleasure shot through my body, and I clamped down on Thayer's cock with my pussy. Thayer growled into my ear, shoving himself deeper and faster into me. My pussy continued to pulse over and over on his dick, the feeling of him inside me almost enough to send me over the edge.

"Fuck, Sina," Gaian growled, pressing my tits together and thrusting up one last time between them. As the head of his cock emerged from between my tits, his cum squirted all over them, covering my cleavage and even my throat.

At the same time, cum filled my mouth, and layers of it spilled down my chest and between my breasts too. I screamed out in pleasure when I could finally breathe again, my legs trembling hard in Thayer's hands.

"Please give it to me, Thayer," I moaned.

"Beg like the filthy whore you are."

"Gods, please," I pleaded, moving my hips back and forth on his cock. "I need someone's cum inside me so badly. Thayer, ple—"

Before I could finish my sentence, Thayer smacked my clit with his large hand, and I came undone. Pleasure rushed through my body, wave after wave of ecstasy making me feel so fucking good.

Thayer stilled deep inside my hole and came against my cervix, as deep as he could get. And I wouldn't even be surprised if the psycho Thayer wanted to get even deeper than that if he could.

48
the vampire

sina

AFTER I FINALLY TOOK OFF THAT mask and thrust it into Calder's pocket—because I didn't think I could be face-fucked any more tonight—I took my time in the bathroom to clean myself up. Lines of drool dried from my mouth down to my neck. My makeup was smeared slightly.

I felt so used tonight, and I loved it.

While I might not have enjoyed the attention earlier in the night, I loved how ruthless my guys were in claiming every inch of me in front of the younger Durnbone crowd. There was no questioning now who I belonged to. And who belonged to me.

Once I grabbed a cloth from Maxine's closet, I cleaned myself up and reapplied some mascara in the mirror. My eyes glimmered underneath her dim bathroom light, the shining light from the almost-full moon reflecting off the mirror.

Vampiric scents drifted through the open window. I inhaled deeply, the odor vaguely familiar but I couldn't seem to place it. My head ached slightly, and I closed my eyes, visions rushing through my mind of the last time I had smelled this aroma.

Six-hundred-year-old vampires stood around me in my bedroom, drawing their sharp nails up my stomach, whispering and communicating with each other in an ancient dialect, touching and groping and using me for their pleasure.

Earlier that night, I had kicked and screamed and begged Dad to stop this torture. I knew what had been going on for weeks, maybe even months now, but I couldn't seem to stop it. The more I begged for him and them to stop, the harder they went.

Snapping my eyes back open, I shook my head to rid myself of the memory and splashed water on my face. My heart raced harder and faster, my mouth drying and my teeth slicing right through my dry lips, cutting them and drawing blood.

In horror, I stared at myself in the mirror. The blood dripped down my chin, where the drool had once been, and slid down the front of my throat. My mouth watered at the sight, my once-dull teeth now sharpened into fangs.

Oh my fucking gods.

What the hell is happening to me? I had to be hallucinating. I freaking had to be.

Once I splashed more water on my face, I wiped the blood away and stared at my teeth, which were now dull again. I mean, they hadn't been fangs in the first place. They couldn't have been. And my eyes … they were my regular color still.

Nothing had changed. I just … hadn't had much to eat tonight. I must've been seeing things now. Maybe all that face-fucking and closet sex had gone to my head. I needed some water to drink and something to fill my tummy.

Clutching my growling stomach, I readjusted myself in the mirror, took a deep breath, and walked back into the party. Heat crawled up my body, igniting every inch of me. But it wasn't the kind that made me want to rip off one of my guys' pants and fuck him senseless.

"Stop it," someone whimpered to my left. "Please, I'm pregnant. Stop!"

I snapped my head in their direction to see a vampire gripping a young woman by the upper arm and dragging her out the back door. It wasn't just any vampire who had any sort of foul stench. I knew that stench from somewhere, yet I couldn't place my finger on it.

This wasn't one of the men who had raped me.

But this wasn't anyone with good intentions either.

"Please," the woman cried. "Someone, help me!"

"Nobody is coming for you, bitch," the vampire said, pulling out a syringe with the same shit that Dad used to give me every single night. I could smell it drifting off the vampire in undeniable waves. "You belong to *him* now."

Before the door could close, I leaped out of it at lightning speed, grabbed the pregnant woman from the vampire's arms, and shoved her behind me. Rage rushed through my body at the mere thought of *anyone* going through what I had for my entire life.

"Sina?" the vampire said, grinning like a madman. "You really did show up to the party."

While I knew that I should've stayed back to ensure that the pregnant woman was okay and to find my guys, I couldn't help the intensifying anger that built inside me. I wanted to stop my legs from moving forward toward that needle and that ugly vampire, but I couldn't.

My mouth dried once more. My teeth ached. My head was spinning. Yet all I could seem to do was focus on killing this man right here and right now. Like other species, except humans, vampires were extremely hard to kill. They were almost immortal.

But tonight, I'd make sure he took his last breath.

Nobody deserved to be used as a sex doll, especially not anyone who was pregnant.

"Sina," the vampire said, his thumb on the syringe. He let a drop of the substance drip down the needle and onto the ground between us.

I sniffed the air, the odor both repugnant and so familiar. My body had learned the hard way that medication made me relax.

It was a learned behavior that I so desperately wanted to get rid of myself.

"Come here, Sina," he cooed. "Have a sip."

I eyed the syringe.

A sip …

Just one sip …

A single slow heartbeat thumped over the blaring music inside the large house. Despite people yelling and shouting and having a good time inside, the steady beat was all I could hear. And this vampire's throat was the only thing that I could seem to focus on. Everything else in my peripheral had turned a dark red, almost-black color.

"Come here," I cooed back to him. "Let me have one sip."

With a smug smirk on his face, he moved closer to me and held out the syringe for me to take. But once he came within two feet of me, I wrapped one of my hands around his throat and threw the needle onto the ground with the other.

I didn't know what happened next. I blacked out.

But the only thing I remembered was the pregnant human screaming at the top of her lungs, blood covering my body, and the vampire lying dead in my arms.

49
the marking

darius

A SHRILL SCREAM ECHOED throughout Maxine's family home. I scanned the party for Sina, my stomach tightening when I couldn't find even a glimpse of her among the many, many dancing figures.

"Where the hell is Sina?" I asked Thayer, who sat at the bar, clutching a glass tightly in his head and eyeing the group of demons in the back, who he must've really fucking hated. Hell, he hated almost everyone nowadays.

"Bathroom."

I glanced over my shoulder at the open bathroom door and growled, snatching his shoulder and lifting him off the freaking barstool. "The bathroom is fucking empty. Where the fuck is Sina?"

Thayer snapped his head toward the bathroom, eyes immediately glinting red. After ripping himself out of my grip, he rushed toward the bathroom and lifted his nose to the air, sniffing her scent.

While I would've done the same thing, there were far too many scents in this room to distinguish any from each other. They were all mixing together, overwhelming my wolf in ways that it shouldn't. But the most I could smell was vampire. Thayer was a half demon, who had a mother who could smell almost anything at any time, no matter how far away. He had better senses than most of us.

Thayer hurried through the party, pushing and shoving people out of the way. The scream came again, so loud that I could hear it over the thumping music. I stormed by his side, needing to find Sina now.

"Where is she?" I growled again, chest tightening.

If someone had fucking taken her again, I would … I would lose it for real this time. I didn't know what I would do without her, especially after what she admitted to me the other night, all the shit she'd been through.

I'd told her that I would protect her, and yet … here we were.

"Sina!" Thayer growled, shoving open a back door.

As soon as he stepped outside, he stopped in his tracks. When I pushed past him, my eyes widened. Sina sat on top of a vampire with his dark blood soaking into her skin and her Halloween costume.

She ripped her fingers into his flesh repeatedly, tearing skin and splattering blood everywhere. "You're not going to lay a finger on another innocent woman!" she shouted at the dead vampire, pummeling her fist into his face. "Never again!"

Before I could stop myself, I wrapped my arms around her waist from behind and pulled her off him. "Sina! Sina, it's me. It's Darius. He's dead. You need to calm down. We need to get you home—"

Sina kicked her foot back, hitting me in the kneecap and sending me flying backward. I landed on my ass at Thayer's feet as she escaped my grasp and lunged forward toward the corpse once more, using her nails—no, *her claws*—to rip off his right arm. She hurled it behind her so hard that it collided with a tree and made an impact.

Thayer grabbed my upper arm and yanked me to my feet, his eyes turning a shade of red. "What the fuck is going on with her? I let her use the bathroom to fucking clean herself up, not turn into a fucking demon."

"Those aren't demon fangs in her mouth," I said, staring at the bloodstained teeth with a pointy edge, fangs that would slip into any human's neck to suck out blood. "And she shouldn't be strong enough to … to kill a vampire with her bare hands."

A pregnant woman sank down against the house, her head in her hands, wailing so loudly that the sound vibrated through my ears. She rocked back and forth, muttering something about how she didn't want to go with him, about how she had a child.

"I'll handle Sina," Thayer said, taking another step toward Sina. "You quiet that woman."

Thayer lunged forward toward Sina, grabbing her by the upper arms to restrain her body. I leaned down next to the woman, not really good with feelings with anyone other than Sina. And *that* still wasn't my strong suit.

"Can you tell me what happened?" I asked her, but she continued crying. "Please?"

As soon as she opened her mouth, Thayer growled, "Fuck it. Never mind, D. I need your fucking help with her. She's—"

When I glanced over at Thayer, Sina ripped herself out of his hold and scratched him right across the face with a sharp claw. Blood poured out of the wound, dripping down his face. Almost immediately, her eyes widened and filled with tears, her body stopping completely and falling to the ground.

"Oh my gods," she whispered, brows furrowed. She glanced down at the blood dripping down the side of his face, her pupils dilating, like a vampire's would. "I-I'm so sorry. I can't stop. I can't control myself. I … you need to run, Thayer. I'm g-going t-to hurt y-you—"

Sina lunged at Thayer. I leaped up from the ground, mind-linked the guys to tell them to get their asses out back before anyone saw Sina like this, and tried my fucking hardest to get Sina away from the blood.

None of this made any fucking sense. Sina had the fangs of a vampire, the eyes of a demon, the claws of a wolf, and the strength of something … else.

Moments later, Gaian and Calder hurried out of the back door, asking what the fuck was going on. But, hell, none of us knew either. Not even Sina as she continued to fight back against both Thayer and me now, trying to get to the blood.

"Get the pregnant woman to safety," I ordered Gaian.

While Sina struggled for a couple more moments, I caught her right arm, and Thayer caught her left. Calder wrapped his hand around her chin and snapped her jaw shut so she couldn't use her fangs on any of us.

Fear rushed through her eyes, yet it seemed like she couldn't control it. She hadn't been able to control herself through the heat either, but this was different. She seemed feral, like she had snapped and couldn't seize back control.

"Please," she whimpered, the word muffled.

Calder pressed his canines against her bloody neck and growled. "Stop this now, Sina, or I'll rip my teeth into your throat and make you submit to me. And I know how much of a brat you like to be."

"I-I can't," she whispered. "I can't."

"Sina," Calder growled, his canines lengthening and pressing into her soft spot on her neck, where we would all mark her one day.

"Do it, Calder," she whispered. "Please, end this. You have to—"

Before she could say another word, Calder sank his teeth into her neck and marked her.

50
the regret

calder

SINA COLLAPSED IN MY ARMS, eyes rolling back in her head and body suddenly relaxed. I pulled my teeth from her neck and shivered at the sight of the mark I had left on her body. From the day she had returned to Durnbone, I'd vowed not to mark her until … until I was ready.

If something happened to her now, I wouldn't be able to live with myself. I wasn't ready, didn't know if I would be ready anytime soon. But Sina had been freaking out, lashing out uncontrollably.

She had become an animal who desperately wanted to stop hurting us, but couldn't.

"You … you marked her," Darius said in disbelief, staring wide-eyed at an unconscious Sina.

Thayer and Gaian stared at us in shock too, the blood seeping down Thayer's face still. But somehow, I felt even more shocked than them.

"Someone, grab the vampire and the woman," I said. "Bring them both back to the pack house."

"I'll get Sina," Gaian said, reaching to take her from my arms.

A low warning growl escaped my lips. "No."

Gaian widened his eyes for a moment, and then his innocent expression turned a shade darker. He had always been the one that Sina gravitated toward, the one of us that she preferred, but she was my mate now. And my wolf wasn't having another person touching her after we just laid our claim.

Once Gaian backed away, I lifted Sina into the air and started through the forest, back to our pack house, without saying good-bye to anyone at the party. It wasn't like many people we cared about were here. Only Sina's friends.

After Thayer said a few words to Xorgor—Sina's friend's boyfriend—he walked past the vampire and hurried toward me until he caught up. "What the fuck was that? You said you wanted to fucking wait."

"I did."

"So, what the fu—"

"She was lashing out," I growled. "If I didn't stop it, she would have torn your face off."

"I wouldn't have fucking let her do that. You just like to be the fucking savior, and it's pissing me off."

"If you had it under control, she wouldn't have fucking wounded you!" I shouted, clutching Sina tighter. "Hell, I wouldn't have been able to control her alone either, and I'm the fucking alpha of this pack. We work together to protect each other, Thayer."

While I believed every word that I'd said, I couldn't help feeling so … afraid. I had held this pack on my shoulders for four years, had tried so fucking hard to take their pain away. Now, I was the closest to Sina, and if something happened to her, I didn't know if they would … take my pain away. I didn't know if they *could* take my pain away.

To my surprise, Thayer didn't bitch back to me. Instead, he stayed quiet as we walked back to the pack house through the dark and foggy forest. Darius and Gaian lagged behind with the vampire and the pregnant woman. We needed answers from her.

When we reached the pack house, I nodded to Darius to dump

the vampire on our couch. "Get as much blood from him as you can. Sina will want to use it to make those potions for us in case her father attacks."

"What do you want me to do with her?" Gaian asked, eyeing the pregnant woman who had stopped crying and was clutching her baby bump.

"Figure out what the vampire wanted from her, then bring her home. Make sure she has people who will look after her and protect her. If she doesn't, then she will stay with us. Sina wanted to protect her for a reason."

Once Gaian nodded, I followed Thayer upstairs to the bathroom. Sina was covered in blood, and I doubted that she'd want to wake up like this tomorrow morning while in my bed. Thayer ran a warm bath, then leaned against the bathroom door as I undressed our mate.

"You're right," he muttered, voice gruff.

I laid Sina in the tub and grabbed a soapy sponge to wipe her off. "About what?"

Thayer growled, walked over to sit on the edge of the tub, and grabbed the sponge from me. He drew it over the blood that covered her collarbone and clenched his jaw. "About working together to protect each other, but it's fucking hard for me. Nobody in my family fucking cares to work together. They only care about themselves."

"Fuck your parents," I growled, tucking some of Sina's hair behind her ear. "We're your family, Thay. And we have to protect Sina, no matter the cost."

As he washed the blood off Sina's chest, he stared emptily at the pink water. "If we're family, so is Sina. You're not going to get anywhere with her if you keep fucking pushing her away even if she now wears your mark. I know you can feel how much she's been hurting because you're a fucking dick to her."

Fear washed over me, the thought of Sina hating me now making me feel nothing but regret. Thayer was right. I had tried to repair our relationship only slightly, but it wouldn't erase the past few weeks.

What if Sina saw my mark on her tomorrow morning and … rejected it?

What if she rejected me?

"Mate will love us," my wolf said. *"She has to. We'd do anything for her."*

But … what if my wolf was wrong? What if she really hated us back? I would finally be able to hear her thoughts and could only imagine how badly she thought of me. Whether I had marked her or not, I would've been fucked either way. Only marking her would make things worse.

"I shouldn't have marked her," I said, reality quickly setting in.

This was so much worse than her father taking her away from us. If she hated me herself, then I couldn't do anything about that. I would have to live with the thought of my mate not loving a single thing about me.

Thayer stopped scrubbing the blood off Sina. "That's not what I meant."

"Yeah, but I shouldn't have fucking done shit to her. She's going to fucking hate me."

"Maybe," Thayer said with a laugh, tossing me the sponge. "But you're the only one of us she seems to submit to, even subconsciously right now. She'll come around, whether she hates you or not. Just don't be a dick to her, and maybe …" He stood and walked toward the door. "Maybe she'll fucking love you one day."

51
the questions

I WOKE up in Calder's large bed alone. Moonlight flooded into the dark room from the window. My head pounded harshly, vision shifting for a moment. After clutching my forehead, I pushed myself up to a seated position and leaned against the headboard.

"What happened?" I whispered to myself.

The last thing that I remembered was cleaning myself up in the bathroom. Everything after that was a blacked-out blur that my brain either couldn't remember or didn't want to remember. And part of me feared that this … had happened before. So many times, I couldn't remember anything about those endless nights at Dad's estate.

What if someone … what if something bad happened? In front of my guys too?

Deciding that I needed to at least see if someone remembered, I shuffled out of bed, realized that I was completely naked, and scrambled to the closet. Fear rushed through my veins, remembering that I had woken up like this so many times at Dad's estate. Naked and unable to remember the hours before.

After taking a deep breath, I let my shoulders roll forward and picked something relaxing to wear from the closet— a T-shirt and sweatpants. It might've happened before with random people, but my guys wouldn't do anything like that to me.

Once I pulled on my clothes, I walked to the door and caught myself in the mirror by the dresser. I stopped dead in my tracks, my mouth drying and my eyes widening as I caught sight of a wound on my neck.

It wasn't just any wound.

It looked like teeth markings, like a …

"Like a mate's mark," a soft voice whispered through my head. It wasn't my inner voice.

I pushed all my hair behind my shoulders and leaned forward, staring in shock as the mark glimmered underneath the moonlight. My heart raced, my chest tightening.

What the fuck is this? How do I have a mark?

Maybe one of the guys had lost control last night. Or maybe … someone else had marked me.

When I grazed my fingers against the rigid teeth marks on my neck, I shivered. I truly hoped it was the former option, as I didn't think my guys would have let anyone else even near me if I'd blacked out last night.

And if one of my guys had marked me …

My lips curled into a wide grin, warmth flooding through my body. I had been waiting for so fucking long—so long. I just wished that I could remember it. I had been waiting for someone to love me —truly love me—for so long.

"What the fuck happened?" Thayer said, his voice drifting through the door. While his voice sounded like a hushed whisper, I could hear it loud and clear. "I still can't wrap my head around what that was last night."

"I don't know," Gaian said. "We could … she could …"

"She was stronger than us put fucking together."

Are they talking about me? Me, strong?

As I lifted my gaze to the mirror once more, a madwoman with red eyes, sharp fangs, and claws stared back at me. I stumbled back, glimpses of last night pummeling into my mind. This wasn't any madwoman, but me.

All I could see in my head was a vampire, a pregnant woman, and me.

Fuck.

Deciding that I needed answers now, I hurried out the door and down the stairs to the living room, where all my guys were gathered and chatting tensely with each other. When I landed on the floor, Calder stood up, his eyes shifting to his golden wolf.

"Mine," he growled possessively through my head.

Yes, through my fucking head.

My eyes widened, and I found myself rushing to Gaian instead of him. Because how the fuck could *Calder* have marked me? Surely, he hadn't. He'd wanted to mark me the least out of all the guys. He wouldn't have lost control. He wouldn't.

I wrapped my hand around Gaian's bicep, clutching on tightly as the others stared at me quietly. From the corner of my eye, I saw a vampire's corpse lying on the couch with vials of his dark blood on the coffee table next to him—vials that I could use to make more potions.

"What happened to me last night? All I remember is there being a pregnant woman and a vampire who wanted to capture her and … oh gods, please tell me she's safe."

Everyone stayed quiet, glancing at each other.

Suddenly, Darius cleared his throat. "You really don't remember?"

"No," I said. "Why? Is she okay?"

"She's fine," Thayer said.

My gaze snapped to him, and I saw a fresh large scar that ran across his face. My nails ached at the sight of him. I opened my mouth to ask what had happened to him, but then I remembered I had done that to him.

"I … I did that to you?" I whispered, dropping Gaian's bicep and rushing over to Thayer. I grasped his face and searched his glimmering red demon eyes, wanting him to say something, but he stayed quiet. "I'm so sorry. I-I didn't mean to."

"It's fine."

"No, it's not," I said, mouth dry.

It wasn't fine that his mate had laid her hands on him, had scratched and scarred him for life. That wasn't what a good mate did or a good person. How could I have done this? How could I have lost control? I … I wasn't a monster, like Dad.

I tensed because … I was. I had to be.

"I'm sorry," I whispered, dropping my hands from his face and stepping back in fear that I would lose control again.

I didn't want to hurt him. I didn't want to hurt any of them. They didn't deserve it. They had waited four years for me.

Four years, and I'd scarred his face.

Tears welled up in my eyes. My knees gave out. I doubled over onto the ground, bending at the hip to curl into a ball. I hated this. I hated this so fucking much. I was nothing but ruined because of Dad. I couldn't even live my life in peace without him.

He had turned me into a monster. He had turned me into a fiend. He had made me so insane that I hurt my own mates, something that he had probably wanted this entire time so he didn't have to do it himself.

52

the monster

sina

I WAS A MONSTER.

Nobody understood the pain that I had gone through every day for years, how much I had tried to believe that Dad just wanted to use my body for sexual favors and not for … this, how much agony this fucking brought me.

My chest tightened as I doubled over and held myself tightly. I wanted to love my mates and had been aching for them to open up more to me, so I could trust them not to hurt me, just like Dad had. I wanted to give them all of myself.

But not like this.

"I-I'm sorry," I whispered, feeling like the ultimate crybaby. I wished that I could just be hard, not feel a fucking thing, continued to live my life without my past constantly haunting me, like it had been.

"It's okay," Gaian said, crouching beside me and gently stroking my back.

"No, it's not," Thayer said, grabbing me by my upper arm and yanking me into the air.

Calder growled at him, canines extending, as if he was ready to snap Thayer in half. Even Darius and Gaian eyed Thayer in caution. I sucked in a sharp breath at the words that had come out of Thayer's mouth. He was rightfully angry with me for what I had done to him.

He stared with those blazing red eyes and growled at me, his canines extended. "You're fucking stronger than all of us, Sina. Stop fuckin' thinking that you're weak because of your father. He wanted to make you a fuckin' monster for a reason, but he doesn't control you anymore, and he's not going to take you again."

"But I-I am weak," I whispered. "I can't control myself. I hurt you. I—"

"You protected a pregnant woman and killed an almost-immortal being, and it took *three* of us to restrain you. Stop believing the lies that your father fed you. He wanted you to believe that you were weak for a fucking reason, and right now, you're still submitting to him."

"I-I'm not."

But everything that Thayer had said was the truth. I didn't believe in myself because nobody had believed in me before, nobody had told me that I could do something. I had lain helplessly in my bed for so many nights that I started to believe that … I wouldn't be able to fight back. Even without Dad's potion in my system.

"You're strong enough to fuckin' kill your father, Sina."

Thayer's words stabbed me deep, right in the fucking gut. I stared into his red half-demon eyes, desperately trying to find any glimpse of him lying to me, of him making this all up to make me feel better. I didn't feel like I deserved this. I had hurt him.

"Don't lie to me," I whispered, but I didn't believe he was lying.

"He's not lying," Calder said.

I gripped Thayer's shirt into my fists and clutched it hard. "Stop it."

"You know I'm not fucking lying to you," Thayer growled down at me, seeing right through the defenses that I'd put up. Something was holding me back, and even he saw it. "You're strong."

"No."

"That's fucking bullshit," he said, raising his voice. "Fucking bullshit, and you know it."

I pressed my lips together, tears threatening to spill down my cheeks again. I didn't want to believe that I was stronger than these guys or that I could kill my father and everyone else who had ever hurt me. I wanted to believe that I was weak. It was easier to accept everything that had happened to me that way.

Thayer gripped my jaw hard and forced me to look up at him. "Tell me you know."

My heart raced, my throat drying. Why was it so hard to face inner demons? Why was it so hard to admit the truth to myself? I had been begging for them to accept me, to love me, when I couldn't even acknowledge the true pain I had inside myself.

"I … I … I know," I finally said.

After staring into my eyes for another moment, he released my chin. "Don't ever forget it, Pretty Bird." He turned away from us and stormed to the pack house door. "I have shit to take care of. Don't let her out of your sight."

Once he disappeared out the door and into the woods, I turned back to Gaian, Darius, and Calder, who were all watching me carefully. I shifted from foot to foot and found myself staring back at Calder.

"*Mate*," the unfamiliar voice in my head growled possessively. "*Mine.*"

Calder's usually annoyed and angry eyes were softer than usual as he stared back at me. He swallowed hard and glanced down at the mark on my neck, the vein in his neck twitching. It was like he wanted to say something to me about the mark on my neck but was torn between speaking his mind and something else.

A couple of moments passed, and he stood. I thought he would walk over to me, wrap his strong hands around my waist, and pull me closer—claiming me. But instead, he tore his gaze away from me and reluctantly walked out of the room.

"*Follow him,*" the voice in my head whispered.

I glanced between Gaian and Darius, grimaced slightly in their direction, then followed Calder up the stairs to his bedroom. He had the door closed, but I didn't care. I walked right into the room because we needed to talk.

With his arms crossed and his jaw clenched, he stood at the window in deep thought. While he didn't turn around, I knew he could tell that I was here with him. I closed the door softly behind me and walked over to him.

I didn't know what I wanted to say to him. I didn't know if I *wanted* to say anything. So, I wrapped my arms around him from behind and laid my head on his muscular back. He tensed, his back muscles flexing, and unfolded his arms.

His breath hitched slightly. "You shouldn't be in here."

"Why?"

"Because," he said, voice unsteady, "my wolf won't let me hold back much longer."

"Then, let him loose."

He tensed even harder. "I can't do that to the guys. They deserve to mark you before I complete our bond. I already broke my fucking promise to them once. They're all hurting to mark you."

We stayed quiet for a few moments, and while my wolf was aching to jump on him now, I remembered what Thayer had said— even though I didn't want to—and forced myself to hold myself back from my inner desires. I was stronger than them ... sometimes.

"Did you mark me because you love me or because you had to?" I whispered, afraid of his response.

Part of me already knew what he'd say. He hadn't wanted to mark me from the beginning. He'd wanted to wait over and over.

He stayed quiet, and I took that to mean he'd marked me because he had to.

Not because he loved me and wanted to mark me.

I wanted to scream, to cry—because he hadn't wanted to get me pregnant because he loved me, but because he wanted to piss off my father. This was sorta, kinda like the same thing, and I hated the fact that it was never me that he thought about first. It was my father.

When I went to pull away from him—because I suddenly felt so … rejected—he quickly turned around and pulled me flush against his chest. Instead of gripping my throat and growling down at me, like he usually did, he kissed me softly.

My breath hitched, and after my surprise, I finally kissed him back. It wasn't a rough, passionless kiss that he always gave me during those countless group-sex nights. This was full of fervor.

Once he pulled away, he rested his forehead against mine. "Everything I do is because I love you, Sina."

53
the talk

gaian

ABOUT TWENTY MINUTES after Sina disappeared into Calder's room with him, I lay back on my bed and closed my eyes to get some rest for the first time all night. Last night might've gone as planned in the beginning, but it had quickly taken a dive into something much worse.

None of us knew what Sina really was.

And I was terrified that we wouldn't be able to protect her. That this time, she would be the one protecting us. She didn't know what she was capable of, and she couldn't even control herself or that inner demon she had—whatever it was.

A light knock came on my door, followed by Sina's sweet scent. "Gaian?"

I sat up to lean against the headboard and squinted my eyes in her direction as the sunlight flooded into the room through the open windows. "What's up, Pretty Bird?"

She shuffled into the room and shut the door behind her. "Can I stay with you for a bit?"

After I pushed over to give her some of the bed, she crawled in with me and snuggled close to me underneath the blankets. Four years ago, whenever we had sleepovers, she'd do the same thing. And, Goddess, I'd missed it.

"What's wrong?" I whispered, noticing her bloodshot eyes. She had been crying.

"Nothing."

Once I tucked some hair behind her ear, she closed her eyes and relaxed in my arms. All night, she had been twisting and turning in Calder's bedroom. We had all been downstairs and heard it. It was like she had been having a nightmare.

"Thayer seemed angry before he left," she said, voice barely above a whisper. "Do you think he … he … blames me for what happened? I mean, I would too, but I don't want him to hate me. I feel so terrible about his scar."

"He doesn't hate you, Sina," I murmured, sinking down deeper in the bed and curling my fingers around her hip. "And if he wanted to, he could have healed the scar you left on his face by now."

Her brows furrowed. "Wh-what do you mean?"

"He healed yours." I glanced down at her chest, where he had carved the initials *CP* for Crispen Pack on one of the first nights we all spent together.

He had been so ruthless with her because he knew she could take it. Hours later, he had felt bad and healed her wound, almost to the point where it completely disappeared. *Almost.*

She brushed her fingers across her chest too, as if she remembered, and sucked in a sharp breath. "He-he healed me. I don't remember it, but he did, didn't he? Why hasn't he healed his own scars then? All of them on his skin?"

"Because he got those while looking for you," I said, moving my fingers in circles around her hip to keep calm. "Calder and Thayer were both so fucked up the night of your eighteenth birthday that Thayer refused to heal himself. He took so much physical pain from our enemies because he thought he deserved it for losing you."

Sina pressed her lips together, furrowed her brows, and let out a small whimper. "Why would he do that? Why would he blame himself?" she asked, but I knew she was the one who blamed herself for everything that had happened to her.

"Because he loves you."

"Do you think you all will ever be able to forgive me?"

"You haven't done anything," I reassured. "What happened wasn't your fault."

"But I lost control."

"We'll teach you how to control yourself then."

"How? Nobody knows what I am. I don't even know the extent of it."

"What do you know?"

She paused for a long time, her body suddenly tensing. When she opened her mouth, no words came out, and she snapped her lips closed once more. "I-I know that I didn't like the vampire, that I … that he seemed so familiar to me. Something—*someone*—told me to kill him."

"Someone?" I asked. "Who? Your inner wolf maybe?"

"No," she said quickly. "I … I don't know who it was, but it wasn't part of me physically. At least, I don't think so. All I remember was thinking of how that woman was going to go through torture, how her baby would grow up in pain, like me, and how she reminded me of … of … my mom."

Suddenly, Sina became quiet again. She swallowed hard and inched closer to me, resting her head on the center of my chest and squirming. Instead of saying much else, she continued to repeat the word *mom* over and over.

"What else do you remember?" I urged, running my fingers into her messy hair and gently scratching her head to calm her. She was working herself up again, her breaths becoming shorter and raspier. "Anything about your father?"

"He was experimenting when I escaped, on other species and on humans, lacing my DNA with theirs, seeing what would happen. I think he was trying to create … another species or … trying to convert humans into … a superspecies."

"A superspecies," I whispered.

Everybody knew that magic and science didn't mix well together. If he was really trying to create a superior species or even a superior mate for other species, then things were bound to get messy. Really fucking messy.

"Why?" I asked, trying to figure it out myself.

"I don't know," she whispered, her shoulders slumping forward.

After she took a couple of steadier breaths, I knew that Sina was about to finally rest well. She needed it after what had happened last night.

Hell, we all needed it.

So, instead of pushing further, I brushed some hair from her face and gently hummed. "Sleep well, Pretty Bird. We can talk about this later if you're up for it. Sound good?" I asked, listening to her mumble in response.

She maneuvered her smaller body until she was lying on top of me and murmured, "You make me feel so safe, Gaian."

My chest tightened, warmth shooting through my body. My wolf purred in response, but I could do nothing but let a stupid lopsided grin stretch across my face. After her father had abducted her, I'd never thought I would hear those words.

But my Sina was back, lying in my arms, and I felt like I was on top of the world.

54

the paragon

thayer

AFTER TREKKING all the way back to Sina's friend's home, I walked up the stone pathway. Red plastic cups littered the front lawn. The music from last night had died down completely. And this place smelled of liquor and piss.

I knocked twice on the front door. "Open up."

Dressed in fuzzy emerald pajamas, Maxine opened the door. "What're you doing here? It's, like, six in the morning. Sina hasn't been here since last night. I thought she went home with—"

"Where's your boyfriend?"

"My boyfriend?" Maxine asked, cheeks reddening. "You mean, Xorgor?"

"You're dating, right?" I stepped into the house. "Right. Where the fuck is he?"

Sighing softly, Maxine closed the door behind me and led me to the back room, where Xorgor was lying on a bed with his junk hanging out everywhere. Jesus fucking Christ, demons didn't have any fucking shame.

Once I cleared my throat, I grasped the door handle and looked down at Maxine, who stood in the doorway. "I need to talk to him privately. It's about Sina." And with that, I slammed the door closed.

Xorgor stirred on the bed and eventually sat up, rubbing the human side of his face.

I tossed him his clothes. "Get the fuck up and get dressed. We need to talk."

"About what?" he asked, voice groggy and deep. He pulled on his shorts to cover his junk and stood up, stretching to his full height. While he wasn't that much taller than me, half his body was always in demon form, which—I would assume—was why he didn't hang out with many other people.

To my knowledge, he had always tried to stay hidden with his magic and rarely made appearances in Durnbone. I didn't blame him either. The people here—especially the demons—weren't accepting of anyone who looked different. Which meant one thing … he would align with me.

"What is it?" he asked.

"The demons don't accept me," I started, balling my hands into fists and thinking back to the other day when I had visited my *mother*. "I can't get close to them, and my family … they won't tell me shit. By the looks of it, the demons don't like you much either. You have royal blood, but I doubt you even have a chance at being leader of our species."

Xorgor clenched his jaw, his one red demon eye glowing. "I don't want to talk about that."

"Yeah, well, neither do I," I said, pausing for a moment to make sure that I didn't hear anyone's heartbeat nearby. I stepped closer to Xorgor. "But we have a problem. A bigger problem than you could even fathom. And I need information on Jaroth."

"Jaroth?" Xorgor said. "He's made big strides to become the next demon leader."

"No fucking shit," I said through gritted teeth. "He's also Sina's ex-boyfriend, and I don't trust him."

Xorgor tensed and swallowed hard. "You shouldn't. He's a liar and a cheat. I get that he's an incubus, but something has never sat right with me about him either. I've only seen him in passing, and I have some shit against him that's my private matter, but … I don't like the kid."

"Where was he last night? A guy like him wouldn't have missed a party like that."

"I heard he was meeting with some high-ranked demons and leaders of the other species to speak about diplomatic matters, about what he'll have to do to become the next leader once Queen Agool steps down."

"Where are they meeting?"

"South of Durnbone."

"That's funny." A dry laugh escaped my lips. "Because he fucking told Sina that he was in the north, trying to figure out how many soldiers her father had, that he'd find out as much information for her as possible."

Xorgor furrowed his brow. "Last I heard, there's an army gathering in the south, not the north. It's a bunch of humans that Jaroth was supposed to meet with to try to stop the war against the other species. The humans want something, but it's not money."

Fury rushed through me. I balled my hands into even tighter fists and growled, knowing that we shouldn't have trusted a word that came out of that fucker's mouth. He had manipulated Sina for far too fucking long.

I stormed out of the room and toward the front door. "They want Sina."

"Why?" Xorgor said, following me. "What could they want with her?"

"They want her because she's the Paragon."

As I rushed past Maxine and back toward the pack house, Xorgor followed, his steps quicker this time. "What the fuck do you mean, she's the Paragon? That's a myth told down through the centuries to demons. It's a fable."

I grabbed him by the throat and pushed him against the door. "If you had seen what I saw last night, you'd know that it isn't a fable.

She's far stronger than even I can fathom. I haven't even been able to heal my wound that she gave me."

Xorgor didn't struggle, but the human side of his face paled. "You can't?"

"No." I swallowed hard and dropped my hand from around his throat, finally coming to terms with what Sina was and the power she held. "That's why Jaroth wants her; that's why Jaroth must've helped her escape from her father. She's the fucking Paragon, the most powerful being alive."

55
the goons

thayer

"XORGOR!" Maxine shouted from downstairs with a slight tremble in her voice. "Xorgor!"

Xorgor shook his head, as if he couldn't believe what I had just told him about Sina, and hurried out of the room. Fuck, I could barely believe it either. The Paragon had only ever been a myth, lore passed down through the demon generations. But it was real. I had fucking seen it.

"Xorgor! Please, come down here!" Maxine shouted again.

A whiff of dirty human drifted through my nose, and I tensed. I had memorized that scent for so fucking long, had burned it into my memory the day that we found Sina's house completely empty on her eighteenth birthday.

I shuffled down the stairs behind Xorgor, staying hidden behind his taller frame. Two of Sina's father's goons stood at the door, staring down at Maxine with guns in their hands and menace in their eyes.

When Xorgor spotted them, he zipped to Maxine and pushed her behind him. I slipped behind a wall, staying out of sight, and looked for a way out of the house. If they spotted me, they'd shoot right fucking at me with those poison-laced bullets.

"Fuck," I growled underneath my breath.

Scanning the house for an alternate escape route, I spotted the back door, where Sina had disappeared through last night while I drank at the bar. Pain shot through me at the mere thought of losing her, of not watching her the way that I should've.

Maybe this all would've been avoided if I had been fucking crazy like Calder and refused to let her out of my sight, even when she had to piss.

After quietly escaping through the back door, I scanned the forest to ensure there weren't any other goons and walked around the house to the front door, careful to stay hidden so the goons wouldn't see me.

There was no fucking way that I was heading home without them. I'd promised Sina that I would do anything to protect her and wouldn't let anyone hurt her again, that I would give her the revenge that she deserved.

"We're looking for a vampire that was last seen at your party last night," one said.

"What do humans want with a vampire?" Xorgor asked, blocking Maxine from them.

Any demon could withstand a regular bullet, but Xorgor didn't know that a bullet from their guns could kill him. I needed to get inside and knock them out before they could ever aim the gun in his direction.

"That's none of your business," the goon said.

I inched closer to the front door, peeked into the house, and pulled Sina's potion from my jeans pocket. She had been dead set on each of us carrying a small potion with us at all times, just in case something happened. Once I flicked the cork off with my thumb, I drank it.

"It's my business if you're at my front door."

"This isn't your house, Mr. ..." The goon stopped and scrunched his fat, ugly nose at Xorgor's half-human, half-demon appearance. "Whatever you are. We're here for Maxine. She has information."

"She has no information," Xorgor said, pushing Maxine back another few feet to keep her out of harm's way. "Now, get the fuck out of here. There wasn't a vampire here last night that fits the description you gave us."

"If she doesn't have information on the vampire, surely, she has information on Sina."

At the mere mention of my mate's name, I lunged into the room from behind the two men. I wrapped my hand around one's face and pounded him into the ground, headfirst and so hard that he immediately blacked out.

The other twirled around at lightning speed, aimed his gun at me, and shot three bullets in my direction. I jumped out of the way of the first two, but the third pierced right through my abdomen. I growled as blood pooled from my stomach.

While the poisoned bullet had taken effect almost instantly with Gaian, Sina's potion seemed to work immediately with me. I tore the bullet out of my stomach, flung it back at the asshole, and let my wolf heal the wound.

He shot another bullet in my direction, but I caught it between two fingers, shifted into my wolf, and sank my canines into his right hand, tearing it off his body. He screamed in pain, and his hand and the gun clattered to the ground.

After staring down at his handless arm, he swayed slightly and passed the fuck out.

I shifted back into my human, grabbed the gun, and nodded to Xorgor. "Keep Maxine safe. They know what Sina is, and they'll do anything to get her back."

———

Thirty minutes later, I stepped onto pack grounds and headed directly for the prison. Unlike her father's other goons, I wasn't going to torture and kill these guys. I'd kick the shit out of them when they awoke, but Sina would kill them.

I wanted to see her true power.

"Get to the prison," I said through the mind link. *"Now."*

Once I chained the men to different cells, I paced outside of them and resisted the urge to just fucking kill them now. I wanted their pathetic lives to be over already, but I needed to wait. I couldn't make senseless decisions anymore.

Not if Sina really was the Paragon.

Gaian and Calder walked into the prison, chatting about Sina quietly. When they saw the goons behind me, they growled and hurried over to me.

"Where the fuck did you find them?" Calder snapped.

"Maxine's house."

"Why were you there?" Gaian asked. "And why haven't you killed them?"

"Because I know what Sina is."

Calder's hard gaze shifted from the men to me. "What?"

"It's folktale, legend, demon lore," I said, shaking my head and hoping to the Moon Goddess that they would believe me. All other species had laughed about it every time they heard it being brought up, none of them willing to believe that there was a stronger species out there. "It's called"—I looked over my shoulder to make sure the men hadn't woken up—"the Paragon."

"The Paragon?" Calder asked.

"The perfect being."

56

the perfect being

calder

"THE PERFECT BEINGS?" I repeated, brows furrowing. "The Paragon."

"It sounds fucking crazy," Thayer said, pacing around the prison and running his hands through his hair. He stared at the ground, his wolfish eyes turning a piercing red demon color. "Because it is. How can a species be perfect? Not even gods can reach perfection."

"I've read about the Paragon briefly," Gaian said. "Isn't it a book in the library? From what I remember, the Paragonian people are a combination of species, almost like you. Multiple species in one."

"The Paragonian people aren't mutts like me," Thayer said. "All the books and lessons we learn during school have been watered down, so as not to cause hysteria, but demon families pass down what they know to be true."

"Then, what are they?" I asked, confused.

Still, I couldn't grasp this reality. Sina had always been human. She had been human four years ago, and she had been human when she escaped her father and returned to Durnbone. If she were anything else, we would've sensed or noticed it on her.

"The Paragons are not just a combination of species with a

mother from one species and a father from another. They have a mother and a father who are Paragons, too, and they come from a *once-thought*-to-be-extinct species, the first species where all other species derive from."

I ran my tongue across my teeth and took in the information that Thayer had presented me. Thayer was batshit crazy most of the time. From the outside, this might've seemed like one of those times, but it couldn't be. I hadn't seen anything like Sina before.

"Wasn't the last known sighting of one five hundred years ago?" Gaian asked.

"So fucking what?" Thayer asked. "Everyone thought they'd die out, become extinct, but they've been in hiding because everyone either wants to kill them or use them for their power, which is exactly what Sina's ex-boyfriend is trying to do."

"You found information on him?" I asked, stepping forward and balling my hands.

"Xorgor told me that fucker had lied to Sina about her father's whereabouts," Thayer said, clutching the silver prison cell bars in his fists until I could hear the sizzling of his skin. "He mentioned he is aiming for the throne once the demon queen steps down. He is weak as fuck, but if he had Sina by his side …"

"He could take over the fucking world," I finished.

All this time, we had known that Sina's ex-boyfriend was lying. We just didn't know about what or why. Now, if what Thayer had said was true, we could protect Sina just a bit more. Or at least, she could protect herself.

I would do anything for her, but she was so powerful that even I couldn't have stopped her last night alone. I wanted to protect her as much as I could, but Sina was still holding something back from us, something that maybe she didn't even know yet.

Only she knew or could sense her father's never-ending danger.

"That means, her father is one too?"

Thayer became quiet. "I don't fucking know. Yes? But then he shouldn't need these fucking idiots to do his dirty work. He shouldn't need poisonous bullets to kill us. He could kill anyone he wants, just like Sina killed that vampire."

After running a hand across my face, I blew out a breath. "So, do we tell her?"

"I think we need more information," Gaian said, crossing his arms and staring at the ground, the way he did when he was thinking. "What if Sina's not one of these Paragons and she is just growing into her wolf?"

"She hadn't even been bitten yet," Thayer said. "She wouldn't have had a wolf."

"What if her father did something to her? What if he wanted to make her a wolf or another species? He was doing experiments on her and was … you know, letting other species basically breed with her."

A blood-hungry growl rumbled from my throat. "Don't you fucking say those words ever again, Gaian, or I swear, I'll throw you into one of these prison cages myself and torture the fuck out of you."

Gaian put his hands up and stepped back. "It's the truth."

Thayer continued to pace the hallway of the prison, then finally stopped in front of Gaian and me. "I'm fucking telling you right now that there is no fucking way her father created that. None of the shit he did makes any sense, but there's no amount of science that could create a superhuman species like Sina."

Gaian shook his head. "So, you're just going to tell Sina with no context at all?"

"Gaian's right," I said to Thayer. "We don't know the whole story. Who knows what her father did or how powerful he truly is? He vanished with her without a trace four years ago and managed to stay hidden for years while experimenting. And who the hell knows what happened to her mother?"

"I'm not sitting back and doing nothing," Thayer growled, shoving me back. "You guys just want to keep hiding important shit from her, protect her, and shelter her. You act like she's the most fragile fucking thing you've ever seen."

"She is fragile right now," Gaian said. "She's slowly regaining horrific memories."

"She just fucking killed a vampire!"

"She can be both fragile and strong," I interjected, placing a hand on Thayer's chest so he wouldn't take his fucking anger out on me. "But if she loses control again and comes after you alone, Thay, she's going to kill you. She almost did last night."

"She won't hurt us. We're her mates," Thayer reasoned, completely forgetting the fact that she had almost really killed him last night. If we hadn't stepped in and tried to stop Sina, then she might've actually taken his life. "We protect her by aiding her, not holding her back. We train her to harness her power."

"And how do you plan on doing that?" Gaian asked.

Thayer curled his lip into a smirk and glanced back at the two goons he had brought home. "I have a couple of dummies she could practice on. And if you don't want any part in it, then fine. But you're not going to stop *me* from watching Sina become one of the most powerful beings on this planet."

57

the woman

sina

I WOKE up in Gaian's bed alone.

After shuffling around in his closet, I pulled on an oversize hoodie that came down to my mid-thigh. Yawning, I walked out of his bedroom and through the quiet house to the stairs, where I smelled yummy waffles.

Darius stood in the kitchen with flour all over his tight black V-neck, drizzling waffle mix into the waffle maker. I hopped onto one of the stools at the island, rested my head in my hands, and watched him.

"How many do you want, Pretty Bird?" he asked, not turning around. "They're for you."

"Just for me?" I said, letting a small giggle escape my lips. "You've made about twenty."

He threw me a grin over his shoulder. "And maybe for me too."

My heart fluttered with excitement, my lips curling into a smile. While Darius and I had never really had a cute relationship, like I had with Gaian, or an intense *want to fuck you right now* thing, like I had with Thayer and Calder, I had been growing closer to him these past few days.

It made me feel really happy for once. Darius was easygoing and made me feel so safe.

Once he placed the last of the waffles on two plates, he sat next to me and poured a shit-ton of syrup over the brunch food. I furrowed my brows at his waffles, noticing the sheer amount of chocolate chips this man put into his waffles.

"You have the audacity to give me waffles without the chocolate?!" I asked playfully, stealing his forkful of chocolate chips and some waffle mix and shoving it into my mouth. "That's more like it."

Darius wrapped his arm around the back of my chair and pulled me closer, growling playfully back at me. "Your sleepy ass didn't tell me she likes a pound of chocolate chips with her brunch."

"Hey!" I said, giggling. "It's not my fault. You could've asked."

"And awaken the monster?" he joked.

While I knew that he hadn't meant the monster that I had become last night—he was just making a silly little joke—I couldn't help but feel all those emotions that I'd had before I crawled into bed with Gaian.

"Fuck," he said immediately. "Sorry. I didn't mean it like that."

I pressed my lips together, forced a smile, and looked down at my waffles. "I know I've apologized already, but I'm—"

Before I could say another word, he shoved another forkful of waffles into my mouth. "You have nothing to be sorry about, Pretty Bird. We all fucking love you and would do anything for you. You're not the monster you think you are. None of us thinks that, so get it out of that pretty head of yours."

"It's hard," I whispered, swallowing the food. "But I'll try."

"You'd better."

After cutting another piece of my waffles, I glanced around the empty house. "Where are the guys anyway? I would've thought that Thayer would be back by now. It's been at least a few hours, hasn't it?"

Darius looked at the back French doors. "They're *taking care* of a couple of people."

"Like … my father's people?" I asked.

Sighing softly, Darius nodded. "Look, don't worry about it becau —" He suddenly stopped and lifted his gaze to the back door.

A pregnant human woman stood at the door and waved to us.

He jumped up. "I actually want you to meet someone."

I straightened myself, vaguely remembering this woman from last night.

She walked into the room and unzipped her light fall jacket. "Hi, you must be Sina."

Nervous for some reason, I stood up and guided her to one of our stools. "Yeah, I'm Sina. How are you feeling? That vampire didn't hurt you at all last night, did he? I tried to stop him. I'm sorry if—"

"No, he didn't," she said, sitting and smiling at me. "I'm Hellana."

"Hellana," I repeated. "It's nice to meet you. Well, is there anybody we can call, so we can get you back home? I'm sure you don't want to stay here with a bunch of werewolves and … whatever the hell I am."

Her sweet smile dropped. "Actually, no. This girl and I are all alone." She cradled her baby bump, drawing her fingers against it. "Alpha Calder said we could stay in his pack for a while. We don't have any family. Her father is … he's not around anymore, to say the least."

"You can stay for as long as you need," Darius said.

"Thank you again," she whispered.

But their conversation slowly faded from my mind. All I could seem to focus on were her words, ringing through my head over and over, like they were playing on repeat, *like they had been* playing on repeat all my life, speaking to me.

Suddenly, a piercing pain shot through my head. I clutched it and leaned against the counter, faintly remembering those words being spoken before, but not remembering who had said them. I squeezed my eyes closed, hoping to find answers. Any answers would do.

The silhouette of Mom cradling a baby—presumably me, as I was my mother's only child—flashed through my mind.

She stood in front of my father at a large desk in my old home, rocking me back and forth. "We don't have any family around these parts. Her father is … he's not around anymore."

But my father was right in front of her.

"I don't have the money to feed her. I don't have any place to raise her," she continued. "I come to you, asking for help. I'll do anything you need, anything you ask of me. Just please, she can't die. It's essential for …"

"For what?" my father said.

"For the sake of my species."

58

the power

thayer

WHEN A GUARD INFORMED Gaian and Calder that trouble lurked at our borders, I walked back to the pack house and decided that I'd show Sina her true power without them. They either didn't understand her powers or didn't believe me.

There was no question in my mind that she was a Paragon.

Sina sat alone in the kitchen, finishing up a waffle for breakfast. The faint scent of the pregnant woman that Sina had saved yesterday and Darius lingered in the air, which meant that they were still relatively close to the pack house and hadn't left Sina alone completely.

When she saw me enter, she sat up and widened her eyes. "Thayer."

"You're coming with me," I said, grabbing her hand and tugging her toward the back.

She tumbled out of her seat and pulled me to a stop. "Wait, I want to talk to you first."

"Whatever it is, it can wait."

All I wanted to do was bring her to the prison to see what she was truly capable of. She had powers beyond belief. And I wanted to know—I needed to know—her true potential. Nobody in my life-time had ever seen a Paragon in real life.

At least … I didn't think they had.

"No, it can't," Sina said.

"What is it then?" I asked, staring down at her. "Be quick."

"I …" She swallowed hard and drew her hands across my face, her fingers tracing the scar that she had left on my skin from last night. It still hurt like a motherfucker. "I … I want to say that I'm sorry. I didn't mean to hurt you."

"It's fine, Sina."

Tears welled up in her big eyes, her bottom lip trembling. "I'm so sorry. I'm a monster. And I … I … I promise to figure it out, okay? I'll do whatever I can. Whatever you want me to do. I'll learn to control myself because I don't wanna hurt you ever again."

"Sina," I said, softer this time because she looked so fucking fragile right now, "it's okay."

After gnawing on the inside of her cheek, Sina clutched my hand tightly and stared at the scar. "The guys told me you can … that you can heal your wounds. You should do that. I don't want you running around with a scar on your face because of me for the rest of your life. It's not fair to you."

While I wanted to tell her so badly that I could heal my scar, I couldn't. But I didn't want her to feel bad. She was already taking this so fucking hard. And she kept apologizing to me over and over and over again.

But I wasn't going to lie to her. She was strong. So fucking strong.

"I can't," I said, clenching my jaw and hoping that she wouldn't freak out about it. I knew that she'd see this scar every day and hurt because she had caused it. That was why I had tried so hard to heal it. "I mean, I can usually heal my scars, but I can't heal the one you gave me last night."

Sina's eyes widened even more. "Wh-what do you mean? Why can't you heal that?"

"Because … it's not from a human. It's not from a demon. It's not from a wolf or a vampire or a fae. It's from no creature that you know. Not even a creature living in Durnbone."

"What are you talking about?" she asked, backing away slowly. Fear swelled up in her eyes. "I'm just human." She stared down at her feet and shook her head. "I'm just a human. I have to be just a human."

"You're not."

"Then … what am I?"

"Your father never told you?"

With all those experiments he had run on her, he had to have known what she truly was.

"No. I mean, he … was trying to make the perfect species—at least, I think so. He did so many experiments on me that I don't even remember half of them. And … I just … I don't wanna be anything other than human."

"Well, Sina …" I drew her closer to me, so she couldn't back herself up anymore and ball up in the corner of the room. She wasn't in this alone. "You're so much fucking more than a human. You're one of the strongest creatures to ever live."

She trembled, looking so helpless and terrified. The Sina who had appeared back in Durnbone weeks ago had so many walls put up, but they were slowly shattering. Every single time we learned something new about her, she became more and more vulnerable with us.

While I didn't do this lovey-dovey bullshit, Sina didn't need an asshole right now. She already got a bitchy attitude whenever she talked to Calder. Right now, I needed her to fucking know that I would do anything for her.

Fucking anything.

So, I gently grasped her hands in mine and brought them up to my lips, placing them on her knuckles. "Humans teach their young to be afraid of beasts even if it's just implicitly. But don't be afraid of your beast, Sina. She's fucking incredible."

When she went to pull away, I grabbed her hands tighter.

"I can't control myself," she said.

"I'll teach you."

"I'll hurt you."

"No," I said with a slight head shake. "You won't."

But still, I wasn't positive. She had the power to kill me and everyone else here. If Sina wanted to hurt me, she could snap all my fingers and my throat in a millisecond. Paragons weren't known to play nice when pissed off.

"You have to believe me," I said, drawing her closer. "I know it's fucking hard. I know you're scared. But to be honest with you, *you're* the only one who will be able to defeat your father when he comes to take you back."

"He's—" Sina started, but then cut herself off. She glanced down at her feet and gnawed on the inside of my cheek. "I think I unlocked another memory from my past. If it's true and real, then my father … isn't really my father."

"But your mother was, wasn't she?" I asked. It was all making fucking sense now.

"Yes," Sina said, voice soft. "She was. How'd you know?"

I grabbed her hand and tugged her toward the back door. "You'll see."

59

the slaughter

"WHY ARE you taking me to the prison?" I asked, nerves nipping at my insides.

Thayer took longer strides toward the small concrete building, dragging me along with him. Two guards stood at the door, scanning the forest for trespassers. When Thayer nodded to them, they opened the doors and let us pass.

I took a cautious step inside and followed him down a set of stairs. It was chilly and cold on the inside, the concrete and the cobwebs making me tremble in fear. I'd never been down here before, but the air smelled thick of blood.

My mouth salivated at the mere scent of it, my teeth lengthening. Something deep and feral inside me wanted to taste it, wanted it pooling in my mouth and rolling down my chin. And that something fucking scared me.

"I really don't think this is a good idea." My stomach was in knots. I tugged on his arm and hoped he would just listen to me and turn back now. What if I lost control here? "Can we turn back? Please, Thayer. I ... please."

When my foot landed on the final step, he stopped. "No," he

said. His reply was short but final. "I'm going to show you what you're made of today."

My stomach twisted and turned even more. I was so fucking terrified of what he had in store for me. After he had told me he couldn't heal his wounds, I had begun to fear that if I had hurt him worse, I would have killed him.

"But ... I—"

Thayer came to a stop in front of a single cell. A man who looked oddly familiar sat in the back of it, chained up and knocked out. I stepped closer to the bars to get a better look and sucked in a deep breath.

"Oh my gods."

He was ...

He was one of my father's men.

He was somebody who had hurt me, used me, raped me.

"What is he doing here?" I asked, my words coming out soft but there was a certain edge in them, one that I couldn't seem to explain.

This man terrified me to no end, but the monster inside me made me wanna rip him apart.

"You're going to kill him," Thayer said, standing behind me with his arms crossed. His words were matter-of-fact, like I had no other option than to ... murder this man in front of me for what he had done to me, to lose complete control.

I had wanted to for so long, but ...

"Don't second-guess yourself, Pretty Bird. Kill him."

After shifting my gaze from the man to Thayer, I grabbed his hand. "But ... what if I lose control? What if I hurt you too? Just like last night." I shook my head, tears welling in my eyes. "I can't do that to you. I love you too much."

The words came out so quickly that I couldn't seem to stop it. I slapped a hand over my mouth and stared at him with wide eyes. Did I just ... did I just say that I loved him out loud? There was no doubt in my mind that I loved these guys and that they loved me too. But was it a bit too soon?

He stood still for a moment, his eyes shifting. Tons of emotions crossed over his face, and I feared that he didn't wanna say it back to me. And that would be okay. I just didn't want to lose him.

"You do? You love me?" Thayer asked.

I scratched the back of my head and chewed on the inside of my lip. "Of course I do."

After a few moments, he smiled. And it wasn't one of his psycho smiles that he had after he murdered someone. But it was soft and loving and … caring. And his eyes weren't so dark and harsh anymore either.

"So, you'll kill this man for me."

I stared at him for a few moments and then turned back toward the man who was slowly regaining consciousness.

He sat up with his head against the wall and stared at me. When he realized it was me, he stood and pulled on the chains. "What the fuck are you doing here with them? Your father will kill you. I came here to return you to him."

Dad still thought that he had control over me. He had none. And as much as I didn't want to lose control, as much as I didn't want to hurt anyone else, he deserved it. And the beast inside me was aching for blood.

My canines lengthened, and my sight became blurry. I let my nails transform into long talons.

"He doesn't own me. And you'll never bring me back to that place again."

No way in fucking hell would I allow that.

I yanked the cell open and stepped into it. I shut the door because I didn't want to lose control and hurt Thayer again. But he just followed me into the cell. He wanted to be close to me. He wanted to see me go crazy, psycho, insane.

"Do it, Pretty Bird," Thayer taunted.

Slowly, I felt myself slipping. I found myself losing control. My consciousness would go in and out, and in and out, just like I had last night. I took my last deep breath and hoped to whatever the fuck I was that I wouldn't hurt Thayer tonight.

And then I transformed into the monster that I was and lunged at the man.

Suddenly, limbs were torn, flying in every direction. The ground was covered in flesh and blood. I ripped my claws into his body, over and over and over and over. Never fucking stopping once. He deserved this. They all deserved this.

They had hurt me. Just like they had probably hurt my mother. Just like they were going to hurt that mother and unborn child yesterday too.

They all deserved to fucking die. Every last one of them.

60

the juicy, hot sex

sina

MY BREATHS WERE short and fast. My heart pounded against my chest. My mind slowly faded in and out of consciousness. And I desperately needed something, someone. More blood. More touch. More everything.

More. More. More. More. More.

My father's guard lay in pieces around the cell. I turned toward Thayer, my canines aching for more, my talons wanting flesh, my entire body needing him. While my inner monster might've wanted him, I feared that I'd hurt him.

"Thayer," I ground out, "leave now."

Thayer curled his lips into a smirk and stepped closer to me. "I'm not going anywhere, Pretty Bird." He grabbed me by a fistful of my hair and tugged it back, so I looked directly up at him. "You're fucking mine."

Unable to stop myself, I snapped my hand around his throat. "You n-need to g-go."

If I surrendered control to my monster, she might see him as a threat and kill him.

Blood from my hand dripped down Thayer's neck. He tugged

on my hair harder and shoved me against the stone wall roughly, stepping closer to me. This man wasn't about to leave, and I knew it.

"You're mine."

"Th-Thayer."

"Give me fucking all of you."

"D-don't push me. I'll l-lose it."

"Then, lose control, Pretty Bird. Show me what you're made of."

I turned us around and shoved him against the stone wall, my hand tightening around his throat. I desperately wanted to stop myself, but I couldn't even think straight anymore. My monster had seized control and planned to do exactly what Thayer had demanded.

His pulse raced underneath my fingers. He wrapped his hand around my throat and tightened his grasp, mirroring me. And then, like the psycho he was, he smacked me across the face harder than he ever had.

A low growl rumbled from my throat, yet I found my pussy pounding. Like he had done to me, I smacked him back so hard that I left a red handprint on his cheek. The excitement in me rose every moment.

"Is that all you've fucking got?" he asked, smacking me again. "Hmm?"

I strummed my fingers down the column of his throat and hit him again, watching his smirk widen even more. As much as he loved abusing me during sex, he loved when I fought back. He loved when I taunted him.

Within a moment, Thayer had turned us around once more, trapping me between him and the wall. I expected him to slap me again, to hit me harder, to play with me, but he tore off my pants with his claws and forced me to spread my legs, letting my wet pussy glisten underneath the dim prison cell light.

I dug my fingers into his throat, hard enough to draw blood. My mouth salivated at how fresh it smelled, and I couldn't stop myself from drawing my tongue across the blood dripping down his throat so I could taste him.

"If you're going to drink my fucking blood," Thayer started, grabbing the back of my head with his free hand and shoving me closer to his neck, "then fucking drink it. Don't be a pussy about it, Sina. Take it all."

Unable to move, I wrapped my hand around the back of his throat and sank my teeth into his neck, sucking his blood. Thayer held my head in the crook of his neck with one hand and slapped my clit over and over with his other.

Pressure rose higher and higher in my core. I clenched, desperately aching for him to be inside me, and sucked harder, his blood pooling in my mouth. He tasted so good—so fucking good. I needed more. More. More.

Another slap to my clit.

"How's that fucking pussy feel?" he growled.

I forced my head back and stared at him with a mouthful of his blood. "Fuck you."

Thayer shoved his hand into my mouth and thrust four of his fingers as deep as they could go. "Say it a-fucking-gain, Sina." He pushed his fingers farther and farther down my throat, leaving my pussy bare and aching. "Say it again."

"Fuck you," I gargled on his fingers.

He pulled his hand out of my mouth and smacked me across the face, then pushed down his pants and thrust himself into me hard. He smacked me over and over and over, my cheeks red and burning.

But I didn't want him to stop. I loved it too much.

I wanted more.

When he pulled away for more than a second, I spit his blood back at him. He pounded into my tight hole and forced my jaw open with his brute strength, and then he spit into my mouth and smacked me again.

Spit. Slap. Spit. Slap.

Over and over and over.

Pressure rose higher in my core. I was seconds from coming undone around him, moments from releasing everything on his cock. I wrapped my hand around his throat, my thumb rubbing over the wound I had made in his neck. Blood gushed out of it.

Desperate for another taste, I coated my fingers in his blood and stuck them into my mouth myself, sucking them off hungrily.

Thayer snapped my mouth closed around my fingers and growled, "You're my hungry little whore, aren't you, Pretty Bird?"

"Fuck you," I mumbled on my fingers, the words muffled because he wouldn't let me open my mouth.

He released his grip on me and chuckled darkly, wrapping both his arms underneath my legs and picking me up into the air. He pounded even harder into me, his lips against mine and his tongue in my mouth, tasting his own blood.

"You're mine," he purred against me, his words so much softer that I found myself coming at the mere sound of them. "All mine."

Wave after wave of pleasure coursed through my body, my limbs numbing for a few moments. I sighed in relief and slowly came down from the high.

Once we finished, I collapsed onto the ground. Pieces of my abuser's corpse lay around the small cell, his blood covering my body and soaking into the concrete floor. Thayer picked me up into his arms and pulled me tight to his chest.

"I love you too, Pretty Bird," he murmured, repeating my words from earlier.

Warmth spread throughout my chest, relaxation washing over me. While I had known it to be true all along, I loved when he said it, and I loved when he stopped being the psycho Thayer for a few moments of vulnerability with me.

After Thayer walked back up the concrete steps with me, the guards opened the doors for us. Thayer walked out with me clinging to him and headed for the pack house. I desperately needed a shower and sleep after that.

"You're mine," he murmured, his face buried into the crook of my neck. "Mine."

Every word he said, his voice became more and more taut, strained even, feral.

"Wh-what am I?" I whispered, staring up at the blue afternoon sky.

Thayer's canines grazed against my skin, a low growl coming from his lips. "Mine."

I rested my head back even further, my inner beast purring at the feel of his canines against my throat. Goosebumps rose on my bare skin, and I shivered in anticipation. Ever since Calder had marked me, I had been aching for another.

"I mean ..." I began, keeping my voice steady even though it was trembling hard. "What kind of monster am I?"

"You're not a monster," Thayer murmured against me, voice tenser. "You're a Paragon, one of the most magnificent fucking creatures to ever grace this world and a woman who I'm lucky enough to call mine."

While I had so many questions about what a Paragon was, I couldn't focus as the tips of his canines pressed into my skin. I inhaled sharply and tensed, anticipating the pure pleasure that would rush through me.

"I'm yours," I whispered.

As soon as the words left my mouth, Thayer sank his canines into my neck and claimed me.

61

the reaction

sina

PLEASURE COURSED through my body as Thayer's canines sank deeper and deeper inside me. My legs trembled. I curled my fingers into his muscular shoulders and let out an unsteady breath.

"You … you marked me," I whispered.

When Thayer pulled away, his teeth were covered in my blood, like mine must've been with his earlier. He licked his lips clean, eyes rolling back into his head, then drew his tongue across his mark to close the wound.

He curled his fingers into my body, a small smile stretching across his face. "Yeah, I did. And I should've fucking done it sooner. No more pissing off and listening to Calder. You're my fucking mate, too, and that was the best fucking thing I've ever experienced."

Heart racing, I laid my head on his chest and relaxed against his body. When the pack house came into view, I smiled. Days ago, I had been begging for them to finally mark me, feeling so helpless and lonely. Now, I wore two out of four marks.

"You're back," Darius called from the back door. When Thayer stepped closer to him, Darius widened his eyes. "Whoa," Darius said, staring at me and him with wide eyes. He opened the door wider to let us in and gazed at my neck. "You marked her?"

"Yeah, I fucking did. Do you have a problem with that?"

"No. I just …" Darius's gaze lingered on my neck for a moment longer, an unfamiliar emotion crossing them.

I wanted to ask what it was, but he quickly averted his eyes and closed the door, stepping away to give us room to pass.

Thayer set me down onto my feet in the living room, where Calder and Gaian were chatting about something that must've happened at the property borders. When they saw me, Calder stopped speaking entirely.

"What the fuck is that?" Calder asked, his canines extending past his lips as he stared at my neck. His mark might've glistened on my other side, but Thayer's mark was fresh. It was still sinking into my skin, becoming a part of it. Blotchy, bright, and red.

"It's my mark," Thayer said, gripping my waist tightly and tugging me to him. With his index finger, he tucked some hair behind my ear to show the mark off to the other guys. Thayer looked at Calder, challenging him, and growled lowly, "If you have something to say about it, fucking say it."

After shooting up from the couch, Calder forcefully took my chin in his rough hand and pulled it to the side to get a better look at my mark. A low and feral growl escaped his lips. "I don't have shit to say about it. It's just …"

It was like he was lost for words too. And he was pissed the fuck off. I might've been all their mates, but he was a possessive asshole who wanted me all for himself. I didn't know why. He was so fucking confusing.

Not wanting him to flip out—because I didn't have the time or the energy for that—I pushed his hand off my chin and pursed my lips at him. "Can you not touch me like I'm an object? I might have your mark on my neck, but you don't own me. We have more important things to talk about, like"—I stared from guy to guy—"what I am."

Calder glared at Thayer and snarled, "You told her?"

"You knew?" I asked, arching a brow at Calder because he was pissing me off again.

Thayer shoved him back and growled, "Don't be pissed because she wears my mark too. She's not just yours. She belongs to all of us."

I crossed my arms. "I don't belong to anyone."

But those two didn't seem like they were listening. All they did was try to posture and alpha over one another. As they stepped closer and closer, I rolled my eyes and pushed them away from each other. I guessed that was what happened when two psychotic, testosterone-filled guys got together.

"What are you?" Darius asked me, ignoring the others.

"So, it's true?" Gaian spoke up for the first time since we had made it back to the pack house. He looked from me to the marks on my neck, and then he clenched his jaw, jealousy clear in his eyes. But at least he wasn't overcome with it, like Thayer and Calder were. Gaian stood. "You're a ... a Paragon?"

I swallowed hard and shrugged, stepping away from the two assholes who couldn't control their tempers, not even for me. "I guess so because I can ..." I started, nerves biting my inside. I still thought of myself as a monster.

But whether I was a monster or not, Thayer didn't care. He wanted me to embrace everything that I was, every species that resided inside me. He wanted me to hone my strength and kill my father.

"I can shift," I finally finished. "It's a shit-ton of species, but only bits and parts of me. My fangs need blood, my claws ache for flesh. And my senses ... there's so much more than that ... of a wolf. When I lose control, everything is more intense—my smell, my movement, my sight. Everything."

"You killed the guard in the prison?" Calder asked, still glaring at Thayer, who shook his head and growled back at him. It was like he already knew.

Had Thayer told him the plan all along? How long had he and Gaian known about this? Darius seemed completely out of the loop.

"Yes, I killed him."

My stomach twisted and turned, the thought making me shiver. Not in disgust. But in pleasure. That fucker had gotten what he deserved.

I stood there, uneasy, shifting from foot to foot. I didn't want them to think of me any differently though.

"Do you guys … do you hate me for it?"

"Hate you for killing that asshole?" Gaian asked, chuckling in a lighthearted manner, but there was something sinister simmering underneath his good-guy persona he had up right now. "No. He deserved it."

I let out a deep breath, my shoulders drooping forward. "That's not all. I had a vision earlier, and I don't think my father is really my father. My vision was of my mother coming to his home while I was a baby and asking him for help, for him to take a stand because my real father was out of the picture. I don't know what that means, but I hope he's not dead. He'd be the only family I have left."

"Your father isn't dead," Thayer said, as if he was sure of it. "Paragons don't die easily. They're more immortal that vampires or demons. If you're a Paragon, then your father and your mother must be ones too."

"He could've been captured, picked apart by an enemy," Darius offered.

"We need to find them for answers," Thayer said.

"Them?" I asked.

"Your mother and father," Calder said, finally looking at me.

"But my mom died. I saw her corpse with my own two eyes."

"Then, we retrieve her body. Wherever your father—I mean, that prick who took you—is keeping her, we need to get her back. If she's really dead, then she's not in good hands. He wouldn't have buried her. He's using her for something," Thayer said. "Something sinister."

62
the jealousy

gaian

"IF SHE'S DEAD, he's probably dissecting her," Darius said.

"Can you all stop saying *if*?!" Sina asked, throwing her hands into the air and shaking her head. "She's dead, has been for years now. If she were alive …" She looked down at her feet. "If she were alive, then I would've known."

"Would you have known, or would you feel guilty for not knowing and leaving?" Darius asked.

Sina pressed her lips into a tight line and pulled her gaze away, shaking her head again. "It doesn't matter," she whispered. "I left her there anyway." After another pause, she looked back up. "Either way, if she's not buried, I need to find her."

I gritted my teeth at Thayer and Calder, pissed that they had marked her but I hadn't yet. "You want us to raid his home to find Sina's mom while that bastard wants to kill us?" I asked, eyeing how close Sina kept moving toward Thayer. She was grazing against his body, her fingers brushing against his knuckles almost subconsciously.

"Yes," Thayer said. "Before Jaroth does."

"Jaroth?" Sina asked. "What does he have to do with any of this?"

"He's no good," Calder snapped. "Forget him."

"Would you like to tell me why?" Sina asked, tapping her foot. "He was supposed to be getting me information this weekend about my father's whereabouts. We could use him to figure out where my father is."

"He's using you," Thayer said. "He wants your power to ensure he becomes the next ruler of the demons."

Sina scoffed. "He told me he didn't even want to be ruler, but that his mother was pushing him to become one. He wouldn't do some shit like that. He hates the demons and his powers most days."

The more and more they talked about Sina's ex, the more her marks seemed to glisten on her fragile neck, and the more I couldn't tear my gaze away from them. Both sides of her throat were scarred for eternity.

I stared at Sina's marked neck and held back a growl. She had been talking with us for the past half hour about what Thayer thought she was and the powers that she seemed to suddenly have. And while I tried to contribute to the conversation, I couldn't hold back my anger.

All these years, I had been waiting for her. I had dreamed of marking her as my mate, of keeping her as my own. Now, she wore two marks that weren't mine, and I couldn't fucking stand it. I didn't want to push her into doing something she didn't want to do, but I didn't know if I could hold up this act anymore.

This nice-guy persona.

The nice guy inside me had died the night I found out about Sina's disappearance. The nice guy had been ripped to shreds and replaced with someone who cared, but someone who refused to lose his mate again, someone who would kill just as ruthlessly as Calder and Thayer.

I wasn't normally a jealous guy. I tried not to be, but …

I ached to have my mark on her neck. She wore the others so

fucking proudly, and I didn't want her to walk around for another day without my mark peppered on her throat, *scarred* on her body.

Sina must've sensed something was wrong because she walked away from Thayer's side and stepped right between Darius and me. When she brushed her leg against mine, I fucking lost it. But I wasn't going to let Sina know how much my wolf fucking ached for her now.

She wouldn't see me as the psycho jealous type, not yet.

I grimaced at Thayer and Calder. "Why don't you guys leave?"

"Leave?" Calder growled. "The fuck you mean? We're in the middle of a conversation."

Inhaling sharply, Sina glanced over at me with furrowed brows. She stared at me for a few moments, as if she didn't know what was going on through my head, but then she turned back to Thayer and Calder and nodded.

"I want to spend time with Darius and Gaian," she said. "Alone for once."

"But—" Calder started, teeth grinding.

"Alone," Sina repeated.

If they didn't leave, they'd both fight to the fucking death for her to spend the night with them, to get closer to them, to touch them, be with them, for them to be inside her. And we would get fucking no time with our mate.

Calder would say that he had control of himself, but we all knew fucking better.

He had the least control out of all of us.

"What's wrong?" she asked when they finally left.

"Nothing," I said, giving her a sweet smile so she wouldn't suspect anything, so she wouldn't know how, with every moment that passed, all I wanted to do was take her harder and faster and more ruthlessly than the others had.

"Come on," she pushed. "Tell me."

"It's nothing, Sina," I said, pushing some hair out of her face and looking down at her marks again. "Don't worry about it."

63

the third mark

sina

SINCE THE OTHERS WERE OUT, being pissed off at each other, Darius, Gaian, and I could have an easy and quiet night. So, I turned on a movie that we used to watch while we were younger and cuddled between the two of them on the couch.

Gaian rested his large hand on my thigh, his fingers curled into my skin possessively. Usually, he wasn't so rough and territorial, but tonight, he wouldn't let up. He kept touching me, kept inching closer, his scent overwhelmingly strong.

I inhaled sharply and closed my eyes, warmth building in my core.

"Pretty Bird," Darius teased, "you're doing it again."

"Doing what?" I asked, trying to suppress a smile.

"What you've been doing all night."

"And what's that?" I looked over at him with a challenging gaze.

Like Gaian typically was, Darius was usually a hands-off guy and not as forward as the two psychopaths who were probably itching to come back home to see me.

Suddenly, Gaian pulled me onto his lap with my back against his front and drew his nose up the column of my neck, his canines grazing against my sensitive skin and making me ache. The beast inside me desperately wanted his teeth to sink into me and for him to claim me, like the others had.

But Gaian had always been the nice guy, the type of person who asked politely before he did something, who respected me and wanted me to make my own decisions about my body. He wouldn't mark me unless he asked first.

Instead, he ripped off my shirt and let my breasts bounce out of it. He groped my breasts in his hands, playing and tugging on my hardened nipples until I squirmed in his lap. Holding me still, he kneaded and slapped my tits, low growls escaping him.

"You know what you've been doing," he growled into my ear and pressed his hardness against my pussy. After slipping one hand into my shorts, he teased my clit and sank his fingers into my wet pussy. "We could smell your wetness since you sat between us."

My lips curled into a smile, and I parted my legs even farther apart, loving the feel of his hands on my body. I had been spending way too much alone time with Calder and Thayer, way too many nights with just them.

Darius moved closer, grabbed my legs, and yanked my ass to the edge of the couch, tearing off my shorts, throwing my legs into the air, and kneeling in front of me. With a low snarl, he stared up at me with dark wolfish eyes, his wet lips trailing up the inside of my thigh.

I rested my legs on his muscular shoulders and leaned back against Gaian, letting my head fall to the left to give him better access to my neck. He drew his tongue up the column, wetting my skin and then sucking lightly on it.

When Darius reached my cunt, he buried his face between my legs and flicked my clit with his tongue. My legs jerked up in the air, my pussy immediately clenching. I whimpered and inched my hips closer to his face, not wanting him to stop once.

He wrapped his arms around my thighs to steady my hips and continued to tease my pussy, licking and flicking my clit until the pressure was too much. I tried grinding my hips up and down, rubbing my ass against Gaian's bulge, so fucking desperate for a release.

My beast was slowly taking control of me, aching to be free in her natural form.

But right now, I wanted to spend tonight with my mates.

"More, Darius," I breathed, grabbing a fistful of his dreads to pull him closer. "Please."

Gaian drew his nose up my neck again and growled lowly in my ear, tugging on my nipples. I squealed, my legs trembling, and threw my head back, needing something inside me but Darius wouldn't slip his fingers into me.

He continued to tease my pussy as Gaian bounced my tits in his hands.

"You're the sexiest fucking thing alive," Gaian growled again, pressing his hips up against my ass. "I want to be inside you."

"Please," I cried, hating but loving how they teased my body.

When Darius pulled away, he stood up and unzipped his pants. "Spin her around."

Gaian picked me up like I weighed nothing and spun me around in his lap, so I straddled his waist. With my hands on his shoulders, I hovered over him and shoved my tits into his face as he stared up at me and whipped out his cock. When I felt the head against my wet pussy, I sank down on him and moaned as he filled me.

As I straddled Gaian, he groped my tits roughly in his large hands and placed his wet mouth on my neck. "Fuck, Pretty Bird," he growled, the sound of his voice vibrating my skin. He moved his lips down my neck to my chest and latched his teeth on to my nipple. "I fucking love these tits."

From behind me, Darius wrapped both of his hands around the front of my throat and tugged on my chin backward, so I stared up at him. He placed his mouth on mine, kissing me, then grabbed my hands and placed them on my asscheeks.

"Spread yourself apart for me," he mumbled against my lips.

I curled my fingers into my flesh and pulled apart my cheeks, giving him better access to me. He let a wad of spit drip from his mouth onto my ass, and then he pushed his cock between my cheeks and rubbed the spit against my hole.

"You're going to open yourself up for me," he growled, his canines lengthening against my lips. My entire body trembled in pleasure as Gaian continued to suck on my breast. "Or I'm going to stretch this tight little ass out for you."

When he pushed the head of his huge cock inside me, I curled my fingers against my asscheeks and whimpered into Darius's mouth. He gently stroked his fingers against the column of my neck and against Calder's and Thayer's marks.

Pleasure rushed through my body. I tightened around them both, my moans turning into whimpers as Darius pushed another inch into my ass.

He pulled me toward him, sliding the rest of his cock into me, and grunted into my mouth, "You're so fucking tight."

They thrust into me at different paces, Gaian pulling out as Darius pushed himself into me. I straddled Gaian's waist, feeling nothing but pleasure shoot through my body, nothing but them pushing me higher and higher into ecstasy.

As if Mr. Nice Guy Gaian couldn't hold back, he roughly grabbed my chin and forced it to the side, placing his canines on the crook of my neck. "Mine," he growled, the sound more feral than I had ever heard it. "You're mine."

I whimpered softly, "Yours."

"Mine," he muttered again, as if he hadn't heard me or couldn't control himself. "Mine."

"Yours, Gaian," I whispered, throwing my head back and tightening around his cock. I desperately wanted him to come with me because I knew if I held out just a bit longer, it would be the best fucking feeling in the world. "Co—"

Before I could finish my sentence, before I could even comprehend what he was doing, Gaian sank his canines into my throat, disposing of the good-boy persona he had for the past couple decades that I'd known him and turning into the feral animal that I'd always known he was.

64

the worries

darius

"YOU MARKED ME," Sina breathed when Gaian pulled his canines out of her neck. Droplets of blood ran down his chin. She breathed more heavily, her chest rising and falling at a quickened pace. "Gaian, you … you really marked me."

When heavenly happiness rushed through her eyes, my chest tightened. By the mere distance between us, I could feel how good she felt. She was my mate after all, except … except I hadn't marked her yet. Except I was the last one to get close to her again.

One day, I hoped to make her at least *half* as happy as the others made her.

I pulled away from the both of them and stared at the three marks that now decorated Sina's throat. They had all happened within a short period, all brutal marks that displayed the utmost ownership over her.

The walls of the pack house seemed to start closing in on me. I sucked in a deep breath to get air into my lungs, but it was no use to calm my racing heart. We might've been in the same room, but I felt so far from Sina.

While I wanted to stay with her, I didn't want to intrude. We might've all been her mates, but this was Gaian's time to be with her. My time would come … maybe. I sucked in another sharp breath and scrambled off the couch, finding my clothes near the coffee table.

Maybe it wouldn't.

My stomach twisted into unruly knots. I yanked my shorts up to my waist and pulled a shirt over my head, not that it'd matter in a minute because I needed to run. My wolf wanted out. He *needed* out.

"Gaian," Sina whispered, placing her hands on his chest and smiling down at him.

Pain shot through my body as I headed quickly to the door.

"Claim mate," my wolf growled through my head. *"Don't leave."*

After taking one last long look at Sina and Gaian, I forced myself to turn away. She was completely lost in Gaian, just like the way that she had always been with him and the others. And I stood at the door with so many fucking nerves.

Why couldn't I just mark her? Why couldn't I do what Gaian had done and not give a fuck?

Maybe because I had always felt like the odd one out of the group, like the one who didn't really matter as much, like the guy who was just there. I knew it wasn't true, but as I slipped out the back door, unnoticed, it sure as hell fucking felt like it.

"Turn back," my wolf howled.

"No."

Without removing my clothes, I transformed into my wolf and sprinted through the dark forest. I didn't run the normal path that our pack took every dawn and dusk, but carved my own one through the thicket and sharp brush.

Sina is my mate. Sina is my mate. Sina is my mate.

I repeated the words over and over again, except they didn't convince me that I should've stayed, that I should turn back. Instead, I found myself running farther into the woods, farther away from what I feared would be rejection.

Truthfully, Sina and I had never been extremely close. Not even slightly as close as the others, especially Gaian. Seeing how he had marked her, claimed her like she was his and only his, right in front of me …

It fucked me up because what if Sina never wanted me to mark her like that?

Trees whizzed by me. The faint scent of human drifted through my nose. I swallowed in desperate hope of moistening my dry throat, but it was no fucking help. My chest heaved up and down, my mind racing with thoughts so loud that I couldn't concentrate.

"What if she doesn't want us?" I asked my wolf. *"What if she's content with the others?"*

"She'll want us," he growled. *"Turn back."*

And while my wolf wanted to run back to her, I couldn't force my feet to move that way. We weren't running away from her forever, but I wanted to give them the privacy that I would want with her, the privacy that I so desperately *wanted* with her.

I just feared that she would always think of me as a friend that she fucked sometimes.

No matter how hard I thought about her, no matter how much I cared, I could never get it out when I was around her. I still felt that awkwardness that the others seemed to have shed away, even four years ago. I had never gotten past it.

I didn't know why. I wanted to be closer to her, but … I didn't know if that was what she wanted because she always seemed to pay more attention to Calder, Thayer, or Gaian. But not me.

"She loves us," my wolf said, trying to convince me.

She might. Maybe.

But was it just as friends? Fuck buddies?

"She opened up to us and told us about her father before the others," my wolf said.

Despite my wanting to keep moving, my legs slowed to a stop. I stared down at the dirt underneath my paws and howled low, still feeling so bad about our relationship.

My wolf was right. We had lain in the same bed as her the other night as she confessed so much of her life that she had been hiding from the other guys. But why me? I'd have expected her to admit something like that to Gaian. Was it because she saw me more as a friend?

"Don't be an idiot. Go back to mate. Now."

"No."

I didn't. I couldn't go back now. I'd head back later on, when Calder and Thayer got back from the pub, so that I didn't intrude on Gaian's time with her. Unlike Calder and Thayer, I knew when to *not* intrude on others.

At least, that was the reason I told myself for not wanting to go back now. Truthfully, I was fucking scared of rejection, terrified of losing Sina. And I didn't know if this feeling deep inside me would ever go away. It had always been inside me, lingering like a beast toying with its prey.

65
the training

sina

THE NEXT MORNING, I woke up next to Gaian with his strong arms wrapped around me. I slowly blinked my eyes open and stared up at the ceiling, somehow feeling even more power than yesterday swell through my body.

Morning sunlight flooded in through the windows. I inhaled deeply and frowned when I didn't smell the sweet, fluffy waffles that Darius usually made in the morning.

"Darius," the monster inside me whispered.

I furrowed my brows slightly and wondered where he had gone off to yesterday. After Gaian had marked me, he had seemed to have completely disappeared from the pack house. I searched every-where for him because it was our time to spend together without the other two.

But he had left without so much as a *good-bye* or *I'll be back.*

Had he come back sometime last night? Was he okay? Or had Dad gotten to him first?

Turning from my back onto my side, I stared at Gaian and nudged his sleeping frame. "Hey, do you know if Darius came back home last night? I … I'm kinda worried about him. I didn't hear him or the others enter."

"I don't know," Gaian mumbled into the pillow, his rough hand still clutching the side of my hip. He pulled me closer so my body was pressed flush against his again. "Go back to sleep, Pretty Bird," Gaian murmured into my ear, his lips tickling my neck.

While I wanted to jump out of his arms to find Darius as soon as possible, Thayer slammed Gaian's door open and stood with Calder in the hall. He crossed his arms over his chest. "I fucking told you that she was with Gaian."

"Fuck you guys," Gaian grunted, snuggling closer to me with his head in the crook of my neck. He hadn't opened his eyes yet. "It's too early for you to be fighting already. Let me spend another hour with her myself."

"It's almost noon," Thayer said, stepping into the room and grasping the large blankets that covered our naked bodies. "Get the fuck out of bed, Sina. We need to practice your power and hone your strengths. Gaian, I don't give a fuck what you do. Sina's coming with us."

When Thayer yanked the blankets off us, I grumbled and pushed Gaian off me. A low, feral growl exited Calder's throat, and he stepped into the room, glaring at my freshly marked neck.

These boys were going to drive me crazy with their jealousy. Why couldn't they just get along already?

"You marked her," Calder said, voice gruff.

I fought the urge to roll my eyes because I didn't want to offend him. I realized yesterday that I might've been a bit too harsh with wanting him and Thayer to leave. He had been through so much, but still … most times, his possessiveness was over-bearing.

"Yeah, I marked her," Gaian mumbled into my neck. "Now, leave. She's mine."

A low growl rumbled from Thayer. "She's ours."

"You guys," I said, shuffling up to the headboard and grabbing another thin sheet to cover my bare chest. It shouldn't have mattered because they had all seen me naked, but I was too tired to fuck this morning. Gaian and I had been up all night, talking. "I don't have the energy for fighting."

"We're not fighting," Calder said, jaw clenched.

Instead of shoving him back aggressively for getting too close to him, like I expected Thayer to do, he laid a hand on Calder's shoulder. "We're not fighting, Pretty Bird. We've just … come to an agreement that's hard to hold out on."

I arched a brow and crossed my arms. "And what's that?"

"That none of us can fuck you until everyone has marked you."

"Pfft, like you guys will be able to hold out on that."

"You're not making it any easier," Calder growled, gaze dropping to my barely covered breasts. "It's hard as fuck, not getting to touch you after we marked you, especially after seeing more and more marks on your throat."

Thayer turned away and walked toward the door. "I swear, we gotta force Darius to do it already. You won't last another fucking day. Anyway, Sina, get your ass out of bed. It's training time."

After I pulled myself out of bed and tugged on clothes to cover my body, I followed Thayer down the stairs to the first floor. I glanced around the pack house, noticing Darius's bedroom door open, but I couldn't find any sign of him still.

"Where's Darius?" I asked, chewing on the inside of my cheek. My stomach turned into knots, the mere thought of him being gone alone not sitting well with me. "Has he come home yet from yesterday?"

"He went out this morning," Calder said, appearing inches from me and staring hungrily down at me.

While I wanted to push him away for being too close, I couldn't help but see the spark in his hard eyes. He might've been the ruthless alpha who was a borderline asshole, but he had a reason to be. And, well … seeing him happy made my stomach flutter.

"Okay," I said, not really loving their answer, but it was the only one they seemed to have for me.

So, after Gaian said he'd catch up with us, I followed Thayer and

Calder out of the pack house and through the woods to the ... prison?

"You're bringing me to the pack prison?" I asked, hesitantly stepping into the cold and dark room. I shivered at the memory of being here yesterday, of killing that man and not regretting a second of it. "You're not going to make me kill someone else today, are you?"

"No," Thayer said, taking my hand and leading me toward one of the back rooms. When Calder opened the door, it reeked of the blood of different species, but especially humans. Torture devices hung from the walls, whips and chains and spikes. "We're bringing you here so we can strap you down and bring out each of the species inside you."

I eyed a steel seat cemented into the ground with heavy cuffs and chains for someone's ankles and wrists. They both nodded to it at the same time, and I grimaced at the steel chair. Once I sat, they bound my ankles and wrists.

"Why do we have to do this?"

Flashbacks of when I used to be restrained, of when Dad would do experiments on me in a chair similar to this one, rushed through my head. I blinked back the tears and pushed away the memories, knowing that my guys wouldn't do this to hurt me.

Gaian stepped into the room behind Calder and arched a brow. "Kinky."

"It's a safety precaution," Thayer said, cutting his gaze to Calder and Gaian. "If I had it my way, you would be free, but because these idiots wanted to be here with me today, we have to do this the hard way. They're afraid of you."

"We're not afraid of her," Calder said.

"Seems like it," Thayer taunted.

"You were the fucking one who suggested restraining her."

"In the fuckin' bedroom, yeah. Not to train her."

Calder growled, "Whatever. But what if we awaken each of the beasts inside her, bring them to their max level, and she fucking goes berserk?"

"You *are* afraid of me." My lips curled into a smile. "Don't worry. I won't hurt you, *Alpha*."

After Thayer chuckled, he continued to secure my chains. I willingly let him do so because they were right. I might've had *some* control yesterday with Thayer, but who knew if I would stay in control today? Yesterday, Thayer had taken one hell of a risk with letting me free.

And with another mark on my neck and more power swelling inside me … I didn't want to kill any of my mates.

Thayer crouched down beside me, finishing the last chain. "I want to see how fucking strong your beast is today," Thayer said, gently gripping my chin. "How strong *you* are, Sina."

66

the truth

sina

WE SPENT two hours luring each species that lived inside me to come out and play—vampire, werewolf, demon, and fae. With each new species that appeared, Thayer would push them to their absolute limits, antagonizing them the way he said demons loved doing.

I struggled through the pain, the hurt, the agony.

It made me stronger. It forced me to see exactly what I was and how I could possibly control my powers in order to kill my father and now, apparently, my ex-boyfriend too. Calder had a field day, telling me what Thayer had learned about him.

Thayer cut his palm and placed it right under my nose, so I inhaled the blood. My teeth lengthened into deadly fangs for the second time today, and I ached to drink the blood from his hand. The mere scent brought back memories of yesterday when he had brought me here and let me suck out his blood as he filled me with cum.

Darius was still heavy in my thoughts, but I had to force myself to focus. A feral growl escaped my throat, and I lunged forward toward Thayer's hand as he swiftly pulled it away. I drew my tongue against the tips of my fangs and strained against the chains.

A screw popped out from the cuff around my leg ankle, and Thayer smirked. "Good."

"Give me blood," I shrieked. "Now."

When Thayer placed his hand against my mouth, I licked the blood from it and sealed the wound closed by licking the wound— just like a wolf sealed a mate's mark. In the heat of the moment and in desperate need of *more* blood, I snapped my eyes toward the door and inhaled sharply.

My monster wanted out—*needed* out—right now.

"Mate," I said, voice taut as my marks began to burn. *"Mate now."*

I didn't know what had taken control of me, but the heat rushed through my body the same way it had a couple of weeks ago when I was alone with Calder. Except, this time … I wanted someone else entirely. I didn't think *any* of these guys could satisfy my hunger.

I needed Darius.

"Mate!" I howled.

Less than a minute later, Darius pushed the prison door open and stepped into the silent room. I snapped my wrists and ankles against the heavy chains, desperate to escape, desperate for him. It was like my beast had sensed he was close.

"Let me out," I growled.

But when Darius looked at me for the first time this morning, I froze. He looked like he had been rubbing his red eyes or as if he hadn't slept at all last night. His beard was unkempt, very unlike him.

"Please, let me out," I whispered, voice smaller than those angry growls, suppressing my inner beast easily this time.

Something with Darius seemed off today, off since maybe even last night. I didn't know what it was, but I couldn't wrap my head around the fact that he had just left me on our night we were supposed to be together.

I had wanted to spend the night with both of them.

After convincing Thayer to release me, I gently rubbed the marks on my wrists and sat up in the torture chair. Thayer, Gaian, and

Calder talked tensely with each other on the other side of the room, going over ways to bring out even other species that might be hibernating inside me.

Once I slipped out of the chair, I walked over to Darius. "Where have you been?"

Darius sighed softly. "Just … out."

"Doing what?"

"Helping Hellana settle into pack life."

Jealousy ripped through me. "Hellana? The pregnant woman I saved?"

"Yeah, we placed her in a cabin near a couple of strong warriors."

I clenched my fists by my sides. "Why were you with her?"

All I wanted to say was that *I* had needed him last night and this morning, when I woke up and when I trained to become stronger. And now, he was telling me that he had been with another woman. Sure, she might've meant nothing to him, but still …

He hadn't had to leave last night without a word. He could've told me where he was going. Why in the world would he keep it a secret? Why wouldn't he come home? Why did something feel incredibly off today?

Before Darius could answer me, Calder grabbed my wrist. "We're taking a break."

"No," I said, standing my ground. "Why don't you, Gaian, and Thayer prepare in the yard behind the pack house? I can practice shifting in a few minutes. I need to talk to Darius, please, Calder."

After Calder told me that I had better get my ass upstairs soon, he walked back over to the others. I turned back to Darius to see him tenser than before as he drew his tongue across his pearly-white teeth and stared at the ground.

"They're stressing me out," I admitted to Darius, hoping to lighten the mood and not come at him, attacking him for this. But I needed to know. I glanced over his shoulder at Thayer, Calder, and Gaian, who all walked up the stairs and talked tensely with each other about what seemed to be … me—or the marks on my neck to be exact now. "We've been at this all morning."

"Yeah, they love you," Darius said, chuckling nervously and scratching the back of his head. While he was usually inviting, he had barely looked me in the eye today, and it kinda made me uneasy.

Did he not want to mark me? Was that why we hadn't said *I love you*?

My stomach twisted into knots, but I swallowed my insecurities and stepped toward him. "I, um …" Nerves zipped up and down my arms. I needed to just come out with it already. "Is everything okay? You seem off."

"Everything's fine, Sina," he said.

He used my real name. Sina and not Pretty Bird.

"Are you sure?" I urged, knotting my brows together. "Something has to be wrong, Darius. You left last night without a word, and now, I find out that you've been with another woman all morning long. Do you … are you …"

I didn't even know what I wanted to say. The words seemed to be trapped in my throat.

"What's wrong?" I pleaded, chest tightening as I thought the worst.

If he had done something with someone else, I would've felt it last night, right? I would've been hurting. Why had he just left me?

"You want to know, Sina?" he asked, becoming … almost *irritated*? "It's you."

I stared at him through wide eyes. "Me?"

"You and," he said, finally looking up at me, "us."

"Us?" I whispered, the word barely getting past my lips. "What about us?"

Darius tore his gaze away from me again and looked back down at his feet. Fear gripped me by the throat. My heart pounded inside my rib cage. The more time that passed by, the more and more I wondered if the next words to exit Darius's mouth would be, *I reject you.*

67
the confession

darius

"WH-WHAT DO YOU MEAN, it's me?" Sina asked, a wave of tears welling in her eyes.

Guilt rushed through me because the words had come out that way. I hadn't meant for Sina to feel bad for marking and mating with the other guys. We were all her mates, but sometimes—hell, most times—I felt left out of the group.

I wanted her to love me just as much as I loved her, just as much as she did the others. Could she ever love me that much? Were all these doubts and insecurities just in my head? Had I ever been built to mate with someone as strong and powerful as her?

"Darius," she whispered, "talk to me."

"I-I'm sorry."

Fuck, I didn't know what else to say. How could I tell her that I felt left out? I found it so embarrassing, so terrible to say aloud. It wasn't like they had done something to make me feel this way. I just was awkward as fuck sometimes.

"Please tell me that you didn't"—she paused for a few long moments, her voice frail and wavering, as more tears piled up in her eyes—"do anything with Hellana. I'm sorry if I hurt you in some way, Darius, but please … you couldn't have."

"What?" I asked breathlessly, unsure if I had heard her. "You think I would cheat?"

A single tear rolled down Sina's cheek, but she quickly turned away from me. Moments ago, she had been training to be the strongest species and warrior that had ever lived in our lifetime, and now … she was broken.

I grasped her wrist and turned her around to face me. "Do you?"

She shielded her face from me and took a step away, wrapping her arms around her body. "No, I don't think so. But honestly, I don't know what to think right now. You barely came home last night, and this morning, you were gone, off with Hellana, another woman."

My chest tightened. "I didn't do anything with her, Sina. I wanted to help her settle."

When I moved toward her, Sina stepped back. "I wanted to spend time with you last night. That's why I asked Calder and Thayer to leave, so you, Gaian, and I could have some fun and …" She frowned. "And you just left without a good-bye."

"I left to give you and Gaian space."

"And this morning?" Sina asked, furrowing her brows. "What about then?"

"This morning, I …" I started, my mouth dry and my throat tight. "This morning, I didn't think you'd want me there. You were in Gaian's room with the door closed completely. What was I supposed to do?"

"Why wouldn't I want you there?" she asked quietly. "You're my mate."

After turning away from her, I glanced down at the bloody prison floor. "Sina …"

"Tell me," she pushed. "Why wouldn't I? I fucking love you all."

"Because, sometimes, I feel like I don't belong," I finally admitted. "Sometimes, I … I … feel like you want to be with the other guys more than me. I don't fucking know why. I've just always felt that way, even four years ago."

Sina took an unsteady breath. "Darius ... did I do something to make you feel that way?"

"No," I said, dragging my hand over my hair. As the word came out of my mouth, I found myself thinking about how stupid I sounded. Sina had done absolutely nothing wrong, and here I was, making her feel like I was blaming her. "You didn't do anything."

When Sina took a step closer to me, I crossed my arms to close myself off. Like the other guys, I didn't like being vulnerable. Being vulnerable meant getting hurt. It had happened four years ago, and I'd tried to turn cold after that.

But I couldn't.

Sina had always held a certain place in my heart, no matter if I didn't feel like I fit in or not. She wrapped her arms around my body and pulled me closer to her, resting her head on my tight chest and closing her eyes.

"I'm sorry you felt like that," she whispered. "But please don't leave me ever again. After Gaian marked me, I wanted you to mark me too. I wanted to feel your canines inside me, *you* inside me again. But you ... you were gone. You left me empty."

"You want me to mark you?" I whispered.

She glanced up at me, hesitation in her gaze. "Not if you don't want to."

I cupped her face and glanced down at the left side of her neck, which only had one mark so far. The space above the crook of her neck was free of a mark and waiting for me, calling to me, beckoning me to mark her already.

Swallowing hard, I trailed my callous fingers along her bare throat. "Sina ..."

My wolf—who I had suppressed all last night and this morning —quickly awoke inside me. My canines lengthened inside my mouth, but the worries were still running through my head, telling me that I didn't belong, that I wasn't good enough for her.

"You don't have to," Sina said, brushing her fingers over my facial hair. Tears trembled in her eyes. "I just don't want you to feel left out because you're not left out to me. If I didn't want you, I wouldn't have told *you* about my father before all the others. I wouldn't look forward to eating those waffles with you every morning. I wouldn't have craved them for the past four years. It was hell without you, and I—"

Before I could stop myself, I dipped my head and kissed her on the mouth. She sucked in a sharp, tense breath, then relaxed in my hold and kissed me back. She wrapped her arms around my shoulders and pulled me down to her.

We kissed until she needed to breathe and pulled away slightly. I moved my lips down her chin, then down her throat, toward the bare part of her throat. My lengthened canines grazed over her soft spot, brushing against Thayer's mark for a moment, then against skin.

"Darius," she whispered, curling her fingers against my chest. "Darius, you don't have to. If you want to wait, we can wait. I don't want to—"

"Tell me you want it, Sina. Tell me you want me."

"I don't just want you, Darius," she breathed, tilting her head to the side to give me better access. "Gods, I need you. Give me your mark. Give me all of you."

I sank my teeth into her throat until my gums reached her flesh. I gripped on to her tighter, pleasure shooting through my entire body. She squirmed in my hold and moaned loudly, her body trembling with pleasure too.

"Darius!" she cried, breathing hitched. "Fuck, I love you so much."

68

the power

sina

WHAT HAD STARTED as an innocent touch turned into something much deeper.

Darius pulled his canines out of my neck and drew his tongue over the wound to seal it closed. I tugged him closer, needing every part of my body to touch him, aching for him—for them all—to be inside me.

"Breed," I whispered. "Please, breed me."

Before I could stop myself, I jumped onto him and wrapped my legs around his waist. When he grabbed my ass with his strong arms to hold me up, I ground my pussy against his jeans, desperate for it.

"Please," I pleaded. "Please, I need it. I need it so badly."

I didn't know what had come over me, but I couldn't stop it. Nor did I want to stop it.

"Goddess, I want to," Darius murmured against my lips, keeping them millimeters away from me, teasing me even harder. The beast inside me craved them so badly right now, even more than when I was in heat. "I want to so badly."

"Darius," I cried, the warmth overtaking my body. "Now!"

While I needed him more than ever, he walked up the prison steps and out of the concrete building toward the pack house with me in his arms. I ground myself up and down on him, rubbing my clit with his growing bulge through our pants.

"*Breed now,*" the beast inside me commanded. "*Breed now.*"

"Breed now," I repeated, sinking my hand between our bodies and into Darius's jeans. I gripped his cock in my hand and stroked it up and down as he carried me. "Darius, you need to take me right now. I'm begging you. I need you."

Heat, power, intensity burned inside me, from the inside out. A deep desire built in me.

"I can't," Darius said through gritted teeth, as if he was trying to hold back. "I made a pact with the guys that once we all marked you, we'd take you as ours together. We've all held up our end, even Calder so far."

"Break your pact," I begged, seeing the pack house come into view. I gripped him tighter and jerked him off faster, my pussy dripping with pleasure. "Please, break it. They've all done it at one point or another. You can break it for me, can't you?"

"Sina," he said, his voice becoming tenser. "As much as I want to take you here, I—"

"Fucking finally," Thayer growled from the back door.

I pulled my hand out of Darius's pants and clutched his shoulders tightly, desperately grinding my pussy against him harder, needing to get off, aching for their cum to be inside me already. I needed them all.

"Breed me!" I whined, throwing my head back.

Darius stepped into the house with me, but I didn't let go of him. Thayer shut and locked the door behind us as Gaian stood from the couch. I glanced from guy to guy, the power only swelling higher inside me.

"Please!" I panted, chest rising and falling quickly. My skin burned everywhere, except the places that Darius touched. This was heat, but worse. So much fucking worse. "Please, come inside me. I need it."

"The fuck did you do to her?" Thayer asked Darius.

Darius didn't let go of me, but held me tighter. "I marked her."

"We all marked her, but she didn't get this desperate," Gaian said, eyes glinting gold.

I stared at him and furrowed my brows. "Touch me, please. Touch me."

Gaian stepped closer to me and gripped my jaw. I leaned into his touch and stared into those golden wolfish eyes.

"Please, fuck me. Breed me. Get me pregnant, Gaian. I need it. I need it so badly."

"She's trying to reproduce to keep her species alive," Thayer said, moving closer to me tensely—almost against his free will. "It only makes sense now that she wears all our marks and her species is dying out."

"Please!" I cried.

Just as he was about to touch me, Thayer balled his hands into fists and fought not to move. "We promised Calder that we'd take her together for the first time after we all marked her. He's held up his end of the deal. He had to go out. He'll be back in a couple of hours."

"No!" I growled, vision blurring. My entire body burned way hotter than it ever had before. I could barely breathe. "I can't wait! I need it now. I need so much cum inside me that there's no chance I won't get pregnant. Please! Please! I'm begging you."

"You can't even get pregnant, Pretty Bird," Thayer said. "Relax. You still have your IUD."

"No," I breathed heavier. "I don't. I pulled it out of me weeks ago, before you took me in the bathtub. I haven't been on birth control. I've been letting you guys fuck me raw because I want to be bred. I need to be bred."

A low growl escaped Gaian's throat, ferocious and needy. "You took it out?"

"Yes," I cried. "For you guys! Now, please!"

Just as Gaian took another step closer to me and Darius, Thayer moved between us and placed his hands on Gaian's chest. "We made a fucking deal with Calder. I know he's an annoying ass, but a deal is a deal."

"He hasn't fucking held up any sorta deal with us. He made us stay away from our mate for weeks," Gaian growled at him, his smoldering gaze still on me. "She's in heat, and I'm done fucking staying away from her." He shoved Thayer back with so much more force than I'd thought he had inside him. "Move."

"Please," I whimpered, my vision blurring even more. "Someone."

Darius clutched me harder, but my hands were slipping from his body.

I closed my burning eyes and whimpered again. "Please."

And then everything went dark.

69

the breeding

sina

SUNLIGHT FLOODED THROUGH THE WINDOWS. It must've been barely five in the morning. My entire body was still engulfed in heat. Had I passed out from the intensity, the carnal urge to reproduce, to have their babies until I physically couldn't anymore?

Feeling hands on my thighs, I blinked my eyes open and glanced down the bed. With his head buried between my thighs, Gaian lay on his stomach, licking and sucking on my cunt, his tongue flicking my clit from side to side.

I went to scurry up to my headboard, but he kept me in place and spread my legs wide, stretching them as far as they would go. I clenched and arched my back, beyond horny and so desperate to have each of them fill my cunt with their cocks and cum again.

"Breed," I begged.

"I've been waiting for you to wake up all night," he murmured against me.

"Please." Unable to stop myself, I scrambled up to the headboard, flipped us over, and straddled his waist. "Breed me." I ground my pussy against the bulge in his underwear and whimpered, "Please, I can't wait any longer. You guys haven't fucked me in days. I'm so horny."

Gaian set his hands on my hips to hold me against his groin and ground his cock against my soppy, needy, aching pussy. "You're desperate for it."

Darius's shirt that I must've worn to sleep last night pressed tightly against me, the design stretching far across the chest and my nipples hard and poking through the material. "Please, Gaian." I grasped my breasts and tugged on my nipples until I moaned. "Please, give it to me. I'm desperate for your cock."

After grinding myself against him for a few more moments, he finally broke, pulled me off the bed, and turned me around so my back was pressed against his chest. With his large, callous hands, he pushed down his shorts to his knees and grabbed my elbows, plunging himself inside of me.

"We really shouldn't be doing this," he murmured against me, his canines brushing against my soft spot. "We should've waited for the others, but I can't seem to give a fuck anymore."

I moaned and curled my hands into the sheets, my tits bouncing against my shirt with every thrust. "It feels too good," I said in a breath. "Too fucking good to wait anymore. They'll come when they—"

"Oh fuck," he said, pounding into me harder.

Pleasure surging through me, I threw my head back. "Oh God! Don't stop, Gaian." My legs trembled, nipples rubbing against my shirt and sending pleasure through my body. I arched my back even harder, giving him better access, and furrowed my brows.

When my bedroom door snapped open and Thayer stood in the doorway, Gaian slammed his cock harder into me.

"I couldn't fucking wait. Her cunt is throbbing around my cock and so fucking needy. She wouldn't stop begging me to fuck her."

Thayer growled under his breath, his piercing gaze on my tits as they bounced against my shirt. He crawled onto the bed, swiped one hand against the clothing, and ripped it off, letting my breasts fall out of it. I reached for the waistband of his sweatpants and stared up at him with wide eyes.

"Feed me," I said. By his waistband, I pulled him closer, then slipped my hand into his pants to pull out his hard cock. I stuck out my tongue, wanting—needing—him inside of me. "Please, feed me."

Thayer snatched my hair in his claws and held my head up. "Fuck waiting anymore. Open your fucking mouth wider. My cock won't fit inside of you like that."

I opened my mouth wider and batted my lashes up at him. "Please, Thayer."

After slipping the head of his cock into my mouth, Thayer released his grip on my hair and took my tits in his hands, groping and squeezing any way that he liked. I bobbed my head on him, taking more of him inside of me.

"Breed," I said with him in my mouth, my word coming out muffled.

He pushed more of his cock into my mouth, pressing his head against the side of my cheek and slapping it lightly. "What was that, Pretty Bird? You want more?"

Hungrily, I nodded. Spit and drool pooled in my mouth and dripped down my bottom lip, rolling down my chin. Thayer pushed himself inside of me as far as he would go, so I was full with two cocks. Gaian tightened his grip on my elbows, breaths coming out in deep grunts.

"Fuck," Gaian growled. "You just keep getting fucking ... tighter."

"She wants us to get her pregnant," Darius said from the door. "She hasn't stopped begging since I marked her."

Gaian slammed himself as deep as he could go and stilled. I curled my toes, feeling his cum spill out of me.

When he pulled himself out, he smacked my ass. "Clench your pussy so it doesn't come out."

"That's not how it—" I started, words muffled on Thayer's cock.

Gaian grabbed a fistful of my hair, pulled me up so Thayer's cock fell out of my mouth and smacked against his thigh, and growled into my ear, "I don't care. Close your pussy up. Don't fucking let my cum drip down your thighs. It stays inside of you."

I whimpered and clenched hard. Gaian released my hair and collapsed on the bed, chest falling as he relaxed. Darius lay back on the bed, grabbed my hips, and sat me on his cock.

Once he was buried inside of me and pushing Gaian's cum deeper into me, he pulled me closer to him and grunted to Thayer, "Calder is going to kill us for fucking her before he woke up."

Thayer moved behind me, shoving the head of his cock into my pussy too. I sank my nails into Darius's chest and whimpered out at the pressure in my core as they stretched me out.

Thayer pushed his entire cock into my pussy and growled, "Fuck me. She's tighter than last week."

"Breed," I begged, bucking my hips back and forth on their cocks.

Strands of Gaian's cum dripped out of my pussy, sticking from my pussy to their balls when I bounced back and forth on them.

Darius wrapped his strong arms around my torso to hold me down, picking up his pace and making my breasts bounce against his chest. Thayer wrapped his hands around my tits, squeezing them and growling into my ear.

"Fucking desperate," Thayer growled.

"Harder."

Thayer trailed his hands up my body and wrapped them both over my mouth and nose like a muzzle, using my body to ram himself into me even harder. I closed my eyes, feeling the pleasure rush through me, arms and legs tingling.

"More," I murmured against his hands.

When I reopened my eyes, Calder stood in the doorway with those dark eyes fixed on me. My pussy tightened around them both, each of them grunting and stilling almost instantly, cursing like sailors and commenting how fucking good I felt.

Thayer pulled out of me first, then Darius, who picked me up and placed me at the edge of the bed on my hands and knees, ass arched in the air and waiting for Calder to push himself into me too. I clenched my pussy, wanting to keep their cum inside of me, just like I had with Gaian.

Calder walked closer to me, grabbing his balls and dick in his large hand. "Four days' worth of cum in these balls for you."

"Please, give it to me, Calder," I murmured.

The other times we'd been together, I had been a brat.

Now, I was a cum-hungry slut who ached to be bred by her wolves.

One hand holding my tit, the other sprawled against the back of my opposite thigh, Calder didn't say anything else to me as he rammed his cock into my pussy and pulled me into the air in a reverse cowgirl position, using nothing but brute strength to hold me up.

Every time he rammed into me, my breasts swayed in the air. I clenched around him, moaning, begging, and pleading for him to come inside of me. He gripped me tighter and picked up his pace, pounding into me.

"Pretty Bird, you've been waiting for this, haven't you?"

I bit my lip and nodded. "Yes."

"You like being bred by us."

"I love it."

He shoved himself harder.

"I love it."

He trailed his hand to my other breast, groping them both and somehow still ramming into me as fast and as hard as he could. He growled, teeth grazing against my soft spot, and sank the first tip of his canine into me.

"I love it so much," I whimpered. "Oh God! Give me your cum. Please, please, Calder."

He swore under his breath and stilled inside of me. Once he finally relaxed, he placed me on the bed beside Thayer. I crawled over to him and onto his chest.

"More. I want more," I whispered, sinking into Thayer's arms.

Thayer laced a hand through my hair and gently massaged the top of my head. "Give us a second to catch our breath, Pretty Bird."

Gaian moved behind me, placing a kiss on my shoulder and gently rubbing my hip. "There will be more. You need to relax for a bit."

"But I … I want it," I whispered. "I need it. So badly."

70
the new entry

sina

WE FUCKED all day and all night.

By eight at night, Gaian had fallen asleep on the sofa, Darius was making dinner, Calder was pacing around the living room and trying to get his dick hard again, and Thayer was taking a bubble bath. Yes, really, a bubble bath.

I sat on my bed, dressed in nothing but Calder's T-shirt, and wrote in my diary.

If it were up to me, I would've continued riding them until I fell asleep. But they had gone so hard for so long that Gaian's bed became soaked with their sweat. I wouldn't doubt that his mattress was soaked through too.

So, here I was, horny as fuck, doing the one thing I hadn't done in a while.

Writing a journal entry about how I wanted them to take me next.

Entry #19.

I stared at the page and pressed my thighs together, whimpering. I hadn't even written a word of this entry yet, but I couldn't stop the ideas, the fantasies rushing through my head. I wanted them to take me so hard, so fast, make me theirs, breed me.

I want Thayer to shove me onto my knees, blindfold me, and bind my wrists behind my back as I try to fight him off. He's too strong for a human girl like me —

I crossed off the last sentence because he had forced me to prove that I was stronger than him earlier. And I wasn't human. But still … I wanted him to overpower me. I wanted him to be rough, like he had been that time in the bathroom while he was covered in blood. He had wanted me to put up a fight with him, to hit him back, and I had fucking loved every second of it.

He'll laugh at me like I'm a pathetic whore and slap me around like one too.

Heat gathered inside my core, and I whimpered. The monster inside me begged to be bred again, begged to be let loose, begged me to sprint right down those stairs and get pregnant with their pups. We needed it.

I forced myself to take a steady breath and continued writing.

As Thayer shoves himself into my mouth, Darius will bend me forward and shove himself into my ass, pounding away until I'm digging my nails into his thighs and screaming in pleasure.

They had all come inside my pussy today, but I wanted to be full with cock again. I wanted every one of my holes to be used so my guys got pleasure. Then, I wanted them to feed my pussy with their cum.

Calder will do nothing but breed me all night and all day, coming inside me over and over and over. He is desperate to get me pregnant with his pup, to continue the alpha bloodline, to make me his property.

Another whimper escaped my lips, and I glanced toward my bedroom door, fucking hoping that one of them had heard it. I didn't know how much longer I would be able to hold out. My monster needed cock, almost as much as I did.

And when I get pregnant and my breasts swell, Gaian won't be able to keep his mouth off them. He'll latch his teeth on to my nipple and tug, grope, and knead my breasts and …

I shoved a hand between my legs and gently teased my clit.

And … suck on my tits so hard until I come all over him.

My pussy clenched at the thought. Gaian was already obsessed with them, stared at them any chance he got. When I got pregnant, they'd grow even larger, and I could only begin to imagine how much he'd like that.

Gently, I rubbed my aching breast and placed my pen down. I was supposed to get my period for the first time since I had been here. Jaroth had always been grossed out by the blood, but I doubted a little blood would scare Thayer away. Or any of the guys for that matter.

At this rate, I'd get myself so horny again that I would force myself on the guys. And I didn't want that to happen. Despite them being rough in bed, they respected me.

So, I tucked my journal away in my side table and blew out a deep breath, relaxing against the headboard.

"Sina!" Gaian shouted from downstairs. "Get down here now!"

Wasn't he sleeping? Maybe he was ready to fuck again.

I leaped up from the bed and hurried out of my room, leaning over the balcony. "Are you—"

"Put on some clothes," Calder growled.

My brows furrowed. "Wh-what do you mean? What's going on?"

"Jaroth's here."

71
the voice

sina

AFTER QUICKLY PULLING ON A BRA—BECAUSE the guys wouldn't let Jaroth see me without one—and some sweatpants, I hurried down the stairs and toward the living room. Through the back French door windows, I saw the guys all standing outside and glaring at my ex-boyfriend. Even Thayer had gotten out of the bath and stood in nothing but a towel in front of him.

I swallowed hard and could only imagine what Jaroth wanted to tell me.

If what the guys had said was true and I couldn't trust Jaroth, then I needed to at least figure out why he had come here. He had to be here for a reason other than my father. But why? Why would he show up this late at night too?

Once I opened the back door, Jaroth glanced over Calder's shoulder at me. I pushed through the guys, who would barely move an inch for me, and stared at my ex-boyfriend, who looked like he had rushed over here in a hurry.

"What's up?"

"Don't talk to him, Pretty Bird," Calder snapped.

But we needed to figure out why he had come.

"I need to talk to you—alone," Jaroth said. "It's important."

"Don't believe anyone other than your mates," a soft and distant female voice that wasn't my own drifted through my head. My brows furrowed momentarily, an uneasy feeling building in the pit of my stomach. *"They all want to use you for your power."*

I stared at the dirt and swallowed hard. The voice almost sounded like … Mom's.

"You're more powerful than them all. You're the only one who can end this."

"About what?" I asked Jaroth, swallowing the nerves.

"Alone," Jaroth repeated. "Please, Sina."

With the sudden weight on my shoulders, I tore my gaze away from the ground and looked up at Jaroth with determination. It couldn't be Mom's voice, but I wasn't that innocent little girl anymore. I hadn't been for a long time.

"It's okay," I reassured the guys in front of Jaroth, ushering them back into the house. "I'm a big girl. I can talk to my ex-boyfriend by myself. No need to be all over me just because we're mates."

"Pretty Bird, he's going to—" Darius said through my mind.

The first voice to ring through my mind link since we had all mated.

"Don't worry," I said to all four of them. *"I know not to trust him. But he's not going to give us any solid information if he thinks you guys are all listening in on the conversation. At least get back inside the house."*

All of the guys, especially Calder, wanted to pick a fight with me about this. But I wasn't having any of it because I needed to get this information from Jaroth and I couldn't have them stop me. We didn't know the slightest about my father's plans—or Jaroth's plans either.

Even if Jaroth was about to lie to me, at least we might be able to uncover something about him. I wasn't sure what that'd be, but I was hoping it'd be something useful because my guys didn't trust him. And right now, I didn't either.

Once they finally agreed, I shut the French doors behind them and blew out a deep breath, brows furrowed. "Sorry about them.

They're suffocating sometimes," I said, making sure my marks were covered by my hair. "Too suffocating. They all want to mark me."

"Don't let them," Jaroth said, looking around nervously. "I don't have time to explain what's going on, but I promised that I'd help you escape your father, so you'd owe me a favor, right, Sina?"

"Yes," I said, crossing my arms. "You did say that, but you didn't help me escape."

"Who do you think switched your father's nightly tea with yours?"

My eyes widened, my stomach tightening. I knew it had been too easy.

"But you … acted like you were surprised to see me in Durn-bone the night I escaped."

"I didn't think you'd come back here," he said, finally looking toward me. "I thought you'd be smarter than to come back to your home, where your father would definitely find you. I thought you'd meet me at our spot."

"At our spot?!" I asked, becoming angry. "Why would I go back there? You cheated on me. I couldn't trust you."

"Well, you're going to have to trust me now," Jaroth said. "You owe me a favor."

I knew Jaroth too well. He had something up his sleeve, some-thing big. When Jaroth was nice to someone, he buttered them up with sultry words and promises of an easy life, and then he dived in and demanded something for his efforts.

He had tried that once before after he cheated, thought that he deserved for me to take him back because he had spent so much time with me and convinced my father to let him whisk me away. The damn audacity he had sometimes.

Now, I knew why he had done all that.

Not because he loved me. Not because he cared about me. Not because he had any ounce of goodness in his heart.

All Jaroth cared about was himself.

"What is it?"

"I can't tell you. Not right now." He glanced around again.

"Look. I have to go. I'll be back to retrieve you and give you the life you deserve, *princess.* No more living out here in the woods, worrying about war."

"What are you promising me? What are you going to do?"

He took my hands and stared me right in the eye. "You're special, Sina. But you have to stay here for a couple more days. Don't leave. Act like you still want those overly possessive assholes. Give them the time of their lives. Then"—he handed me the liquid my father used to slip into my drinks—"poison them with this on the third night. I'll be here for you."

"You want me to poison my mates?" I asked, sensing they were listening to every word.

My mind link went wild with growls from the guys. And I bet they were holding Calder or Thayer back right now so they wouldn't burst through the back door and rip this man's head clean off his body.

"Yes," he said and stepped back into the woods.

"Yeah, okay," I said as Jaroth disappeared through the forest. I tucked some hair behind my ear, revealing the marks on my neck that he hadn't seen. "I'll stay here, where it's safe. With my mates, who'd do anything to protect me."

But I didn't know if their protection would be enough for the beast inside me.

72

the queen

thayer

ONCE THAT FUCKIN' asshole left our property, I grabbed Sina's hand and led her right to the front door. She squirmed in my hold and gently pulled her wrist away from me.

"What's going on? It's late. And I'm still horny."

"Well, hold it the fuck in, Pretty Bird. Something isn't right."

Pissed, she furrowed her brows and crossed her arms. "Of course something isn't right with Jaroth. Nothing ever has been. But that doesn't mean I can tell the monster inside me to slow down. She's—"

I grabbed her chin in my rough hand and forced her to stare up at me. She was damn cute and all, but we had a problem that needed to be figured out now.

"We'll fuck you when we get back. This is serious."

After she finally snapped her mouth closed, I wrapped her into a coat because it was getting chillier down in Durnbone, especially at night, then nodded to the guys. The only person who might have some idea about Jaroth was Xorgor, Maxine's boyfriend.

We walked through the chilly fall forest toward Durnbone, the sounds of the night echoing around us.

Sina stepped closer to me and wrapped her hand around my forearm. "Where are we going?"

"To see Maxine."

"Maxine?" she asked, eyes wide. "What does she have to do with this?"

"Not her, but her boyfriend."

"You think Xorgor knows something?"

Branches snapped around us from a couple of small squirrels scurrying through the woods with nuts. I pressed my lips together and stared ahead at the horizon of lights illuminating from the town.

"He knows more than I do."

Once Sina pursed her lips, she nodded and looked at the ground, tensing so suddenly that she came to a full stop on the outskirts of the woods. She wrapped her arms around her body and glanced around. "Something feels … off."

"Off?" Gaian asked, stepping next to her.

"I don't know," she whispered, staring at Durnbone. "I can't explain it. I feel … energy."

"Energy?" Calder asked, stopping feet ahead of us and glancing over his shoulder at her.

Her gaze drifted from the middle of town toward the demon sector. "Yes."

I grasped her hand tighter again. "Well, we don't have time to waste. We have to talk to Xorgor. If it gets worse, tell me, and we'll stop."

After sucking in a sharp breath, Sina nodded. "Okay."

We continued into Durnbone, finding the quickest path to the other side of the town.

"I can't believe that fucker wants Sina to poison us," Calder growled. He looked down at Sina and held out his large hand. "Give me the vial."

When she stared at him through wide eyes and raised her brows, I tugged her along.

She frowned up at him. "Are you being serious? Why do you need the vial? Do you actually think that I'd poison you guys?"

"No," Calder snapped and grabbed the vial from Sina's hand. "Next time he shows up on my property, I'm going to kill him with this."

Sina surprisingly pressed her lips together. "Good."

"Good?" Gaian asked, suddenly chirping into the *lovely* conversation.

"What? Do you not want that asshole dead?" I growled at him.

"I do," Gaian reassured. "But I didn't think Sina did."

"He's pissing me off," she said, staring at the ground.

Through the mate bond, I could feel the way her chest tightened, as if she was thinking about the past with him.

"He's always been a liar, a cheat."

"Yeah, well, he's in the past," Darius said, walking beside us. "You got us now."

Her lips curled into a wide smile. "I know."

As we approached the demon sector—or more specifically, The Inferno—Sina tensed again, her nose scrunching.

"It's stronger," she whispered, clutching her head. "I feel it rushing through my veins, pounding in my head."

"The fuck is that?" Calder asked. "Why're there so many people at The Inferno?"

I glanced toward the club, my eyes widening slightly when I saw how many demons stood at the doors to attempt to gain access. What the fuck was happening there?

It wasn't like I could march into The Inferno and ask Mother anything. She had fucking banned me from coming back and denounced me as her son because werewolf blood ran through my veins—because *she* had hooked up with a wolf and gotten pregnant.

Plus, Xorgor had royal demon blood. He had to know more about Jaroth than us.

"Don't look at me. I don't fucking know," I said, snatching Sina's hand tighter and tugging her past the club so whatever was happening to her would stop. It seemed like the influx of demons here was making her sick. "But we need to get Sina away from here."

Once we finally made it out of the town, Gaian touched Sina's shoulder. "You good?"

"Yeah, I'm fine now."

I nodded to myself and retraced my steps to Maxine's old home.

We marched up the sidewalk, and I banged on the door. "Maxine! Open the fucking door. I need to talk to Xorgor right now. It's important."

A moment later, the door swung open, and Maxine pulled us into the room quickly, slamming the door behind us. "Don't scream my name! Xorgor isn't here. He… We…" Maxine paused, guilt and… *blood* on her face. "He's out in town right now. He should be back soon."

"What's going on?" I asked. "Why do you have blood–"

The front door opened again, and Xorgor stepped into the room, cursing.

"The fuck is happening?" I asked him. "Jaroth just showed up at our house. Is he working with her father or not? And why the fuck are all those demons at The Inferno? We could barely get by."

"Sina's father and Jaroth are not working together," Xorgor said, running his forked tongue across his jagged teeth. "Jaroth only works for himself. He would never work with a human, especially one like Sina's father."

"What the fuck does Jaroth want?" I growled, pacing Maxine's living room, arms crossed.

I'd expected Jaroth to arrive in Durnbone and attempt to cart Sina out of the town, straight for her father. But he had told her to stay put, *with us*, where she'd be safe.

Xorgor ran a hand through his shaggy hair and murmured a demonic curse under his breath. "I don't know and I don't have time for that right now. The underworld is in chaos. The demon queen is dead. *Murdered.*"

73
the throne

MURDERED? I mouthed.

Sometimes, a human in Durnbone was hard to murder, but how could someone terminate the demon queen's life? Surely, she had security, people to protect her. And she was supposed to step down soon anyway.

"By me," Xorgor said.

"You killed her?" I clarified.

Maxine frowned and glanced nervously at me. "S-She deserved it for what she did to Xorgor."

"The fuck you mean?" Thayer asked Xorgor. "What did she do to you?"

"I don't want to talk about it," Xorgor growled between jagged teeth.

"So, you're going to do it?" Thayer asked. "You're going to lead the demons?"

"I don't want to lead, but she gave me no choice in the matter."

"You fucking have to do this, or the demon world will go to shit," Thayer said.

"Like it hasn't already," Xorgor snarled, nervousness crossing his features. "There will be a rebellion soon. I suspect tomorrow at the latest. And the kingdoms can't even fucking accept me looking like this, a half-human and half-demon face stuck like this forever. How will they… How will they accept me as their new leader?"

Maxine pulled her hand away from me and took Xorgor's face in her hands. "I accept you just the way you are, Xorgor," she whispered. "They will too."

He stared down at her for a long time, hard gaze softening. And finally, he dropped his head and rested it against hers, his body tense. "I can't fucking do it. I don't want to do it. They've done nothing but belittle me since I was a child."

My heart clenched at the brokenness in his voice. It reminded me of Maxine's after she was attacked by werewolves years ago. She had come to me in tears and told me that nobody would ever love her, that nobody would ever look at her the same. But I hadn't seen her any differently just because she had a couple of scars on her chest.

Maxine was my best friend either way. She always would be.

And now, Maxine was that person for someone.

Thayer stepped forward. "You fucking know that if anyone else claims the throne, they'll banish you from the demon kingdom and make Maxine a sex slave," he started, catching Xorgor's attention now. "You know how demons are. You know that they'll backstab you, even family."

Xorgor mumbled underneath his breath.

"Just like Jaroth has backstabbed all of us, even me," I whispered.

"You have to," Maxine whimpered to him, grabbing his hand again. "Please, if not for yourself, then for me. I don't want any incubus who has your brother's ill manners to touch me ever again. Do this for us."

"For us," Xorgor repeated quietly, as if he didn't believe the words coming from her.

It was as if he had never had anyone stick up for him, had never had anyone believe in him before Maxine. While we all had our own problems, I couldn't even begin to imagine the shit that Xorgor had faced all these years.

In the most honest way, Xorgor was an ugly monster with the kindest heart.

"For us," Maxine repeated.

"Okay," he whispered.

After a couple of moments of silence, Xorgor looked back up at the guys behind me. "But this is not the reason why I rushed over so quickly. I believe that Sina's father will attack Durnbone soon. Nobody knows for certain, but after I killed the demon queen... I looked through notes that I found scattered in her office. She had intel about your father, Sina. And apparently he had been planning to start a war in Durnbone. Soon."

My eyes widened, and I sucked in a sharp breath.

He might've just been a human, but he had Paragons at his disposal. At least, he'd had me. He had taken my blood and paralyzed me, made alliances through letting other species rape me until they were pleased. He had used me to advance his position in the world, and he wasn't even my real father.

"He's coming to Durnbone with an army of warriors that are stronger than everyone else," Xorgor said. "I don't know what that means, but it's what I found."

My heart pounded against my rib cage, horrid thoughts racing through my head. "Humans ... humans that are advanced. Regular humans might not be able to protect him and fight for him ... but a Paragon could. One is all that it'd take."

74
the birth

sina

XORGOR CONTINUED TALKING to my guys, but my vision became fuzzy. I clenched my fists by my sides and stared at the ground, trying to keep myself steady. But the longer time went on, the fuzzier my vision became, and the farther away their voices sounded.

Until, suddenly, everything was gone. When I reopened my eyes, I had almost been transported to another place.

Mom lay on a dingy mattress with thick metal chains wrapped four times around her wrists and her ankles, bounding her to the bedposts. She wore a white bra that seemed to be stained with years' worth of sweat and blood, making it an off-white, almost-gray color.

Like so many times when Dad had paralyzed me, Mom wasn't wearing any underwear. Unlike me, her stomach was heavily swollen, as if she was pregnant, and decorated with more stretch marks than I had ever seen on her belly.

. . .

Had she had more kids? No, she couldn't have. She had died. This was a dream.

I walked into the bedroom and stared down at her as she stared up at the ceiling, her eyes dull, as if she didn't have any fight in her left. Wanting her to feel something again, I brushed my warm fingers against her cold yet sweat-covered cheek.

She widened her eyes and shifted her focus to me, mouth parting in disbelief. "Sina," she said, her voice sounding parched. "Sina, you found me. You really, truly found me. I ... I never thought I'd see you again."

"Mom," I whispered, tears welling up in my eyes. "Mom, what's going on?"

"Your father isn't your father, sweetheart. He—"

"I know," I said, nodding. "I know he's the villain, the enemy. He's done so much to me."

"What has he done to you?" she asked weakly.

"Used me for experiments, let his friends ... touch me—"

Suddenly, Mom's eyes filled with tears, and her body trembled on the stained mattress. "I'm sorry I couldn't protect you from him. This is all my fault. I should never have gone to him after they took your father. I should've raised you myself. I'm so sorry! I've done this to you!"

While her body flailed on the bed, she yanked on the chains around her wrists and ankles, only tightening them more and making herself bleed from the raw skin profusely. I sat on the edge of the bed and took her face into my hands.

"This isn't your fault."

"It is, Sina. Please, don't tell me that he still has you," she asked, tears glistening in her eyes. But then she shook her head. "No, he couldn't. I wouldn't be able to talk to you through here if you hadn't mated."

"What do you mean?" I whispered. "This is just a dream. You're not real."

"Sina," she whispered, lips trembling. "Oh, my Sina. There is so much I didn't get the chance to teach you about who you truly are, about the power you wield, about the family and species you come from."

"Mom ..." I whispered, still attempting to understand what she had just said.

She scrunched her face and grunted out in pain, her grunt turning into a scream. "The baby ..." She looked down at her stomach and grabbed the thick chains in her hands. "You have to get out of here, hide somewhere. They're coming for you, Sina. They're coming soon."

"What are you talking about? What's—"

Mom let out another scream and spread her legs. "Sina, go! Only you can stop this. Find your real father."

Suddenly, the door to my left opened. I didn't want to leave Mom, but I couldn't let them see me. Whoever it was, wherever this was ... I needed to figure out what was going on even if this was just a dream.

I crouched behind a large dresser and hoped that the men wouldn't see me, seeing as the room was basically bare otherwise. Three large men walked into the room along with the man who had told me to call him Dad.

For fifteen minutes, I crouched quietly in the corner of the room and desperately wanted to leap out and kill those men right here and right now. Mom's screams echoed through the small room as she birthed twin girls.

Dad handed the babies to one of the guards. "You know what to do with them." He nodded to another man who began to unbuckle his belt and stepped toward Mom. "Get her pregnant again. She has one more pregnancy until she's disposable."

With tears in her eyes, Mom shook her head. "Please, don't. Let me see my babies."

Instead of answering her, Dad walked out of the room and left Mom alone with this burly human man. I stared at him in horror as he crawled up onto the bed and between the legs of a woman who had just given birth.

Mom tried kicking her chained legs at him, her shrill screams echoing through the room. I couldn't fucking watch another second of this. I stood up and lunged at the man, grabbing him by the front of his throat before he could insert himself into her.

Before he could even let out a scream, I sliced my wolf claws into his throat and sank my fangs into his neck, sucking out as much of his blood as I needed before the man fell to the ground, dead.

Rage rushed through me, and I snapped my head toward the door, where the others had disappeared. This torture needed to end. Now.

Mom shook her head. "Don't go out there, Sina. They can't catch you."

"They won't."

"Sina," Mom scolded. When I reached the door, she whimpered, "Sina, I love you."

After slipping out of the door, I followed the voices toward a room I had always known as the laboratory, where they had done experiments on me almost every night. I stopped at the door and glanced around it and into the room.

Dad sank a needle into one of the crying baby's hearts and extracted blood. The blood whooshed through a small tube and connected with a needle that had been sunk into one of Dad's guard's hearts.

The baby screamed at the top of her lungs, the shrill sound echoing through the room. Then, suddenly, it was gone. The baby stopped crying, stopped moving, stopped breathing. My eyes widened as I took in what they were doing, as I finally figured it all out.

Dad was creating an army, an army of Paragons, using babies.

Babies!

75
the stomach

darius

WHEN I NOTICED that Sina's eyes had glazed over during our conversation with Maxine and Xorgor, I hurried over to her. She stayed still for a moment, then began to sway from side to side. My eyes widened slightly as my stomach twisted.

I didn't know what was going on with her, but I wasn't going to wait and find out. I placed my hands on her waist, clutching it tightly to stop her from swaying. She whimpered and shook her head, closing her eyes.

A moment later, she collapsed. I caught her before she fell onto the ground and picked her up into my arms. Her eyes were closed completely now, her body relaxed, as if she had just passed out. Everyone snapped their heads over to her.

Maxine ran to us, pushing some hair off Sina's sweaty forehead, her eyes wide in fear. "What … what happened to her? What's going on? Ever since the Halloween party, Sina has seemed off. Please, tell me. I've waited four years for her to return too."

After peering at Calder, Thayer, and Gaian, I cleared my throat and stared down at my mate, passed out in my arms. I didn't know what to say to Maxine or what we *should* tell her about what our mate really was.

"She's been experiencing things," Gaian started. "I don't know if you know or not, but she's not human. And her father …"

I glared at Gaian, not wanting him to say another word. Sina wouldn't want him to say anything either. She had kept it a secret from us for so long; I doubted that she would want one of her best friends to know.

It wasn't because she didn't trust Maxine, but because she wanted to protect her.

Like she had wanted to protect us.

"Sina's father wants her back," Gaian said.

"Bring her home," Calder said to me. "We'll figure things out here. You go too, Gaian."

After taking Sina to the front door, I walked out of it with Gaian toward our property. It might've been on the other side of town, but I decided to go the long way so we didn't run into that demon crowd again.

As much as we all wanted to kill Jaroth, we first needed to get Sina somewhere safe.

Almost a half hour later, when we reached our house, Sina shifted uncomfortably in my arms, twisting from side to side and sweating profusely now.

When she began muttering, "No," over and over again, I nodded to the back door.

"Open it up, Gaian. We need to get her—"

Suddenly, Sina snapped her eyes open and stared up at the dark night sky. Tears began pouring down her face, her cheeks becoming blotchy. "No!" she said, shaking her head and twisting even more in my arms. "No! They can't."

I didn't know why she was crying or what kind of daydream she'd just had. I wasn't as good with emotions as Gaian was, but I clutched her tighter so she wouldn't thrash around so sporadically.

"What's wrong?" I asked.

"They … they want babies!" she shouted, her cries becoming

louder and completely controlling her body. Her breathing became heavier, her voice raspy. She looked around frantically. "They want babies!"

"Who wants babies?" Gaian asked her.

Instead of answering him, she jumped out of my arms and looked around the forest, shaking her head. Strands of her brown hair whipped around under the moonlight. "We need to stop them. They want the babies."

Gaian peered over at me, and I looked right at him, unsure of what was going on and what Sina really meant. At the moment, there were only a couple of baby pups in our pack, but if anything had happened to them, someone would've contacted Calder.

"Which baby?" Gaian asked. "What are you talking about?"

She ran her hand through her hair over and over, making it messy. And then she tugged on it, hard, as if she was punishing herself for some godforsaken reason. "Gods, I should've known. I should've fucking known! Where … where is that woman? That's why the vampire wanted her."

"Which woman?" Gaian asked.

My body stiffened. "The pregnant woman. Hellana."

Sina ripped herself away and sprinted through the woods toward our pack houses. She knocked on every door until she found the one that smelled the most like Hellana. Stopping in front of the door, she stared up at the second-story window.

"This woman …" she mumbled to herself, shaking her head again. "She must be a Paragon, just like me. I didn't realize it before, though they must've only taken Paragons. That's all my father ever wanted—Paragons—so he could rule the world."

She clutched the door handle, but Gaian grabbed her wrist. "You can't just barge into somebody's house, Sina. They—"

Once she pulled herself away from Gaian, she snatched the handle again and yanked on it hard. The door trembled in her hold, and then, finally, she ripped it open and right off the hinges. Without calling to see if Hellana was even home, Sina sprinted up the stairs to the bedroom.

Unsure of what Sina had seen, I walked up the stairs behind her until she started to scream at the top of her lungs. When I rounded the staircase and glanced into the hallway, Sina dropped to her knees in front of the master bedroom.

"No!"

Gaian and I sprinted toward her and looked into the bedroom. My stomach dropped, my mouth drying. Hellana lay on the bed, muffling her sobs with a pillow over her mouth and clutching her stomach, which bled profusely.

At the waist, her clothes had been ripped and stained with blood. And when I took a closer look, the flesh on her stomach was ripped apart, and her baby was gone. Completely and utterly torn out of Hellana's belly.

76
the plea

sina

I WISHED that this wasn't real. I hoped it was all a dream.

Hellana lay in her bed with a gash, big enough to tear out a baby, in her stomach. Blood soaked through the blankets, sheets, and mattress. I scrambled to my feet and stumbled toward the bed, collapsing on the side of it and taking her in my arms.

"Get Thayer!" I screamed, knowing that he wielded magic to heal wounds. He had done it for me with the engraving he had cut on my chest for the Crispen Pack so many weeks ago. "Someone, get Thayer!"

"On it," Darius said.

Tears streamed down my cheeks.

If what I saw was real—and it was based on Hellana's baby being stolen—then Mom really was alive. She was raped and forced to bear children so that evil, vile man could create an army of his own brainwashed soldiers.

"My baby!" Hellana shouted, her cries shrill.

"I'm going to do everything that I can," I whispered to her.

I didn't want to give her false hope that I'd find her baby alive because I had seen what they did in my daydream. The process happened quickly—so fucking quickly. If they had her baby, they could've killed her by now.

My stomach churned at the mere thought.

"Please," she cried, placing her cheek on my shoulder and clutching my elbow. "You have to get my baby back. We need to continue our bloodline, our species. You know what happens when they take them."

Gaian stared at me in confusion. "What does she mean by that?"

I pressed my lips together and looked down at the wooden floorboards with tears in my eyes. I didn't even want to say it out loud. I couldn't bear the thought of hearing it come out of my mouth. What he was doing to those babies … it was pure torture.

What I couldn't understand through this all was why he hadn't tried to get me pregnant. Why would he force people to rape me every night and not want me to get pregnant like the rest of the females, like Mom, like Hellana?

He didn't want me pregnant for a reason. He didn't want me to mate for a reason.

"I'll tell you later," I said through the mind link. *"I can't say it aloud. Not here."*

Truthfully, I didn't want to say it through the mind link either.

"You have to save her," she sobbed.

"I'm going to do everything I can," I repeated again, picking her up into my arms and handing her to Gaian. "Take her to the pack doctor. He can keep her alive until Thayer comes. Then, Thayer can heal her wounds, like he healed mine."

Once Gaian nodded, I hurried out of the house and back to the pack house. I wasn't supposed to be walking through the pack alone —or anywhere for that matter—but we had bigger problems on our hands.

Babies were being taken and used for that fucker's own wishes. He was stealing life and making humans into Paragons, a more supreme species than demons, wolves, vampires, fairies—hell, *every other species* combined.

"Darius," I said through the mind link, *"once you find Thayer, please track the baby."*

After I received a slight hum for a response, I hurried into the pack house to gather as many vials of vampire blood and herbs as I could find. Something told me that we would need them soon.

Those fuckers had snuck onto our property and stolen a baby. They were getting desperate. They needed more blood in order to build their army, more blood than what they already had.

And I needed to save everyone, even Mom.

She didn't deserve that life, no matter how much she blamed herself. She deserved to live out the rest of her days in peace, not heavily pregnant and being raped constantly. It wasn't fair to anyone.

Once I retrieved the vials, I hurried back to the front door, about to exit the house, when Darius rushed into the room with sweat dripping down his forehead and a worried expression on his face.

"Sina ..."

"You're supposed to be tracking the baby," I said, furrowing my brows.

What was he doing here? What could be more important than this? Granted, they didn't know what my *father* was doing to the kids. If someone stole a pup from their pack, they'd be on their tail quicker than anything.

"We have a problem," Darius said.

"I don't care if we—"

Calder stumbled into the house with blood gushing from a gaping wound in his neck and spurting from his mouth. He dropped to his knees in front of me, eyes rolling to the back of his head and body smacking against the wooden floorboards.

"Kill him," he grunted, voice parched. "Kill Jaroth."

I collapsed on my knees next to him, a cry escaping my mouth. What the hell had happened? Who had given him this—

When my knees hit the ground, I spotted Jaroth lying in a puddle of his own blood behind Calder with his body shredded to pieces from what looked to be Calder's claws.

77

the paralyzed

calder

PAIN SHOT THROUGH ME, my neck searing and my arms and legs aching like they never had. I slowly opened my eyes and stared up at the ceiling in Sina's bedroom. If it wasn't for the pillows drenched in her sweet, thick scent, I would've thought I was in my room. I couldn't turn my head or move my muscles an inch.

"Calder," Sina whispered from my side. "Can you move?"

I opened my mouth—or at least tried to—but I couldn't say anything. I couldn't even scream.

She hovered over me, her head tilted to the side slightly and her eyes wide with tears. "I'm sorry," she whispered. "This is my fault. I shouldn't have ordered Darius to go find the baby."

I wanted to tell her that it was okay, that this wasn't her fault, but I couldn't even speak through the mind link. The last thing I remembered was walking home from Maxine's house and finding Jaroth lingering around my pack borders and fighting him. My teeth digging into his flesh. My claws in his neck.

What had happened after that? Had we captured him? Thank the fucking gods that he hadn't taken Sina.

"Should you give him more medicine?" Gaian said to Sina's left, his face barely in view. "The vampire blood and herbs?"

"I've already given him the dosage I usually took," she said, chewing on her inner cheek, the way she did when she was nervous. "I don't know what will happen if I give him more. It usually takes effect by now. It's been hours."

"Well, fucking try," Thayer growled.

More tears welled up in Sina's eyes. "I-I don't want to kill him. I don't know what Jaroth gave him."

Thayer leaned over the bed and snatched my chin. "You might be an asshole, Alpha, but you're not fucking dying today." When he released me, he turned back to her. "Fucking do it."

Sina pressed her trembling lips together and crawled up onto the bed next to me, taking the vial of medication from Gaian's hand. She gently cupped my chin and pulled my lips apart, placing the edge against my mouth.

"I love you," she whispered, tilting the vial so the liquid rolled into my mouth and down my throat. "I'm going to fix this. You're not going to be paralyzed forever."

Paralyzed forever?

As the last drop rolled down the back of my throat, tingles shot up and down my arms, through my body. It was the only thing I could feel. Then, everything turned dark.

———

When I woke up again, it must've been midnight. I turned my head toward the window, a sharp pain lurching up the side of my neck. I grunted in agony and stared into the dark night sky. Everything fucking hurt, but at least I could make small movements.

"Sina!" I called, my voice hoarse.

Is she still here? It sure smelled like it.

"Sina."

The door opened quietly, and Sina's scent drifted through the room. "Is that you calling me? Are you awake?"

"Sina," I breathed, moving my fingers slightly. "Come here."

Sina closed the door softly behind her, then hurried over and crawled into the bed with me, wrapping her arms around my shoulders. I wanted to hold her back, but I still couldn't move my arms or legs.

"What were you thinking?" she whispered, tears streaming down her cheeks. "Darius told me he was trying to track the scent of the baby and found you and Jaroth going at it in the middle of the forest. Why would you try to capture him alone?"

"He was lurking near my property. I'd do anything to protect my pack and my mate." I turned my head toward her and winced, another shot of pain running through me. "I'd do anything for you."

Gently, she grabbed my face to hold it still. "Don't move," she whispered. "He sliced your neck nearly down to your spine. It's a fucking miracle that you're alive."

"I'd do anything for you," I whispered, tears in my eyes. I kept repeating the same thing over and over to her, but I fucking meant it.

I had been nothing but an asshole to her, but I'd had my reasons. I needed to protect my pack. I needed to protect her.

If anything happened to her again, I didn't think I'd survive it. It'd nearly killed me last time.

"You almost got yourself killed."

"I know," I whispered, ignoring the nagging pain in my neck. "And I'd do it again. You're my fucking everything."

"But, Calder ..." She wiped some tears from her cheeks and glanced down at my body, gently moving her fingers against it, and then she sighed softly. "How do you feel?"

"Better."

"Can you move?"

"My fingers. My toes. My head."

"Nothing else?" she asked quietly, chewing on her lip again.

"No."

She bit back a sob. "I'm sorry. I've tried to heal you. I've tried so hard. I gave you more than the regular dose of vampire blood and herbs. You might … you might not be able to walk again."

My throat closed, my wolf howling lowly inside me at the thought of never being able to shift again.

"Even Thayer has tried," she cried.

"It's okay," I whispered, gliding my fingers over any piece of skin of hers that I could feel. "I'd do it again for you."

She dipped her head and rested it on my shoulder. "We're going to lose this war. We can't win without you."

"That's not true," I whispered. "All this time, I've been trying to protect you. I needed to keep you safe. Now, it's your turn. You're the only person who can end this. Find those babies. Kill your father. Bring your species back. Then, come back to me and let me love you."

She shook her head. "I'm not going anywhere without you, Calder."

78

the confrontation

sina

CALDER LAY IN MY BED, staring up at the ceiling. His neck had been severed so deeply that I hadn't thought he'd make it through last night. I had cried so hard into Thayer's, Darius's, and Gaian's arms at the mere thought of losing my mate.

But he was alive. And I had revenge to get on the man who had made him like this.

"Jaroth is awake, Sina," Gaian said as I closed Calder's door to let him rest. "Thayer has been torturing him in the prison all morning for answers about what he gave Calder, but he hasn't spoken a single word."

I swallowed hard, my stomach twisting, and hurried past Gaian toward the back door. I didn't know why Jaroth had shown back up on our property before he said he would. I didn't know why they had gotten into a fight. I didn't know what the hell he was up to.

But I needed answers. Today.

As soon as I stepped foot outside, the smell of blood filled my nostrils. I followed the scent all the way to the prison and inhaled sharply when the guards opened the doors. Thayer must've let Jaroth bleed out all morning; the stench was repugnant.

"Sina!" Jaroth wailed when he saw me. Chained to a wall, he was naked with his dick cut clean off his body and hundreds of lashes across his abdomen. "Tell them to let me go. I haven't done any—"

"What did you do to him?" I shouted at Jaroth. "What did you give Calder?!"

Jaroth's eyes widened. "I don't know what you're talking about, Sina. I didn't do—"

My monster took control of me, pushing my guys out of the way and lunging toward Jaroth. I seized his neck in my grasp, my claws sinking into his pathetic neck, and lifted him, cutting off air to his lungs.

"What the hell did you do to him?" I roared, my voice shrill. "Tell me!"

"I-I didn't do anything! Let me out!"

"You want out?" I asked, breathing hitched. "You want out of these fucking chains?"

"Yes, Sina. I'll give you anything you want. Please."

"Sure," I said, grabbing his arm at the shoulder and tearing it clean off his body.

He threw his head back and screamed, his pleas lost in the hatred I had for him. So he really couldn't move or escape, I grabbed his opposite leg and ripped it off his body too.

"You're free."

He collapsed to the ground, blood gushing out of his wounds. "What have you done?!"

"Have fun running your fucking demon kingdom," I said between clenched teeth, crouching to his level. "That's why you pulled me away from my father. That's why you helped me leave, isn't it? You wanted my power to help you secure your place as king of the demons?"

Instead of answering me, he grabbed his arm wound with his opposite hand. "Please."

"What did you fucking give Calder?" I asked. "Or I'll rip off your other arm."

"The juice that paralyzes someone," he said.

"And what else?"

"Nothing!" he shouted. "I swear."

"What else?!"

"Nothing else was in the syringe. It was a stronger dose than your father usually gave you. When Calder attacked me, I sank it into his spinal cord at the nape of his neck, but I did it for us—"

I slashed him across the face with my claws, opening up another wound. The sweet smell of blood drifted through my nose, stronger than before, and my fangs ached for it. "There is no us! There will never be an us. You paralyzed my mate. And for that, I will kill you."

"Please," he cried, wincing away. "I can reverse it."

My chest tightened, and I forced my monster to stay still. "How?" I growled. When he didn't respond, I held out my hand toward Thayer, Darius, and Gaian. "Give me the syringe that Jaroth gave me last night. I'm going to do the same thing he did to Calder."

When Darius handed me the syringe, Jaroth furiously shook his head. "Look, I don't know how to do it, but I know what might work. You know that your father has been putting the blood of Paragon babies into human men. You might be able to do the same with Calder."

"I'm not sacrificing an innocent Paragon baby," I said quietly, though the thought lingered in the back of my head.

If it can save my mate …

My stomach twisted even harder.

What the fuck am I thinking? I can't do that!

"Not a baby," Jaroth said. "Your blood."

"How?" I asked between gritted teeth. If I could save him, then I would. "How do I do it?"

"It's not as simple as just giving him some of your blood," Jaroth said. "There is an entire process. I don't know what it is. I've only seen a glimpse of what your father has done. Only in passing. I swear."

I stepped toward him with the syringe. "If you don't know how it's done, then you're no use to me."

"Wait! Please!" he shouted. "I know someone who might help."

"You're lying."

"I'm not! I know who your real father is!"

I stopped inches from him and tilted my head. "What do you mean?"

"Your real father," he said in a hurry. "Demons captured him years ago and bound him in the ice pits up north. He has the strongest power of Paragonian magic that the world has ever known. He could help you transform Calder into a Paragon too."

Gripping the syringe tighter in my hand, I stared at this man in front of me who had kept these secrets from me for all these years. Why hadn't he told me? Why hadn't he helped me? If he'd ever truly cared about anyone other than himself, he would've said something.

So, I grabbed a fistful of his hair and yanked it down so he stared at the ground and I had a clear view of the nape of his neck. Without hesitation, I stabbed the syringe into his spinal cord, the same way he must've done with Calder, and paralyzed him.

"Thanks for the information," I said. "But I would never let you go. You asked me to paralyze all my mates. You asked me to give up my life for one where I'd be stuck with you forever. You paralyzed Calder and nearly ended his life. As soon as you sank your syringe into him, it was over for you, Jaroth. I'm not the girl you can push around anymore. I'm mated to the four strongest wolves in Durnbone." I dropped the empty syringe on the ground and stood, kicking him straight in the jaw. "I'll kill you later. For now, enjoy your useless life."

79

the need

AFTER LEAVING Jaroth to rot in the prison, Thayer, Gaian, Darius, and I decided what needed to happen next in order to end my fake father once and for all.

Fifteen minutes later, I stood at my bedroom door, nervous as fuck to tell Calder what I was about to do.

I peeked my head into the room to catch him glaring at the ceiling and gritting his teeth.

"What's wrong?" I asked, stepping in and shutting the door behind me.

"I've always been the person that my pack leans on, that the guys lean on," Calder said with his head turned toward the window. "I've never been someone who can just fucking lie in bed all day and let everyone do fucking everything."

Once I stepped into his line of vision, I frowned at him, my stomach in knots.

"I hate this. I can't even fucking move."

"Maybe it's the Moon Goddess's doing," I suggested. "To give you some rest."

"More like the fucking devil," he growled. "I don't need to rest. I need to go out there and fight for my pack, for us, for you."

I slouched down on the bed next to him, lying on my side, and gently played with the ends of his hair. While I didn't want him paralyzed at all, he needed the rest. But I could tell that it was already weighing on him.

Being cooped up in my bedroom all day and all night, unable to move barely any part of his body, was taking a huge toll on him. And he was getting *just a bit* moody. What would he do when I told him that I'd be leaving with Thayer and Gaian to find my father?

Probably shout. Maybe scream.

When he became quiet, I let out another low breath. "You're not going to like this," I whispered, stroking my fingers through his thick hair.

"What?" he asked, turning his head toward me, eyes glinting in the golden sunlight.

"Please, don't be mad."

"What is it?"

"Jaroth gave us information about my real father's whereabouts," I whispered, my heart racing faster and faster. Still, I couldn't believe that either of my parents were alive. "All this time, I'd thought that they were dead. All this time, it had been a lie."

"What's the information?" Calder asked, almost as if he knew what was coming.

"The demons chained him decades ago up north in the ice. Thayer confirmed it with Xorgor that the demon queen—or the previous demon queen—had spoken about it to all those with royal blood."

"So, what the fuck does that mean? You're not leaving me, are you?"

"I've already talked with the others. I'm going to leave with Thayer and Gaian tomorrow night to find him, so I can spend tomorrow with you. Darius will stay to help you and Hellana out. We still haven't been able to track the scent of her baby yet."

I chewed on the inside of my cheek and stared at him, not wanting him to be upset with me. But how could he? This was my father, who had many secrets about the Paragons. My father, who I had never met.

Instead of yelling and screaming at me like I expected, Calder pressed his lips together and furrowed his brows, his eyes filling with tears. I rarely ever saw this man cry, but whenever he did … fuck, it broke me.

So fucking badly.

"Please, don't go," Calder said.

"I have to go."

"This pack needs a luna," he said, fingers twitching to brush against mine. "We've all been waiting four years for you—and not just the guys. My entire pack has been waiting for you to lead with me, with us. And I can't do it myself anymore."

"My dad might be able to help you," I said. "We need to find him."

"I can't do it, Sina," he said, voice actually breaking. He shut his eyes, a single tear falling down his cheek that he couldn't even wipe away. "I can't fucking do it again. I can't lose you. What if … what if you don't come back?" The more he talked, the quieter his voice became until I couldn't even hear it anymore.

"I'm going to come back to you," I whispered.

"In front of the guys, I try to be tough. I take all the pain, all the heartache, act like a fucking alpha should. But as cliché as it fucking sounds, I'm fucking breaking on the inside. Fuck, I'm already broken. I can't even move anymore."

"You're not broken, Calder." I pushed more hair out of his face. "And even if you were, I'd love you. I'm never going to leave you like I did."

"Stay with me," he pleaded. "Let Thayer and Gaian go alone. They can handle themselves, but if your father decides to attack our pack while you're gone with all his Paragonian warriors, Darius won't be able to defend us alone. We'll be eliminated. Dead."

My stomach twisted, my heart fucking clenching.

As much as I wanted to find my father, Calder had a point. What if I came home and Calder and Darius—I bit back a sob—were gone? I was doing this for them too. I needed to find my father, so we all survived.

While I wanted to stick up for myself and tell Calder that I would find my father myself, I didn't have it in me to break his heart. He might've been an asshole to me, but he had been carrying all this weight on his shoulders for so many years.

I wasn't sure if the others really understood how much this affected him, how strong he was being for them and for me. All this time, I'd chalked this up to him being an annoying alpha-hole, but I was wrong. So wrong.

"Okay," I whispered. "I'll stay with you."

80

the tortured land

"DON'T WORRY, PRETTY BIRD," I said the next evening, peering back at Jaroth, who lay on the ground behind me.

His arm and leg were chained together behind his back, so he couldn't move. Not that he'd actually be able to anyway with the dosage of that shit Sina had given him yesterday. Since Sina had decided to stay back with Calder and Darius, I'd decided that we needed a third *good friend* to bring along on our journey. Cue Jaroth.

"He's in good hands."

"Let me fucking go," Jaroth said between gritted teeth. "Now!"

I chuckled at his pathetic pleas and turned back to Sina.

Gaian wrapped his arms around her smaller body and pulled her into a tight hug, squeezing her until her breasts were pressed flush against his chest and her eyeballs jutted out. She gently hugged him back.

"I'm going to miss you," Gaian said to her, sucking in a deep breath of her scent. "We'll be back as soon as we can. It should only be a few days' trip. And when we return, your father will be with us."

"Don't be making any promises." I looked at Sina once Gaian finally pulled away from her. We both knew that I wasn't a hugger, so I grabbed her by her throat and yanked her toward me, placing my lips millimeters from hers. "We'll try our best to find your father."

She smiled against me, her soft yet sharp breath making my chest tighten. How the fuck was I going to be without her for these next few days? It felt like her birthday four fucking years ago, and I never wanted to experience that loss again.

"I know you will," she said, closing the distance between us and placing her warm lips on mine. She grasped my free hand and intertwined our fingers, her brows furrowing lightly. "And I'll be here, waiting for you both to return in one piece."

"And me," Jaroth said. "I'll be back too."

"Be happy if you return in pieces," Gaian growled.

But Gaian didn't know what I had planned. We might've been heading for the north, near the ice pits, but we had to pass a couple of other *happy* places, where we could let Jaroth rest. And by fucking happy, I meant … well, he'd see.

"Your royal blood won't save your ass this time," I said to him, kissing Sina one last time, then releasing her and snatching a fistful of Jaroth's greasy-ass hair that hadn't been washed in what seemed like fucking months or some shit. "Not this fucking time."

Once Sina walked back into the pack house, we started our trek through the woods. I dragged Jaroth by his hair, intentionally walking over sharp rocks and through streams to give him a good taste of what death would feel like for him.

He coughed up water, and his body was cut in various places from the rocks and twigs. We walked for what seemed like hours until the path forked into two ways. The right path led north, straight for the ice pits. The left went … another way.

So, I turned left and continued dragging Jaroth's body along.

"I thought it was this way," Gaian said, nodding toward the path on the right.

"It is, but we have to make a stop."

"Do we need to?" Gaian asked. "We told Sina we wouldn't waste time."

"Oh, this time won't be wasted. That, I promise you."

I yanked Jaroth along harder, hoping he'd finally fucking notice where I was taking him. I wanted to hear him scream and beg for me to stop, for us to turn back, for his fucking life, like Sina must've done every single night that she stayed with her father.

"And once we take care of Jaroth, we'll find Sina's father."

Jaroth glanced up from the ground, his eyes widening. "No. Gods, fucking no. Not here."

My lips curled into a smirk, and I dragged him along deeper into the forest. The gray fog that hung between the trees thickened, the brown dirt slowly turning into red rock and the sky glinting pink. Hellhounds howled in the distance.

"Anything but this," Jaroth said.

Monsters of all kinds—who especially loved to devour demons —lurked in these forests. They didn't really enjoy feasting on any half-breeds, like me. And, fuck, I could only imagine what they'd pay for a demon with royal blood.

Too bad he wasn't worth anything to us anyway. I wouldn't accept a single fucking coin for him. All I wanted was to see him in the saliva-covered fangs and the sharp talons of a monster who'd rip him to shreds.

Not pieces. Shreds.

Once we made it deep into the land, I whistled to garner the attention of the monsters. After dropping the grip that I had on Jaroth's head, I walked with Gaian to the nearest tree and sat down on the hard red ground, leaning against the bark.

"Take a front row seat," I said to Gaian. "You're going to enjoy this."

Four-legged monsters crawled out from the forest, their bodies covered in mud and their skin wrinkled. With their four-inch claws, they walked up to Jaroth, their large snouts sniffing at his limbs and his body.

Jaroth lay in the middle of the path, completely paralyzed. "Please! Stop this!"

In a fury, twelve monsters were on Jaroth's pathetic body, tearing him to shreds.

Gods, I wished I'd had some popcorn.

"You bring anything to eat?" I asked Gaian.

He pulled out a pack of M&M's out of his pocket—*fucking savage*—and poured a few into my palm.

I rested my head back against the tree and pointed to Jaroth's half-eaten body. "Don't forget the head. Gotta eat the head too."

A monster opened his mouth, stuck Jaroth's entire demon head inside it, and chomped down, ripping his head off his throat. When he tore the flesh apart, blood squirted everywhere. I chuckled and popped an M&M into my mouth, enjoying this without regret or remorse.

This fucker deserved every last bit of torture.

Gaian sat beside me and smirked. "I wish Sina had come to see this."

"Me too, Gaian. Me fucking too."

81
the villain

sina

ONE DAY HAD PASSED since Thayer and Gaian had left. I stood in the doorway to my bedroom, watching Calder sleep soundly for the first time in what must've been almost half a decade now. His eyes were shut softly, his lips parted.

"Hate to interrupt, but you're going to want to hear this," Darius said, grabbing my arm and tugging me out the door. Instead of shutting the door and speaking to me in the pack house, he continued to the back door. "One of our warriors caught the scent of Hellana's baby."

My eyes widened. "Wh-what? Are you serious?"

"If we hurry, we might be able to find her. She's closer than expected."

"But it's been a few days since she was taken," I said, furrowing my brows and trying to make sense of this. "My *father*'s men should've taken her back to his estate by now. Why are they still hanging around here?"

"I don't know. Now, come on."

As he pulled me along through the woods, I desperately tried to figure out what his plan was. Why would they leave the baby close to our property? What were they trying to do? Were they going to—

I stopped and snatched his elbow to force him to halt. We stood in the quiet forest.

"What if this is a trap?"

"What if it's not?" Darius asked. "This is Hellana's baby, a newborn Paragon."

I pressed my lips together and glanced at the ground. "Don't do that to me. You know I want to find the baby, but if this is a trap and we walk right into it, then we're all going to be screwed. I made a promise to Calder that I'd be your luna and protect this pack."

While I wanted to badly break that promise in order to find the baby, I couldn't. I had to think logically, not emotionally. We wouldn't be prepared for a full-blown attack. I didn't know how many warriors my *father* had.

"We'll meet up with my contact," Darius said. "See what he has to say. If we conclude that the information leads to a surprise attack or that your father is waiting for you to find the baby so he can snatch you, we'll turn right back around. I promise."

My stomach twisted, but I nodded. "Okay."

This was the least I could do for Hellana. I'd promised I'd do everything in my power to return her family back to normal. She had lost her baby the same way that Mom had lost hers in my daydream-reality thing that had happened.

So, we snuck through the woods, careful not to step on twigs or branches or crunchy fall leaves. We couldn't draw any attention to ourselves, and we needed to be on full alert at all times. I couldn't risk having that man capture me too.

Everyone was depending on me to survive. Mom. Dad. Hellana. Calder.

Suddenly, before we could even make it to Darius's contact, voices echoed through the woods along with a baby's cry. A familiar voice that I would never be able to forget. A voice that haunted every last one of my dreams and nightmares.

Darius covered my mouth with his hand, pulled me behind a

large rock, and held me tightly to him. He sniffed the air and tensed behind me. *"Don't say a word, Sina. Don't even take a sharp breath. They'll know that you're here, that we've found them and we are onto them. You were right. This looks like a setup."*

Thank the fucking gods that we had a mind link or else I would've been losing it by now, going absolutely insane. They were using a baby to lure me out because Dad knew that I'd try to find it, that I'd be looking. He knew I'd do anything to protect the innocent because nobody had protected me.

"You can't do anything by your-fucking-self," *Dad* sneered at one of his men who must've stolen Hellana's baby. "You're fucking useless."

When nothing happened and the silent moments passed quickly, I knew deep down that this really was a setup. *Father* wanted me to come out and show myself—to try to save the baby and the helpless men he had brainwashed, who he had let rape me.

He was sick and twisted.

I swallowed hard and tensed in Darius's arms, biting my lip to attempt to stay in control. All my monster wanted to do was rip that man's head off and feast on his body. He deserved every minute of pain, every moment of torture that I would one day give him.

But I didn't know how many guards that *Father* had in this forest, how many men he'd be willing to risk in order to capture me again. Who the fuck knew what he was up to or what his plans were?

"Give me the needle," *Dad* ordered one of his men.

The needle had to be filled with poisonous liquid that'd paralyze the guard who *couldn't do anything by himself.* I squeezed my eyes closed and wanted to shut my ears, too, because I knew that *Father* had more than just paralyzing him up his sleeve.

After a horrid scream from the guard went through the forest, his body smacked onto the ground with a hard thump. A shiver ran down my spine as the feelings of paralyzation rushed through me. I knew what was going through that man's head, how helpless he must be feeling. He might've been the one to steal Hellana's baby and do horrible things to me, but it was under *Father's* control.

"Release the Paragon," *Father* said. "Let her feast."

Suddenly, a monstrous screech pierced through the forest. I placed my hands over my ears to stop the ringing and winced at the sound. When I peered from behind the rock at the scene unfolding in front of me, bile rose in my stomach.

A guard uncuffed a Paragon, who must've only been seven years old. She stood with her head dropped, long, unkempt brown hair covering her face, her body so thin that I could see her rib cage.

"This is your reward, Warrior Number Thirty-Four," *Father* muttered to the girl. "Remember this when the other Paragons act out of line. Remember what you receive when you're a good girl for me."

Rage rushed through me, those exact words whistling through my head. The first time I'd heard them, I couldn't have been older than this girl. It was the first time that … the first time that he had let someone slip inside me.

My monster took over.

When I went to leap out from behind the rock, Darius grabbed my elbows and held me back with all his might, his grip tighter than it ever had been. *"Don't do it, Sina. Do not let him get underneath your skin. You need to survive."*

"He needs to die," I growled through the mind link.

Darius grabbed me harder. *"Stop it, Sina!"*

Before I could charge out there and stop the girl from doing whatever she was about to do, she gently rubbed her wrists where the chains had once been and licked her lips, her fangs extending from her mouth.

She lunged forward at the paralyzed man and began feasting on his flesh and tearing off his limbs, killing him within a single moment. I stared in horror at the sheer amount of damage that this girl could do and shuffled back against Darius.

And this girl was Warrior #34. Who knew how many *Dad* had already?

82
the agony

darius

WARRIOR #34 flung pieces of flesh behind her while hungrily feasting on the human's innards. His screams had died out only a couple of moments ago, but I could still hear them ringing in my ears. This young girl was a cannibal, a beast who had been starved.

We needed to get out of here now.

Right fucking now.

"Let's go, Sina," I said, tugging on her elbows to pull her away.

She shuffled back another few feet, but then a baby's cry echoed through the forest. After tensing, she ground her feet into the forest floor and refused to allow me to pull her back another inch. *"We have to save the baby."*

"We have to go."

Before I could tug her back, she yanked me forward. *"We need to save it."*

"No," I growled.

How couldn't she see that we wouldn't be able to survive this? Who knew how many Paragons this man had at his disposal in these woods, searching and hunting us down? He wouldn't have come alone, not when he knew how powerful Sina truly was.

Sina struggled in my hold, desperately wanting me to set her free so she could kill the man who called himself her father. And after what I had just seen that little girl do to a grown man, I wanted to let her go too.

But if I released her, we would all die.

I felt that in my fucking soul. The Moon Goddess was whispering to me to hold her tight, to keep her safe because this man was anything but nice, anything but sweet. He was worse than cruel.

"Let me go, Darius!" she screamed through the mind link. *"I need to save them!"*

"You saw what that girl is capable of," I growled back at her. *"She just tore a grown fucking man into pieces and feasted on his body. I'm not going to let her do that to you too. You're mine. I-I can't lose you again."*

Calder, Thayer, and Gaian had trusted me to protect Sina. I refused to let her go. I had waited so long for her to come back, for her to tell me that she wanted me like she wanted the others, for her to let me mark her.

My canines lengthened, my wolf taking control.

"We don't know how many more of those creatures they have here," I roared.

"She won't attack me. She's a Paragon, just like me."

"She's not under your control. She's under his. Just like you were."

Suddenly, she stopped squirming in my grasp and twirled around to glare at me. Tears lay heavily in her once-bright eyes. She shoved me hard into the boulder and showed me her vampire fangs.

"Don't hold that over my head. I know what he did to me. I lived through it every fucking day for years," she screamed through the mind link, her words trembling with anger and agony. *"And that's why I need to save her and save Hellana's baby."*

"Chain Number Thirty-Four back up," he announced. "And then we'll move out."

When Sina lunged forward, I seized her waist again and slapped a hand over her mouth. No fucking way was I about to let her jump out there and get herself killed over a girl and a baby. She was more important to me—to us—than anyone else.

A guard clasped chains around the girl, who licked the blood off her lips. I grasped Sina tighter and sank my nose into the crook of her neck, gently setting my teeth on her mark, hoping that I wouldn't have to bite her to control her.

Sina struggled harder and harder, almost escaping my grasp. So, I cursed to the gods that I had to do this and slipped my teeth into her neck, growling at her through the mind link to stop. We didn't have the warriors ready for this.

Slowly, the men cleared out with the young girl and the baby. When they were gone completely, Sina ripped herself away from me —my teeth tearing her skin—and rushed back toward home, thankfully not after the guards.

As soon as we stepped into the pack house, Sina slammed the door and twisted toward me. "We could've saved them! We could've fucking saved them!" she screamed. "Why did you stop me?! I could've taken them all on!"

"You know why I stopped you, Sina," I growled back.

"Why?!" she shouted, fangs extending. "Do you not believe in me?"

"I believe in you and what you can do, but—"

"But what?!"

"But I'm not going to lose you again! I fucking refuse!"

She broke down in tears, collapsing onto her knees and throwing her head into her hands. "I could've saved them. I could've fucking saved them. Now, he will take them back to his estate and do what he did to me. He's going to let grown men rape them, and … and … I should've stopped it."

Sina was trying to blame me for this to take the blame off herself. If she had really wanted to, Sina would've thrown me off her and ripped through her *father's* guards one by one. But she knew that it wasn't a good idea. She had known we wouldn't win.

We needed more intel.

"If you thought we'd make it out alive, you would've ripped yourself out of my hold."

"Stop it."

"You know it's true."

"Stop it," she begged. "Please, stop! I can't ..." Another heart-breaking sob. "I c-can't handle it. I could've stopped it. I could've stopped it, and I didn't because ... because when I saw his face, all those memories came rushing back. I wanted to kill him, but I know I can't. He's done so much to me. So fucking much to me."

She continued to scream and cry in the middle of the living room floor as Hellana appeared at the back glass door, knocking.

I ran a hand over my face and hurried over to it. "Listen, I can't talk right now, Hellana."

"My baby," she whispered. "I heard that you caught the scent of my baby."

I sucked in a sharp breath and glanced over at Sina.

"Tell her," Sina cried harshly. "Tell her."

"We couldn't save your baby," I said.

As much as it hurt me, Sina hurt worse. Her father had struck cold-hearted fear right into her, and I didn't blame her. I didn't want her to feel worse about what she had done, especially now that Hellana was here. It wasn't her fault.

She hadn't chosen to get abused by him all those years.

"Sina wanted to save the baby, but I stopped her," I whispered, swallowing hard and glancing down at my feet. I didn't want Hellana to know that I was lying to her. I wanted—needed—to protect Sina at all costs. "We were outnumbered, and I—"

"Stop it, Darius," Sina cried, looking up at Hellana. "It's not his fault. It's mine." She curled up into a ball in the middle of the floor. "It is all my fault. I could've stopped this. I could've stopped this, and I didn't. Your baby is gone because of me."

83
the girls

sina

I LAY ALONE in Calder's bed with the door locked and the blankets piled on top of me. It had been seven hours since Hellana had left, and I refused to leave this room. Calder was in my bed, Darius downstairs.

My entire body ached, not only with pain from letting my father leave with the baby and the girl, but also with the agony of what he had done to me. It was like I had relived my entire life over again when I saw him.

Paralyzation. Fear. Rape.

It stung me so fucking deep.

When I squeezed my eyes closed, I faced all those tortuous memories. When I opened them back up, I saw the pain in Hellana's eyes after I told her we couldn't save the baby. It was constant torment that I'd never push away.

Someone knocked on the door. I sank further down in the bed and pulled the blankets over my head, sobbing into them. I hated myself. I could've been strong; I could've saved them. Instead, I was still just a weak human. All of my guys would be so disappointed.

"Sina!" Darius called. "Open up."

"Go away," I cried. "Please, I want to be alone."

After a few quiet moments, the door was nearly blasted open. I tore the blankets off my head to see Xorgor standing next to Darius and Maxine. She rushed over to me and crawled into the bed, tears streaming down her cheeks.

"Sina," she whispered, taking me into her arms. "Why didn't you tell me what happened with your father? If I had known, I would've done something more than just … than just … help you return to Durnbone."

I rested my head on her shoulder and looked over at Darius. He mouthed an apology to me for telling her all my secrets, but I closed my eyes and enjoyed my friend's warmth. He had nothing to be sorry for. Honestly, I was glad that he had told her because I wouldn't have been able to.

Hell, I had been back for weeks now, and I'd barely told my guys.

Not because I hadn't wanted to—maybe that was how I'd felt at first—but mainly because it brought back so many bad memories. I had suppressed them and pretended that they didn't exist, but seeing that monster today … had made me feel even worse than when I had been with him.

"I'm sorry," she cried. "I'm so sorry. I should've done more."

"It's okay," I whispered, hiccuping. "It's not your fault. It's mine."

"Stop blaming yourself," Darius said softly.

"How can I?"

"Because this isn't your fault," Maxine said, voice breaking. "You didn't ask to be abused. You didn't ask to be … to be taken advantage of. You didn't ask to be paralyzed and used for your father's sick experiments. We're going to fix this."

"How?" I asked, harsher than I'd meant to. "The only person who can fix this is me."

"That's not true," Xorgor said, leaning against the doorframe, next to Darius. "As of last night, Jaroth has been declared missing by the demon people."

"Don't worry about him," Calder called from the next room. "He's dead."

"What do you mean, he's dead?" Xorgor asked.

I swallowed hard and sat up taller in the bed, still holding on to Maxine tightly. "He snuck onto our property the other day, paralyzed Calder, and—"

"He fucking paralyzed Calder?" Xorgor growled, rushing out of the room and to my bedroom, where Calder had been lying for the past few days now. After a string of curses, Xorgor returned to the bedroom. "Do I even want to know how?"

"With the same liquid my father used to give me."

Maxine held me tighter, gently stroking her hand against my arm, like she had done when we were just kids. She leaned her head against mine. "Is Jaroth in your prison? Did you capture or kill him?"

"Thayer and Gaian left to find my father in the north. They brought him along."

"In the north," Xorgor repeated, almost as if things were starting to register in his head. "You mean—fuck. I knew Thayer was a fucking psychopath, but I wouldn't have thought he'd bring Jaroth to the pits with him."

"What pits?" Maxine asked.

"Where monsters who love feasting off demon flesh live," Xorgor clarified. "If they brought Jaroth there, he'd be more than dead. I doubt an ounce of his flesh and blood is still out there. Those monsters devour every last bit of demons."

84
the father

gaian

"IT'S COLD AS FUCK," Thayer growled, wrapping some fur from a wild animal he had killed around his body and shielding his face from the treacherous winds that burned our bare skin. "Not going to fucking lie. I wouldn't be surprised if we found Sina's real father dead up here."

I cut my gaze to him and pulled up my hood, the cold searing my ears. While I hoped that Sina's real father was alive, I didn't know how anyone could survive here for years by themselves, chained up.

After stopping, Thayer pulled out his phone, which I was surprised still had any battery or service. I hadn't seen anyone for the past ten hours around here, not even another animal, besides the one he had killed.

"If this map is correct, he should be about a mile farther," he said, stuffing his phone back into his pocket and picking up his pace toward the north. "Let's fucking go. I want to get back home. We're going to fucking freeze out here."

Once I started after him, we trekked up the side of a mountain that loomed over the forest below. The snow that lay upon the slope had frozen over into solid ice. Thayer slowed down enough, so he wouldn't trip and fall on his ass.

Carefully, I stared down at the ice, so my eyes wouldn't burn, leaned forward to balance myself, and took steps up the mountain. The farther we made it, the colder it got up here, and Thayer had to keep talking shit to keep himself warm.

I just kept Sina in my mind, desperate to reunite her with her biological father, the man who had lived his life chained in the ice pits and a Paragon who must've been one of the strongest people alive if he had survived *this*.

Thayer slipped face-first into the ice and began sliding down the mountain side. I gripped on to a sturdy tree branch to steady myself and grabbed the back of his arm just as he passed me to stop him. He grunted and scrambled to his feet.

"If you don't shut up, I'm going to let you slide all the way down next time," I said.

He shook the ice off his coat. "Has Sina seen this side of you?"

Biting back a snarky reply, I gritted my teeth and continued a mile up the mountain until we reached a level clearing. Thayer blew out a cloud of cold breath from his mouth in an attempt to sigh and crossed his arms, scanning the area around us.

"He's not fucking here," he growled.

"Well, where the hell is he? You have the map. You're part demon."

"That doesn't mean I know shit about where he is," Thayer growled. "My mother doesn't give a fuck about letting me in on the demon gossip or rumors. She's a no-good, lying piece of shit."

Before I could finish my sentence, the mountain rumbled, shaking the trees violently around us. I ground my feet and bent my knees slightly to stay put and not shake with it, but Thayer—yes, fucking Thayer—was picked up by the winds and thrown down the side of the crumbling mountain.

As the mountain began caving in on itself, my feet slipped from the spot, and suddenly, my body was flying through the air and following Thayer's hundreds, if not thousands, of feet down into the darkness.

We landed with a thud on hard concrete. Above us, the mountain that had caved in on itself began closing overhead, trapping us within its center. And when the darkness completely consumed us, I stumbled to my feet and grabbed ahold of Thayer.

"What the fuck was—" he started, then looked behind me and froze.

"I would've let you find your way down here yourselves," a man with a deep voice said behind me, "but you two together are quite annoying. Who would've thought I'd say that after not seeing anyone for the past twenty-three years?"

I turned around to face him, my eyes growing wide. A Paragon with eyes burning bright stood, chained to a single pole, his body spewing flames to keep himself warm in the midst of these ice pits.

"You fucking did that?" Thayer growled.

"Ah, boy, I didn't just open up the mountain and let you fall inside it. I created it."

"You created the mountain?" I whispered in awe.

Thayer growled. "You made us walk all the way up the fucking mountain in the cold when you could've just made this land disappear so we could find you more easily? What the fuck was tha—"

Before he could say another word, I elbowed him hard in the ribs. "Shut the fuck up."

If this was Sina's father …

"Ah, it must have been hard for you to trek through the ice pits for three days. You can only imagine what it must've been like for the past couple decades. I'm sure you can understand why I used the little power I have left to make myself a warm home."

While Thayer gritted his teeth, I yanked him back, so he wouldn't attempt to kill Sina's father. The cold had pissed him off just a bit too much, and I didn't blame him. But we needed her father to save Calder.

"We're here to help you escape from your chains and bring you to Durnbone."

"Durnbone …" he hummed. "Haven't heard of it."

"It's a town to the south, filled with monsters of all types."

"And whose orders are these?" he asked. "How do I know you won't try to kill me the moment you release me from these chains?"

"Because you're a Paragon," I said. "There is no defeating a creature as strong as you. If we attempt to kill you, you'd snap our necks and bury us in an avalanche outside. Unlike Thayer here, we're not all that naive."

Thayer growled at me. "Watch it."

"We? All?" he said. "Have you brought more with you? Who is your leader?"

"We don't have a leader."

"Who's your leader?" he repeated, the flames burning brighter.

"Sina."

"Sina? And who is she?"

Thayer ripped himself away from me. "Sina is your daughter."

85

the trek

thayer

WIND SEARED the sides of my fucking face. I followed Gaian and Sina's father through the icy snow fields on the path back home. We hadn't had to say much to him after we admitted that Sina was this man's daughter. His eyes had gone wide, and he'd immediately stood and walked with us out of the mountain after we released him.

Snow pounded down sideways around us, blocking my vision. With this kind of fucking weather, I was surprised that I hadn't almost fallen on my ass and down the mountain again. I was trying to keep my focus while standing next to the father of the woman I loved.

I didn't know what to fucking say to him. I wasn't good with these kinds of things.

But ... Gaian wouldn't shut his mouth. They both went on and on and fucking on, all the way down the path that we had taken here. It was so fucking cold, and my fingers were about to freeze off, and these fuckers wanted to talk.

Of course, Gaian wanted to make a good impression. This was Sina's father, and Gaian had to get him to believe that he was a good guy who didn't just want to get into his daughter's pants. And Sina's father was eating up Gaian's good-boy persona, like everyone did.

"Will you shut the fuck up?" I growled, canines lengthening past my lips.

Gaian shot me a look that told me to be quiet. Her father had more power than I'd thought. If he wanted to, he could break me in half with a snap of his fingers. And while I wanted to make a good impression too, all I cared about was actually making it back home to see Sina again.

What the fuck was this all for if we died out here?

After growling quietly one more time, I stared ahead of us at the long trek we had home. I didn't know how long it had been since we had left the mountain, but the walk back seemed so much longer than the one here.

"Our friend is hurt," Gaian said to Sina's father.

"Our alpha," I corrected.

"Our alpha, your daughter's mate, is seriously injured," Gaian continued, stuffing his hands further into his pockets and looking over at the Paragon. "He's paralyzed. And we were hoping that maybe … you could help him."

"Another mate?" her father exclaimed. "That's three of you now. How many more does she have?"

"She's strong." Gaian laughed. "Too strong for just one. She has four altogether."

"And that had better be it," I growled.

Of course, they both ignored me and continued on with their conversation. I pressed my lips together and decided just to keep my mouth shut because I wanted Sina's father to heal Calder just as much as Gaian did. If I kept being pissy to him, he might decide not to help us.

Though I couldn't help it.

I hadn't gone this long without Sina since she had left four years ago. Between the haunting memories of finding her house empty that day to the frigid air burning my face off, I couldn't be nice right now. No matter how hard I tried.

"We were told that maybe … you would help us," Gaian said to Sina's father, testing the waters. "He's devastated that he can't move, and so is she. If you could do something … anything … it would really help. We know how powerful you are."

After letting out a low sigh, Sina's father frowned. "If there's really a war approaching Durnbone—a war that my daughter needs to fight and a war with my people—I won't be able to participate if I help your friend. I don't know if I could make that sacrifice."

"Sacrifice?" I repeated.

Gaian tore his gaze away from Sina's father and stared down at the ground. I balled my hands into tight fists, my claws sinking into my flesh.

"We should've never fucking come up here," I growled through the mind link to Gaian when nobody responded to me.

While slow to respond, Gaian stole a glance at me. *"Maybe he can't help Calder, but if he can help end this war before it starts …"* Gaian trailed off because he knew that I was right.

Sina's father didn't know the first thing about what the enemy was capable of.

If he had truly lost a lot of strength, being bound to the mountain all these years …

"What, you're not fucking strong enough to heal him and to fight? Aren't Paragons supposed to be the strongest creatures in all of existence? You're making that extremely hard to belie—"

Gaian elbowed me hard in the ribs and growled more ferociously than I had ever heard him. He wanted me to shut my mouth again, but I couldn't. I had grown up on stories about Paragons and their strengths. Demons almost *feared* them. And demons didn't fear much.

"It's okay, Gaian," her father said. "Thayer is right. But every year that I was bound to those chains, more and more of my power was sucked out of me. Every time a true Paragon dies in this world, my magic dwindles. I don't have much left."

I pressed my lips together, kinda feeling bad for the guy, and glared ahead of me.

"I'll make my choice when I see my daughter."

"You're actually thinking about helping him?" Gaian asked.

A solemn look crossed Sina's father's face. "That's right …"

I stared at him for a long time, but he didn't say anything more. But there was more to the story, more that he wasn't telling us. That look of pity, sorrow didn't go away. Something was wrong.

"What aren't you telling us?" I growled.

Her father looked over at me and widened his eyes just slightly, as if he had been caught or as if he hadn't thought I would notice or call him out on it. That asshole had been chatting nonstop with Gaian this entire time, and now, just … silence?

"Tell us. What the fuck is it?" I urged.

"Thayer," Gaian growled, telling me to shut my mouth again. "This is Sina's father. You can't just—"

"It's okay, Gaian. I've been stuck here in the mountains for decades. I might not be sure how much magic I have left, but I know it's enough to make your friend into a Paragon, like me, so the lineage of the greatest species around will continue forever, if I decide to do so."

He stared off into the white blanket of snow that stretched for miles ahead of us, as if he had just made a grand speech and everyone was cheering for him. But he hadn't answered my question. But honestly, I wasn't sure any of us wanted to know the secrets he held.

86
the first meeting

sina

IN MY BEDROOM, I lay next to Calder with my head on his shoulder and my leg draped over both of his. I wrapped my arms tightly around his torso, not that he could actually feel it, but it comforted me.

I didn't know how long it'd been since I had last seen that asshole who had raised me. Since I let him take the baby. Since *I* let the baby *die*. I hadn't been keeping track of the days. I didn't even know what time it was. Day seemed like night, and night day.

If it wasn't for Darius, neither Calder nor I would have eaten anything. Hellana had even forgiven me—though if I were her, I wouldn't have—and come over to help us out with Calder too. I should've been the one helping her out—she needed it more than I did—but I couldn't seem to get over the terror I felt inside me.

After closing my eyes and seeing the man who had abused me daily, I reopened them and stared up at the bland ceiling again. Every night, I had nightmares of him. Every night, I dreamed that he would come back and find me, paralyze me, and rape me again and again and again.

I didn't want that to happen. I couldn't let it happen. I was finally somewhat happy with my guys. That was all I'd ever wanted. I didn't wanna be a Paragon. I didn't want to save the world. I just wanted to be happy.

But with him still alive, I would never be truly happy. Nobody would know happiness ever again. He was torturing innocent people, making them his slaves, and ripping their lives away from them.

"Are you okay?" Calder whispered.

I didn't answer him. Instead, I continued to stare up at the bland ceiling like I had been for who knew how long and pressed my trembling lips together to stop myself from crying.

"Sina …"

"I don't know," I answered honestly and hoped that he would just drop it. "I don't know how I feel. Part of me doesn't want to feel anything. I just want this all to be over. I don't know how much longer I can endure this torture, knowing that he keeps stealing Paragon babies."

A long silence fell over the room, and then, finally, Darius sighed from the corner. "I want this all to be over too," he said, sitting in a chair and staring out the window with a book in his hand. Moonlight bounced off his wolfish eyes.

"What are you reading about?" I asked, sitting up slightly.

Darius held the book up so I could see the cover—*Paragons: The Myth*.

My heart swelled at the thought of Darius reading up on what I was. Thayer knew a lot about me and my kind, but the other guys didn't. I didn't know what to say. He was doing more research on me than I was.

He gave me a heartwarming smile. "Somebody's gotta help figure you out."

I let out a low, empty laugh, Calder following.

Another chuckle bubbled in my stomach, but I held myself together. I didn't laugh again because I didn't want to feel happy. I was a fucking paradox. I did, and I didn't. There was nothing to feel happy about, but something deep inside me, something about being with my mates, made me feel just a bit giddy.

My life had been a fucking mess lately.

Maybe it was because I hadn't seen Gaian and Thayer in a while too.

Just as I thought I was feeling a bit better, the front door shook, as if somebody was trying to break into the house. All three of us looked at each other, and Darius stood. All hope of a happier life left my body because I wasn't ready. If this was my father—no, my abuser—then I couldn't fight him like this. I couldn't. I would try my hardest to stand for my people, but he would kill me or take me away from my newfound family.

Darius walked to the bedroom door. "Stay here. I'll see what's up."

I didn't know why, but I stood. "No, I'm coming with you."

I wouldn't let Darius die because of me. He didn't deserve it. He was the sweetest person I had ever met. None of my mates deserved this.

"Sina," Calder growled, glancing over at me.

"Sina, please," Darius pleaded. "Let me do this myself."

The door shook again, and then suddenly, someone slammed it open. My heart pounded against my rib cage, my breath ragged. I wasn't ready for this, but I needed to protect my pack. I couldn't protect Hellana's baby, but I could do this.

A growl rumbled through the house. "It's fucking cold out there."

At the sound of Thayer's voice, I let out a sigh of relief. They were home. Finally.

"We're home," Gaian announced. "And we brought company."

Breath catching, I stared at Darius with wide eyes. Had they really, truly found my father? If the rumors were true, it had been years, decades that he had been bound to that mountain with no food or water. How had he survived?

Before I could stop myself, I sprinted down the stairs, nearly tripping over my own two feet. When I made it to the landing, I scanned the living room until my eyes landed on a middle-aged man with glimmering eyes and a smile that seemed so familiar, but I had no recollection of it.

He smiled at me. "Hi, Sina."

87
the war

calder

"WOW," Sina's father said to Sina, staring her up and down in the pack house living room.

They had barely said two words to each other in the past fifteen minutes, just trying to get over the sheer fact that they were actually meeting for the first time.

While I felt like a fucking joke, unable to move and meeting Sina's father the first time, I found myself sitting in the living room —thanks to Thayer's help—watching Sina interact with him. There was no doubt that they were related—their bright and glimmering eyes were a straight giveaway.

"I can't believe it's actually you," Sina said.

Thayer crossed his arms and leaned against the wall. "I can. You both don't know when to shut the hell up."

Sina cut her gaze to him, as if to tell *him* to shut up, but she ended up smiling at him. He growled but then caught himself smiling back at her. I could only imagine how hard it must've been for him in particular to leave Sina this past week.

"Shut up," Sina said playfully, then turned back to her father. "I have so many questions."

"So do I." He glanced from Gaian and Thayer to Darius and me, then back to his daughter. "I never had a chance to meet you. I was taken away from your mother just before she was about to give birth, and I was bound to the ice. How is she?"

"Mom …" Sina trailed off. "I think she's alive. I saw her in a vision, I believe?"

"Ahh, yes. The Paragon vision. It's similar to the mind link that all wolves have with their packmates, except we can visually see other Paragons that we've met before, no matter which family they belong to."

"So, why couldn't you see her?" Sina asked.

"As I was telling Gaian and Thayer, my power has"—he gulped —"dwindled."

"Dwindled how?" she asked, brows furrowed, leaning against the chair I sat upright on. Almost instinctively, she grabbed my hand, intertwined her fingers with mine, and set them in her lap. "Not completely, right?"

After staring at us in silence for a long few moments, her father pressed his lips together and shook his head. "No, not completely." He turned toward me. "Gaian told me that you were in an accident and became paralyzed."

I moved my fingers a mere millimeter against Sina's, barely able to feel her touch, and gritted my teeth. "It wasn't an accident. I was poisoned by a liquid that can paralyze any species. He gave me too much of it, and now, I'm like this for good."

Sina's father gulped again. "It's called Transfixel. They used it on me over twenty years ago, but it wasn't as powerful. That's how they were able to capture me and bind me. They took away most of my power."

"Is there any way you can … help him?" Sina asked.

"Sina," I said, feeling so fucking bad about myself.

I knew she hadn't meant to make me feel this way, but that was how I took it.

"It's nothing to be ashamed of," he said to me. "I had to deal with those same feelings all alone for years. Once you get rid of them, you'll become stronger mentally. Don't feel like anything I do is because I pity you." He turned back toward Sina. "But, yes, I can help him."

Sina squeezed my hand tighter and stared down at me with tears in her eyes. "Do you hear that, Calder?" she whispered. "You … you might be able to get a bit of yourself back. I hate seeing you look so upset over the way things are."

Thayer shot me a look that I couldn't quite decipher, as if he knew something that nobody else did about Sina's father and the help that he was offering us as an entire pack.

He cleared his throat and stepped forward. "So, that means you won't be able to fight."

"In this war?" Sina's father clarified. "No."

My mate's face dropped. She glanced back at her father and furrowed her brows. "If you heal Calder, you can't help us defeat the man stealing, abusing, and raping innocent Paragons? Your power has dwindled that much?"

"Don't worry about defeating them," her father said. "You're strong enough to do it yourself. I can tell just by sitting in the same room as you that you have my power inside you, but you're afraid to use it."

Sina suddenly dropped my hand and stood, furiously shaking her head. "No. No, I can't do it. I could try a million times to kill him and stop this madness, but I … I can't. I've seen it play out in my head so many times."

He walked over to her and gently grasped her face. "You can do it."

"No, I can't."

"You can. You have my power. That's why they want you."

"Wh-what's your power?" Sina asked, voice trembling.

"To lead."

Sina laughed emptily. "You think *I* have the power to lead? Who am I going to lead if we have nobody but ourselves by our—"

"Leading Paragons is different from other species. Leading Paragons means you inspire them internally to fight. Leading

Paragons means you can not only save them from the horrors of this world, but you can also control them."

"Control them?" she repeated, voice just above a whisper.

"If they're using a baby to create soldiers with Paragon blood rushing through their veins, you have the power to control them. That man needs you alive so you can lead his army. They might follow him into a couple of battles, but he can't command them. Only you can."

Sina parted her lips, then pressed them back together about a dozen times. Then, she shook her head, as if she didn't believe it. "M-me? But I—"

Sina's father grabbed her face again. "Stop waiting for him to come to you. The war has already begun, and it's time for you to stand your ground. You're a Paragon warrior, and we never stop fighting."

88
the beginning

sina

I SPENT the next two days training with Dad and Thayer, desperately trying to become stronger in order to end my abuser's life once and for all. I refused to think of his name anymore and cursed myself for ever calling him Dad before.

Now, I stood in my bedroom, where Calder lay, with my mates and my father, about to embark on the scariest fucking thing in my entire life—facing the man who had pimped me out and used me for my power.

"As much as I wish to travel and fight alongside you, I must stay here," Dad said, cupping my face in his large, cold hands and forcing me to stare up at him. His eyes glimmered under the sunlight that flooded in through the back windows. "You will thrive, my daughter."

While I had only just met him a couple nights ago, I couldn't wait to return from this war and live out the rest of his years with him. He had mentioned that he had become weaker over the past couple of decades, and I didn't know exactly how long Paragons lived.

Whatever the case, we would make the best of it.

After pulling him into a lasting hug, I closed my eyes and enjoyed it. The man who had raised me never once hugged me, and I honestly couldn't remember the last time Mom had hugged me either. It had been over a couple decades at least.

My stomach fluttered. For the first time, I felt like I had my life together, like everything was actually beginning to make sense, like I had found what I was fated to do in this world—save Paragons from those who hurt us.

When Dad finally pulled away, he nudged me toward my mates. I found my way to the bed and sat on the side next to Calder, staring down at the alpha-hole who had forced me to live with him weeks ago. I was so fucking glad he had.

"You must all go," Dad announced to Thayer, Gaian, and Darius.

I took Calder's hand.

"I will stay with Calder and heal him the best I can. Don't worry about him. He'll be back to the way he was for you."

With all his strength, Calder squeezed my hand. "You know I would try to stop you if I had my strength. I wouldn't let you go at it alone." He gestured for me to move closer to him and lowered his voice. "You'd be bound to *my* bed and carrying my pups."

"Stop it," I scolded softly, peeking a glance over at Dad, who leaned against the doorframe with his arms crossed and one brow raised. "You can't say stuff like that while *he's* here."

"I can say whatever I want, Pretty Bird. This is my pack house."

"Not when I'll be the one caring and healing you while my daughter is gone," Dad said, though I could see the slight amusement in his eyes.

When I returned for war, I'd have pups, but they wouldn't be true Paragons. True Paragons had two Paragon parents, like me. My pups would be half-breeds, and while I wanted to help continue the bloodline, I could never even consider leaving these guys.

No matter what, I was with them until the very end.

After stifling a laugh, I gently placed my hand on the back of Calder's neck, leaned down, and kissed him on the lips. I didn't know how he and the others had done it, but they had changed me from the Sina who cried from just thinking about her *abuser* to someone who'd go fight him.

"Thank you," I murmured against Calder. "For everything you've helped me become."

"Come home to me," he said, his eyes softer this time. "Promise."

"I promise."

Once we gathered everything we'd need in this war against my abuser—mainly potions to prevent paralyzation—I gave Calder one last kiss and headed to the front door with my guys and with my father.

"Keep an eye on Calder, will you?" I asked Dad. "Make sure he doesn't get too out of hand."

"He's not going anywhere," Thayer joked.

I arched a single brow. "Calder is always a surprise. You never know with him."

Dad chuckled and pulled me into a hug. "I'll fix him for you, Sina. He's not going anywhere."

"I'll see you soon," I said with a smile on my face. I stared at the guy who had not only given me the physical power to fight, but also the father who had inspired me to eliminate the man who had pretended to be him. "Very soon."

"Good-bye, Sina," Dad said, gently squeezing my shoulder.

"Bye, Dad."

89
the death wish

calder

AFTER SINA LEFT to travel with the guys to her *father's* estate, her real father didn't return to Sina's bedroom, where I lay until almost midnight. He walked in with a large glass bowl, herbs, and some blood in a container.

I eyed it, then scanned him, wondering what he'd been up to.

"Why'd you really stay behind?" I asked. "With the power that you possess, you could've stopped this war for good. That man who calls himself her father is only human. He might be smart, but he doesn't have your strength."

"Sina must face her demons alone," her real father said to me with his back turned. He placed the bowl on Sina's dresser and began pouring in ingredients. "She will get nowhere in life without pushing herself to become a better and stronger Paragon every single day. She must do this herself."

But I could tell that it was only half the story.

"What's the real fucking reason?" I asked.

He hummed softly to himself, as if he hadn't heard my question, and stirred the ingredients together until the liquid turned a dark blue color.

I growled, "I asked you a fucking question. Why'd you stay?"

"Sina can face that man alone. Like you said, he's only human."

"You might've been able to bullshit everyone else, but I see right through you. Why?"

He grimaced and stirred the potion in a big glass bowl. "To heal you."

"You could've healed me later."

"Not in front of my daughter," he said, clenching his jaw and averting his gaze. "She'll never forgive me for what I'm about to do. I've only just met her. I wouldn't have been able to see the hurt in her eyes."

I swallowed and clenched my fist as hard as I possibly could, which was just fucking pathetic. What the hell did this fucker mean that his daughter would never forgive him for what he was about to do to me? What was he planning?

"The fuck does that mean?" I growled, canines lengthening.

While I expected him to show me just as much aggression—because whatever it was didn't seem too good for me—he stood at my side, calmly stirring the glass pot with his lips pursed.

"It's the only way," he muttered, more to himself than to me. "I have to do it."

"Do what?" I growled, heart pounding.

Again, this fucker ignored me and grabbed a ladle. After filling it with the potion, he brought it to my lips. "You must drink it. Sina deserves this more than she deserves me. I haven't been in her life."

He pressed the ladle to my lips, but I used all the strength I could muster and knocked it away with my chin. It splattered all over me and soaked my T-shirt.

I growled, "Don't feed me that shit until you tell me what it's for. Why?"

Sina's father stared at me for a few long moments before setting the ladle inside the bowl and sitting on the side of the bed. "Because in order to fully heal your wounds and mold you into the man you once were, I have to trade my life for yours."

My lips parted in disbelief. "You're … you're fucking lying. You can't do that."

"Despite the popular belief that Paragons live forever, we don't. I've been alive for nearly three hundred years. I've witnessed women give birth and the final breaths of my most beloved. I've felt the pains of battle and of love. I've lived my life the best I could, but my only regret is that I don't have more time with her."

"I can't believe I'm fucking saying this," I said between gritted teeth, but Sina meant more to me than anyone ever before. If I had to stay like this for a couple more weeks or a couple more years, then I … would do it for Sina. "But wait until she's home. Spend more time with her. She's never had much of a parental figure in her life."

"You misunderstand me," he said. "There is no waiting. I don't have long left, only mere days, if I'm to be honest. Since they bound me to the ice, I've witnessed my power diminish. I have counted the days until my death. If your warriors had waited another week to find me, my power would've given out, and I would've frozen to death."

"You should've told her," I growled, rage rushing through me. "When Sina comes home and finds out that you died, she's going to be devastated. She would've understood if you had mentioned something."

He stared down at the bed between us and shook his head. "She has too much heartbreak inside her. She would've been distracted the entire time that she was fighting in the war. And she wouldn't have had a shot at winning with something like that on her mind."

"Still," I said through gritted teeth, "she should know."

As much as I wanted to live, as much as I wanted to be the same alpha that I had been, this felt so wrong. How could I take the little power that he had left in his body and face Sina afterward?

"It doesn't matter. I have made my decision."

"What do you expect me to tell Sina when she comes home?" I asked.

"Tell her the truth—that I love her and did this for her."

I pressed my lips together and glared at this man who had deceived all of us. This wasn't fucking right. This was one of the worst fucking things that could've happened. We'd found her father. He refused to fight. Now, he'd take his life to give me strength.

Sina's father stood and grabbed the ladle once more, filling it with the potion.

"Tell me …" I started, staring at the spoon as he brought it to my lips. "What will happen?"

"For me, healing you will mean that I will pass on to the next life. But for you, you'll inherit the powers of the Paragons, and while you won't be one yourself, you'll be able to reproduce as if you were one. The Paragon bloodline will continue because of you." He paused, then brought the ladle to my lips. "Now, drink."

90
the abuser

sina

"I'M NERVOUS," I whispered, clutching Gaian's hand.

We approached the highly guarded estate with Hellana, Xorgor, our warrior wolves, and an entire guard of demons who looked like they wanted to rip someone's head off. They weren't friendly in the slightest, as I didn't think they actually wanted to be here. But they had no choice. Xorgor had forced them to come. Besides, it didn't matter to me—they weren't the scary ones because Thayer had frightened them off from looking in my direction.

"There's no reason to be nervous," Gaian responded, squeezing my hand.

If Dad thought I could defeat this abusive piece of shit without his help, then I ... had to do it. I trusted in myself all the way up until we made it within a mile of the estate and spotted the guards spread throughout the woods.

"Believe in yourself, Sina," Darius reassured. "You must kill him."

"The Moon Goddess did what she did to Calder for a reason," Thayer said. "Because he'd kill him for you. You wouldn't grow into your full potential if he were able to walk still. You're the only person who'll get in close enough to kill him."

"Okay," I whispered, heart pounding inside my chest.

After commanding his army to be silent, Xorgor and Maxine walked over to me.

"We don't send in anyone until you signal for it," Xorgor said to me. "We haven't fought against a Paragon army in decades. We don't know what this group is capable of or if they are capable of anything at all."

"They are," I reassured.

I didn't like the thought of heading into the estate with only a few close people, but Xorgor was right. Never in a million years would I put his people—and my pack—in danger without trying to eliminate the threat myself first.

Last night—without Calder—we had agreed that I would walk onto the estate first to get my father's attention. If I could take control of the Paragons like Dad had said I'd be able to, then I would try as hard as I could and freaking hope that nobody else would have to die because of me.

After taking Hellana's hand, I made contact with her through the Paragon vision. I'd tried it out the other night after Dad told me about it because I knew that it'd be useful. It definitely took a few tries to make contact at first, but I got it in the second try now.

"You'll see everything that I see," I said to Hellana. "Send in the warriors when I say."

She'd know and inform the others about what happened inside the estate, preparing them for the worst. Before I released her hand, she pulled me into a tight hug and rested her head on my shoulder.

"I know you still feel shame about not having the courage to save my baby, but I … I've come to terms with it. I can have another to continue the Paragon bloodline—as long as we survive. I need you to be strong. Okay?"

"Okay," I whispered once she pulled away. "I'll do this for us. For Paragons."

"For Paragons," she repeated, giving me a trying smile.

This was all on my shoulders. The outcome of everything weighed on *me*.

I had to kill him.

I had to avenge all those who had died.

I had to breathe life into the next generation of Paragons.

From afar, I stared at the mansion that lay upon the estate in the distance. Hundreds of guards must've roamed around the forest, looking for any sign of trouble. I wondered if that asshole was actually here.

Probably or else he wouldn't have this many guards with him.

It was now or never. No more waiting.

After sighing, I threw my arms around Gaian, Darius, and Thayer. "I love you all so fucking much. Thank you for everything that you've done for me over my entire life, but especially these past few weeks."

"Don't fucking say that shit," Thayer growled. "You're not going to die."

"I just wanted you to know," I said.

"We know," Darius said.

"No need to thank us, Pretty Bird," Gaian said.

Thayer broke off the hug, grabbed my shoulders, and ushered me toward the estate. Only he and I were going to *act like* we were sneaking around the property until someone *accidentally caught us.*

"You'll kill him," Thayer said once we were half a mile onto the estate. "Then, you're not leaving the pack house until your belly is full with pups. You know, this is the last bit of freedom you will have for the next nine months, so make the most of it. Kill that motherfucking basta—"

"Are you talking about me?" someone hummed behind us.

At the sound of his voice, I froze. My heart thumped against his chest.

"I knew you'd finally return, sweetheart," he purred. "Turn around and give your father a hug."

Slowly, I turned around and spotted him standing a few yards away from me with his arms extended and at least ten guards surrounding him. Before we could even react, a bullet sped through the air and pierced through Thayer's abdomen.

I didn't doubt that it was a bullet laced with poison.

"Stop this," I growled, wanting to help Thayer but knowing that he wouldn't be hurt for long. He had taken some potion beforehand, so the poison should whiz through his system before we knew it. I glared at the man. "Now."

"Stop?" He chuckled. "We're just getting started, Sina." He motioned to the guards. "Take her."

91
the fight

thayer

I GRASPED my bleeding abdomen and stumbled back a few feet, the poison seizing control of my body. My legs trembled, then suddenly gave out completely, and I hit the ground on my knees with a thud. Desperately, I tried to catch myself with my arms, but I couldn't move them either, so I continued to fall face-first against the ground.

"Take him to the prison," Sina's *father* ordered a guard. "Get as much information out of him as you can. They don't leave anyone's sight. There has to be more of them around here. They aren't stupid enough to come alone."

"Maybe we are," I growled through my canines, glaring into the dirt because I couldn't move even my head a couple of inches to the side. My entire body was stiff and numb, to the point where I couldn't feel a thing.

But if Sina's potion worked—gods, I hoped it did—then I wouldn't be like this for long.

A large guard—way too big to be solely a human—picked me up and tossed me over his shoulder as if I weighed nothing. I seethed through my canines, loathing the fact that he was manhandling me, but not being able to do anything about it.

"Stop!" Sina cried, hurrying after me.

"I'm fine. I can move. Just playing the part," I growled at her through the mind link, completely lying to ensure her safety. If she thought that I could defend myself, then she'd be able to think clearer and accomplish what she needed to accomplish. Plus, this should wear off soon, right? I stared back at her as they took me away. *"Don't follow—"*

Before she could move another foot, her *father* seized her arm tightly and dragged her in the opposite direction. "You're coming with me, *dear*. We have *much* to catch up on. I'm not letting you out of our sight again."

"Be strong, Sina," I said through the mind link. *"For all of us."*

When she disappeared from my view, I growled and bared my canines at the man still walking with me down to the prison. I didn't want to fucking be like this—useless and paralyzed while my mate was in danger.

Now, I fucking realized how Calder must've felt.

After a couple of moments, the guard entered the prison, which reeked of feces, and dumped me into a cell. He took one of my wrists and locked it up to a chain hanging from the ceiling, then did that with the other one too so I hung from my arms.

I glared at him as pins and needles pierced my flesh. "Let me out, you fucker."

He chuckled darkly, walked over to a closet in the side of the room, and grabbed a knife. The silver blade glimmered underneath the dim cell light that hung overhead. Even from a distance, the silver repulsed me, made me ache all over.

But I could do nothing.

Moving closer, he drew his finger across the blade to the tip and smirked at me. "Do you remember me?" he asked, stepping closer to me. "You killed my comrades when we came to find Sina, bathed in their blood."

"So, what's this?" I asked, glaring down at the blade. "You want payback?"

He sank the blade into my bullet wound and drew it up my abdomen, at least an inch deep. I gritted my teeth, the pain piercing through my body and the numbness slowly disappearing.

Over and over, he slashed my stomach and opened up the wound more and more. I grasped the chains and held myself up, taking all the pain and all the wounds he inflicted.

"Let me out," I growled at him.

Sweat rolled down his chest, soaking through his shirt. My blood splattered all over him.

He didn't stop. He continued and continued and continued, cutting so deeply that he cut through my muscle to my innards. When he hit my insides, I roared, yanked the chains from the ceiling, and lunged at him.

I slashed my claws across his throat and split open his artery. He stumbled back and widened his eyes.

"Y-you can move?" he whispered as blood leaked out of his body.

When he landed on the ground, I straddled his waist and hurled my fists into his face over and over again until his head was bouncing against the concrete. His hard-ass head bruised my knuckles, but I didn't stop until his heart stilled.

92
the paragonians

sina

"DON'T LET her out of your sight," Dad told a couple of guards when they thrust me into a cell on the opposite side of the estate where Thayer had disappeared.

Across from me, Paragon children sat, huddled together in a cell, malnourished.

"I need to find the others that they must've come with."

"We came with nobody," I said.

Dad chuckled, as if he knew I was lying, and disappeared.

Two guards stood at my cell, glaring me down like I was nothing to them. I closed my eyes and reopened them, staring at the children and tapping into the Paragon vision to Hellana outside.

"Do you see this?" I asked.

"Yes. You should try to connect with them. Those guards won't let you out alone."

"Connect with the children?"

"Yes," she said. *"Connect with them. Inspire them, as your father taught you. They're impressionable, and they can easily be swayed to our side."*

After closing my eyes and dropping the vision so I could focus on the children, I inched closer to the bars and stared at the girl who that asshole had brought out the other day. While she had been ferocious outside, she looked so fragile behind these bars.

I closed my eyes, searching through the Paragon vision to find her.

"Warrior Number Thirty-Four," I whispered.

She looked over at me and furrowed her brows.

"You don't deserve to be here. None of you do. I want to help you escape."

She didn't respond.

"Escape. Freedom."

I didn't know if she understood me, so I closed my eyes and hoped that I could send her one of my thoughts—an image of us freeing ourselves from the guards and living outside in peace with the other species.

Her eyes widened slightly.

"Please, I will help you if you help me."

Another long bout of silence before she sat up taller. *"How?"*

"Are you all Paragons with powers?"

"Yes."

"If you work together, you can escape your cell. I will distract the guards. You all escape, kill the man in front of me, and set me free. I will bring you to get revenge for all the people, all your family and friends, that your master has hurt."

They all looked at each other, as if they were talking to each other through the Paragon vision too, a liveliness in all of their eyes again. I didn't need an answer from them because I knew that they would help me, and if they didn't, I still needed to escape.

"Hey, you fuckers," I growled, standing up and gripping the prison bars directly in front of the children. "Over here!"

The guards walked toward me and shoved me back and off the cell bars.

I lunged toward them and grabbed one by the throat, sinking my claws into his neck and yanking him even closer. "You're going to—"

Before I could even finish my sentence, the cell door swung open across the hallway, and Paragons leaped out of the cell, jumping on the guards and taking large bites of them with their pointed fangs.

The guards struggled for a moment before they both collapsed onto the ground and became nothing but corpses. Warrior Number 34 grabbed a key from a guard's pocket and unlocked my cell.

"Freedom," she said. "Please."

"Freedom."

———

Once I thrust myself through the door and exited the mansion that my father and his minions had attempted to hold me inside of with the other *true* Paragons, I froze in my spot. Demons and werewolves were fighting across the front lawn against that asshole's guards, who he had turned into Paragons with babies' blood.

My heart pounded inside my chest as I scanned the battle happening before my eyes. From afar, I spotted Gaian and Darius had both shifted into their wolves and were fighting off two Paragonian guards while a couple of their packmates lay dead on the ground beside them.

So much loss. So much fucking death.

A Paragonian guard ripped a demon into two and dropped him at my feet. I stared in horror at how strong they were, but I knew we couldn't fear them. If I tried hard enough, I'd be able to take control of them. I could stop them, but first, I needed to stop that asshole.

Continuing to scan the area, I spotted that asshole trying to depart to safety. I gritted my teeth and balled my fists, extending my talons enough to rip right through my skin. My body boiled in anger, my fangs aching for his blood.

"Stop him!" I growled, inspiring the younger Paragon children, who were much stronger than some measly guards, to fight for their parents who had died because of that asshole, to get revenge and seize their own lives back. "We don't let him live!"

The children sprinted through the battle, killing anyone who stood in their way even if they had Paragon blood, and headed straight for that asshole who ran desperately toward a small concrete building just outside his estate.

I bet that fucker had a bunker in case something like this happened.

"Don't let him make it into the building!" I shouted. "Bring him to me!"

As the children picked up their pace, I turned back to the battlefield and gripped my hands into tighter fists. I wasn't sure how or if I'd be able to control them completely because they weren't true Paragons, but I had to try.

"The wolves and demons are not your enemies!" I shouted, walking through the battlefield. Rage boiled through me as I witnessed the horrors these creatures—my kind—could do to other species, but I forced myself to stay calm. "Stop fighting them!"

While words weren't much, especially to creatures who feasted off violence, some stopped attacking the other species and glanced my way. In their eyes, I could see their internal struggles to continue fighting. The asshole had controlled them up until now.

Now, I wanted to release them from his curse.

"You don't have to fight!" I shouted louder. "We aren't here to kill you!"

More stopped and glanced over. I didn't know how it was possible, how they listened to me, but Dad had mentioned that his power to inspire the Paragons to fight for him had been passed down to me. It was my turn to make the decisions, make the choices that would keep us alive.

"Must fight," one growled, dropping a demon and turning toward me. "Must fight."

"No," I said gently, shaking my head. "You don't need to fight."

He barreled toward me quickly and seized my throat in his large hand, pulling me into the air. "Must fight."

While I wanted to kill this fucker right here and right now for touching me, I gently retracted my claws, stared into his angry eyes, and placed my hand on his wrist. "I will not fight you," I whispered. "I don't want anyone here to die, except the owner of the estate."

"No," he said, shaking his head. "We must kill everyone, before they kill us."

"No," I reassured. "Nobody wants to kill you. I want to free you from his mind control."

"Free us?" another said, stepping forward, brows furrowed. "From him?"

I nodded. "Yes."

The Paragonian guards broke into a whisper and stopped showing any sign of aggression toward the wolves and demons. He dropped me from his hold and turned back to the others, as if looking for guidance.

After a couple of moments, the group went silent.

He turned back toward me, his canines lengthening. "We want freedom. Freedom for us and our families."

"I'll give you it," I promised. "But you must let me kill your leader."

Another flare of whispers, and then he nodded. "Kill him."

When I turned back around to head toward the children, they were returning toward me with blood dripping down their mouths while dragging a body behind them. They dropped that asshole at my feet, who was drenched in his own blood and piss.

Small bite wounds and claw marks covered his entire body. He scrambled to his knees and immediately collapsed back down on the ground, unable to hold himself up because of what seemed to be blood loss.

"Get up," I growled.

He tried to stand once more, but fell flat on his stomach.

"Gaian, Darius," I ordered. "Make him stand."

My mates shifted back into their human form and hurried over to him, each picking up an arm and lifting him into the air. Fury rushed through my body, completely taking hold of me, like it had the other day when in the prison with one of his guards and Thayer.

My teeth sharpened into fangs. My claws extended from my

fingernails. My vision darkened, a black film blocking out everyone who wasn't this asshole abuser who had ruined my entire childhood.

I lunged forward and slashed my claws across the front of his pants, ripping them off and humiliating the *poor old man*. I continued slashing his privates over and over because he deserved it for letting everyone rape me.

Every single one of his shouts, cries, pleas satisfied me.

This was how I had felt every night at his estate, and nobody had come to my rescue. As nobody would come to his either.

When his cries died out, I ripped his dick clean off his body and fed it to him, shoving it deep down his throat and loving the way he choked on it. When the bulge reached the front of his throat, I ripped my claws into his neck and severed his head, watching it fall to the ground in front of us.

It was over.

It was all fucking over.

93

the restoration

sina

"YOU'RE FREE," I announced to the group of Paragons who had been under that asshole's control for far too long. He had used innocent babies to create some of them, and while I had wanted to kill them for it, I had realized that it wasn't their fault. "You're all free."

I expected them to leave this place, roam the world, and make lives for themselves. Instead, they just stood there and stared at me, as if I still had control of them. But Dad was right. I didn't have complete control of them, but I had the will to inspire their deepest wishes—to reunite the Paragons, save the world, and be free.

They hadn't been born to fight each other like this. They had been bred that way.

"You can leave," I announced again. "You're free."

"Where shall we go?" one asked, looking around. "We don't belong with any other species. We're different animals, different creatures. We don't have a home of our own. Nobody will accept us into theirs."

I glanced around at the entire group, who seemed to agree, then peeked over at Gaian, who shrugged his shoulders, as if to agree with what I was thinking even though I hadn't said a word out loud or through the mind link. He understood me so deeply.

"We can start a life together," I whispered, smiling at Gaian, Thayer, and Darius. "Paragons need a place to live, thrive, and breed, so we are never on the verge of extinction again. I have a place we can go."

"Gather your things," Darius said to the group. "We'll leave in a couple of hours."

Once everyone departed, I walked over to my guys and placed a hand on Thayer's abdomen, hoping that he could heal all his wounds. "Are you okay?" I whispered, brows drawn together. "I'm sorry."

"Don't apologize," he said. "I loved the pain. Jolted me awake."

"I should've known," I said playfully, glancing back at the mansion. "I need to go find my mom and help her collect her things. She's coming with us." I ordered Gaian to take care of Thayer, who growled that he didn't need help, and jogged to the mansion.

While I had lived here for four years, I hadn't been able to explore every inch of this place. There had to be a dungeon where the asshole kept Mom. I had gone there in my Paragon vision.

After exploring the place for ten minutes, I found my way through a secret passage and into the dark corners of a dungeon. I lit a torch and walked through the hallways, desperately trying to find a light.

When I found a light switch, I flicked it on and found myself in a long hallway with plenty of doors. I retraced my steps from my vision to Mom's room and gently opened the door.

"Mom?" I whispered, spotting her lying on the bed.

"Sina?" she asked, widening her eyes and grasping her stomach. "Sina, what are you doing here? You shouldn't be down here. He'll find you and—"

"He's dead," I whispered, my lips curling into a smile. "I killed him."

She widened her eyes even more, then began sobbing. "Oh, thank the gods! But what about … what about your father?" Mom whispered, sitting up against the headboard and placing her hand on her stomach, where a new baby bump had formed. She gently closed her eyes and sighed softly. "Have you found him? You seem so much stronger."

"Yes," I whispered, butterflies fluttering in my stomach. "He's somewhere safe."

"Where?" she asked, brows furrowed. "I can't feel him through the Paragon vision."

"He's at my pack house with my mate."

She reopened her eyes and took my hand. "Are you sure?"

I furrowed my brows. "Yes, I'm sure."

"Please, contact him. I-I need to talk to him. I haven't spoken to him in years."

After moving onto the bed with her, I leaned against the headboard and closed my eyes. Like Dad had taught me, I tried to contact him through the Paragon vision. And while I was able to reach and connect with the Paragons outside, getting healed, I couldn't reach Dad.

My heart pounded against my chest. "I … I can't," I whispered.

Desperate to connect to inform him about our win, I squeezed my eyes shut even tighter and breathed deeply. Nerves zipped through my body as I waited and waited and waited for him to answer, but I couldn't come up with anything.

If Dad wasn't allowing me into his view, something must've happened. So, I did the only thing I could and tried to contact Calder through our mind link. If that asshole had sent Paragons after him before this started, then we'd be fucked.

Calder would be in danger too.

My stomach twisted, bile rising in my throat.

"Calder," I said desperately. *"Please, answer me."*

I knew we were far away, but this needed to work.

Mom grasped my hand. I reopened my eyes to see tears in hers, threatening to spill over and fall down her cheeks.

She gripped her stomach tighter and shook her head. "He's gone from this world, isn't he? I … I wanted to apologize"—she glided her hand across her stomach once more—"for this. It wasn't my fault. I tried my hardest to—"

"He's not gone," I whispered, shaking my head.

"Calder, answer me!"

"What is it, Sina?" Calder said, his voice colder than the last time I had spoken to him.

"Tell me that my father is okay," I whispered.

Silence.

"Calder!"

"Sina, I … I can't."

I froze, opening and closing my mouth over and over, unable to form any words for this. So many thoughts ran through my head that I couldn't even articulate one of them.

What had happened to Dad? Was it that asshole's doing? Where could he have gone?

"You need to come home, Sina," Calder said. *"Now."*

94
the confession

sina

GAIAN and I made it back to the pack house in record time, heading onto the property only a few hours after I had chatted with Calder. He'd refused to tell me what had happened over the mind link. Darius and Thayer stayed behind to wait for the other Paragons to gather their belongings and lead them back to the pack house, but I couldn't wait any longer. Calder and Dad might've been in trouble.

When I leaped onto the back porch, I snapped open the door to a quiet home. It was almost too quiet, too eerily quiet for both Calder and Dad to be here. I stepped into the living room and released Gaian's hand.

"Calder?" I shouted. "Dad?"

"I'm in here," Calder said, walking out of his bedroom.

My eyes widened, and I rushed up the stairs toward his room. "You're healed!"

"Yes, I'm—"

Before he could finish his sentence, I wrapped my arms around his torso and pulled him into a tight embrace. For days, I'd feared that I would never see Calder move again, never mind walk around the house!

"I can't believe it," I whispered. "He really healed you fully."

"Sina," Calder said, dropping his hand from my body to grab mine. "That's what—"

"I need to thank him," I said, my mind racing with hundreds of thoughts about how we could be together in peace once more.

Mom and Dad could meet for the first time again in years, and we could live as a family.

My real family.

"Where is h—"

"Sina," Calder growled more sternly this time.

I snapped my gaze up to him and widened my eyes, my stomach twisting and turning again today. Something was wrong; that was why we had come back. But … nothing seemed to be broken into or ruined around the pack house. Which meant …

My throat dried. "What happened?"

"It's your father," he whispered, tucking some hair behind my ear. "Your father …" Calder trailed off, his words getting lost in the deafening silence.

It wasn't like him to hold back what he wanted to say. Like Thayer, Calder was usually unapologetic about his words and how they were taken.

Fingers curling into his chest, I stared up at him. "Tell me."

"He's dead."

My heart stopped beating for a second, and I found myself shaking my head. Over and over.

I ran through all the rooms. Screaming his name. Shouting that this wasn't a funny game they were playing on me. Needing him to come back.

"No," I said, running through the house again. "Where is he? Where is my dad?"

Calder walked down the stairs to Gaian, speaking a couple of muffled words to him. I tumbled down the stairs, nearly tripping over my two feet multiple times, and hurried over to them both.

"Where is he, Calder?" I asked again.

"He died for me," he whispered, grasping my hand once more. "I tried to stop him, but he refused, and I couldn't move. He gave me every last bit of his soul that he had left for me to be with you, for me to continue the Paragonian life with you."

Tears welled up in my eyes. I shook my head again.

"No," I sobbed, my knees weak.

Calder caught me before I collapsed and wrapped his strong arms around my body. I lay so helplessly in his arms.

"No, you're lying. Tell me you're lying. I just … I just met him."

"I'm sorry," he whispered.

And while Calder spoke those words, I heard Dad's voice for the last time, drifting through my ears, apologizing to me about what he had done, the choice he had made to help Calder live, the need for me to forgive him.

I pressed my lips together and pulled away from Calder, wiping my tears with the backs of my hands. "It's not your fault," I whispered, staring at the ground between us. "He wanted to do this one last thing for me. It's okay."

"But—" Calder stuttered, eyes widening.

After lifting my gaze, I gently placed my hands on his chest and smiled up at him. "It's okay," I said. "We're all okay now. This was how it was all meant to turn out. We have a pack, a family, and now …" I gazed out the front door window at the Paragons that Thayer and Darius were now leading to the spare houses on the property. "And now, we have time to focus on us."

"On all of us," Gaian said.

Calder looked from him to me to the others outside. "You did it."

I snatched his hands and squeezed. "We did it."

95
the last journal entry

sina

"WE'RE GOING to play a little game with you," Thayer growled in my ear.

I teetered from foot to foot and whimpered, a sleeve of silk covering my eyes and shielding my vision. My hands were pulled behind my back and bound around a large tree trunk in the forest behind the pack house. I had been standing here—completely naked and unable to move—for almost an hour now. Waiting for one of them to touch me.

Over the course of the last week, since I had saved the Paragons, we had enacted every entry from my journal, except this one. And I had been begging—aching—for them to complete my fantasies.

"Please," I pleaded. "Breed me."

My inner monster had been in heat all week, desperate to be filled with her mates' cum every single hour. I needed it more than I had needed anything in my life, and this time, I refused to stop until my belly was full of babies.

"We're going to untie you," Calder growled. "And you're going to run as fast as you can."

Leaves crunched beside me.

"Don't let us catch you," Gaian warned.

"When we do, we get to touch, tease, taunt you as much as we like," Darius said.

Thayer drew his fingers up and down my sides. "And when we catch you, Pretty Bird, you're going to beg us to stop. Fight us. Refuse to let us slip inside you."

Calder chuckled darkly. "As much as"—he moved a single finger down the center of my chest and over the ropes they had used to tie me up, and when he flicked my bare nipple, I whimpered—"you can, which, for a woman *like you*, won't be much."

Silence among the wolves again.

Someone drew their claw around the rope that bound me to the tree, but not to the one that bound my hands together. I landed on my knees in the dirt and caught myself before I fell forward and flat on my face.

"Run," Calder ordered.

I looked up and scrambled to my feet, still blindfolded and tied up. "B-but I can't see or—"

"You have five minutes to get as far as you can."

Without them having to tell me twice, I lightly jogged through the woods. I collided with a couple of trees, stumbling forward, but I kept my pace. My heart pounded inside my chest, my pussy tight with pleasure.

I ran. And I ran. And I ran.

Harder. Faster.

Branches snapped under my feet. Leaves crunched under my toes. Howls erupted through the dark woods.

The four wolves were coming … for me.

Heart thumping even faster, I continued to run. The pounding of their feet running through the forest toward me echoed through my ears. And before I could run another few feet, a wolf enveloped my arm in his strong jaw—not enough to draw blood, but enough to tug me down.

I tumbled to the ground with a thud and landed on my knees and shoulder, ass in the air. Another low growl came from behind me. The wolf placed his paws on my backside, his body transforming into that of what felt like a human.

"Perfect," Darius growled behind me.

A wad of spit dripped onto my ass, and he slowly pushed a finger between my cheeks. I dug my shoulder into the ground and looked back at him, vaguely making out his human figure through the blindfold. He pumped his finger in and out of me before adding another one.

As they had asked me to, I threw one of my legs back and hit him in the stomach hard, fighting back with everything that I had. He caught the second leg that I hurled back at him and put pressure on them with his knees.

I threw my hands from side to side, trying to get them loose so I could really fight back, but Gaian had tied the rope way too tightly for me to escape easily. I scrambled in his hold, my tits swinging against the dirt.

"Let me go!" I shouted.

Darius inserted another finger into my ass, opening me up even more.

The other wolves padded up toward me, stopping near my right and transforming into their humans. And soon, there were four sets of hands all over my body, touching, groping, grabbing, and slapping me.

Darius removed his weight from me and glided his knees onto the outsides of mine. When I kicked him again, he pulled my legs back so I fell flat onto my stomach. Then, he slammed his cock into my ass and began fucking me in the prone bone position.

"Open your fucking mouth," Thayer growled from above me, slapping me hard on the cheek.

My skin stung, and I growled back at him in response, refusing to open my mouth. He slapped me hard on the cheek again, slipped a finger between my lips, and pulled my jaw open.

Before I could stop him, he collapsed onto his knees, grabbed a fistful of my hair to pull my head up, and plunged himself inside my mouth, grunting. His balls glided against my cheek, smacking me in the face with every thrust. He spit and smacked me over and over, becoming rougher each time.

Someone snatched my hand and wrapped it around their cock, forcing me to stroke it back and forth. Wads of drool and spit ran down my chin to my mouth. Darius continued pounding into my ass and reached an arm around my waist to rub my clit.

My pussy pounded as I clenched and unclenched on nothing.

"Please," I said on Thayer's dick. "Breed me."

Thayer pulled out of my mouth, grabbed a fistful of my hair to lift me, and smacked me hard against the cheek. "Shut the fuck up. We'll breed you when we're done using you, you fucking bitch."

I clenched harder. "Thayer, please—"

Thayer filled my mouth again, but this time, either Calder or Gaian plunged inside me too. I opened my mouth as wide as I could to take them both and sucked aimlessly, becoming more desperate by the moment.

Fuck fighting them back. I needed them so badly.

I bobbed my head back and forth, swirling my tongue around their heads and covering them in my spit. Darius continued to rub my swollen clit as someone else took one of my tits in his hands, kneading the sensitive flesh and twirling my nipple around against his palm.

When he seized my nipple, I cried out. Ecstasy exploded through my entire body, the pleasure pumping through me. My pussy clenched over and over, aching to be filled with cum already. Darius held my trembling body steady and slammed his dick deep into my ass, stilling. He grunted and slowly pulled out of me.

"Fill my pussy," I begged.

The other three moved around, one pulling me into the air with my back and arms against his taut chest. He spread my legs and slipped into my pussy while another stepped closer to me and pressed the head of his cock against my pussy lips too.

Thayer growled behind me, his teeth sinking into my neck hard enough to draw blood. I tilted my head against his and clenched hard as the other slipped inside me.

"More," I begged. "Give me your cum. Fill me with it."

Someone—who must've been Gaian—dipped his head and took my nipple into his mouth, sucking on it. His teeth glided against the hardened bud, and he gently bit down and tugged.

"Your tits are bigger," he growled against me.

I clenched harder on them, desperate and whimpering, "P-please!"

"Fucking huge," he grunted, sucking on my other breast.

Another moan escaped my lips. "Gods, Gaian, don't stop," I whispered. "Please, don't stop. It feels too good."

Gaian groped both my breasts, squeezing harder from my chest to my nipple. Pleasure ran through my body, my tits tingling. The sensation wasn't like anything I had felt before, and Gaian had never been so hungry for them. He sucked harder, teeth latching on to one.

"Fuck," he grunted. "You taste so good."

I furrowed my brows. "Wh-what do you mean?"

"Don't stop fucking her," Gaian commanded, sucking harder on my tits, moving from left to right and squeezing, almost *milking* them. He took my nipple between his teeth and tugged gently. "Your tits are going to make me fucking come, Sina."

My pussy clenched hard on Thayer, and I felt him still inside me too. When he pulled out, Calder immediately grabbed my hips and thrust his cock into my pussy with Gaian. He held me so strongly in his arms, using my body to make himself feel good.

"Fill me with your cum, Calder," I begged. "Please, breed me."

"You're already fucking pregnant, Pretty Bird," Calder growled into my ear.

"H-how do you—"

"Oh-oh fuck," Gaian grunted, louder than he ever had before, and stilled inside me, his mouth still latched around my nipple.

Calder pulled my blindfold undone. When my eyes readjusted, I caught Gaian giving my nipple one last long suck. He pulled back and opened his lust-filled eyes as a dribble of milk ran down his lip.

"Pregnant with our pups," Calder growled, still pumping into me. He sprawled a hand over my stomach and thrust deeper and deeper. "Soon, your belly will be so swollen that you won't be able to move from your bed, and we'll be able to fuck you whenever we want."

My pussy clamped down on his cock, and he slid his hand down to my cunt, cupping it.

"You're ours now, Sina. Forever."

The end.

If you'd like to read the epilogue, sign up for my newsletter.

also by emilia rose

Contemporary Romance

Stepbrother

Poison

The Bad Boy

Detention

Excite Me

Paranormal Romance

Submitting to the Alpha

Come Here, Kitten

Alpha Maddox

My Werewolf Professor

The Twins

Monster Lover

also by emilia rose

Scan the QR code with your phone to view all of Emilia's books!

about the author

Emilia Rose is a *USA Today* best-selling author of steamy romance. Highly inspired by her study abroad trip to Greece in 2019, Emilia loves to include Greek and Roman mythology in her writing.
She graduated from the University of Pittsburgh with a degree in psychology and a minor in creative writing in 2020 and now writes novels as her day job.
With over 18 million combined book views online and a growing presence on reading apps, she hopes to inspire other young novelists with her tales of growth and imagination, so they go on to write the stories that need to be told.
Join Emilia's newsletter for exclusive giveaways, early chapter releases, and more!